THE MAGIC OF FOUR

CELIA LAKE

Second World War, from the perspective of young adults who have a good idea what their parents did during the war years and what that cost.

The last book in the Land Mysteries series, it includes a number of characters who have appeared in other Albion books, but can be read in any order. Unlike most Celia Lake books, *The Magic of Four* is not a romance - they're all fourteen.

Content notes are available on my website.

Cover design by <u>Augusta Scarlett</u>.

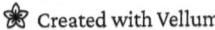 Created with Vellum

MINERVAL TERM

CHAPTER I
LEO ON AUGUST 31ST, 1946

L eo took a last look around the sitting room. He'd put all the books away in their proper places, or stacked them on Mum's and Dad's desks. The table was clear, save for a few autumn flowers in a vase for decoration. There was a bottle of cider in one of the chilling containers.

He could have spent the night in his dorm. That was one of the privileges of living at Schola out of term time. Leo had appreciated his Head of House, Professor Hammond, making it clear earlier in the week.

Tonight, there'd be just a few people there. The fourth and fifth year prefects were back a day early so they could get everything ready for the new firsties as well as for everyone else swarming back. Leo had helped them all afternoon. There was a lot of work to be done, and Leo had sorted papers for the firsties and helped make sure all the dorm beds were ready.

But he'd wanted one more night here, in his own bed, in what had been his own bedroom since he was born. Not that Mum would be around. She'd be up late with the other

3

Heads of House, doing whatever it was that placed seventy new firsties into the right House for them. Tomorrow, through a very practical application of magic and physical effort, everyone's trunks would end up in the right place. They'd all start with at least one set of clothing with the house colours and patches attached.

Dad hadn't come back yet either. He was keeping the firsties busy into the evening. Exhausting them now meant tomorrow would be easier on everyone. All the new students were at the tail end of a week living in cottages on the east coast of Schola's island, getting to know each other. And, as Leo remembered clearly from last year, worrying a lot about what their five years at Schola would be like.

Leo mostly remembered this week last year as a swirl of exhausting complexity. At the same time, he'd been bursting with energy. Everyone had been, even the people who had turned out to be quiet and laid back later on.

Of course, last year had a lot of reasons for high spirits and for nerves, both. They'd all been waiting for the announcement that the war was over, truly over. The end of the war in Europe in the spring had been a huge relief. They'd been able to stop worrying about bombs dropping from the skies, or U-Boats east in Cardigan Bay, or west in the Irish Sea. But there was still war going on, off halfway around the world. It had taken a couple more days, but they'd got that news on September second, when the school was caught up in the second day of classes.

This year, the world was different. And also the dates worked a little differently. Today was Saturday. Every older student was likely at one last family supper, gathering, or outing. Tomorrow, they'd come back, by portal or ferry, mostly portal. There would be regular runs of the pony carts and the village carts up here with trunks and cases and whatever people might bring. There'd be cases and bohort and pavo gear, duelling gear, musical instruments, or whatever they needed for their lives at school.

Tomorrow's supper would be the opening feast with the announcements of the firsties into Houses. From there, he knew how it went. There'd be a gathering at Bear House to welcome theirs, and with each year to help them get settled in. And there'd be tons of catching up, though of course, Albion wasn't a huge community. People had seen each other all summer at the Midsummer Faire and bigger events, even if they weren't close friends.

Leo and his yearmates would be in a new dorm, which was another change. He'd been to look at it today, while he was helping set up things. It was more or less a mirror of last year. This time, instead of windows overlooking the keep and courtyard, the windows had views over the southern fields and coast, down toward the village. He'd claimed his own cubicle already, but he already knew no one else particularly wanted the one at the far end. He'd had the good sense to ask last spring. Leo got along well enough with the boys in his dorm, but he was desperately looking forward to third year, when they got their own rooms. This year, they at least each had their own work-room or study room.

Leo was still trying to figure out how to arrange his. They could bring in furniture if they wanted, and Leo knew where a lot of useful furniture was. There was plenty in the storage rooms across from their rooms here in the Keep, for a start. Or Mum had been making noises about Leo getting the desk Ursula had been using.

But Leo first needed to figure out what he wanted to use that space for. He preferred studying with other people in the background. Most often that was in the library's quieter spaces, when he wanted that, at the group tables with his friends. Or he found a table in the House library when he wanted people around, but not to be interrupted too often.

He was going to have a lot of need for space to set up for ritual work and leave it up. That didn't leave much room for furniture, necessarily. It wasn't like the workrooms were big, though he'd been able to get the central slice of the tower room. Absolute luxury, compared to his sleeping space. But that wasn't actually very big for some of the ritual work he was hoping to be starting later in the year. For the ordinary class exercises, any of the rooms would have done, but he was hoping to work on more than that with Uncle Alexander as he got time.

The dormitory cubicles weren't cramped, ten feet or so. They were long enough he could have his trunk at the end of the bed, have the curtain closed, and still have room to change or bend over. But it wasn't much space for a bed, trunk, wardrobe, dresser, and whatever books he could fit into shelves along each of the dividing cubicle walls.

In his dorm last year, no one had bothered much with the curtains during the day. Mostly they were a handy way to indicate someone was sleeping, or trying to. And they did have charms on them that actually muffled the noise, or it'd have been a lot worse to be in the dorm.

Besides all that, second year had other changes. They added a new set of classes, beginning to work on particular types of magic. Leo was looking forward to his, especially Ritual and Incantation, but all of them really. Well, not Alchemy. He wasn't taking it, even though Uncle Garin had roared about it. But second year was also the year the secret societies picked people. Whatever that meant for Leo or his particular friends, it was going to cause a lot of strain and nerves in his yearmates.

Leo was trying not to think - not too much today anyway - about everything else that meant. He was a second year; he was supposed to be figuring out what he wanted to do with himself, what he wanted to specialise in. He already had some ideas, it wasn't as if he hadn't talked about it with Mum and Dad and Uncle Alexander and other people some, but he didn't know how to get from where he was now to where that was, whatever it looked like. Mum had suggested last year that he think about whether going to Oxford - and the magical Academy - might suit. That would mean a lot more work over next summer and the years after, for the non-magical exams. So he didn't have to decide today, but he needed to by next spring. And that was both close and forever away.

Anyway, all of that new meant he'd wanted to spend one last night in the family rooms, tucked into the fourth floor of Schola's keep. Only, right now, with it empty, he was sort of regretting that. It'd be different if Ursula had been here. If she'd still been at Schola, she'd have been with the other prefects in Fox House tonight. But she'd finished school in June and she'd been living with their Uncle Garin at Arundel since the beginning of July. She was doing whatever it was she did on a Saturday evening now. Her not being here was no longer entirely strange, but Leo still missed her.

His sister was annoying sometimes - it was apparently required of sisters. Also brothers. Leo tried to keep up his end of that. But she also had a lot of sense, and she saw things differently than Leo did. He was really missing having her to talk to at times like this. Things were changing, they were in the middle of changing, and he didn't know what was coming. Not really.

Before he could get entirely tangled in his own thoughts, there was a sound at the door and a shift in the wards. It was properly dark out now, well past eight. Dad pushed the door open, his hand coming down from where he'd opened the warding. He had his satchel over his shoulder, a walking stick in one hand, and he looked tired. Maybe exhausted, but not like he had through the war, and through most of last year. Not that bad.

"Leo. I wasn't sure." Dad rubbed his hand through his hair, and it came out in odd waves, like Leo's did. Same dark hair, same waves, same sort of face, though it looked better on Dad. Dad thought Leo would grow into it nicely. Dashing was one of the things people had called Dad when he was young. And - as he said - far more dissolute than had been a good idea, even at the time.

"Cider for you? Mum left a little hunk of cheese and a couple of apples." There wasn't bread to spare, or much flour for biscuits. The United Kingdom had just gone to full-on rationing for flour, along with everything else, thanks to a miserable wet summer. Albion had too, because they weren't sure how much of the crop could be coaxed through the wet yet, even with a lot of magical skill thrown at the problem.

"Bless. Do you mind fetching it?" Dad hesitated.

"One of the lighter potions?" Leo knew that expression. It was one of the things people paid attention to, or at least Leo did. Ros and Avigail did the same with their parents. He'd been noticing that this summer, the few times the parents had been around while they were together. Whatever Jasper noticed from his mum and dad, Leo thought it came out differently. Maybe he worried about entirely different things. They'd never really talked about it. Jasper could be right private. Leo was never sure how much to ask about. He didn't know whether Jasper would find it rude to be asked or feel like he had to answer, even if he didn't want to, because Leo came from posh on Dad's side. Mum's side wasn't a lot of help either, because the current bit of family were civil service or crafters, and that was different too.

"Yeah. Please." Dad lowered himself into his usual chair, toeing the footstool over and leaning back. "Wrenched my knee in the field." Which explained the stick, the potion, and the tired. Dad would have been masking that for however long he'd been out in public. Leo went trotting off to the storage cabinet, then stopped by the kitchen to slice up the apple and put the cheese on the same plate. It wasn't much, but it was something. Once he'd handed everything over to Dad, he had to decide what to do. Dad waved him at a chair. "Unless you had something else to be doing?"

"I was trying to figure that out when you came back. Haven't seen Mum since mid-afternoon." He hadn't expected to. She had things to sort out in Horse House, where she was Head. They'd have started the discussion or whatever it was by eight. He was pretty sure of that, even if it would likely run past midnight. And she'd had supper at the high table, and Leo had eaten with the prefects.

"No. She said she thought it'd be a little shorter this year, maybe, than yours. Different class, different divisions." Dad shrugged once. "I think at this point, familial obligation means I'm supposed to sternly ask you if you're ready to excel this year. Do you mind if we don't bother with that?"

Leo laughed, leaning back in the chair. "Did Uncle Garin lecture you again?"

"He tried to. And then I reminded him he should still be making it up to you, and he gave up. He's getting better at picking what he fusses about, anyway. Retirement is good for him." Uncle Garin had retired from the Council last winter, and it had meant a lot of changes.

A fortnight ago, Uncle Garin had formally declared Ursula as his Heir, instead of Dad. Leo had been expecting it'd be years before they did that, though he'd hoped they would sooner than later. Dad had admitted later he'd thought the same, or he'd have warned Leo. But Uncle Garin made decisions when he made them and didn't much worry about anyone else's sense of timing.

He'd now had a bit to get used to the fact they'd made the decision that fast. Leo was glad of it. For one thing, Dad had been vastly relieved. He could help Ursula out with learning the Heir's role in the land rituals, but he didn't have to be responsible for all that, as well as everything he did at Schola. And it meant Leo could go into this year without that over his head, all those expectations.

When he looked up, Dad was watching him. "Yes?" Leo kept his voice steady enough, that was good.

Mum was clear. Dad should use his words, they were very useful. Dad had been brought up in the Great Family tradition of never saying anything that might be used against him later. And, well, Uncle Garin was sometimes an excellent example of that. Mum, on the other hand, felt it was a lot more practical to actually say things rather than guess.

Dad snorted, though he had a drink from his cider before saying anything. Once he'd put the bottle down, he asked, "Have you decided if you want to make it public?"

"Everyone will know at Solstice, Dad. I could wait, but there'd be a fuss then. If I mention it now, it'll just go into the first rush of everyone coming back." Leo spread his hands, mock-quoting. "How was your summer? How's your sister? Oh, she's great. Uncle Garin named her Heir a fortnight ago. We're all thrilled. Did you see the book list for Ritual?"

Dad laughed. "You've talked to your Mum about it, then."

"Uncle Golshan, last week. He's better with gossip. Setting it up right." Mum was good at a lot of things, but for managing gossip, Leo would go to Uncle Golshan or Uncle Alexander any time.

"I needn't ask if you're ready for class. Alexander thinks he can clear a fair number of Sundays, so long as the bohort matches don't run too late. An hour before or after supper, can you keep it open?"

"Of course, Dad. And it's all right with Professor Leonard?" He could probably still get away with calling her Aunt Borea tonight. They were technically not yet in term time. But it was about her as his teacher, so he'd be formal. Growing up at Schola, basically every professor was like that for him. Their teaching faces - and robes - and their personal ones were the same and different, always.

"There's a workroom, next floor down. We can set it aside for you. And she says she's open to sorting out time in the Ritual classroom when you get to needing more space. Given Alexander." Uncle Alexander had been the Ritual professor at Schola before her, back when Mum and Dad were busy falling in love. Leo knew how lucky he was to get Uncle Alexander's time on the regular.

For the last eight years, he'd been to and fro dealing with Council matters. Even when he was in Albion, he'd never known much in advance if he'd be available any given day. Or hour. The idea of having time scheduled regularly, even if Uncle Alexander had to cancel sometimes, was wonderful. And he knew Dad would enjoy it. Uncle Alexander had trained Dad, back when Dad was at Schola, though much more in duelling than in ritual. Which reminded him, actually, to check on that.

"And then Tuesdays for duelling with other people. And Thursdays with just you."

"Just so. You, Avigail, Theo Lefton. Maybe only you three. I'm thinking about whether there's anyone worth adding. It might depend on how much people did over the summer that made a difference."

There were a number of people who wanted to be in Dad's special training, but he didn't usually take people on as first or second years. Leo knew Crimson Hettleburgh hoped for it. It'd be a mark of distinction for him. Crimson had a lot to live up to - he was Heir to his father's title and the land magic. But he wasn't naturally gifted at duelling like Dad was, and he wasn't dedicated to getting better, like Leo was.

Anthony Phipps and Malcolm Hector both wanted that sort of attention, too. But they wanted to be flashy and showy, and that didn't actually make for good duelling skill. More to the point, it didn't make them very safe partners to learn more complicated techniques with. Oh, Leo would have class with them eventually, but hopefully a couple of years after he'd got the basics solidly down without interference.

Leo grinned. "At least I might have slightly fewer bruises. No Artemis." Artemis, Theo's older sister, had been in Ursula's year. Artemis had gone right into Guard training, like her Mum. Theo was a tremendous dueller, especially working with her, but she was the more aggressive of the two. Theo was now a fifth year in Bear House, but for all his own skill he did, in fact, usually leave fewer bruises on his opponents.

"I'm thinking about Tiberius, too. Or maybe I'll ask you to come into some of his, some of the time." Dad ran his hand over his face. Then he shook his head. "I know that's more complicated, socially. No, I think I'll bring you into his. I'll let you know in good time."

"Sure, Dad." Leo wasn't going to argue. Tiberius Warren was a good sort, but very much of Fox House, absolutely standing upon his dignity. Tiberius's father was Leo's Uncle Claudio, one of Dad's earliest students and now a great friend, but that kind of fondness wasn't transitive. Leo didn't dislike Tiberius, but they didn't seek each other out, either. Being a year apart and in different houses, that wasn't uncommon, anyway. "Secret teaching, then?" He offered a grin, because it was and wasn't. Other people not having a real sense of your skill was a good protective move.

"Don't you get ahead of yourself. We'll be stepping things up a bit for you and Avigail. And you've pavo and bohort practice, too." Doing both wasn't common, but both games were great training for magic on the fly, and that was something Leo wanted to get a lot better at, since his own tendencies were for slow and deliberate. Dad had been an amazing bohort player in his own youth, and Leo felt he had to live up to that. Or at least try. Pavo was just fun, especially with three friends who were all amazing riders. Leo was decidedly not in their league, but he was steadily working on competent, and it was good to learn how to do that, too.

Leo leaned back a bit more. "Lots of learning. And lots of subjects. I'll do my best, Dad. You can tell Uncle Garin you gave me a sufficient lecture."

Dad waved a hand, then considered the bottle. He'd devoured the apple, apparently, in bites when Leo wasn't noticing. "What do you say to a bit of time up on the top of the keep, looking at stars?"

Leo considered. Dad made a good effort at stars, but he was - well, Leo was maybe reliably better there. But Leo had grown up with Mum teaching him about them from before he could talk. "You just want to amuse Mum when she comes in."

"Yes. But also it's a nice night, it's our last one without any obligations for the term, and it's actually clear. Might as well take advantage. It was a little chilly coming in, though. Bring your cloak. Let me leave a note for her."

Five minutes later, they were out on the top of the keep. Dad slid them through the warding smoothly. Leo got to work figuring out where things were in the sky that might be interesting to look at, so he could point them out to Dad.

CHAPTER 2
ROS ON SEPTEMBER 1ST

Ros looked around and was satisfied with her unpacking for the moment. She'd want to rearrange the books later, most likely. Right now, they were in order by subject, but of course that wasn't how they fell in her week. On the other hand, with classes on different days, she couldn't just put them in order by the day of the week. She'd be constantly shuffling everything over, and that was hard on a book's spine. Papa had taught her better than that.

She had set out what she needed immediately, though, and the notebooks to go with them. The first day of class would be busy, but at least this year she knew where everything was, near enough. And how to get there efficiently. She flicked through the items on top of the shelf one more time, nodded, and went down to see who was in the House library. Or, specifically, if Peter had already gone to find a table in the back of the main library to claim for his own.

Ros nodded at a few people in passing. That was part of what was expected of her. The Carillon family reputation was for making and remembering connections. It came out in the pleasant sociability Mama brought to all the necessary philanthropy she did. Papa was more complicated, but his public face was all about his particular interests and sharing them with people who enjoyed them. The private, of course, had a lot more to do with sharply refined pattern-matching, Intelligence work, and a range of skills for managing secrets that neither Mama or Papa talked about.

Now, that brought her to thinking about how the space changed the people. This year, their dorm was on the other side of the House, with a rather gorgeous bit of sea view. That was especially true from her workroom. Fox assigned them out based on marks and good reports from professors the previous term. Peter had barely beaten her out in overall marks, but she'd earned several comments of note from professors about helping with things in class, and they'd more or less tied. Fortunately, they didn't want the same thing in a workroom, so it had been easy. She got her fabulous sea view. He got the room next to her with a bit more space.

No, there he was, at a table near the back of the House library, a couple of books stacked in front of him. He looked up, a little warily, as he heard a noise, then visibly relaxed when he saw who it was. Maybe before they left school, she'd have managed to teach him not to show his reactions that blatantly.

She'd been talking to some of the third years at supper, and he'd been down near where the new firsties sat, so they hadn't had a chance to talk yet. "Rough afternoon?" she asked, before adding, "And how was your summer since I saw you?" He'd invited Ros out for a day in London at the beginning of August. He'd done the same for Leo and Avigail on other days, and he'd also invited Jasper, but

Jasper had been busy with horses. Though Jasper was on average always busy with horses.

"Busy. Lots of reading, in between other things, I'm ahead on that. Only of course, I don't know what a lot of it means, or how to apply it. Remind me why taking everything seemed like a good idea?"

"Because you want to know everything." Ros grinned. "You and Avigail, wanting to take everything you can. At least Leo and I are skipping one or two."

Peter snorted, running a hand through dark brown hair, and then frowning. "When are your free periods, then?"

Ros had been expecting this, and she pulled out the book she'd been working on so hard all summer. It was only just begun, the making of it and the two charms. But Papa had said it'd work best if she used it, even if it was just to tuck notes into right now. She opened it, carefully.

"That a journal?" The magical journals were wonderful, and she did, in fact, have one. It was in her trunk. She'd write Mama and Papa before she went to sleep tonight. They also cost enough - still - that most people her age didn't have one, and someone from Peter's sort of family definitely wouldn't. Leo didn't have one, either, or Jasper. Though money wasn't the issue with Leo, so she wasn't actually sure why he didn't.

"Family tradition. A book of charms, embedded. We start working on them about, well, after our first year at Schola, and keep working on them. Mine's only got a real simple charm or two. There's one that's handy for seeing if anyone's listening. Papa has one that will muffle sound, one to help trace lines between people, lineage. All sorts of other things."

Those were the two Papa had said she could talk about. She was working on sketches for a third. Hopefully she'd get to set that over solstice hols. And her sister Merry said she'd help, too. Though Merry was busy with her own things as a fifth year in Seal House, even if she didn't talk a lot about what they were.

The images by themselves - even if she'd had more than two right now - wouldn't have been informative. The second of hers was one to improve memory and focus, an aid to study. It didn't replace doing the work, but it meant if she were tired or distracted or any of a dozen other things that came up all the time, she had a better chance of remembering what she'd read or studied or heard in a lecture later.

"Anyway," she said. "It's where I put my timetable. Here. You've still got Latin every day? First thing?"

Peter nodded. "Latin. I'm in the Monday Arithmetic section, then lecture on Wednesday."

"I'm Wednesday and Thursday there. That's no good." They turned out to have the same Trivium schedule but not the same section. So they'd both be free on Mondays and Fridays, but Avigail had riding scheduled on Wednesdays before lunch. "And you're taking Sympathetic when I'm free."

"Why aren't you taking it?"

Ros shrugged. "It's - I could? Of course." She didn't need to justify herself or her marks to Peter, of all people. The two of them - and Iseult Crane - reliably vied for top of the class, depending on the subject. "But if I want to do languages, I need some time to study them. And do my assignments. Sympathetic was the thing I could give up most easily. Not Materia. And Alchemy's useful and Papa has someone I can do some work with next summer if I do well."

"Ah." Peter bit his lip. "Nothing like that for me. There's not much alchemy in eels. Or dockyard sums."

"No, but there's a lot in the shipping charms. And..." Ros considered the connections. "Papa knows someone who's in with the Pelagiuses. I suppose that's the plural, even if it sounds wrong. I mean, it's a family name. If you wanted, I could see if they're taking anyone on for a summer. Maybe not next, but going into fourth or fifth."

Peter went entirely still. "I'd not want to owe a favour."

"Me asking Papa isn't a favour. And if you turned out to suit, you'd be doing them some of a favour. I can ask Papa if it's worth asking about. They don't see each other terribly often, but he will sometime in the next month or two, probably."

"You Great Families and the interconnections." Peter frowned. "Not a marriage connection?"

"Council. Well, now retired. Magister Cyrus Smythe-Clive's sister is a senior Healer, Rhoe Belisama. She's married to Magister Hugh Pelagius, and he's been running the shipping line since his older brother - half-brother, I think that's a first wife - retired." Ros dropped in the full names automatically, both because it was a lot more clear and because Peter wouldn't place them immediately. Avigail would have, and not just because of her own Papa's Council seat. But of course, she wouldn't have had to explain it to Avigail or Leo.

"I repeat. Great Families and the interconnections." Peter was good-natured about it, given that she had all that information more or less at her disposal. She'd learned it from the nursery, and he had only really understood it existed a year or so ago. "What languages? Did you sort out all four?"

"All four, yes." Ros was going to be very busy indeed.

"Arabic with Professor Ward on Mondays - when you've got Arithmetic. French with Professor Knox, when you've got Latin first thing."

"You're braver than I am." Peter was still a little unsure about their Head of House, who was sharply observant.

Ros grinned. "But I'm going to have four languages." She shrugged. "Latin with Professor Leonard, that's on Thursday, that's the one we were trying to sort out last time I wrote. Papa traded favours for the others, but he doesn't know her as well."

"How does your father know Professor Ward? Or, wait, who's the other one?"

That involved lowering her voice, because this was a little sensitive. "German with Professor Wain. A lot of the astronomy literature, and a fair bit of other things, it's either in German or Latin. And she's fluent, because of the astronomy."

"Even with the war?" Peter didn't exactly look upset, but he looked confused.

Ros considered how to put it. "It's not the language that did the damage. And Papa says, if we don't understand the language, how can we begin to mend things? He's fluent in it, Uncle Alexander's perfectly conversational. One of the alchemists I might spend the summer with, he's German originally. Been here since 1935, though. So it'd be handy to get it conversational by then, even if I can't do academic work in it." She wanted to make that very clear. "And Papa sorted it with Professor Wain."

"Professor Wain makes sense, what you and Leo have said about his parents, and where they spend time. Your parents, Avigail's. And Jasper, by association." Jasper's father ran Papa's stables, so yes. The same and different. "Professor Ward?"

"I know you know Mistress Ward, down in the village with the bookshop. She was in Owl House with Papa, when they were in school, and they've been friends since."

Peter laughed. "So not Great Families, the same way. House connections, like you keep telling me, might be useful some day." He considered. "You at least explain it."

"I mean, most of ours aren't very obvious. Sometimes deliberately. It's not like Crimson Hettleburgh or Iseult Crane or the people who'd like to get close to them," Ros pointed out.

"Hettleburgh's all right, I suppose. It's got to be queer, not knowing if someone likes you for you, or because you're going to inherit the land magic," Peter said. "And Crane doesn't like me."

"Iseult Crane wants to be top of our class, and you keep getting in the way of that. She thinks there can only be one person who's most excellent. And Philemon Hestelbloom's good, but he's not as much of a danger." Hestlebloom was a steady academic sort. His mother did something in the diplomatic corps of the Ministry.

Ros sort of understood how people got competitive about it, how there could only be one at the top. She'd talked to her older brother, Edmund, enough about it. That didn't mean she approved. Many people could be excellent, it wasn't like there could be only one excellent and everyone else middling.

"So why don't you do that? Or aren't like that." Peter flicked his fingers, agitated, and Ros let him talk it out. "Your father's a Lord, your brother is his Heir, people want you to be their friend? Why bother talking to me?" Peter lowered his voice even more, and after a moment Ros reached for her book and brushed her fingers over the charm. She'd only cast it a handful of times this way. But now she could see the shimmer on the raven wings in the illustration for just a moment before the border turned a translucent blue. No one near enough to overhear. Peter's eyes widened at it.

Ros shrugged. "I think it's more fun if a lot of people are excellent. There isn't a scarcity, only so much to go around. Crimson needs to live up to his family's expectations, or at least he thinks he needs to. Iseult does too, only hers are about being the best Owl ever, top of her class in everything. I want to know a lot of things, but I don't have those expectations. Mama and Papa have both been very clear about that. Or, say, there's Jasper, who's really good at horses, but he might well be really good at other things we haven't figured out yet. Or had a chance to learn yet." She had a theory it was the second one, but Jasper didn't believe her.

Peter hesitated, looking at where her fingers rested on the page of the book, then back at her. "I don't know how to make sense of that. But you keep talking to me, so I'll keep learning."

"Glad to be an informative resource." Ros grinned at him, before deciding it was time to lighten things up. "Right. Back to the timetable before we forget. I'm riding Monday and Friday after classes. Tuesday? Avigail and Leo are both busy then. If we want time for all of us, plus whoever looks interestingly clever this year, it can't be then. But it'd do for just us."

Peter nodded. "Tuesday and Thursday, five to supper." It'd give them two solid hours, or close to it. "What's Leo not taking? Or Jasper?"

She glanced at the schedule. "Leo's not taking Alchemy. His uncle threw a fit and a half, I guess, but Leo held firm. Extra duelling time, though, and he's training for both bohort and pavo." She wrinkled up her nose. "Horses are better."

"You keep saying that. I have enough trouble following bohort with everyone on their own two feet."

Ros had grown up with pavo all over the place - it was what Papa specifically trained his horses for. Both games needed quick wits, a lot of magical skill, and a lot of self-control, but pavo also required riding ability and a good bit more physical strength and flexibility. She was hoping to make the team properly this year instead of the reserve. Jasper already had the upper body strength for it, and he was likely to just get better.

"Anyway. Leo's not taking Alchemy. And his dad has him in duelling Tuesday and Thursday, so who knows how tired he'll be." Leo's papa was the Protective magics professor. Ros sort of envied Leo the chance to see him twice a week like that, but she also knew Professor Fortier made Leo work for everything he learned.

"And Jasper?" Peter fiddled for a moment with the pen in his hand.

"Taking less. Latin - he'll be with you, I bet. Extra Trivium, though he was doing a lot better by Floralia term last year. Not taking, um, Arithmetic, Astronomy, Sympathetic, Alchemy, or Ritual. So Incantation and Materia. Mostly, that's what he wants to go into."

Peter considered that. "And a lot of time in the stables, I guess?"

"Lots of time in the stables. He was saying last week, after we got our proper timetables, that he's got a solid two hours every day. And pavo practice Saturday and whatever time he wants Sunday, too. I guess he's taking on some training for Master Held. That counts for all his chores time, anyway."

"What'd you get this time round?" Peter rummaged. "Library shelving for me."

"That's just because someone noticed you know where everything is, anyway," Ros said. Though she might have mentioned it to Professor Knox, even if he'd already spotted it. "Clearing up after breakfast and helping with some of the food preparation. Mama thought it'd be good. And there's great gossip and treats, as they get the baking going for the rest of the day."

"Huh. Not what I'd have expected. Avigail? Leo?" She could tell Peter was trying to figure out what the range of things was.

"Avigail's helping tidy the classrooms - Quadrivium, nothing fancy for the magic. I think she said Thursdays before supper. And Leo's, well. Leo's a special case. He's helping Professor Ward with the Materia inventory and storage. Not usually a student chore, but Leo's been helping with it since he was about nine. Susanna's a prefect now, so she's got other things to be doing."

"Huh." Peter then blinked. "Wait, isn't Susanna in Seal, and Professor Ward's her Head of House? Her dad?"

Ros shrugged. "They make it work. And apparently it was a unanimous decision by everyone else, and Professor Ward gave in? My sister Merry told me all about it, and she absolutely didn't want to be prefect again. She said last year was outside of enough." Merry was not fond of obligatory timetables, it turned out. She wanted to throw herself into whatever she was doing without having to stop to make sure everyone was where they ought to be or deal with some minor crisis.

"You're not exactly being subtle about demonstrating the benefits of a well-established network," Peter said, finally. "But I take your point. And ta, for the information."

Ros hesitated, though she decided on saying, "You're welcome. You're a friend, right? No trade needed." Then she tapped her fingers on the desk. "Someone told you, I hope, about the secret societies? They pick people this year, whoever they're picking. I don't know much about it yet, Leo hasn't wanted to talk about it. I got stories from Edmund and Merry about what happened their second years, but I don't actually know if they're in societies. People don't say, even to, y'know, sisters."

Peter snorted. "Professor Knox mentioned, last June. He gave me a little to read. I suppose that's the sort of thing I should ask him a bit more about now?" Ros was clear Peter was actually asking about the timing. Peter wanted to know everything he could. Sequencing, however, especially how other people interpreted it, still confused him.

Ros nodded. "Yes. Because I'm really curious what he tells you now. Tell him you did the reading, ask him to talk it through with you, we'll talk after? And maybe Leo will tell us more this year." Then she considered. "Right. What about classes?"

"Do you think you could have a look at my Latin? And I'll have a look at whatever you like in turn. Except your languages. We don't want that."

"Deal. And you're still planning on helping out Jasper, right? I'm glad to, but it's better if it's you too. You know different things, for one. Did the Society and Culture reading over the summer make sense to you? I read everything, but I got bogged down in the comparisons between the comedy of manners novels, Albion against the non-magical, and I'm sure I'm missing something. I meant to ask Papa, and then I forgot."

"Sure. And of course, Jasper. He's a friend, right? And I

learn things better when I explain them. Do you need to grab notes?"

Ros shook her head. "Got what I need with me. Until curfew?"

Peter nodded, nudged a chair out with his foot. He waited until she was sitting down before launching into an explanation of what exactly it was the non-magical needed distraction from in the late 1890s. Entirely different things than Ros was used to factoring in, apparently.

CHAPTER 3
JASPER ON SEPTEMBER 7TH

J asper was glad enough to be back at school. It helped that his schedule this year had been arranged so he had a lot more time in the stables. Two hours every day, and a bit more on weekends. Last year, he'd gone up with the others after pavo practice on Saturdays. Today, he'd brought a packed lunch down, and helped Master Held out all afternoon. They'd had the farrier out, and another set of hands to hold and calm down horses did a lot of good.

Of course, he couldn't do it how Dad did. Dad had the Horseman's Word. He also had more than twenty years as Lord Carillon's head of stables, breeding and training up horses for pavo play and for regular working use, both. Jasper had grown up with free-roaming New Forest ponies nuzzling him for attention as soon as he could walk on his own. Now, that was the one thing he knew, all the way down to his toes, that he was good at. Not as good as Dad, but he could learn to be, and maybe earn his way to the Word.

Here, there were the individual student horses, quite a few of them, as well as the school's own. Riding wasn't nearly as necessary these days, but it was still an important skill for anyone who wanted to go into Materia, or any of the professions that often took people into places roads - and automobiles - couldn't easily go. This year, Jasper was helping make sure all the lesson horses were well tended. And of course, the ordinary sort of work doing his share of mucking out stalls and feeding for his own Dorothy and the other student horses.

He was coming back up from the stables, taking the curving path around to the front of the castle, when two people stepped in front of him. He could see a couple of others behind them. No one from his House was visible, and all of a sudden, he was sure that was deliberate. They weren't yet up within the curtain wall, and there didn't seem to be anyone else right nearby. Phipps. Hector. What he thought was a firstie, and someone who might be another third year. Not in Jasper's year, and a little too tall to be another firstie.

The last of them - a third year, someone whose name Jasper didn't know - sniffed. "You smell something unpleasant, Phipps?"

Another sniff. "Yes. Pity, isn't it? Blemish on a perfectly good day. I hope the smell goes away before the bohort trials tomorrow."

Jasper felt his shoulders tighten. On the one hand, he'd been wondering if they'd try something. He hadn't come in for bullying directly last year. Phipps and Hector had also been firsties, and nervous about throwing their weight around. And Ros had been pretty sure the bullies had been nervous of what Ros or Leo in particular might do about it. But Jasper guessed the new school year made them braver.

And if they'd found a third year or two, that wouldn't help at all. He cleared his throat. "Just going back to wash up before supper."

He could try to be civilised. They wouldn't be the same back, but Jasper had to live with himself. Well, they had to live with themselves, but that apparently wasn't worrying them. More to the point, if things got bad - and they might - he wanted to be able to speak truthfully if someone asked him. It'd be easier if someone used truth telling, honestly, but that wasn't simple to do. He'd heard that story from Mum and Dad, part of how they met, making a proper court and space for it in the courtyard that Jasper knew every inch of.

None of the other boys were fast to reply, it looked like. Maybe they wouldn't make the bohort team. Any of them. After a moment, the third year, who was taking the lead, shook his head. "Won't do any good. Some things don't wash off."

Jasper didn't know how to handle this. Every version of this he'd done in his head, practising the way he did for anything he needed to do in public, they'd been better at taunting. Even if he hadn't been able to imagine the specifics, he'd filled in a gap in his head with something that smarted. He tried again. "Can I get by, get out of your way?"

They lined up, more firmly shoulder to shoulder, blocking the path. It didn't give Jasper a lot of choices. It was what, six. Maybe quarter past. Supper was at seven. All the professors were likely doing whatever it was professors did in the late afternoon. Marking or talking to students or whatever. He wasn't sure, he just knew they usually weren't very obvious this time of day.

After supper, he bet Professor Wain and Professor

Fortier would be coming out and down this road. He knew they went down to the pub most Saturday nights, if there wasn't anything big getting in the way. Tradition, Leo had said, that went back to before they'd been married or whatever they'd done before that. But second years weren't allowed down in the village on their own, just in groups in the afternoon with a prefect handy.

So it wasn't like Jasper could sit down in the road for two hours or so, waiting them out.

Jasper could go back to the stables, but Master Held had probably gone off to his own supper. Also, Jasper didn't want these boys following him down, where the horses might get hurt. Or Jasper himself, though that mattered less there. Master Held had a cottage not far from the stables, but Jasper couldn't turn up there. He'd not been invited. And Jasper wanted Master Held to think well of him, that he could solve his own problems. That Jasper was mature enough not to get into fights.

And besides, turning his back on a predator wasn't smart. He wasn't in a herd, he couldn't kick and use his feet, not and get away with it. They might not be terribly competent or clever predators, but that didn't actually matter much. Jasper was clear on that.

He'd have to see if he could talk himself out of this. Or at least, talk long enough someone else came along. There might still be a group coming up from the village, he didn't know. One of the professors might spot them, the five of them were being pretty obvious now. And maybe Professor Fortier had some way to know if something like this happened. Leo hadn't talked a lot about the protections on the castle, but Jasper knew there were some. A lot.

"If you're not going to move, you're going to miss supper." It was the first thing that really came together in

Jasper's head. It wasn't a great line, it certainly wasn't a strategy. It did, however, visibly confuse them. All of them were blinking. They weren't matching up to the script in Jasper's head, but he wasn't following theirs either.

He tucked his hands behind his back, out of sight, but where he could move if he had to. Jasper had experience falling, a lot more than they did. Maybe he could fling himself to the side and scramble up behind them. He was pretty sure they were used to flat and tended roads, not bogs and furrows. Or whatever the heavy gear of the Army had done to the poor New Forest for five years.

"Were you talking to us? Were you daring to talk to us? Getting above yourself." That was the lead third year again. "Phipps and Hector told me you like the horses so much you're down there all the time."

It was true, so Jasper just shrugged. There wasn't anything wrong with horses. No, wait, that wasn't quite right. Most horses - and most ponies, and most donkeys and mules - were just grand. Some of them had had bad experiences, or they hurt, or no one had taught them manners, and that wasn't so great. These five were like balky colts who didn't want to walk on a lead rein or learn to start under saddle. It gave him a better way to think about them, but it didn't actually change anything right now.

"I know where I am with the horses." As soon as he said it, he wanted to wince. It just left him open to all sorts of other attacks. Maybe not physical - he wasn't sure if they'd try that. But they could do a lot without ever touching him.

Now it got a braying laugh. "Why are you even here, then?" The third year gestured behind his shoulder. "Your place is wasted on you."

That was the thing. Jasper didn't know why he was at

Schola. He knew enough about his exam scores when it came to the magic. He also knew he was behind a lot of his classmates in the academics. Or not behind, exactly, when it came to actual class assignments, but things they seemed to have picked up effortlessly, and he had to work for. Stories and how things worked in different places. Even though he was familiar with one of the landed estates, that wasn't enough.

Or possibly, how Ytene ran, at least these days, wasn't like other places. That made a bit more sense. It would be a good question for Master Benton, when Jasper got a chance over winter hols. This was not the time for that. Jasper shrugged. "I assume they had some reason, the people with the exams and the choices." He didn't understand that, but he didn't entirely need to.

Phipps took a step forward, as if he were going to do something. Just at that moment, Jasper caught a flicker of movement, one he knew at a distance, even in silhouette. He whistled, the repeated melodic stutter of the woodlark. Not a bird anyone should expect around here. They didn't live this far north, and Jasper knew that, even if he suspected these bullies didn't. Well, it was unfair to blame the firsties. They hadn't had much of the Natural History class yet.

He didn't have to purse his lips for it, really. When he and Ros had taught themselves this one, they'd figured out it was at least as much in the tongue. Jasper warbled back and forth about the pitches, repeated it. They were outside. He held his breath then there was an echo off the stone wall, and - the five ignored it.

A moment later, there was a sound behind the boys, and Jasper could see Ros coming down the path toward them. "Oh, there you are, Jasper!" She turned to call back to someone behind her. "Wait up a min, Daphne, would you?" Then she turned back to look at Jasper. "Goodness, did you lose track of the time? You said you had that question for Professor Hammond about the assignment for him? He said he'd be in the library until supper. You probably have time to wash up and change if you come now."

Ros was a force of nature. Not as much as Avigail was. Ros did it differently, anyway. Her older sister Merry was a tempest on the ocean when she got going. Avigail was a strong wind that buffeted. Maybe Ros was one of the ancient trees who wouldn't bend. Or a river. She didn't get stubborn, not the way Jasper did. But she was implacable.

The five boys parted ways, as if her mere voice were some great ship sliding into port, perfectly managed. Jasper followed her. He could hear them laughing behind him, the sort of nasty laugh that meant the next time would be worse. He'd have to watch his back and his things.

It wasn't until they were well up toward the keep, maybe twenty feet from it, that Ros spoke. "Don't need to tell you to have a care."

Jasper shrugged. "No." Now he felt prickly, and it wasn't Ros's fault. "None of them's in Horse."

"Phipps is in Fox - ugh, he's awful to Peter and a couple of others. Hector in Boar. Who were the other three?"

"I think two third years. I was thinking the middle one might be Owl, but he wasn't very clever about any of it. Or witty. And the other might be Salmon. But I don't know them that well." There were places people overlapped, in the Houses of course, and in the clubs and musical and theatre groups. Or the bohort and pavo teams, of course. But Jasper didn't do most of those other things, and they didn't share a House and Jasper had never seen either of them near the stables. "I'm not sure about the firstie, but definitely not Bear House."

"I didn't get a good look at him. Maybe Owl. Have they given you trouble before? Third year. I can ask Daphne about it, anyway." Daphne would be the Daphne who was Avigail's cousin, then. She and Ros got on well when it came to academic details. She was a third year in Owl herself.

Jasper's shoulder twitched. "Not directly. You know that. I'd have told you."

"If I'd have figured it out." Ros was too sharp for her own good again. "If they're going for you, who else?"

Of course, she'd be worried about Peter. Who was too clever for his own good sometimes, not a problem Jasper had. But Peter also came from the sort of family where the bullies thought he shouldn't be here. They'd talked about it, a few times, when the others weren't right there. Peter put up with them cheating off his papers, but was mostly spared the other nastiness, and he understood why Jasper didn't make a fuss about it. Making a fuss just drew more attention, and not the good kind. That was the sort of thing Ros would probably never quite understand.

"This was the most they've tried, all right?" Then he broke off. "I really do need to wash up. See you after supper?"

"Sure." Ros twisted away. "The concert, right?" There was a vocal group coming in to perform that evening, and Professor Hammond had suggested it'd be informative, as well as pleasant to listen to, all multiple-voice harmony. Jasper wasn't sure what it was he liked about the music, but something there made more sense to him than most of his classes. And the professors liked it when people turned up at the lectures, and that wasn't a bad thing either, with his marks like they were.

"Yeah. See you after supper." This time he didn't make it a question. Ros wasn't upset. Or not at him. At least he didn't think so. He didn't have time to worry about it now.

CHAPTER 4
AVIGAIL ON SEPTEMBER 10TH

Avigail claimed a table in the library, making sure there was room for at least five. Leo would be a bit. She'd finished supper a few minutes ago, right as the half-hour chime went, and he hadn't even made it into the Great Hall. Their duelling session had run long, or rather Leo and Theo's had. Professor Fortier had dismissed her at quarter to seven, with enough time to go wash up quickly before supper.

Theo was still getting used to not having Artemis right there. Leo had almost got a smidge of advantage twice, even if he hadn't been able to hold on to it. Avigail could also see how Leo was struggling with learning something new. She'd wanted to stick around and watch, but she never liked other people watching her in that state. The kindest thing she could do was go away. Leo would turn up in a bit, she was sure, and she knew he had his own stash of bruise salve and liniment in his dormitory.

Likely enough, it'd be her turn to get pushed next week. Last week, Professor Fortier had gone lightly on her, figuring out where she was after the summer. This week he'd had her working on drills for dexterity. Growing an inch and a half had changed a lot of her balance and foot-work. Likely, she still had a few inches to go, but who knew? She could reasonably end up anywhere between Mama and Rowena. It was useful, though, to be able to look at Rowena and Anthony, both out of school now, and have a sense of what the range of options might look like. Older siblings were, in fact, helpful that way.

Academics were a bit more complex. Avigail was taking everything she could, which made for busy days and a need to get to the library as promptly as possible. Peter was taking just as many classes, but he handled his time differ-ently, and of course he wasn't doing extra duelling or riding. Now, she pulled out her notes to work through what she needed to turn in, and when, while she was waiting for people to actually study with. Ros and Leo were taking a little less, but Ros was making up for it with language tuto-rials, and Leo with duelling and private tutoring in Ritual.

Which brought her back to the question of friends. Papa had been on his own most of his time at Schola. The Papa she knew now understood how to be charming. She'd watched him do it, quite a few times just this summer. Mama had kept to herself at Schola, but she'd had a couple of people she was closer to. Especially after Morah Avigail had taken her in. Avigail had never met the woman she was named for, but she'd been Mama's apprentice mistress. And before that, once Morah Avigail had realised Mama was an orphan, she'd given her a home, and people.

Avigail had come in to Schola having friends, knowing people, trusting them. But that felt like a risk now, because they were all going their own ways. She and Ros and Leo and Jasper studied together, with a couple of others. Mostly that meant Peter Wallace, who was clever and asked interesting questions. But they weren't in the same sections half the time and Jasper wasn't taking nearly as many of the academic courses. They were all starting to specialise in ways Avigail didn't understand, except for Peter.

That much, Papa had actually explained to her. If she was considering going into the Penelopes, like Papa, when she left school, having a broad range of knowledge was an excellent start. After all, when going into a line of work that was all about untangling what other people had done magically, every bit of learning could be useful. And more to the point, learning how to think in a variety of ways was. Being a Penelope wasn't about being clever, exactly, it was about being versatile.

Figuring out what she could be brilliant at would also help, but Mama and Papa pointed out that was a lot to figure out when she was fourteen. She had some time for that. In the meantime, well, wanting to know everything was a sign the Penelopes might be a good choice, later. But not knowing felt to Avigail like she was failing at something.

Mama and Papa had both been certain how they were spending their adult lives by the end of their second years, even if that had had some unexpected bits. Avigail's sister and brother had been too, with Rowena following Mama into being a Portal Keeper, and Anthony going into the Guard like Grandpapa and Uncle Magni.

Avigail still wasn't at all certain. Part of her wanted to be a Penelope, to be that kind of clever and sharp and helpful all the time, to have a place where it mattered. But part of her wasn't sure if she was up to it, if she could be as good as Papa or Aunt Mason or Aunt Witt or Aunt Doyle or any of the other Penelopes. Even the younger ones were so good at so much.

And the rest of her life wasn't exactly helping. She got on all right with the other Salmon House students in her year, and the year or two above. But the older students were usually deep in their own projects. Avigail had picked up a couple of crafting skills from them last year. A bit of leatherwork, though materials were hard to come by. Also, a bit of dressmaking suitable for adjusting clothing or mending, which was just useful given the clothing coupons.

The problem was, there was a difference between that and friends. And Avigail wanted people to laugh with, and tease, and do something that wasn't schoolwork with. Besides duelling. Duelling was in her schedule, and so was riding, so she was sure she was getting that.

While she'd been thinking, she'd missed three of the girls in her year coming in, taking the table the next set of shelves over. They weren't being quiet, either. The three of them were chattering over the day. How Professor Fortier had come in to supper late, and what had he been up to, he looked even more dashing this year. There was a fair bit of twittering about a couple of the fifth year boys, none of whom were likely to spare a second year much attention unless they were siblings or cousins or shared some particular interest. She knew the fifth year boys on the pavo team, by virtue of knowing them last year when they were fourth years and she was a firstie.

The tittering got to her, though, especially when there was another loud proclamation from Tessa McAllister, wondering where Professor Fortier had been. She was in Owl, and Avigail kept wondering why, because thus far, she hadn't shown a great deal of an Owl's expected logical reasoning.

Avigail pitched her voice to carry just enough. "He has duelling training until seven, and they ran late today."

"Why would you know?" Oh, that was an outright sneer. "Don't tell me you go in for something like that." Ah, duelling was one of those things, in their eyes, that was manly and virtuous - pun intended - in a man, but not in a woman. Alcesta Berring had taken the lead. She was in Fox, like Ros, but Avigail knew the two of them were cordially ignoring each other. Trouble in the actual dorm room was an awful lot of fuss.

Avigail stood, brushing her uniform skirt out smooth, and came around the bookshelf. She respected libraries, and also making older students angry wasn't a good strategic decision basically ever. "Because I'm in that session. Professor Fortier was finishing up with Leo and Theo Lefton. He sent me off so I'd be on time for supper." Avigail shrugged. Specifically she let them see the shrug. She couldn't charm them, she knew that. She'd failed at it last year, and you didn't exactly get to erase history and try again.

"It's not proper." Alcesta sniffed. "You'll never marry someone decent like that." So this was about that, then. Papa came from an ancient family, he was Grandpapa's Heir to the land magic, and he was on the Council. Even if people had wanted to argue about social status with the first two, the third meant they had more sense. Mama, though, her parents had both been Bengali, making do with what work they could get on the London docks. They'd both died when Mama was young, and it was only a set of coincidences - and Mama's particular gift with a rare sort of magic - that had changed that. Avigail didn't much want to marry anyone at the moment, but she was going to choose for love, like Mama and Papa, not social status.

Then there was the question of the duelling. She'd have thought that coming through a war, people would respect skill in that sort of thing, the ability to actively deal with a problem. It didn't work that way. Even so, Avigail could name two dozen socially respected female duellists of the last twenty years off the top of her head, though not all of them indulged at this stage in their lives. A few were dead. Nor did she want to model any part of her life on the late Livia Fortier. Except maybe the level of skill.

Everyone agreed that Lady Fortier - Professor Fortier's sister-in-law, Leo's aunt - had been brilliant at what she did, even if she was also highly skilled at terrifying people. She'd probably saved dozens of magical artefacts from being taken in the invasion of Paris the day she died. Papa respected that. Avigail knew that much. And he held the Council seat that had been hers. Papa had a lot of thoughts about Livia Fortier even if he didn't talk about them much. "I don't think I'd want to marry someone who didn't want me to be good at things."

It was lacking something in the rhetorical department. Avigail was good at her Trivium classes, more than enough to analyse things once they were actually out of her mouth. The three other girls looked shocked. That, now, that was the sort of puzzle Avigail didn't exactly want to spend time on understanding. But she knew, with the sort of moth to a flame desire that both Mama and Papa talked about sometimes, that it mattered. Finally, after the shocked silence had stretched out a little, Alcesta Berring coughed. "You can't just say something like that. It's not, people will, you just can't."

Avigail considered her options here. "You can't. Or at least for the sake of the discussion, I'm glad to work with that. But that doesn't mean I can't."

"Men don't like women who are better than them. Why haven't you learned that? Where did you go to tutoring school, anyway? You keep..." Melitta Henning broke in.

"I didn't. The one they were going to send me to was near Southampton, and it seemed like a bad idea in 1943 for some reason." The Blitz had been over, but everyone knew that invasion might still happen. Also, she might have laid out an argument to her parents and grandparents involving charts, diagrams, maps, and a dozen reasons why she wasn't leaving Veritas. They hadn't argued, though they had made a number of suggestions for more persuasive chart design next time something like that came up.

"Oh, well, that explains a lot, actually." Alcesta leaned back in her chair. "And I suppose your sister was at school, and your mother..." Now her voice got careful.

"Mama was doing quite a lot of war service and travelling. I spent a lot of time working with Grandmama. Lady Edgarton." And no one, but no one, had ever accused Grandmama of bad manners. Not even Grandpapa's mother, apparently.

Alcesta considered that information. "Well. Point is. We were taught that boys don't want someone who's better than they are at what they're good at."

"Is that why you don't talk in class?" Avigail didn't understand why someone wouldn't do well in school if they could. Mama and Papa had both been very clear that her duty right now was to learn things, whatever that looked like. Just like their duties were to the Council and the Penelopes for Papa. And making portals and tending them, for Mama. Or just making things better in general for both of them. But she could understand someone not showing it, even if that didn't make a lot of sense to her.

Melitta Henning glanced around, like she was afraid

someone might see. But also, she looked like someone who desperately wanted to explain all the ways Avigail was wrong. The two desires were chasing around in her expression, like a fox going after a badger who was going after the fox. "No one sees my marks but my Head of House." Which was true, though that meant Owl House didn't assign its workroom spaces by who had the best marks. On the other hand, that was probably sensible for Owl. There would be a lot of people clustered at the top, at least if House stereotypes held true. "It'll matter for my apprenticeship if I do one, but no one sees those either. And it means I can do as Mother wants, in public."

It was an annoying argument, but it had a logical consistency Avigail couldn't figure out how to break open. "And you're all right with that?" She didn't know what to make of someone who'd come to Schola and then not apprentice and presumably master at least one form of magic. She had skills and gifts, she had the chance to come to Schola. It was her obligation, more or less, to figure out how to use them. Mama had been very clear about that, from the time Avigail was tiny.

"Oh, yes." Melitta looked up, then blinked several times, her face and posture shifting swiftly. "Crimson, oh, I was hoping you'd come by. Could you explain the Incantation exercise to me again? You got it so quickly yesterday." Crimson Hettleburgh was, well, exactly the sort of young man Melitta's family thought would be an excellent match. He was Heir to his father's title. He was in Fox. And while Ros had high standards about who she spent her time with, she agreed Crimson wasn't actually awful at all. Not very interesting, maybe, but not awful.

Avigail took her cue. Also, she could see Ros and Leo and Jasper and Peter all coming in together. She slid back into the chair she'd already claimed as they joined her. Ros raised an eyebrow before bending over to take out her books. "Anything we ought to know about?" She kept her voice pitched low, so it wouldn't carry.

"Totally different outlook on life." Avigail drew in a breath. "One more reason to figure out what I'm actually good at. Some other things."

"Right. Cryptic utterances. Where are we starting tonight? Everyone good on the Incantation exercise, or do we want to start with Materia?" Ros got right down to their task. They were all taking both of them, and Avigail and Ros and Peter could figure out time to talk Alchemy later if they had to.

"Materia. I keep feeling like I'm missing a layer." Avigail glanced at Leo. "You have a better idea what Professor Ward was talking about, the secondary and tertiary actions?" Leo was moving a little stiffly. She was sure he had bruises, or he'd strained something.

He grimaced once, but nodded. "Yeah. Someone got a bit of scrap paper or a slate?" Ros produced both slate and chalk, and he set to work tracing out a series of boxes and patterns, diagramming out the range of interactions for mint.

CHAPTER 5
LEO ON SEPTEMBER 24TH

Leo was just taking a breather and a sip of water when Dad's chin went up. They were more than an hour into their duelling time. Avigail had just started attacking Theo with a particular sequence of charms, so Theo could try out a new defensive technique. Dad held up his hand. "Hold."

Everyone immediately stopped, hands up, before lowering them slowly. Dad let out a huff of a breath. "That can't wait. Someone's—" His eyes half closed. "I don't even want to know how someone got stuck in the wards from there. Theo, you mind lending a hand? I'd rather not roust Ibis out." Dad was distracted, not to say 'Professor Ward'.

Theo bobbed his head. "Of course, sir."

Then Dad glanced at Leo and Avigail. "Leo, do you mind cleaning up in here? Put things to rights for tomorrow? Benches and equipment away, whatever cleaning can't wait. Don't worry about the rest of the charms, just lock up. I hate to ask you, but..." Dad was shifting from one foot to the other.

"Of course, Dad." Leo didn't normally call him that

45

around other people, but the salle in near-private was different. Just as Leo was 'Leo' here, in this space, and 'Fortier' everywhere else as a student, except with his close friends. Even with Mum and Dad. Anyway, Leo knew where everything went, and he knew how to lock what needed locking, and he knew how to set the wards when they left.

Dad waved a hand. "You're welcome to stay and chat, Avigail. Right." He took off in long loping strides for his office to grab his bag. Theo immediately went to wipe down his face and grab his own, still in duelling togs. Theo held up the towel for just a second, and Leo waved a hand. He could throw that in the laundry basket easily enough. Theo nodded, and then stepped off next to Dad as Dad came out of the office at speed.

Leo watched them go, not moving until they were both out of the salle proper. When he looked back, Avigail was frowning after them. "That happen often?"

"It's a bit early this year. Usually something like that, it's one of the secret societies getting clever about figuring out who they're interested in." Leo considered, then started with beginning to haul one of the targets they'd used earlier out of the centre of the salle, back to where it normally lived. Without being asked, Avigail came around to take the other side, which made it much lighter work.

Avigail was quiet until they'd moved that target and the second one into place. "Secret societies." Her voice was a little uncertain. "Ros and I were talking about that, wondering about it."

Leo snorted. "You could ask, you know. So could she. What do you know already?" Leo glanced over as he went to grab the broom to sweep the dirt out of Dad's office and back into the salle. There'd be tidying up the towels and tools, then raking.

"Less than you do, I bet." Avigail grinned at him, suddenly. "Care to even that up any?"

"You just want to know everything. I don't know all of it. No one does. There's a lot that you only get a fragment of, here and there."

Avigail turned to face him, hands on her hips. "And you've been picking up those fragments since you were tiny."

It made Leo laugh. "Well, yeah." He considered. "Seven societies, some more secret than others."

"I know about the Nine Muses. They're not really secret at all, are they?" It was, to be fair, difficult to be properly secret when producing musical and theatrical performances every term with the society name listed as the sponsor. Avigail glanced around. "What can I do to help right now?"

"Help me wipe down the woodwork? There are rags in the bucket under the end there, and clean water next to them. I'll refill it before we go." Leo went to grab the cleaning spray. Someone earlier today had apparently been doing something questionable with mud that had splashed all over the benches on the courtyard wall of the salle. If he cleaned it now, it'd be fine tomorrow.

Once they got started on that - Leo with the spray and an increasingly muddy rag, Avigail following along with a damp one to clean up the rest - Leo sorted out his thoughts. "The Nine Muses do have secret parts, but everyone more or less knows who they are. They're one of the largest, too. They invite seven or eight people most years."

"And the invites are in the spring, so that's a large group for the spring concert, right?" Avigail wrung out her cloth and got it clean to rinse again.

"Exactly. Initial invites usually go out in Vestal Term,

though it can happen any time. But most likely the end of January, early February. The invite just turns up some-where, and it tells you what you need to do if you want to be considered. A series of tasks, some sort of challenge, something like that. Sometimes it's a set, multiple notes." Leo jerked an elbow toward where Dad had disappeared. "Sometimes it's stupid prank stuff. Sometimes dangerous stuff. A lot of the time it's sort of silly, or it's something that's actually useful to the society. Like for Nine Muses, part of it's helping with the Vestal Term concert or produc-tion, or whatever it is."

"That one at least makes sense." Avigail agreed. "Here, is this too much water? I don't want to spoil the wood."

Leo laughed, rather amused. "Not much can damage the wood in here. It's charmed and protected to within an inch of its life. If you like, you too can come spend a Saturday afternoon sometime re-waxing everything."

"You don't mind it, though, do you?" Like a lot of Avigail's questions, it wasn't actually a question.

"No. Sort of soothing, really. Like helping Uncle Ibis - um. Professor Ward, with the Materia. I know what each part is doing. I like setting things to rights. Like this, too. Dad's careful not to ask very often, though. He doesn't think that's fair to me." Leo went back to scrubbing at a bit of stubborn mud with the corner of his rag. "Anyway. The next in order of secrecy is probably the Dwellers at the Forge."

"They keep turning up in the papers, don't they? Only I know sometimes the papers aren't always right. Or some-times they are." Avigail frowned. "I wish Ros was here. Her Aunt Laura's close in with the Dwellers. Ros's uncle, her husband, is one, and his friend. She likes them, I haven't met them, really. A picnic or two, that's not enough to actually get to know anyone." She considered, giving Leo space to continue.

"Uncle Garin hates them. Says they don't know what they're doing, they're playing with fire. Which is, really, a hilarious pun, and I can't decide if Uncle Garin means it or not. They're meant to be the fire Prometheus brought down from Olympus, in one sense, wanting to make sure things get better, not worse. The Dwellers are a lot smaller at Schola, though. They don't add a lot of people every year. Usually two, occasionally one or three. But if you keep an eye on those newspaper stories, they stick pretty close as adults. They help each other out. It's not always the same people mentioned."

"And the other societies don't? Though it sounds nice. Having people you know will have your back. Rather than bullies and people being snobs and whatever." Avigail frowned at her cloth. "Is there more fresh water?"

"Let me fetch it. The sink's in Dad's office. The wards won't like you." Leo glanced at the bucket, which did need a refresh. He trotted off with it, dumped it out in the great stone sink, and then filled up an extra, bringing them both back out. Avigail was stretching a little, which made sense. She'd been working hard in training. Also, Avigail didn't stay still much.

"I think it depends on the society, honestly, how much it's a community?" Leo had to stop, to figure out how to put this into words, and Avigail came and got her rag damp again, going back to scrubbing the wood without rushing him. Leo let out a breath. "I like having friends. I'm not so good at figuring out more than the five of us. Or being cordial to people, but that's not friends. And I can't think of it as allies, like Ursula does, trajectories of influence?"

Avigail snorted. "Leo, as far as I can tell, no one thinks

of that sort of thing like your sister does. Even Grandmama and Aunt Charlotte, who both do the Great Families politics very well." She waved the rag. "But if you joined a society, it'd be for the people, the community, not the, I don't know. Status? Power?"

Leo blinked at her, that she'd put it that way apparently so easily. Then he nodded. "Yeah. Should I keep going about the others?"

Avigail nodded, turning away, so that at least Leo wasn't focused on her looking at him. That was distracting, to be the focus. He took a breath.

"The other societies vary a lot. The Nine Muses tend to ebb and flow. It depends on what's going on artistically and who they need for what parts. Dius Fidius and Animus Mundi are mostly really formal about it. From what I gather, it's a few meetings a year, and then people make connections privately. Maybe the other three do things, but they're all more private still."

"All right. That's not really a community, no. Who's next?" Avigail dipped her rag in the fresh water again and wrung it out, waiting for Leo to pick up his cleaning.

"Dius Fidius are, well," Leo glanced around, and then took a breath. He didn't have remotely the sense of Schola that Dad did. Not yet. But last winter, his parents had shown him something that meant he was starting to get faint hints of it. Now, he usually could figure out where Mum and Dad were, roughly, compared to where he was. And he certainly knew Schola's spaces well enough to know what that meant.

Mum was upstairs. He could feel the height distance, though he couldn't tell if she was in the family rooms on the fourth floor or her office two floors up from there. Dad was well off to the northeast corner, and Leo thought he was on the outside edge of the curtain wall, not somewhere in the depths of Owl House. "Here's the thing. I'm sure Mum isn't in any of them, she's said. Dad won't say, but I've got my suspicions about Dius Fidius. Ursula noticed when he was gone. And it was a bit more obvious who else was disappearing when she was a prefect."

Avigail took a moment to sort through that. "And they're supposed to be all about good governance, aren't they? Or that's what the public face is."

"Yeah. There was an older society, before the Pact. After, they formed something that was all good public works. Ursula's got a whole spiel about this. You can guess what she's not a member of. Mostly, it's a few meetings a year, and they don't seem to do much. Drink, smoke cigars, trade stories about how they were slightly more generous to one of the staff than was strictly necessary." Leo understood how that sort of person worked - he was related to enough of them, though mostly more distantly, through Dad and Uncle Garin. That didn't mean he liked it. "I mean, nearly all posh Fox House. And about four men to every woman, if Ursula's right, which she probably is."

"You really shouldn't hide how you feel about things, Leo. I'm sure it doesn't do you any good." Avigail said it sweetly, then somewhat spoiled the effect by grinning and laughing immediately after. "So they're going after Crimson Hettleburgh and Anthony Phipps, whoever else they approach. And Animus Mundi?"

"Focused on ritual. I'm actually a little curious there? Only I don't know what they actually do. Do they just sit around and talk about ritual methods? Do they figure out new rituals or methods or whatever that might actually do something useful?" Leo shrugged and focused on scrubbing. Talking about Animus Mundi felt a bit uncomfortable.

It was like a coat he was supposed to grow into that itched the back of his neck and pulled oddly across his shoulders already.

Avigail grinned again. "And one of those you're maybe interested in, the other not at all." She cocked her head. "I don't think Daphne's a member there. She's not that good at keeping secrets, honestly. Rowena's much better."

Leo snorted. "Rowena sets a high standard, you've said so yourself. And yeah, about what's interesting to me. Can you try cleaning this bit now? I think I've got all the mud off." Leo stepped aside to let Avigail do her part. "That leaves the last three. They're all a lot more private. Many Are The Waters isn't actually a name, it's a phrase. Anyone who knows anything about the societies knows that much."

"Rowena told me about them." Avigail said. "Don't think she's a member, though again, Rowena, how would I know? She doesn't tell most people a lot of things, even family." Avigail snorted. "Or rather, she sometimes tells one of us, but not the rest. And she trusts we won't tell those bits, and we don't. Anyway. There's a lot of Seal House there, from what she said. And people who want to go into healing, too."

"Yeah. There's a sister group - and they always say sister, though I think maybe they're more or less balanced, men and women and all?" Leo wasn't sure how anyone could figure that out when they weren't public, but Ursula hadn't ranted about it, which was sort of a measurable feature. "Anyway. Sister group at Alethorpe. And probably some people at Forvie, though oceans are a totally different kind of water. Sometimes you'll see the name pop up, some of the notable healers. Healer Belisama, Mum mentioned once, though she's not showy about it."

Avigail grinned. "I've met her a couple of times. Papa and Mama have had the Smythe-Clives over every couple of months. And a couple of times Healer Belisama and her husband too. He's got some fascinating travel stories. I mean, running the Pelagius liners, you would." Then Avigail added impishly, "Papa said Healer Belisama lets her brother take all the shiny bits."

Leo grinned back at that. Magister Smythe-Clive had just resigned last winter from being Head of the Council, so Avigail absolutely would know that sort of thing, given her father was on the Council.

"What about the other two?" Avigail went back to washing a bit of the wood.

"The Four Metals goes in for crafting, and honestly, I think a lot of them have to be Salmon House? It'd be easy to tuck things away there. And maybe something in the village. We don't have a proper forge up here, but I don't think it's all metal work." Leo paused. "It gets a lot of Materia specialists. Uncle Ibis sort of didn't say something last year, when I was helping over winter hols. I don't know if he's a member, but maybe he helps them? They're more collaborative, but they aren't very public about it until there's something final to show off."

"Oh, now there's a really good question of which ones of our professors are members, and of which one. You said your mother isn't, and your father is. Now I'm going to have to diagram it properly. Gather information and evidence." Avigail's eyes had lit up, and honestly, Leo was sure he'd be right in there helping. There wasn't a lot in the library about them, not on the open shelves, but Leo knew where most of it was. And maybe he could talk Mum into more information.

Leo set that aside for the moment. "Anyway, the last

one's Society of the White Horse. The little bits I've heard, it's about the landscape. Not the land magic like your father and Ros's, but something bigger than that? I don't know the right words. But they're right private, and not just when people are at school."

"Also, not at all something we've covered in class yet. That might make a really good research project, though. Because you'd think people who really wanted that would be at Snap, right? So who's doing that sort of thing here, caring about it?"

Leo spread his hands. "Don't know. Don't know that we're going to get an answer. Though honestly, I wouldn't be utterly shocked if they tapped Jasper? Not just because of the horses, but you've seen what he's like about the New Forest when we visit." He glanced along the benches. "Want to get this last bit, and I'll start raking the floor?"

Avigail nodded, agreeably finishing up, then taking the buckets over to by Dad's office, leaving them for him to dump. Leo raked half the salle before dumping and refilling them. Then he worked his way pass by pass up toward the door where Avigail waited for him. Once he'd got all the way to the door, he hung the rake up. "See you at supper after we've washed?"

She nodded, then went bounding off, as full of energy as she had been when they started training.

CHAPTER 6
ROS ON OCTOBER 12TH

Ros swung her leg over Merla's hindquarters, landing on both feet with a bounce. She managed the two steps to grab the ball she needed from the ground, shoving it in the top of her jumper. She took another two strides, flung herself up, and slid back down. Merla stopped a step later, peering at Ros with a puzzled expression.

"Good idea on getting your hands free, Ros. Let's work on the vaulting, though." Marguerite, captain of the pavo team this year, was running things today, though Master Held was watching. There were lots of pavo skills that Ros was doing well at. Vaulting was not one of them. Flinging herself off Merla's back was easy enough. She'd known how to fall off a horse safely since she was five and still on a leading rein. She reliably landed evenly on her feet these days, unless she meant to roll. But getting back up was another problem.

Pavo needed both. Parts of the puzzle, whatever it was that was needed to win the match, usually involved getting down and up again at speed. No one had time for stirrups or standing still. Ros could stick like a burr to Merla's saddle. She was a lot less likely to drop something in her hands, she could manoeuvre with seat and knees, not needing the reins. But the vertical was defeating her.

She steered Merla over to the side of the ring, out of the way of the others, while she considered what to do.

Jasper rode over to join her, tilting his head. "You're better than you were." He offered it a little cautiously, as if he weren't sure what she'd do. He'd got more touchy about that this year, and Ros was trying to figure out why. She didn't think it was anything she'd actually done, but the looming bullies had made Jasper more skittish.

That was a bigger problem than the vaulting. "I'm not going to blame you for being good at it." Jasper had height on her, he had leg length on her in specific. More to the point, he had better leverage from his shoulders. Also, less in the way of a bosom to get in the way of things. None of which was his fault, and none of which helped her. "I just don't like being bad at it. Different problem."

It did get a smile out of him. That was something. Then he tilted his head. "Look, how about we work on it when everyone else works on the flexibility exercises? You don't need that." He glanced around. "Leo, too, maybe."

Ros nodded. "Thanks." She considered, then trotted back out into the ring to tell Marguerite that and get her approval. They spent the next twenty minutes working on other things, Ros partnering with one of the older girls to do some of the dexterity drills. Casting charms on horseback was difficult about six ways round, but she was decent at that one, at least once she had the charm down pat. Today they were just doing coloured bubbles at specific spots, to practise precision.

"Right, everyone split up. Jasper, you're here with Ros.

Leo and Avigail, I think we want you with us for the flexibility today. Everyone else, come out to the poles up field." They had a set laid out, tight enough to test everyone's ability to weave through them.

Jasper waited until the ring was clear. Master Held was, apparently, staying here, because he came over with a lunge line, a long strap that'd keep whichever horse circling. "You want to demonstrate, Jasper? Your Dot up for another few minutes, yes?"

His mare was a stocky chestnut with a broad chest and feet like dinner plates. She wasn't the sort of elegant conventionally attractive mare that sold well, but her tail had always delighted Ros. It had every colour a horse came in threaded into it when she looked closely, from bright red chestnut through gold and copper and silver down into deep brown and black. She was like one of the great war horses of the Middle Ages, scaled down to just barely Ros's current height - five foot - at the withers. She was too round for a proper pavo mount, and Papa and Jasper's father probably wouldn't breed her. But Dot was smart as anything, and that counted for a lot at the moment.

"She's not bored yet." Jasper patted her on the shoulder. He dismounted with a slight bounce, fastening the lunge line to her bridle, tying the reins up safely and crossing the stirrups over her withers so they wouldn't bounce against her side. "Ready when you are, sir."

"Heyup, Dot." The mare moved out. She had moods - well, horses often did, just like people - but was obliging today. Master Held got her up to a canter, the rolling gait. Off hind, then the near hind and off fore together, then the near fore. Over and over they went, round once, before Jasper joined her. He took a few steps to match speed with her, hand resting on the saddle. Ros concentrated. This was what she knew intellectually but couldn't get her body to do.

Jasper made it look like magic. She was pretty sure it wasn't, but it looked like it. No one should be able to get that kind of height from the ground. He rode smoothly for a couple of strides at the canter, then flung his right leg over her hindquarters again, landing with a bounce on the ground and repeating it.

Ros paid attention to where his hands were, but she thought that wouldn't work for her. His left was on Dot's mane, a solid handful, and his other was on the front right of the saddle, just beyond the pommel. Ros tried that, and she thought her chest would get in the way, or there was something about the angle of her hip.

It worked on smaller ponies - Papa had tried her on some this summer. She could vault, respectably enough, on anything under about thirteen-two. But that was a full five inches shorter than Merla, and those five inches made a terrible lot of difference. That was the problem with pavo. A pavo player wanted sturdiness, longer legs, for some things. And that ran counter to wanting a manageable height for the vaulting.

Jasper did another couple of vaults before calling out, "Let's give Ros a try, sir?" He brought Dot to a walk, and then steered with his knees to bring her into the centre, so Master Held could unclip the line. Ros brought Merla into the centre, to get her set up. Jasper hopped off and handed Dot's reins to one of the girls who was looking on. She was a firstie who was down at the stables as much as anyone would let her. The Jasper of her class, that way, and he was as good with that as he was with any of the actual horses.

"Right. What you've been trying isn't working, so what can we do different?" Jasper turned to Ros.

Ros snorted. "What you do different is you have springs in your ankles. Where'd you get them?"

Jasper laughed at that. "There's an image. Though, I mean." He considered. "It's not actually outside the lines of pavo to do that. Or to have it on your boots. You'd have to get used to it, and I don't know how to cast that kind of charm. But I bet Leo does, or Professor Fortier."

Master Held started chuckling. "Unconventional solution. But let's see if we can get anywhere the ordinary way. Can you show me once or twice what you're doing now? And then we'll try some things." He got Merla moving. Ros rolled along at the canter for a full circle, then vaulted off.

As always, that part went well. She tried the positioning Jasper had been using, mane and right of the pommel, and everything just felt wrong. She made her best attempt, got halfway up, managed to get her toe in the stirrup, and scrambled on. But Merla had stiffened up, not liking it. And it had absolutely no room for error. If they were in play, Merla would have slowed, possibly shifted in a way that could be a problem. It wouldn't do.

They tried again, with just about the same results, plus a stubbed toe. Ros got herself mounted, but Master Held brought Merla down to a walk almost immediately. "What do you think, Carillon?" he asked.

"It's not working, sir." She was frustrated, but that was no excuse to be rude. Actually, it was even more reason to be polite. She patted Merla on the withers, too. "It's not fair to her." That was the heart of it, but Ros made herself add something else. "And I don't like being bad at it." Last year, it hadn't mattered. She'd been shorter. Almost no firstie made the team anyway - Jasper was the first in seven years. And Ros had been good at other parts. This year, though, it stung.

Jasper was considering something. "Have you tried from the right? The last year or two?"

"No?" People didn't. People got on and off horses from the left. Well, except for Avigail's Papa, who trained his horses for it. She'd never done that with Merla. "Why?"

Jasper shrugged. "Give it a try? At a trot or canter, whichever you want. Do you mind, sir?"

Master Held shook his head, bringing Merla in to the centre to turn her around before setting her up circling clockwise. Merla picked up a canter easily enough again. Ros took a breath, let it out, let the rocking feel remind her of how even Merla's gaits were. Then she flung herself off to the right. She'd dismounted this way plenty of times. It was good training to be able to get off in both directions. Sometimes that was important.

Getting back on, though, that was trickier. After a moment, she got one hand on Merla's mane, right at the withers, the other on the back of the saddle. It was tricky to do both hands on the saddle, there was a decent chance it'd twist, and that was right out as an idea. Then she kept her head down, took a couple of strides, bounced, and her leg was swinging over Merla's hindquarters with room to spare.

She nearly spoiled the whole thing by going too far over in startlement, but caught herself, then whooped with joy. Merla, thankfully, took it in stride. She'd been well trained to deal with noise and fuss around her.

Jasper called out, "Do it again. Not just a fluke." Ros gathered herself up, and then she was off Merla, running alongside, then up again, more securely this time. She was grinning, her face about to split, when Master Held slowed Merla down.

"Good work. Both of you. Well spotted, Jasper." Master

Held clapped him on the shoulder. "You two can have a bit of a free ride until the end of practise, I think. Thirty minutes."

That was enough time to go up the road along the cliff and back, not too far. In a moment, Jasper was mounted again, and they set off at a trot, before bringing the horses to a walk once they were well away from people.

"Why'd you think that?" Of course that was what Ros wanted to know first.

Jasper shrugged. "You're maybe a little too much like Lord Carillon, sometimes? I don't know, the way you hold yourself." That didn't make sense. Ros made an uncertain noise, and Jasper snorted. "He favours his left shoulder. Not that I've ever seen him vault, but I was wondering if it made a difference. Maybe it didn't, when it was smaller ponies. No reason it should matter, but it seemed worth testing."

Ros swallowed hard. She knew Papa had had a bad injury there, during the Great War, but that was about all she knew about it. It wasn't something he talked about, though she'd seen the scars when they'd been swimming somewhere. There wasn't any reason it should carry down to her. Only, well, Jasper had been right. She let the mares walk on a few more strides. "Papa hasn't vaulted in years." To be fair, he was over sixty, and pavo was in fact a much younger man's sport, even with healing magic on offer.

"Like I said. Shouldn't have mattered, but maybe it did. We'll have to talk it over with Marguerite, but it might be an advantage in other ways, too. Being able to vault when others can't, not being the expected side. Or maybe you'll sort it out on the left, now you can do it on the right? No idea." He seemed rather comfortable with the uncertainty there, in a way Ros never was.

On the other hand, Ros really hated being bad at things.

And pavo, in particular, somehow. It was letting Papa down, in some important way she didn't know how to describe. Now she just straightened her shoulders. "Thanks. Do you want some help with your essay later?"

"Oh, please. I know what I want to say, but it comes out all awkward. And Avigail said she'd find time to explain the Incantation assignment. Peter has questions about it too." Ros nodded. If they were helping him, less likely that certain people would be awful. They weren't willing to risk it with her around, from everything she'd seen, not that she and Jasper had talked directly about it since that thing a few weeks ago. Jasper kept shying away from it. And Ros knew if she pressed too hard, he'd shut her out, and he'd probably be right to. Even if she hated that. She worried he'd do that, close himself off from everyone, keep himself distant.

The silence hung there, slightly awkward, before Ros had an idea. "Try writing it from the end. Paragraph by paragraph?" It was more or less equivalent to what Ros had just tried. She saw it register on his face, then he was laughing.

"Canter, and then we'll circle back? And yeah, I'll try that." Before she could answer, he and Dot picked up an easy canter, heading up to the point of the island and making further conversation impossible.

CHAPTER 7
JASPER ON OCTOBER 25TH

J asper had been looking forward to Friday afternoon all week. As soon as he'd finished in Incantation class, he'd changed into riding gear, and twenty minutes later, he and Dot had been on their way. Sunset came earlier and earlier, but he had enough time to do a loop up across to the west side of the island, then up through the northern fields and orchards.

Something in him had wanted to be outside and on his own, and this was the one time in the week he had a chance at it. What he'd do when the sun set even earlier, he wasn't sure. For much of November and December and January, the sunset was too early - right around four - for him to get out on horseback after class. His morning riding time on Wednesday and Thursday was partly about helping train horses or help out with a little teaching. Saturday was given over to pavo. Sunday morning he did the more involved training with Dot, when it was quieter.

Maybe Sunday afternoon, but he'd discovered last year that people noticed if he wasn't at bohort. Besides, he wasn't interested in playing it, but cheering on his House mattered. And Leo had made it on the reserve for his House team this year and Avigail might next. Seeing the matches meant he could keep up with the conversation at meals better.

He set it all aside. That was for later. Now was for enjoying the autumn air, the scent of the sea, the smooth dirt roads with very few people visible. It wasn't the New Forest; it wasn't home, but it had its own pleasures. He and Dot had a good solid warmup getting over to the west coast, then picked up a steady canter along the cliff road, moving to the north and east. Jasper let himself fall into a comfortable awareness of the land. Schola wasn't brand new to him, not anymore, but it was still only his second autumn, and there was more to learn about the island.

He could see the seals down below, and a few of the merfolk. He waved at them, because he'd been told that was polite, though he'd never talked to any of them in person. Leo said they all signed, rather than speaking, since sound worked differently under water. But they understood a wave, and they waved back. Jasper hadn't seen that many of them, all out like a group before, but they must have a reason for it. When Professor Ward had talked about them in classes last year, he'd made it clear they had their own ways of doing things, some of which made sense to people on land, some of which didn't.

Now, they seemed to be clustered in a spot off the coast on the northern side of the island. He could barely see that one would pop up, another would dive, cycling through most of the group. He thought some of them might be keeping an eye out, but he didn't know a lot about what sort of threats there might be in the water. It made him think of rooks or crows, reacting to something on the land, the way they were one and many, working together.

By the time he and Dot got within sight of the orchards, he pulled her down to a walk. The trees sometimes hid people moving around. There might be sheep grazing in the field beyond, and either way, startling Dot wasn't kind. A few steps later, that turned out to be a good idea. Dot's ears pricked forward. He felt her hindquarters bunch a little under him, all the signs that there was something dubious ahead.

Of course, what horses - even very clever ones - thought was dubious didn't always match reality. Jasper patted her on the withers, murmuring to her, while he scanned to figure out what was actually happening. Not sheep, no, at least not yet, but Professor Wain. She had a beige apron on, a woven wicker basket over her arm, and she was climbing down from a ladder propped against one of the apple trees.

Jasper considered. Maybe she liked the quiet too? But it would also be rude to go by and not say anything. While he was trying to figure it out, she must have heard something, because she turned, hand over her eyes against the sun behind him, and then waved. Jasper rode over slowly, as she came down to the edge of the road, and then nodded, touching his cap out of instinct. "Professor Wain."

She smiled up at him. "Getting a bit of a ride in before dark? Hello, Dot. You've a bit in. You shouldn't have a snack." It was companionable, and something in how she handled it made Jasper a lot more comfortable. Last year, his first day in Horse House, he'd asked if she rode. He'd seen her a few times with Leo's mare, Story, but this was different. She knew how to meet Dot on her own ground, and something in Jasper eased up, something he hadn't known he was nervous about.

"Thank you, Professor. She does like a snack, but she's supposed to have better manners." Then he frowned. "Is there a problem out here? Can I help with something?" He didn't think she'd been up this way last week, or the week before.

"I was out checking the apples and the bees. It looks like it might rain tomorrow, and our staff meeting's starting a little later, so I thought I'd do it this afternoon." Jasper knew - Leo talked about it sometimes - how professors had a lot of other things to do. But he hadn't really thought about meeting schedules.

"Yes'm." That came out automatically, and Jasper bobbed his head again. "Anything I can help with?" Then, he heard himself ask, "I didn't think you'd be responsible for apples. Or bees."

Something in that made her laugh. "Well, there are days when the number of apple varieties seems like the stars in the sky. So many, slightly different, and not nearly enough time to get friendly with them all." Then she waved a hand at the orchards. "It's one of my duties. It's partly about rationing and making sure we have enough food. But I actually picked up tending to them when I got married. Dad's family has a line of orchard magics, and Mum's has honey. Between the two..."

"Apples and bees." Then Jasper frowned. "But not the land magic."

"Not the Fortier kind of land magic, no." Professor Wain didn't seem uncomfortable putting it that way, but now Jasper wasn't sure about asking more. She gave him a moment, then said, "I'm glad to talk about it. Most people don't ask."

That put the problem back on Jasper's shoulders, and he had to stop and think. "May I ask, please, what you were doing today? And then what you're doing generally? I know the Forest magic. The New Forest, I mean. This is, I think it's different?" He stammered his way through the last bit, haltingly.

"Ah, that's a good question. Mind walking with me up this way? I want to check on the Old Man of the Orchard before I head back." She picked up the basket. It had at least a dozen apples in it, maybe two dozen, and at least three or four different varieties. She swung it easily, as if the weight weren't any bother, but she kept it in her off hand, well away from Dot's mouth. Jasper considered, then swung off Dot's back to take her reins and lead her. He'd have better control that way.

They walked along in silence for a little, down the road that ran north to south, back to Schola itself. There was a little indentation, part way down, a path that led from the edge of the road deeper into the orchard. "I've come to understand," Professor Wain said, her voice quiet, "that there are a number of kinds of land magic. You've grown up seeing one of them, in Lord and Lady Carillon, and Edmund, as their Heir. Leo's grown up watching his father and uncle. And now Ursula as Heir, which we're all grateful for."

She took a few more steps, and Jasper didn't interrupt. "But there are other ways to understand the land and the magic. My family, it isn't the land magic that we talk about with titles and demesne lands and the Council. There's a magic that comes with each farmer, each crofter, each person who tends their chickens or pigs or sheep or horses or who makes use of their forest rights. Everyone who's got a garden that grows anything." She smiled more broadly. "And we are a nation of gardeners, magical and non-magical, even before growing our own veg was so necessary."

Jasper couldn't help smiling. "You know a bit about those, Professor?"

"Not as much as I know about these apples or our bees. Or the orchards and bees and livestock I grew up with. But a little." She shrugged once, still agreeable. It was like Dot stamping one of her feet. Nothing upset, just a little movement. "You heard the lecture last year about how astronomy is maths in time and space? Apples are like that. Anything that's harvested is, maybe. There's the progression of time through the seasons. And there's what gets produced in this place right now. Which flowers the bees find and collect pollen from, which is some set of what's growing near enough."

That made sense to Jasper, too. "Local. Specific. Not..." He frowned. "Not half the New Forest, or, um, West Sussex?" That was where Arundel was, the Fortier demesne estate.

"Exactly. So today, I was out seeing how much more of a harvest we have to get in, and when we should do that. We've a dozen different varieties, chosen and nurtured, so we have apples for eating, for cooking, for cider, all that. And getting some for the staff meeting, since I was here. Meetings go better when people have a snack. Not just because hungry people are cranky." That came with a broader smile. "These days, that's not such an issue as it was once. But also snacks mean people take a pause in talking, and that's useful."

"It's, um, a very Horse approach, Professor?" Then Jasper ducked his head. "But other people don't mind it?"

"It is, and they don't. Rationing makes the snack part tricky. So many of the foods we can do easily don't lend themselves to finger foods well. Apples, though, I'll make the most of the apples as long as I can. Besides, they're delicious." She pulled a couple out of the basket. "This one is Gwell Na Mil, English-speakers call it Seek No Further or

Better Than A Thousand. It's a wonderful eating apple. This one's unique to Schola, we think, we call it Merlin's Toy, though there's some academic wrangling about if that name actually applies to this variety properly. Apples are tricky that way. And this one's Hebson's Jewel, that's another that's unique to Schola. The lore goes that one of the original teachers here, the ones who started the village, brought cuttings from his home and grafted them here. It's probably not true, exactly, but it is probably a descendant."

"Huh." They'd been told the history of Schola, last year. How a group of magicians, all sorts of specialities, had moved here over a couple of decades, looking for somewhere quiet where they wouldn't be bothered. It wasn't Avalon, the isle of apples out of legend, but it made sense there would be apples, really. "All the history."

"All the history, and people tending it, year after year, like we've tended and built the school. I find it reassuring, really. These aren't the same trees, of course. But we have varieties that go far back, that have seen us through all sorts of other chaos in the world."

It put a new flavour on the school's history. Jasper nodded. "And the rest of it?"

"The bees because we do like the honey, and because it's grand for all the growing things on the island. My mum's family makes mead, and I keep the tradition up. We use it for celebrations and gatherings - births, weddings, funerals. We'll be hosting a gathering for Ursula being named Heir this winter, and the mead will be at that. Funerals, as well, though I hope we'll have less of those for a while."

Jasper opened his mouth, and then he couldn't ask. Maybe Leo would talk about why Professor Wain's tone had changed to something brittle.

"Anyway." She went on briskly, though her voice smoothed out a bit more when she got back to an easier topic. "The other part, and maybe no one explained this, is that here, we don't have a Lord or Lady, not the same way. Our land magic, in that sense, is tended by the head of the school. With some help. My husband and I both do our bit. Linta - she was Head of Horse in my day, and she's still a dear friend, though almost entirely retired finally. She was the Flora professor, and she's been tending our gardens and making sure everything goes well there, or as well as any gardener can. All of us like that, really."

It was a mode of land magic Jasper really hadn't considered, even though it was very much like his Dad did. "One person, or a Lord and Lady together, they can't do it all?"

"No. They can be the focus for part of it, a lot of it, even. That's Helena, of course, the Headmistress. But there are other parts that need the Council, or people who understand the waterways - the rivers, the coasts, the merfolk, the selkies." Professor Wain gestured back. "And there are people who understand buildings on the land. Locks and dams, but also what it means when the castle is in ruins, or someone builds a new manor house on this bit of hill. We're back to the land being like stars."

Jasper snorted. "Yes'm." It was at least a consistent metaphor to work with. Then he considered. "I saw the merfolk coming back along the coast, they were very busy with something."

"Huh." Professor Wain considered that. "I'll tell Isembard and Ibis, just in case. Thank you for noticing, it's always a help to know that sort of thing, just so we can check if something needs more attention." She gestured at the orchard. "And of course, sometimes there's tending that needs doing. Pruning, or taking down branches that are rotting." Jasper stiffened slightly, unsure what she meant. "Or just things not going as they ought and needing to figure out how to get it flowing better." Now he was fairly certain she was alluding to bullying, without asking him straight out. Maybe she knew if she did, he'd say everything was fine. Even when it wasn't, it was a nervous worry in the back of his head all the time he was out where that knot of people might get at him.

"Yes'm." Jasper hesitated, then offered, "And easier to do with different people, different sets of skills?"

"Just so. We can't all do it all by ourselves." She seemed like she might say something else. Then she looked up, eyeing the angle of the sun. "I'd best get back, given I've only got my legs. I'll leave an apple for you to try when you get in, with Mistress Dowland. How's that?" Mistress Dowland kept an eye on the House, since Professor Wain taught late at night, and her rooms weren't in the House like all the other heads.

"Thank you!" Jasper hadn't expected that. "And for explaining."

"Ah, well. I'm a teacher. Hard to get me to stop, some-times. Have a good ride." She waved, heading off deeper in the orchard, to pause by a massive ancient apple tree, where she bent to do something Jasper couldn't see. An offering, maybe, of some kind. Orchards had traditions, he knew. He turned Dot around, walking her back to the path, and then mounting easily. Professor Wain had given him a lot to think about.

CHAPTER 8
AVIGAIL ON NOVEMBER 1ST

Avigail was at loose ends. That was potentially dangerous, she knew that. And perhaps especially at this time of year, when everything was far more liminal. That ran from last night and All Hallows - or perhaps a little before that - at least through the anniversary of the Pact on November seventeenth. Or through the end of the month, depending on how one felt about the shift from the Julian calendar to the Gregorian. It was of some interest to Avigail - some of the older rituals needed adjusting - but not actually relevant right now.

What mattered right now is that many of the students were busy with their own private memories. Some hadn't been in classes yesterday, either for their personal preparations or to go back to their families for a couple of days. There had been no evening activities other than a variety of rituals in half a dozen formats. They ranged from the chapel down in the village to an outdoor ritual to whatever private and personal rites people made to their ancestors and named dead.

Leo had spent the evening with his parents, not just

their weekly tea on the Thursday, but through supper and into the evening. Not that he'd talked about it at all, and she hadn't pressed. He'd looked like he had a headache in their Geometry class at nine. It seemed to have improved by Music at eleven, but perhaps he'd just got a better potion from Matron.

Avigail had gone to none of those. Her family did that sort of thing mostly in February, for Parentalia and Papa's traditions, and in September or other times in October, for Pitru Paksha and Mama's. She'd made her own offerings privately this year, tucking it in around her classes and obligations. Part of her felt that such things were a family affair, not something to share outside of it, in a way she didn't have words for. And while she knew people who'd died, most of hers weren't people she'd been close to.

There'd be more of it, too, for Armistice Day. Then, at least half of their classes would be cancelled, too. There were too many of the staff who had people to remember, former students or others in their lives. Leo had mentioned in passing last year that his dad disappeared for the day, without any comment, he had for as long as Leo could remember.

Anyway, about half of her classmates weren't in class. That meant that they'd done some review for their end of term exams, nothing that couldn't be easily made up. And now it was late afternoon, and nearly no one was out and about. She'd been nosing about in the House library when she realised she wasn't alone.

"Oh. Tobias." Tobias Wilton was a second year, like her. And, like her, he had a Council connection, though not nearly as direct of one. His aunt had been on the Council a couple of years longer than Papa. She'd have thought him of the sort of family likely to take the day off, or go back to the family cemetery or something of the kind.

"Avigail." Tobias bobbed his head. "Looking for something? Several of the fourth years checked out the books I was looking for on Wednesday, and they haven't brought them back yet."

Tobias had a tendency to disappear into one or the other of the crafting rooms, more or less in rotation. Avigail wanted to do the same with the ritual and magical workrooms, so she understood the impulse. "Which ones?"

"Leatherwork. I can't properly do metal yet, and besides, I'm interested in making latches and buttons and fastenings. That's more delicate. My mother's arranging for me to get some proper training in it this summer."

"To go into talismans, or crafting in general?" Tobias had options, there. And either one of those would be a respectable line of work, as his family would count it.

"Crafting." He tilted his head. "Maybe also talismans. I don't know yet." He shrugged. "Anyway. I wanted to do something now, to catch the eye of the Four Metals before we go home for solstice."

Avigail considered her options here. She wasn't exactly friends with Tobias, but they weren't antagonistic, either. If that was the word she wanted. Mostly, they just moved in very different circles. He liked one or two people around, and she was close with her friends and wandered through other circles when she needed distraction. "Why's that? Or, no." She flushed, that was put badly. "I mean. I know the obvious why, and you don't need to tell me the less obvious."

Very clumsy. Not quite as bad as actually falling on her face in the Great Hall, but certainly not at all deft. Tobias turned around and then considered. "Come up to the leatherwork room? I've got something you might find interesting."

Now she wasn't sure if she wanted to. They were fourteen. She wasn't interested in boys, not that way, though Rowena had said she might find herself to be this year or next. Or possibly girls. And if she thought girls, talk to Rowena first.

But Avigail was absolutely of the age - well past it, actually - where people's parents were contemplating the matches that might advance their own family. And Tobias Wilton's family was definitely in that category. Which meant that it couldn't just be an entirely intellectual question for Avigail, because it wasn't for other people.

He saw her hesitation. "Leather. The project I'm stuck on. Maybe you'll have an idea?" It didn't give her any more information about whatever else he or his family might think, but she shrugged. "Sure." Besides, supper was in an hour, she'd have an excuse to break off and look for Ros. Tobias stood up, brushing his hands. He held the door for her, automatically assuming he should, and then scooted past her to go to the leather crafting room. She wasn't cleared on it, and when she joined him on the door, he was opening the warding with his palm. She kept her hands properly tucked behind her back.

Not that leather was going to leap up and do something disastrous. And she was cleared on the sewing room and what everyone referred to as the tinkering room, with various bits and bobs to be combined in different ways. But the leather workshop had a second room for dyeing, and those could be dangerous if combined the wrong way or disturbed in the process. He led the way to a workbench, pulling over a basket of materials. "Here. This was what I was trying to do." He pulled out something shiny, and also a long band of black leather that was still being worked.

What Avigail saw was a copper disc with a dimpled surface. After a moment, he flipped it over, and she saw the engraving on the back. Copper would be easier to work with than a number of metals, and certainly cheaper than gold or silver. "What were you trying to do, then?"

"Make it into a belt buckle, attract the right sort of attention. No compulsion, of course. For one thing, that'd get the wrong sort of attention. And for another we haven't learned how yet." Not in class, but Avigail was fairly sure that Tobias had learned quite a few things not yet in their formal curriculum. She certainly had. Papa had said that assuming the person she was talking to was roughly as skilled as herself wouldn't be insulting. It was a sensible rule of thumb, except for the times when someone did something exceptionally stupid or foolish she would never have considered. Those made it notably harder to maintain the assumption.

She tilted her head. "May I touch it? Hold it?" Now she was curious about what he'd actually done, or more usefully whether she could figure it out. He handed it over, and the copper had more weight to it than she'd have guessed by just looking at it. Avigail peered at it, leaning lightly on the top of the bench, turning it back and forth in her hand to see how the engraving caught the light.

After thirty seconds or so, she at least had a question. "What's it not doing that you want?"

"What I want is for the Four Metals to think I'm worth inviting. Some of that's classes, and going to the right sorts of lectures and workshops. I'm doing all that. It's not like it's hard to figure out which they'd care about." The evening lectures were optional, unless one of the teachers actually required it. And it made sense the societies would pay attention to who showed an interest when they didn't have to be there. Especially for something like the Four Metals, who had a particular bent.

"Um, who was it? Magister Singh, two weeks ago. And Magistra Leung, who was talking about the embroidery?" They both had been fascinating, honestly. Magister Singh had talked about the ritual items of the Sikhs, and their implications for someone of Albion. Having a set of magical tools on hand at all times, as part of a solid way of being in the world, certainly had made a lot of sense to Avigail. Even if that particular mode wasn't for her. Magistra Leung had talked about the intersection between Chinese embroidery and Western methods, and the intricate ways one could create clothing with talismanic or protective effects. Again, not a line of work Avigail wanted. She could hem something simple or sew on a button or make simple objects, but embroidery bored her most of the time.

Tobias nodded. "Like that. And coming up with interesting questions. It's not like the Nine Muses, you can't just audition for things. All the crafting projects tend to be invitation only."

It made Avigail wonder how Tobias spent his time, then. He wasn't down in the stables; he was in a different group for the house magics than she was. Hers was mostly about talking about different ways to spot magic, to make sense of what was going on. "Volunteer, when we get a chance to help with something."

"Well, of course." He said it like he'd thought of that months ago, which he probably had. "But making something. I'm pretty sure Daedalus Tilton is one. He's got this amazing device up in his room that tells him what he ought to be studying. You put a marble in at the top, and it works its way through a series of gates and rails, and lights up a charm by brushing by it. Then he does what it says. It's clever. Funny, too. Besides the practical."

Some people - Avigail, for example - handled the question of what she ought to be working on by looking at her notes about upcoming assignments. But naming might be destiny in this case, and one probably couldn't expect someone named Daedalus to come up with simple answers. She nodded. "So. See if he needs someone to hold bits in place for whatever he does next?" It seemed obvious to her, but Tobias smiled.

"Thanks. And that?" He gestured at the copper.

She considered it. "I don't have notes here or anything, but you might want to check this bit. I think you've got the sigil for water here, and I'm pretty sure you wanted light, yes? You're using Parkinson's Eight, right?"

Tobias bobbed his head. "I am. Are you sure? No, wait, you just said you weren't. I can check it after supper, though. I thought I copied it straight from my notes. How did you know?"

Avigail didn't have any idea how to explain it. It was just where the thing silted up and got mucky and didn't flow. It was like the otter in the river causing havoc last summer. Papa and Claudio had taken her out for the day to see what she made of a problem, and it had been an otter. And now the copper was like the otter, something out of place and making chaos. Or not making chaos, in the case of the belt buckle, but not doing as it ought.

She had to say something, and thankfully, something came to mind. "There's something about the flow. Do you remember what Professor Hammond was saying about cadences? It's the wrong cadence, only it's the magic, not in notes?" She hoped that didn't sound too horrible. Now, though, she wanted to talk it out with Peter. He had more of a natural understanding of water than she did. He'd grown up right next to the Thames, after all.

She'd have to write the whole thing up for Papa now. He'd told her to do that. There was an hour of her evening gone. Before she could say anything else, there was the ringing of the bell, the half-hour before supper. "I should drop my bag and set things up for tonight. Do you mind?"

Tobias was already bending over the disc. "Of course not. Thanks, though. Gives me some ideas. Close the door on your way out?"

Avigail diagnosed someone who was going to miss supper, but that was his lookout. She wasn't going to nursemaid him, and besides, the charms on the House meant Professor Morwen would know he was here. Or that he hadn't left for supper, maybe, if she checked. She nodded, and went out without saying anything else, and managed to set out half her report for Papa before the second bell rang to call them in for supper.

CHAPTER 9
LEO ON NOVEMBER 11TH

Leo had been up since well before dawn. It was one of his riding days, and normally he'd have grabbed breakfast and been down at the barn at nine. Today, though, he'd had a roll he'd kept from last night.

By half-seven, he'd been in the right place to see Dad walk out of the Keep, through the courtyard, and down the road toward the portal. He was wearing his uniform, the Great War one, and it still fit well, thanks to a little magical tailoring. There was the poppy, shining blood red despite the dawn light, in his buttonhole.

Yesterday had been Remembrance Sunday, with the memorial service. Schola had her own traditions for that, some shared and some more private. There was a gathering in the Great Hall, with a solemn reading of the names of those who had been part of Schola who'd died in the two World Wars. Mum had said there had been a debate about going back far further. But while they had the lists of names, Schola alums had died in every conflict since the founding of the school. Near thirteen hundred years meant a tremendous number of people. Most of them would just be a drone of names.

Both Mum and Dad had stories about the Great War. It wasn't just people they'd gone to school with, but there were a few Mum had taught in her very first year as a professor. But it was the recent names that hurt more. Leo hadn't known all of them, not always more than their names and faces. But he had - unlike most of the current students - known them at least that well. And it was far worse for Mum and Dad, who'd taught basically all of them one way or another.

It meant that both Mum and Dad cancelled classes on Armistice Day proper, because whatever Remembrance Sunday was for them, it was all public. Having the right face on for today's students was important, being a comfort to the ones who'd lost fathers or brothers or uncles or cousins. And these days, mothers and sisters and aunts, as well.

He didn't know what Mum did. He'd never dared ask. Whatever it was, she was completely private about it. She just couldn't face anyone. But Dad left the Keep at dawn and came back well after sunset. In between - he'd picked this up from Uncle Seth and Uncle Golshan - he went to the Cenotaph in London. Then Dad went to the memorial in Trellech, before coming to rest with a small group of other veterans who understood. He finished up with a private drink with Uncle Alexander, if Uncle Alexander was in the country. He'd be back late, visibly drained but able to go on with the demands of the school. And by then Mum would be up on the top of the tower looking at stars if it were at all clear. When she came down late, she'd be not exactly better, but able to go on.

For his own part, Leo went down to the barn, losing

himself in the honest labour of mucking out stalls and helping with the morning feeding. Once he was done, he went back up to the Keep, and it was only about ten. Rather than washing up in Bear House, he grabbed a clean set of clothes and his kit and went off to the bathing rooms under the Keep. He wanted to soak, and he wanted quiet, and he was pretty sure one of the private baths would be free. His favourite one was, tucked in the back where no one would stumble across him.

Leo soaked a long time, long enough that he felt the reverberation of the bell for the two minute silence before he expected to. He folded himself over, thinking of the students he'd known who'd died, the people who didn't get a chance to do what they'd wanted in the world. When the bell rang again, he slowly got dressed, charm-drying his hair. Making sure no one was around to spot him, he bundled the dirty clothes up in the satchel he'd brought with him. Then he turned right, down to the end of the hall and the storage cupboard. He brushed his fingers against the wards on the wall, waiting for the door and the stairs to appear.

A handful of moments later, he was down, further below the keep than anyone went routinely. Mum and Dad knew about it, and a couple of others. But only a couple. Mum and Dad had brought him down here last winter. To begin, the room was utterly dark, no hint of light coming through from above. There was just the cool, damp, stone smell of being deep in the bedrock of the island. But he could also sense the magic, a pulse of it, or maybe the sort of low hum you felt more than heard.

Leo waited. It always took thirty seconds or so. The blue magic began to glow, highlighting the lines around the model of the Keep itself, the curtain wall that held the

Houses and the library, all the spaces of the school. This was the heart of Schola, Dad had said.

Some of it was practical, a way to see what buildings needed attention, if a wall was beginning to leak or crumble. Some of it was feeling how everything was connected, how Schola was a living being. Instead of fingertips or toes or elbows, she had the branching walls and interior rooms and the later additions to the Keep. Being down here was peaceful, but it was also a way to reassure himself that all was well. Honestly well, even with the grief of the day. Leo wasn't fooling himself about that. When he was here, he knew he wasn't, even if that feeling of certainty got away from him at other times and in other places.

He couldn't stay down here forever. But the breathing space mattered. He made a slow circuit of the room, looking at all the spots he and Dad had been keeping an eye on, and nothing had changed. There was an odd little flicker along the far border, off on the north edge of the island, but it just twinkled sort of like a star, then went dimmer. Everything else seemed in good order, otherwise. He'd mention that to Dad, tomorrow at duelling, just in case it needed attention, but he didn't think it did.

By the time he'd done that, he was starting to get hungry - a roll didn't last all that long, really. It was almost time for lunch, so he went back upstairs. He stopped to listen, as he always did, before opening the door from the storage room, and he heard a sound he couldn't place immediately.

Then it hit him: someone crying. Not right by the door, but down the side hall. It was about the most private place anyone could find in the entire Keep. Most people didn't know it was there. Leo closed the storage room quietly, making a note to get Mum to teach him the charm for doing that better sometime soon. He took a few steps to the shadowed hallway, just a few charmlights glowing along the whole length. There was someone sitting on the floor, a firstie by the size and uniform trousers, knees pulled up to his chest and his head buried in his arms. Leo could hear how the sobbing that had caught his attention had shifted to gasps of breath.

He considered his options, then scuffed his shoe back toward the main hallway before he called out, "Hey." Leo thought about what else to say, but everything else sounded stupid in his head. Ros would be much better at this, though Ros might also terrify whoever this was.

The head came up, and Leo could see how the shoulders shivered.

"I'm Leo Fortier. Look, there are more comfortable places to have a bit of quiet and a cry. I can show you where. I know pretty much all the good spots."

There was a pause, then a hesitant question. "Professor Fortier?"

"That's my dad. And Professor Wain is my mum. So I grew up here." He kept his voice even and steady. He'd learned that one from Jasper, watching him work with a couple of less than well-mannered horses last month. "Somewhere a bit more comfortable?"

"People will see."

Leo shook his head. "We can duck into the salle without anyone seeing us, and no one's there today. Won't do you any good other times, but I can make up tisane, if you like?" Making tea was sometimes very handy. While it wasn't the only reason Dad had set the wards so Leo could get into the office, it was useful more often than it seemed.

The boy considered, then stood up, like he'd been there too long and had got stiff. Leo went slightly ahead, to make sure they didn't run into anyone else, but it was all pretty quiet. Getting on for lunch, definitely. They came up the corner stairs closest to the salle. Leo did one more check to make sure there was no one in the hallway, before gesturing the boy along into the salle. "Let me put on the kettle." He didn't make it a question. "You can sit here. No one will see you in here if you're on that side."

Five minutes later, there was hot water, mugs of tisane steeping, and Leo came back out. The boy had settled on the bench, one foot tucked up, the other dangling an inch above the ground. Still really small, then. Leo held out the mug. "Give it a minute to have flavour, but it's nice to wrap your hands around something warm, isn't it?"

That got him a wide-eyed look. "I'm. I'm Miles. Miles Kester. And I..." He stopped then, before he stammered.

"And you're having a rough time, details unspecified," Leo filled in. He settled on the bench, feeling the ground under his feet. "Can I ask a couple of questions about what kind of bad time?" He took in the uniform, the House badges. Seal House, which meant Uncle Ibis, if he needed to go to the Head. Or Susanna, who was a prefect this year.

Miles shrugged. "All of it? Classes. Chores. I don't really know what I'm doing. People."

"All right. What's the trouble with your classes?" Leo pulled a foot up, taking an encouraging sip from his mug. Little by little, Miles started talking. He liked his classes, but in that intense way that didn't make friends. More like Avigail than Ros. He wasn't as far behind, coming in, as Jasper had been. From what Leo sorted out, Miles had gone to a reasonable enough tutoring school, but his family tended to end up at Dunwich or Forvie, not Schola. So he felt - metaphor entirely intended - like a fish out of water.

And while there were things about Seal that obviously

fascinated him, Miles was also smart enough to know people weren't telling him everything. They weren't. That was how the world worked, and Seal maybe more than most. The others in his year were fine - no bullying, at least nothing Miles even hinted at - but they had their own interests. And he was definitely struggling in a couple of places. Not with what they were actually getting graded on, but what it was building to. Miles had enough sense to see that it was laying foundation - that's the way Leo felt it went best - but not how.

"All right. I have a couple of thoughts. I think I know someone who might be willing to study with you. Second year, he studies with us sometimes. I think he might be good at explaining, and he grew up in London, right on the Thames, so he understands that kind of water. Different from the ocean, yeah? But..."

"But still the water." Miles smiled now, a little shyly. "And?"

"And I'm going to make sure you and Susanna and I get a little time together real soon. Yes, the one who's a fifth year prefect. She's more or less my cousin. We both grew up here, and I'm thinking maybe we see if we can go down to the shore and introduce you to the mermaids. But she's better at signing with them, and besides, well. She gets bored easily. It's good to give her someone new to talk to." Leo said it lightly, but it was true enough.

Miles hesitated. "It's not a bother?"

"Not for me, not for Peter, not for Susanna. Shall we go find lunch and Peter? And I'll catch you at supper after I've talked to Susanna."

Miles didn't argue, at least. Leo didn't have Ros's force of personality, but he liked this better, seeing a way forward. Once he'd put the mugs away, they went off to the

Great Hall, pausing for Miles to wash his face and tidy up. Peter was thankfully easy to find, and Leo made a couple of suggestions about topics of mutual interest before leaving them to it.

Susanna was in a knot of other fifth years, but he got her attention. Sign language really was handy, he could make it clear it was both about her House and timely. A couple of exchanges, and they made arrangements to go down to the shore Saturday afternoon.

It was a decent morning's work, really, for a day where Leo hadn't expected anything like that. And it was something that would make Mum and Dad pleased when he told them about it at family tea on Thursday, when they could actually catch up. It didn't make up for the reason for Armistice Day, the many reasons. But it was like the poppy, something beautiful growing out of that. Maybe enough.

CHAPTER 10
ROS ON NOVEMBER 21ST

"Miss Carillon, here we are. Tea's just ready." Ros made her way into Professor Leonard's office, flipping the sign on the door to indicate the professor was busy. It was time for her weekly Latin tutorial, but she had other things she wanted to ask about. Learning four languages all at once - even if she was actually only starting from scratch on one and a half of them - was a lot.

Latin was the easiest of the four, because Mama and Papa had both worked with her on it for years. And she'd had a fair bit of Greek, though she wasn't continuing that at school, but it helped with the Latin. French was next, Mama and Papa were both fluent, so she'd been having conversations in it on and off all summer. Arabic was harder because that was Uncle Alexander and he'd been so terribly busy. And then the German she'd just started with Professor Wain. It was a good thing she already had the concept of both conjunctions and declensions down, but it was an entirely different family of vocabulary. As it was, she set her notes down and murmured her thanks for the tea.

It had become part of the ritual of the learning. Each of the professors teaching her languages offered her tea - they were, whatever else they were, also British. But the approach to it was decidedly individual. Professor Ward apologised regularly for the lack of sugar for his. It would normally be the strongest black, with mint and sugar cane, in crystal glasses that showed the colour properly.

Professor Knox liked a green tea, delicate and distinct. She'd noticed he didn't care much for either strong flavours or scents, and she suspected that was because of the precision of smell that helped in Alchemy. He had the sort of translucent bone china that made people with sense worry it'd shiver into nothing as soon as they touched it. Even if Ros knew it was stronger than it looked. Most of the time.

Professor Leonard favoured a mix of black with herbal - more mint, in this case, though about half and half, in sturdier china teacups painted with designs. And Professor Wain liked a herbal, rose hips and hibiscus and dried red berries and apples. That came in hearty pottery mugs, glazed with the blues of the night sky and the greens of a flourishing field. Though sometimes she'd be drinking the nettle nutritional tisane that was served to help keep up everyone's strength and health.

Now, Ros settled into her chair and waited politely for Professor Leonard to be ready to talk. She was perhaps in her middle sixties. Ros knew she'd raised a family before being widowed early. Mama had got the background from both Uncle Alexander and Professor Wain. Professor Leonard had been teaching at Schola for twenty years this year, and she was fully comfortable in the role. Her office also had all the detritus of research that marked her as an Owl - books stacked sideways on shelves, always a pile or two actively in use. Often, she had to clear books off the table for their tutorial.

"You asked an excellent - if complex - question in class yesterday." There, that was an opening sentence fit to challenge a nervous student.

Which Ros wasn't. She grinned, suddenly, because this was going to be fun, and she wasn't going to hide it. "You did give me house points for it. They were very pleased last night." It had been a noticeably generous amount, actually, more than she'd expected.

"You earned the points for bringing it up in class, and not saving it for doing well on your essay. Now we're in private, though, I'm curious how much of that you worked out for yourself, and how much you learned from other people."

"Uncle Alexander or Papa, you mean." It wasn't like Professor Leonard didn't know about both of them or their skills. Papa had apprenticed with a friend of Professor's Leonard's apprentice mistress, though Ros didn't actually know how the dates fit together. Papa had mentioned it to Edmund when he'd been about to start at Schola, that he approved of her background and style. And that Uncle Alexander did too, though there were places they didn't overlap at all.

"Just so," Professor Leonard said, amused.

"Mama, more than either Papa or Uncle Alexander." Ros let that settle for just a moment. Mama had also taught her a fair bit already about the art of pacing, though she wasn't remotely as good at it as Mama was. Yet. "We were talking over the summer about assumptions in ritual structures. And then you were talking in class about the different kinds of ritual, erm, architecture, though you didn't call it that."

"That part, I am quite sure, is from Council Member

Landry, yes." Professor Leonard said it dryly, but she was smiling broadly. Uncle Alexander did have a tremendous amount to say about ritual architecture, it was true. "I am hoping to get him to come give a lecture about it to you all in the spring, if his schedule allows. When the rest of your class will have some context to better appreciate it."

"He'll like that." Uncle Alexander lit up when he was teaching, and that was the sort of thing Ros's entire family liked to encourage. "So will I. And thank you for letting me know in advance. It means I can bargain with him for how difficult my questions will be."

It made Professor Leonard laugh loudly, and clap her hands together. "Oh, that I'd rather like to see, actually. Do let me know if I can help with whatever your negotiations involve." She then considered the original topic. "Assumptions. That's a good word, but not one I expect to hear from second years, even those with your background."

Rather primly, Ros replied, "There aren't that many who have it. Edmund and Merry, of course. And Avigail and Anthony and Rowena." Her brother and sister and Avigail's, of course she knew their takes and training well.

"And only two of those are particularly inclined to Ritual as anything like a specialty." Professor Leonard countered. Edmund and Avigail, of course. The other three were all entirely competent at it, but it wasn't where their interests lay. Merry wanted all the navigational magics, both practical and philosophical, and a dozen things about the coastline and the ocean. Though she wasn't opposed to a river, either. She'd spent a few weeks last summer on a canal boat with a friend and her family, in addition to visiting Peter.

Anthony was a duellist, and he'd taken to the protective and martial magics like a great raptor. And Rowena, well.

Rowena kept her own counsel, but she'd gone right into portal keeping like her mother as soon as she could. That had a little ritual to it, but a lot more about intuition and the feel of the stone or the tree or the water.

Ros grinned. "Still. Mama suggested that I read both Phillida Wright's *The Spiral Stair* and then also that collection of Professor Lollard's articles and *Conversation*." She let that settle.

"My twice-over predecessor." Professor Leonard wrinkled her nose. "And my own Ritual professor, actually."

"I wouldn't expect you to speak against him, of course." Ros said promptly. "De mortuis nil nisi bonum and all that. I don't properly remember the Greek it comes from, though."

That made Professor Leonard snort, and she set her teacup down carefully. "You knew that bit of Latin long before we started." Then she nodded. "Your mother was nudging you to look at the contrast between the styles. I can recommend some additional reading. Some of it is a bit over your head yet. Not because you won't understand the words, but because I'm fairly sure you don't have the practical experience with it yet."

"That's what winter hols are for?" Ros suggested.

"Take it up with your parents, then." Professor Leonard waved a hand. "Explain where you got to the comments in class, please."

Ros wasn't trying to be difficult, honestly. She would be going about it entirely differently if she wanted to be difficult. On the whole, though, she didn't want to do that with any of her professors at the moment. They had different approaches, certainly different interests, but they all cared about their subjects and helping people learn them. Ros had heard enough stories from her parents to know that was a big change in the last decade or two.

"We'd been talking about how Mama goes about some of the social planning, as opposed to how Papa does. It was right after the Midsummer Faire, which is very busy for us, in terms of the horses and the stables. Lots of people come by the tent, and this year I was helping Mama, making sure everyone had tea or drinks and a place to sit. Things like that."

Professor Leonard nodded encouragingly. Ros went on. "But after, I was asking why the tent felt the way it did, and Mama had me read those things. And I realised that it's two different takes on making a space, a defined space. Posit the tent as a cover. Papa knows some people who know the Jewish side of that, how it's built into their rituals. Or some of the land magic techniques, not that I do those myself, other than the family parts." That was for Papa and for Edmund. It would almost certainly pass her by unless she married into another landed family. A bit for Mama and somehow for Uncle Alexander, not that Ros would ask about that. Some things it was best to not ask Uncle Alexander about. They required careful consideration about the possibility one might not actually want to know the answer.

"That is fourth year work, for the record. Which I'm quite sure your parents know." Professor Leonard leaned back. "And?"

"And then Mama asked me to think about the other tents, and how they felt. What I thought their structures might be like. If they had ritual work behind them in the first place, and what it might be. She didn't expect me to know the methods, of course, and I didn't. I haven't had time to learn them all yet. But I was rather accurate about which had ritual underpinnings, and, um. Which style, is that the word?"

"Style will do for the moment. There's more precise language we can get into at some later date." Professor Leonard considered. "Do you want to do more of that sort of thing after you leave school?"

That was the crux of it. Ros wanted something in that misty shape of what she felt and understood. But she didn't want Ritual, per se, the way she thought Leo might. Not that she was sure. It wasn't something he talked about, even with the three of them. Or four, he was fairly relaxed with Peter Wallace this year. She wanted something that Ritual had a relationship with.

After a long moment of consideration, she spoke. "Uncle Alexander and Papa both suggested I think about diplomatic work, or upper level Ministry work. And there's a lot of unspoken ritual in that, the protocols and how to use them. As well as the more obvious parts. That's what I think I'm interested in, maybe. But I don't know." She was only fourteen, after all, she wouldn't be fifteen until winter solstice.

"Mmm." Professor Leonard nodded. "That does explain the interest in languages. Learning how other cultures go at a topic would be helpful for that, even if you were doing your work in English." Then she cleared her throat. "Speaking of, we should get started. Pull out your copy of your translation. I have my notes here."

Ros had expected that. Both the discussion, and that Professor Leonard would leave it alone after a bit. She pulled out her own copy of the translation she'd been set for the week. She'd turned in one for Professor Leonard to review yesterday at the end of class. It made the tutoring much less flustered. They could both see what they were doing, and Professor Leonard had time to make whatever notes she wanted as well. She began at the beginning. "I don't understand the use of the ablative here."

"Oh, that's the ablative of attendant circumstances. Here, let me give you some other examples." Professor Leonard leaned over, precipitously, to snag a book from a pile on her desk, and thumbed through it. Ros pulled her notebook over and settled in to take proper notes.

CHAPTER II
JASPER ON NOVEMBER 30TH

J asper was busy when he first heard the noise start up. He'd been asked to help with the set construction for the performance at the end of term. None of it was terribly difficult work. It was all nailing canvas tight onto frames so it could be painted and then attaching braces. Professor Hammond was around, but off talking to some of the musicians, trying to figure out the best seating for them.

It all seemed like so much chaos to Jasper, like things were being done far too close to a performance for good sense. He was used to the rhythm of preparing pavo players and mounts for a key match. The training built up to it, of course, but it was no good hurrying the last stretch. That had a much bigger chance of failing. Or worse, people or horses getting hurt, and Jasper didn't want any of that.

Even if the stakes were a little different here - outright physical injury seemed less likely, maybe - it seemed like poor planning. No one had asked Jasper, though. And it wasn't like he actually knew how to do it better. He just strongly suspected there was a 'better' that wasn't being done.

On the other hand, he wanted to try different things out. He'd volunteered to help with the sets because Professor Hammond had asked. But also because Jasper knew how to make things, how to mend things, and a lot of people apparently didn't know that. Posh families had people for that. Which made sense, if they had a specialist for furniture, of course they'd want them to do the work. On the other hand, it meant people who could help put a set together were in shorter supply at Schola.

And as much as Jasper liked his friends - he did - he probably needed to spend time with more than a handful of other people. He'd started this with the hope that maybe the bullies would lay off. It had worked on the one hand, when he was here, Phipps and all weren't. On the other hand, he hadn't really got to know any of the others well. Everyone had their own bits of the production to work on, and it hadn't allowed a lot of talking. Most of them already had their own friends, anyway.

Jasper kept on with his work, steadily. Not foolishly. He stopped every twenty-five minutes or so to stand up and stretch and get a bit of mint tea to drink. Dad had warned him about the ways people could get hurt, doing the same thing over and over without a pause. Dad hadn't told him, in so many words, but Jasper had learned to spot the old injuries, how they acted up. Stan, his older brother, had pointed it out to start. And they'd both learned how to volunteer to do the heavier work on the days Dad's shoulder was bothering him, or he was more achy.

It felt good to be doing something physical. And for that matter, to be doing something he was good at that didn't involve a horse. He was nearly through his fourth term at Schola, and he didn't feel so completely behind as he had, but all his classes continued to need a lot of focus and attention. And he definitely needed to keep up with the extra tutoring in Latin, in writing, and studying with Ros and Peter.

Jasper was in the fourth or maybe fifth round when he heard voices behind him. Professor Hammond had disappeared, maybe into the costume storage, and so had a number of the other students who'd been milling around working on other things. Most of them were older. Jasper only knew a couple to talk to.

"Oh. I suppose that explains things." It was one of the older girls. She had that sophisticated cut-glass tone down in a way that usually meant a fifth year. "Don't we have people for that?"

"Darling, obviously we do." That was another girl, a more alto voice, the sort of rasp to it that made Jasper wonder if she smoked a fair bit. "I suppose it's kind to give them something to keep them busy."

There was a male voice, just behind them, joshing and joking with someone out of hearing range, and Jasper braced his back. The next step was standing up, so he could set the piece on end. If there had been anyone else around, he'd have asked them to lend a hand, and now he wasn't sure. He didn't want to leave it, either. Instead, he just stood up.

"Can I help you with something? Professor Hammond's just through in the costume stores, I think." Jasper knew how to be polite to the sort of person who'd sneer at honest work. He kept his tone to what Mum and Dad would approve of, which also was the sort of thing Professor Wain approved of. The politeness, anyway. She'd given a talk on Wednesday, during the House meeting time, about self-deprecation and the problems it could cause when it came to magic, along with a couple of the older students.

It was hard to imagine any of them had actually had a hard time with it, though. They'd all seemed confident. Cool and collected. They weren't feeling anger rising up. Jasper knew he got that from Dad. He had to tell himself they weren't worth losing his temper over.

"You? I don't think so." The first voice belonged to a blonde girl. Woman, really. She was definitely using either cosmetics or charms that did the same thing, which seemed a bother while at school. "That set doesn't look like much. Shouldn't you have someone supervising?"

Jasper cleared his throat. "I've proper training in construction." He'd spent a lot of the summer helping Stan and Dad and workers from the estate expanding and fixing up the family cottage. Or, to be more precise, the one Dad had grown up in, which hadn't had anyone living in it regularly since Dad married Mum. "And Professor Hammond checked out my work."

That just got sniffs. "Didn't expect to find you anywhere other than mucking out stalls." She stalked over to the tea urn, getting a mug for herself. "Make yourself useful, then. Go get Professor Hammond."

Jasper could feel his weight shift before he made himself pause. "Is there something urgent? He's busy with other students right now." He kept his voice even, or at least he was trying. Jasper was pretty sure it wasn't actually working, these were the sorts of people who would pounce on any hint of weakness or nerves. But he didn't want to take their orders, and that was something he hadn't known about himself until right now.

"Do what you're told. Tell him Miss Ritt is waiting for him." She considered. "Lowenna Ritt, of the Norfolk Ritts."

Jasper did know that name, though he thought not her family directly. Lord Carillon didn't sell to them, though Dad had been more neutral about it. That meant it was politics and not solely how they treated their horses. Though if this was the way they treated their staff, he definitely felt sorry for the horses.

"I'm sorry. I have to get on with my own work, or these won't be done on time. Costume store, just through there." Jasper didn't turn his back on them. He had more sense.

It meant he got just enough warning to see the boy with them, the man, come and shove him. It wasn't subtle; it was flat out vicious, in a way Jasper hadn't actually expected. He'd been on the lookout for one of them to trip him, or mess up his work.

He landed hard. Not as hard as most people would have. He'd learned how to fall tumbling off a short-legged pony in the arena, over and over again. But he could feel it jar through his shoulder, across his back, and he was going to regret breathing tonight. He ended up on his back, one knee bent, staring up at them, and not able to scramble out of the way fast enough.

Before he could do anything at all, there was a voice from the doorway. He more or less recognised this one: Richelda Evans. She pitched her voice to carry, and she'd had proper vocal training somewhere along the line. "Professor Hammond? You're needed." No please or thank you.

She gestured at Jasper to stay down. He knew she was one of Professor Wain's Time and Place students, looking to go on in Astronomy. He stayed. At least whatever happened next would have a witness who might at least be neutral. Maybe. And there'd be a professor to do something.

There were the sounds of footsteps, then a "What happened?" Again, it was sharply framed, no buffering words, no space, or rather it claimed and held the space immediately, like a Bear. Previously in Jasper's experience, Professor Hammond had been amiable. Mild wasn't the right word. He had the sense none of the Heads of House could actually be described as mild, even if some did a bit better at making a show of it than others. He was intense about music, not about being note-perfect, but in feeling it. And he had high standards. Jasper had never heard him raise his voice, not more than very briefly, to be heard above a noisy room of chattering students.

Now, the silence rang out. It was like Professor Hammond was everywhere in the room, a bear looking around ready to take on all comers, defending his territory. The three who'd come in - Ritt and her friends - stepped back. "It wasn't us, Professor. We didn't do anything."

Professor Howard whistled twice, a particular sort of whistle, and three more students came out of the back. "Please escort these three to see the Headmistress, if you would. She's in her office downstairs right now. Let her know I'll be along in a few minutes with more information."

Ritt and the others started to argue, and Professor Hammond raised his hand, then said something. The word wouldn't stick in Jasper's head. He didn't know what it was, but he knew what it did. They were all mouthing words, no noise coming out. He added, to the three students he'd called out of the back, "If they give any trouble at all, you know what to do."

There were murmurs of "Yes, Professor." Then they were gone. Evans and the others weren't making trouble, at least not here. If the Headmistress was in her office - even though it was Saturday - they didn't have far to go. Just down to the ground floor and into the offices tucked next to the stairs that went up and up into the keep.

"Are you hurt, Pride?" Professor Hammond's voice was much gentler now.

Jasper considered, before giving an answer. "A bit tossed about, sir." He didn't even know what he was trying to ask. "Bruised, I don't think anything broke." There, he'd been honest enough. He knew what the bad hurts felt like. He'd fallen off horses often enough. "I, um."

Professor Hammond snorted. "Go to Matron if you've any concern. As to the rest, there's a charm that lets me hear what's going on on stage, when we're backstage. Very handy for all sorts of reasons. I do apologise. I didn't expect they'd do that. We were almost done."

Being tripped was one thing. Jasper knew how to deal with that. Being apologised to, however, like that, was something new. Jasper pushed himself upright, steadily, doing all the little checks to make sure he hadn't hit his head, and he wasn't dizzy. A moment later, Professor Hammond had taken a few steps over to him, offering him a hand up. Jasper accepted it. He didn't actually know how to refuse it.

"Anything you want to tell me I didn't hear?" The question was quieter, spaced out a bit, like Dad working with a skittish yearling.

"I wasn't going to come get you. Though I suppose you heard that." Jasper tucked his hands behind his back, because he felt like he was going to fidget or something worse.

"Quite right, too." Professor Hammond considered. "I'll need to go down and talk to the Headmistress for a bit. Twenty minutes, probably. Maybe thirty." He took half a step back, giving Jasper more space, and then pitched his voice to carry again. "Evans, would you run things up here, please, keep everything moving along? Pride, if you need a break, you take one. That's the only order I'm giving you. But if you are able to get the rest of the set done, ready for painting, we'll be very grateful."

"I think in a minute or two, sir." Jasper tested his balance. He needed a bit more tea, probably, before he tried anything with a hammer.

One of the others who'd come out of the back said, promptly, "I'm glad to hold things. I don't understand how it goes together properly, my geometry's just awful too. But I can hold them."

Jasper swallowed. "Obliged, um." Then he had to ask. "Pardon, I don't know your name?"

"Grant. Philodorus Grant, most people call me Phil." It was indeed one of the more long-winded First Family names Jasper had heard. Mind, that didn't tell him if Grant wanted first names, and Jasper was not up to figuring that out unless someone actually told him.

Professor Hammond had been making a few other brief comments. Now he strode off to go downstairs. "Back in a bit. I'll see if I can get something out of the kitchen for a snack on the way back."

It wasn't until he was gone, the door closed behind him, that the chatter broke out again. It was chaos for a little, everyone with their own opinions about Ritt. None of them liked her, none of them much wanted to work with her or her set. 'Stuck up snob' was one of the things tossed around, as well as several bits of slang Jasper didn't know but could guess at. Jasper let it wash over him, trying to figure out why they were saying it, why it seemed to matter to them that he heard it.

He didn't chime in. It wasn't safe for him to do that; he knew that much. People like him didn't get to share their opinions without consequences. He might do that sometimes, but he didn't care that much here, other than not wanting to get pushed around.

Instead, Jasper finished his tea and went back to work, getting another frame done more quickly with Grant's help. The others went off to various other tasks, a few on the stage - not leaving Jasper alone - but not talking much. After they'd been working for ten minutes, Jasper finally felt he needed to ask. "What'll happen to them?"

"For pushing you or for lying about it? The pushing was bad, the lying was at least three times worse. And the Headmistress can compel truth, not that she needs to, with Professor Hammond hearing it all." Grant considered. "I don't know, exactly. Some sort of suitable punishment, probably. The kind of thing that's annoying and tiring to do, that'll wear them out. Not the stables." He added that with a smile. "We wouldn't want to do anything to make the horses uncomfortable. Or the chickens or the sheep or the cows. Maybe the goats, though. Goats don't care much, and they can hold their own."

Jasper had stiffened up at the first part, but the last got him to a laugh. Goats didn't care. "But I should watch my back?"

"Mmhmm. Though there's a decent chance the Headmistress will charm them to stay away from you. None of them are in Horse, they're not in your year. That's pretty easy to manage."

The fact it was an even an option took a moment to register. It wasn't like people could do that in the village school. He hammered another few nails in, then said, carefully, "Schola's a whole new place, isn't it?"

When he looked up, Grant was grinning at him, like he'd said something that mattered. But Grant didn't press, just let them go back to working together in agreeable silence. Professor Hammond was longer than he'd said, but he came back with a variety of snacks - mostly vegetables, but still tasty. And by the time everyone had enjoyed those, Jasper felt he could get on with his tasks again properly.

SOLSTICE HOLIDAYS

CHAPTER 12
AVIGAIL ON DECEMBER 22ND

Avigail was waiting as patiently as she could manage. They'd been there since early afternoon, and the initial formalities were almost over. Inside half an hour, maybe, the dancing would start up. First, everyone had to finish the offerings. Each of the Lords and Ladies in various combinations had to present the gifts of their lands. It was only the third time she'd seen it, instead of hearing about it.

This time had been different, and Avigail was trying to figure out how. There were a great many obvious changes, but she didn't know how to make sense of the less obvious ones. Hopefully Grandmama would be up for talking through it tomorrow or the next day.

To begin, of course, there was a new Head of the Council, Silvia Warren. Council Head Smythe-Clive and Council Member Teague had retired right after the summer solstice, and there were two new people who'd challenged. They were standing at the end of the row of the Council, twentieth and twenty-first. The rest of the row was Council

Member Warren, as the head, then Council Member Landry as the most senior. That was Ros's and Leo's Uncle Alexander. Right now he didn't look very avuncular, he looked guarded. Though he was smiling at people as they made their bow and whatever little socially appropriate comment they'd come up with.

Grandmama had explained that it was good to have four or five in rotation, because of course, people could hear what got said to the Council Members nearby. "Happy Solstice" was unimpeachably correct, but rather tedious. And in most cases, you might have personal comments for some of them, but not all of them. Avigail had been amusing herself with thinking about what she'd say to the Council Members she knew.

Papa was the easiest and the hardest, maybe. She had plenty of choices, but whatever she said would have to be suitable for the moment. Ros was much better at coming up with those. But Ros was over with her mother and her sister across the room, while Lord Carillon and Edmund made their way through the line, just behind Grandpapa and Anthony. Anthony, because of course Papa couldn't actually be in two places at once, as both Heir and Council Member.

Council Member Landry would be easier if he weren't standing next to Council Head Warren. Because whatever Avigail might say to him, Council Head Warren would hear, and so on. It made Avigail want to sigh and write out a logic problem or something of the kind, to come up with an acceptable combination.

Orion Sisley was more fun to think about. She knew him better than the other people on the Council. It was his brother making the offerings, because Orion's son was too young to be Heir yet. Papa had Orion and Claudio and

Hypatia and Cammie over for supper a number of times by now. Sometimes even when Avigail had been permitted to eat with them.

She'd ask him about how the beehives were doing, or his project to renovate some of the buildings on the estate to balance the flow of the land magic better. Or she'd say something about Claudio, depending on who else was nearby. Orion was four down from the end, now, and near enough Papa that whatever she said in this hypothetical offering might make Papa smile.

People kept moving up the line. They were maybe ten minutes from everyone going through. Avigail turned to say something to Rowena to discover she'd disappeared. So had Mama, which meant they must have seen someone to talk to. Instead, there was Claudio, Council Head Warren's son, but much more interestingly Papa's apprentice, offering a glass to Grandmama and then one to Avigail. Grandmama's was obviously wine. Avigail's was some sort of squash, black currant. She murmured, "Thank you."

Claudio gestured at the chairs. "May I join you?"

Grandmama nodded. "Of course. Are you hiding from your mother's omniscience, or is there some other reason?" She was teasing, of course, but Claudio flushed. He'd been Papa's apprentice now for a year and a half. Honestly, he ought to know what Grandmama was like with people she considered family by now.

"Both, Lady Alysoun, of course. As always." He glanced up at the line, as if making sure his mother hadn't moved from the head of it. Papa had been taunting Claudio's mother for years now. He considered for a moment. "You might not have heard this part. Mother's a tad put out that I didn't challenge for either of the two open seats."

Avigail tilted her head. "I'm sure you had reasons. Good reasons. Or Papa would have argued with you about it."

Claudio paused, going very still, and then he was laughing. Grandmama shifted her hand instantly, one of the charms that muffled sound, so it wouldn't alert people near them. Or, the way Claudio was laughing, halfway down the room, and it wasn't like this keep's great hall was tiny. When he caught his breath, he coughed. "Good point. Excellent, in fact. Do tell your father about it, preferably when I can watch."

"Are you coming round this week?" Avigail hadn't been sure of the scheduling. There were an awful lot of fancy parties scheduled, and unlike this one, she wasn't old enough for those.

"Oh, yes. At least once, I need a break from Mother. And probably staying over after the bohort match, if that's not a problem." He glanced at Grandmama, who smiled.

"It's lovely to have the house full, honestly. And we'll have plenty to talk about." Grandmama glanced up toward the line of Council. "Honestly, I'm hoping Gabe at least gets a breather for a bit. And I know he wants some time in the workroom with Avigail."

Claudio glanced over. Avigail said, mock-primly. "He promised to help me with a project." Then she immediately went on. "Last winter, I was very good and didn't come up with a better form of itching powder for people who really do deserve it. Still."

Avigail still didn't understand the pretty princesses, not one bit. Over the autumn, she'd at least figured out how to position herself so they didn't irritate her too much. They weren't inclined to be bullies, not directly. But they were cliquish, they blocked off learning new things, and Avigail didn't like it. They'd mostly ignored Avigail, just like they were ignoring both Peter and Jasper, and that was both easier to manage and uncomfortable, all at once.

"And why didn't you?" Claudio leaned forward.

"For one thing, Papa would have figured out I'd made it almost immediately. He'd probably have had you help." That was the thing about Papa with apprentices, even if Claudio was the first one she'd really got to know as a person. Isobel was lovely, but Avigail had been a lot younger then. And there had been a lot she hadn't been able to follow fast enough to join in conversations.

With Claudio, there was still tons she didn't know, but Papa made a point of checking and explaining or telling her what to go read. They were all dancing around the idea that she might apprentice as a Penelope when she left school. Not to Papa, of course. The Penelopes worked differently than the Portal Keepers, where Rowena was apprenticed to Mama.

Right now, it was a malleable sort of future thing, but the reading was pretty much always fascinating. Time with Papa was a delight, and Claudio was also really good at filling in gaps in her knowledge. He knew different things than Papa, too. And he was more orderly about his explanations, though that wasn't hard in comparison. And that meant it was fine for Papa to teach her things or set her puzzles to be going on with.

Claudio nodded. "And it'd have put out Isembard and Thesan, and that's not really kind, either." They were here, too, and Leo was somewhere around, but Avigail hadn't spotted him in ages. Leo's Uncle Garin had retired from his Council seat last winter. That was the one Orion had now. But he and Leo's sister Ursula had needed to make the offerings for their estates. And so Leo's parents were here for that, making a show of their support.

It did make Avigail pause, though. "I was thinking about different kinds of interactions." She glanced over. But this was something Grandmama liked, and Avigail got a nod to go on. "Like how I call you Claudio, and Orion is Orion. But you're Uncle Claudio and Uncle Orion to Leo. And Professor Landry, when he's that." That was what she called him when it wasn't entirely public. He liked it better. At least from her.

"Well, some of it's just constellations of people. Thesan's got a nice line of explanation about it. You should ask her sometime, when it's social time." Claudio considered, giving her a moment before he said anything else.

"I mean, that one's also complicated, because it's Professor Fortier and Professor Wain, but they're also Leo's parents. I don't know how he manages that one at school." Avigail really didn't, but Leo seemed to keep it straight. Mostly by a series of rules, so far as she could tell, about what role someone was in at the moment. Though outside of actual classes, he did usually refer to his parents as Mum and Dad.

Which was a whole other thing, actually, and now Avigail was frowning. Claudio raised an eyebrow. "What's that thought, then?" When she hesitated, he added, "We've got another fifteen minutes or so before Mother will want me for the opening dances."

That also had to be odd, honestly. There were a whole set of formal dances, done in pairs, starting with some very old ones and moving up as far as a waltz. They made specific patterns, magical ones, though the Council didn't talk a lot about the details. For Papa, it was simple. He danced them with Mama. And Hypatia with Orion, they'd got properly married last summer. But Professor Wain usually partnered Council Member Landry for them, and

Claudio's father had died when Avigail was really young, just two.

Avigail considered how to put it. "Different names for people. Parents, I mean. How it's Mama and Papa for me, but Leo calls his parents Mum and Dad." And there were all sorts of implications there, class implications. Even though if she were being technical about it, the Fortiers were a very ancient, very posh family as Albion counted it. More than the Warrens. Also more than the Sisleys, like Orion. But not more than Avigail's Edgarton side.

"Ah." Claudio leaned back a little in his chair. "I know a little about that, actually. And I think it's all right to tell you." He glanced at Grandmama, who merely smiled. "Isembard had a very formal sort of family, growing up. Very distant, and it wasn't just because a number of them died right around the time he was born. His father inherited the title, Garin was right around ten, his parents had very separate lives."

"Leo said once that his..." Words were complicated. "His father grew up in the Essex house that's theirs now. Not Arundel, mostly."

"Like that. And that's where his mother lived, most of the time. Unless it was something like this." Claudio gestured at the whole ever-shifting event. "He said something in passing to me, that he'd hated Sunday evenings for a long time, without realising why, because he'd get called in to justify himself to his parents. Told be more like his brother." Claudio considers. "He decided he didn't want to be that parent. And that's definitely not how Thesan grew up. Her parents are lovely. And most of her siblings."

"Most?" Avigail had heard stories about Leo's family on that side, but she was curious what Claudio would say.

"Her older sister is very, um. Rigid is the word they use.

Wanting things just so. Mostly it's fine now, but it was rough for a while. Your father would have had comments about it, if they'd ever interacted." Claudio glanced at his mother, they were down to the last five or so working their way down the line, so almost done. "Like he's been doing for Mother."

"And you call her Mother." Avigail said it quietly, but she said it.

Claudio winced. "You are very perceptive, Avigail. Don't stop, just."

Grandmama saved him, at least a bit. "So what you're saying, Claudio, is that Isembard and Thesan deliberately chose the least formal mode. They wanted to be reminded, every time they talked to Leo and Ursula, that they were doing things a certain way. More like Thesan's family than Isembard's."

Claudio was nodding along. "Exactly like that. And to be fair, raising children somewhere unusual, with the rest of the Schola staff right there. All those aunts and uncles by choice." He grinned at Avigail then. "Like you, just a different set."

Avigail had indeed grown up with a whole set of people who weren't at all related by blood, and it didn't matter. Some of them lived at Veritas, some of them just visited a lot. And that didn't really matter either, they were still family. "And Papa and Mama are in the middle. Not as formal as Father and Mother, but not as informal as the other." She couldn't imagine using Mum and Dad. Ma, maybe, with Mama, that was the word Mama used about her own mother. But she did it with the lilt of the Bengali behind it, and Avigail couldn't do that reliably at all.

"Just like that." Grandmama's voice was quiet. "Your grandpapa called his parents Mother and Father. Mind, there's a difference in generations there, but it's also telling."

Avigail nodded. "Did Grandpapa have the same kind of thing as Professor Fortier, then?"

"Called down from the nursery, scrubbed up? Oh, yes." Grandmama smiled, the fond smile she got when talking about him. "The point when I knew we were definitely doing things differently was when I came upstairs to the nursery one day. Gabe was six that summer. And Richard was there reading to him, talking about animals and birds on the estate. Very different from what he'd had as a child. Different from me, too, though my parents were more involved. Tea every day, unless they were away, not just once or twice a week for a few minutes. And here's the thing for you to think about, what that changes now. When people know how to have those kinds of relationships younger. Like you and your friends, more secure in your families."

Avigail was about to say something else, but then the noise in the room changed. Claudio pushed himself upright. "Time for me to do my bit. Lady Alysoun, Avigail, happiest of solstices, if we don't speak again today." He took off, not directly for his mother, but pausing to speak briefly with his son Tiberius - a year ahead of Avigail, in Fox - and his wife. Avigail considered, and was suddenly fairly sure Tiberius called his parents Mother and Father, and that was a tangle she was going to have to think about a lot more.

Grandmama made the same comment in return, and then tilted her head. "We can talk more about this while you're home. Right now, why don't you go find your mother and sister and let them know the dancing's forming up? I think they went into the side room that way. With any luck, your papa will make it here when they do."

"Of course, Grandmama." Avigail was glad to do that sort of thing, and besides, it would let her get a good look at who else was here. And she could see Grandpapa and Anthony coming back, so Grandmama wouldn't be on her own for long.

CHAPTER 13
LEO ON DECEMBER 23RD

Leo came back upstairs whistling, though he stopped right outside the door. It was cracked slightly open, and he could hear Dad talking to someone. A moment later, he heard Uncle Alexander.

They'd still been asleep when Leo had gone out this morning. Or if not actually asleep, lounging around in bed and not getting up. But Leo had promised Aunt Helena that he'd help with the chickens and the goats and the horses in the stable. He'd grabbed lunch downstairs with the kitchen staff. Then he'd taken a nice long soak in the baths under the keep, because he'd wanted to get cleaned up before tonight's festivities. Doing it early would mean Uncle Alexander could have the second bath up here and take his time.

It was Mum and Dad's anniversary, actually, but more importantly, it was one of the series of seasonal feasts for Schola. It was a time when everyone who lived in the keep tried to be handy for a festive meal. It was tucked between solstice and Christmas for people who did that. Which his family did, though mostly in the sense of excellent food and getting all the aunts and uncles and cousins on Mum's side in one place for once. That was tomorrow and the day after. Tonight was for the people of Schola, who made their whole lives here.

Leo made a titch more noise before pushing the door open. "Afternoon, Dad. Uncle Alexander."

Dad cut off what he was saying, but he did it with a broad smile. "Leo. Come in. We were sorting out some bits of the schedule." Uncle Alexander cleared his throat. "Among other things. Grab a mug of tisane? I have a question or two."

Questions were always interesting, if not always exactly good. Being told to grab something to drink suggested they might be the more lengthy sort. "Anyone need anything?" Leo knew the protocol for that, but Dad and Uncle Alexander still had mostly full bottles of cider and waved him off. They continued talking quietly, too quietly to hear from the tiny little kitchen up here.

A couple of minutes later, he came out with his mug and a sliced up apple or two that were starting to go wrinkly. They'd been out of the stasis charms a tad too long. Dad had both his arms draped along the top of the sofa on his side, his feet up on one of the footstools. Uncle Alexander was on the one at right angles. Leo considered, then sat on the other. "Mum upstairs?"

"Finishing up some of her admin work, yes. She'd like it to be done, so we can enjoy the rest of hols." Dad stretched a little. "I wanted to ask you about last night, before we do the family things on that side on Boxing Day."

Leo knew exactly where this was going. "Uncle Garin." It wasn't a question.

"Uncle Garin." Dad's voice dropped. "He was talking to you for quite a bit."

He had been. Uncle Garin had been in a mood last night. A different mood than usual, but still definitely a mood. He was still getting used to being at the Council festivities with only his Lord hat on, as Mum put it, and not his Council Member hat. This was only the third set of rites since he'd actually retired. Mum and Dad had both been busy talking to people. And dancing, and Leo liked seeing them dance.

It had given Uncle Garin an excellent chance to snag Leo while Ursula was also busy and Uncle Alexander had disappeared into half a dozen other necessary conversations. Leo considered his options, because it wasn't like Dad and Uncle Alexander weren't, in fact, experts at reading people. "It wasn't anything new, Dad." Absolute truth.

"Still. I'd like to know how much I should go tell him to mind his own business." Dad leaned forward now, elbows on his knees, a particular kind of banked ferocity in his eyes. Very Bear House, actually, now Leo had seen that a few times in action from Professor Hammond. "Not whether. How much, and what about."

There was no good way to squirm out of answering. Leo hadn't wanted to make a thing of it. It was going to be awkward now. "The societies."

Both Dad and Uncle Alexander glanced at each other, so Leo had been right about what they'd been talking about, too. It was the logical topic, with him as a second year. "Would you tell us what you said?"

It was a very polite request. Other people's parents would make demands, Leo knew that. Maybe not Ros's or Avigail's or even Jasper's. But a lot of people thought children were an extension of themselves. "Should Mum be here for this?"

"Not for the moment." That was a much more decisive answer than Leo had actually expected. And it made him almost certain of something now. Dad nodded. "Go on, please."

Most people his age would probably have fought it. Leo knew perfectly well Dad was going to win this one. What Dad had taught him is that if he couldn't win the way he was planning, see if he could do something else. Whether Leo could do it with Uncle Alexander sitting right there was another question entirely.

"He was careful to not come out and actually say it. But he made it clear I should be looking for something from Dius Fidius, and that I knew what to do about it." Leo spaced the words out. "Nothing that anyone overhearing would have put together like that, of course."

"Of course." Dad's voice was utterly neutral now, and that was almost worse than Uncle Garin had been last night. "What did you say?"

"We were in the Great Hall at Dinas Emrys. You and Mum both taught me manners. And besides, it's not like arguing with Uncle Garin does any good, anyway." Leo let a tiny hint of his frustration here show. He knew what answers Dad probably wanted. That was the thing. "He thought I agreed with him for long enough. Probably. He didn't come talk to me again."

Something in that made Dad grin, then chuckle. "No. He came to talk to me. What do you think about what he said, then?"

It was a straight out question. Leo considered his options at this point in this duel, and it was a duel. "You also know who's likely to get an invite." He made his gaze open enough to watch Uncle Alexander, too. Uncle Alexander's face always moved quickly, but Leo caught the flicker as he went on. "Both of you."

It was still Dad who spoke, of course. Uncle Alexander wouldn't interfere, though he'd accept a handoff, by whatever method it was they used to signal that. "What makes you think that?"

"Oh, come on, Dad. You're both members. You and Uncle Alexander. Along with Uncle Garin." Leo let out a breath, slowly. Dad had a point, not having Mum here, because she certainly wasn't. If he hadn't been pretty sure already, this would have been confirmation. Dad would be reacting differently if she were. He hesitated one more moment. "Uncle Claudio, too, but not Uncle Orion."

"How?" It was just the one word, and it could be taken a number of different ways. Dad's face was still, now, a mask of neutrality.

Leo answered the obvious looming elephant, 'how do you know we're members?'. "Honestly, Dad. I pay attention to things. You and Uncle Alexander disappear at the same time a few nights a year, the same mysterious notes on your calendar. Or near enough." Dad's just said 'out' and Uncle Alexander's said 'Schola' or 'club row'. But wherever he was at Schola wasn't anywhere Leo could see, and Uncle Alexander only went to Club Row in Trellech for necessary business. "You should at least pick different things sometimes. And twice you mentioned seeing Uncle Claudio when he hadn't been here, and you hadn't been other places."

Then Leo considered. "And you said, several times, that Uncle Orion took a while to figure himself out, and he and Uncle Claudio got closer, um, Uncle Orion's fourth year. So he might not have got an invite in his own right."

Dad rubbed his face with his hands. "Does your sister know?"

"Who do you think I worked it out with? Her second year, actually, she was paying really close attention to when people were in and out of the dorms. And it's not like she stopped after that." Leo might have snuck out of bed to look out the windows a few times, and see if he could figure out who was going out or coming back.

"Oh." To Uncle Alexander, Dad said, "Remind me that it's a pleasure having brilliant children?"

Uncle Alexander promptly said, "Have you told anyone else?"

"Avigail. Just that I had suspicions, not that I was pretty sure." Leo considered. "That day you got called out of our duelling session, Dad, in October? We got to talking about the societies then."

"Ah." Dad rubbed his face again. "You should decide what you want to do. Whatever invite you may or may not get. You don't need to please me with it."

Leo swallowed hard. "Would it please you if I did?"

Dad honest to goodness flinched, and Leo had never seen that before, not ever. Dad closed his eyes and took a breath. Uncle Alexander hesitated for just a second, then he started speaking. "We both know what that kind of expectation feels like. And what it's like when other people are making you into a shape that's all right. But maybe not what you'd want, if you had more choice."

Leo tilted his head. "I know Dad - you've said you should have been Bear. Like me." He hadn't really thought about Uncle Alexander that way, and now he frowned. "Owl?"

Uncle Alexander, very solemnly, let out an excellent imitation of an eagle owl. Leo had only heard it a couple of times, the 'bubo bubo' of it. Then he smiled, and Leo started laughing. It was entirely too ridiculous.

When he'd caught his breath, Dad had managed to find words again. "Bear, yes. And Owl. And that's part of why I'm so glad you're where you are. It seems to be the right fit for you. You know the houses are - they are choices. Most people would fit a couple, better or worse, or it would take them to different places."

"Mum?" Leo ventured asking, it was barely possible he'd get an answer.

"Ask her about it yourself, but she'll tell you that Horse has done well by her. But she might have done well in Salmon or even in Owl. She'd have come out a different sort of person, though. She says the instincts that Horse trains up, those are good for teaching, for one thing."

It was hard to argue with that. Leo had heard enough stories about how Schola was before he was born, the first few years of his life, to know things had changed. They'd moved from someone from Fox as Head of School, to Aunt Helena, who was also Bear. And she'd listened a lot more to Mum and Dad and other people who wanted to do things another way. Generatively, as Mum liked to say, not focusing on ambition or only a few people winning. Like the feast tonight, actually, that was part of tying the seasons together, specific to Schola herself.

Leo came back to the question, though. That was fair. And it was also kind, really. Even if Dad wasn't going to push about it more. "Dad, when you come back on those nights. You're often in an odd mood. Not upset, not angry, but odd. It feels, um." He had at least some language for this. "Herrick's Sixth, the way something echoes weirdly? An unresolved chord progression."

Dad rubbed his face again. "I'm glad to have the

demonstration you've been paying attention both in duelling and in Music class." He drained the rest of his cider a bit abruptly. "I am often in an odd mood. With echoes. Not really because of Perry, it's more about those expectations. I'm not going to tell you what to decide. If you get an invitation, and if you do what it requires, I'd be glad to have you there. But if you decide you want to do something else, so long as it's good for you, I'll be just as happy. Does that help?"

It did. Having Dad saying it helped even more than knowing it, weirdly enough. Knowing he didn't have to keep ducking around it. "Can I get you another bottle, Dad? And Uncle Alexander, there are some things I'd love to work through with you. Maybe, um. Dad, when are you and Mum doing anniversary things?"

Dad laughed, suddenly more relaxed. "The twenty-eighth, this year. Since the bohort's on the twenty-seventh. And yes, Alexander's free then. You can have the evening to do whatever you want. Your Aunt Borea has said you can use the Ritual classroom, so you'll have all the space." He considered, then said, "No more cider, but would you put on the kettle again?"

Leo pushed himself upright. "Uncle Alexander?"

"Tisane for me too, please. No need for us to get maudlin. And we do have a feast to look forward to. There will be mead for that, your mother's made sure of it." As Leo went off to go deal with the kettle and tidy up the bottles, he heard them pick up about what they were looking forward to tonight. And the next few days, with various combinations of family.

CHAPTER 14
ROS ON DECEMBER 24TH

It was a delightfully comfortable evening. They'd had a late supper, and Ros was curled up in the library, with the fireplace making things cosy. Mama and Papa were settled on the sofa in front of it, and Ros was on the floor, near Mama's desk.

Merry and Edmund had gone off to catch up one-on-one. That was fine. She'd get her chance to talk to Edmund sometime in the next day or two. Ros was confident he'd make time for that. He always did. Merry was still working out what she wanted to do after leaving school, or rather how to do it. Edmund had a lot of thoughts about that, now he was at Oxford and the Academy properly.

Also, Ros knew they were expecting Uncle Alexander sometime soon. She didn't want to go up to bed until she had to. He'd been staying out at Schola, with Leo and his parents, during the Council celebrations. They had a pattern now of the traditions. He was there until Christmas Eve, here overnight. Then he'd visit the extended Wain family for an afternoon meal, back at Ytene for an evening feast, and then a brief appearance at the Fortier family gathering on Boxing Day. After that he'd be here through the twenty-eighth, and then back at Schola for a few more days before Leo's parents had to go back to teaching.

It was a little complicated, but everyone got to see him. And it wasn't as if Christmas proper were particularly religious for any of them. Culturally, yes. And Papa's parents and grandparents had moved a little more in the non-magical community, at least when it came to the arts, and it was easier to build that into their schedule. Time they weren't expected to be elsewhere, anyway.

At about nine, there was a flurry of noise from the hall, one of the staff, and then the door opening. "Hail the hall." Uncle Alexander was in an extremely jovial mood, the sort of thing that went with a cloak and scents of changing weather coming in with him. Papa got up immediately, embracing him, then Mama, as Papa went to pour him a drink without asking. Uncle Alexander raised an eyebrow at Ros, and she waved a hand back, a little uncertain now whether she should go upstairs.

Uncle Alexander settled down on the sofa, with Papa next to him, and Mama on the other side instead. "Do stay, Ros. Are Merry and Edmund somewhere?"

"Upstairs." Ros grinned. "Being them."

"Well. Presents later." Uncle Alexander was looking very pleased with something. Smug, even.

"Presents tomorrow morning, Uncle Alexander." Ros had learned that one of the roles of the youngest in the house - at least in this household - was as the keeper of traditions that others might want to change. Uncle Alexander had been the one to teach her that, when she was seven or so, not long before the war. Papa's face, while he was doing it, had gone through a dozen different expressions. Finally, he'd mildly commented about Uncle

Alexander being an excellent teacher and also entirely made to dispute the obvious.

"Indeed, indeed." He rubbed his hands together now. "I have had a lovely meal, the promise of two more tomorrow, even with the rationing. A little heavy on nut roast. And I have not forgotten, Ros, that I do also owe you a birthday present. Which we might in fact discuss today."

Ros tilted her head. Her birthday had been on the twentieth. Uncle Alexander was usually busy that night, whether or not it was the actual Council Rites. The solstice moved, of course, just a little from year to year. She'd had a pleasant evening with her parents, a number of books as gifts, and a new saddle and bridle for Merla. But she never knew what to expect from Uncle Alexander.

"Yes?" She leaned forward on one hand, waiting.

"If this does not please, I will gladly convert it into shopping time in a bookshop of mutual agreement." Uncle Alexander glanced at her parents, then focused on her. "But I thought you might be interested in a handful of experiences spread out across the year. One or two during the winter hols, one or two over the spring, and a few over next summer."

Ros didn't know what to say to that. "What sort of experiences, please? There's not nearly enough information to make a decision, Uncle."

It made him chuckle. "It is a week for admitting to things." Of course, he didn't explain that at all. "I have a series of, hmm. Conversations I would like to have now that travel is an option again. In a number of cases, I will also be meeting with them more privately. But to begin, it would actually be rather handy to have a meeting that must remain nominally casual. An outing to a museum, to a cafe in London, to some concert with a chance for a small treat before or after. It would be a chance to meet people from a wide range of backgrounds. America, certainly." He glanced over at Papa first. "Theodore thought he'd make it over in March."

"Ah." Papa was being rather quiet. He and Mama weren't interfering. Ros could assume from that they'd already talked about this, and it was in fact her choice. Though maybe Mama would give her a little more information later. "Go on, Alexander."

Uncle Alexander nodded. "Some of it will depend on who actually visits. If it's convenient, I might arrange a day or two where you can come from Schola, or where perhaps they come out there. Some of them I trust, within their scope. Some of them I absolutely don't. I promise I will tell you which, well beforehand. You will get a biography and background on them when I set things up. Which may be weeks or months in advance, or might be only a day or two, but that is the life of a diplomat."

Ros snorted, then settled back a bit, her hand behind her to brace against. "Is that what you think I want to do?"

"I don't know that 'want' is the right word for anything like that. But you show an interest in it. You wanted all the language study - I did gather from Ibis that your Arabic is coming along nicely."

He shifted into that smoothly, his accent a bit different from Professor Ward's. But that was the thing. She knew Mama and Papa weren't fluent in it. They had only a few customary phrases. Uncle Alexander had been clear about that when she started. "I do mean this as a gift, because I think you will appreciate it, the range of what is visible and hidden. You have an eye that delights in that, from your father, and you have a talent for understanding which parts matter, from your mother. And there are parts that are all yours, and I would see what you make of the chance."

She did, in fact, follow all of it, and that surprised her. Though none of the grammar was challenging here, and he was deliberately using fairly simple vocabulary. Or he'd been conspiring with Professor Ward to make sure she had the vocabulary most relevant to his interests, which honestly wouldn't be a surprise. Ros considered, then replied, also in Arabic. "What sort of people would I be meeting? And how would you..." Her grasp of verbs failed her for a moment. "How would you explain me?" she tried. It did well enough.

Uncle Alexander chuckled, switching easily back to English. "There, you do ask good questions. Most of them have some diplomatic function in Albion, official or less official. Your papa and I met Theodore in Berlin." Ros had been tiny, but she'd heard the stories when she was old enough. Well, some of them, some Papa and Uncle Alexander skipped over. Both of them. There was no hope when that happened. "How I'd introduce you would depend a bit on the person. With Theodore, as Geoffrey's daughter, out for a pleasant afternoon with me when we were done setting up other conversations for later. With Ekaterina Petrova, that I am instructing you in the first steps of the diplomatic dance, to see if you take to the art form. With one of my father's cousins, that you have some gifts I wish to encourage. You would need your French with him, mind. He refuses to speak anything else."

Ros considered that. "Theodore sounds like a British name. But not British?"

"American. And Ekaterina Petrova speaks excellent English, fortunately for me. Russian is not one of my gifts. Depending where we meet, we might try German, but that needs a good bit of privacy. Others, as I say, depending on when people are here, and when you are free. And when I am free, which is always a good question."

Ros had known what she was going to say, more or less immediately. She would always take an afternoon out with Uncle Alexander, under whatever circumstances she could get it. "And you'll tell me what to be prepared to talk about? I don't actually have a lot of vocabulary yet."

He chuckled. "Yes. Preparation, as I said. And I'll tell you how I plan to introduce you. If you think that's not an option, you're to tell me in advance. We can make sure you have some suitable clothes, the sort of properly dressy thing for tea in a hotel or a cafe."

He glanced up at Mama, who snorted. "You don't ask for much with the clothing rationing. But I'm sure Cassie and I can work out something. A nice blouse and skirt will do for some of it, anyway, with a decent coat. I'm fairly sure we can take in one of my old ones for that, have it look good as new."

Ros peered up at her. "You think it's a good idea, Mama?"

Mama leaned forward. "He did ask before he proposed it to you. A couple of weeks ago, even, we've had time to think about it. I think you'll find it interesting. If you turn out more like Merry, and you want to travel, you'd know more about the places you might visit. If you want to go into diplomacy or the Ministry, it would be an excellent start. And we know - all three of us - that sometimes it's the personal connection that opens a door for something more impersonal."

That was something Ros was going to chew on for a long time to come. Probably starting with staring at the ceiling tonight. Finally, Ros nodded. "I'd like to try, please.

Though I think I don't know nearly enough to have a reasonable conversation about a lot of things."

Uncle Alexander chuckled. "I might also lend you some books. Current geopolitics. And I'd like you to start reading the newspaper regularly. Both the Trellech Moon and the London Times, and I'll send you other pieces from time to time." It would mean more reading, but that wasn't generally a problem for Ros. She read fast. "And I'll explain things to you while I'm here and you're home." He leaned back, stretching an arm along the back of the sofa, and Papa smiled. "Here's one to start with. You were up at the Council Keep, for the public rites, of course."

Ros nodded carefully.

"And you were there when Cyrus was still head, this summer." She had been. Everyone had known he was going to step down. He hadn't made a secret of his coming retirement.

"That's like a microcosm of the larger world. I amuse myself, sometimes, in the more tedious meetings, about making members of the Council into nations. Don't tell them. I suspect they wouldn't like it. Gabe knows, mind." Uncle Alexander waved a hand. "It is, however, a method that sometimes kicks something loose in another realm. And I am not primarily a diplomat, except when I am."

"So you're constantly keeping things in your head, not because of what's going on right now, but what, um, might be relevant sometime?" Ros felt that wasn't a well put together sentence, but it would have to do.

"Exactly. It's also a little like bohort or pavo that way, thinking several steps out. Knowing which goals you're aiming for, and which you might need to put off, or delegate, or see if you can solve a different way. When we're doing the matches on the twenty-seventh, you watch and see what you make of that."

Papa chuckled at that. "It'll be good for your pavo play, too. Speaking of, while Alexander's out tomorrow, I thought we might do a bit of work in the arena. I'd like to see more of how you're getting on with your skills, you and Jasper."

"Jasper's much better," Ros said promptly. Then she grinned up at her parents. "I'm getting better, though. Unconventionally, but better." Then she stood up. "Thank you, Uncle Alexander, but I'm sure you have things to talk to Papa and Mama about now. And I'll get to see you tomorrow."

"I'll be back by four at the latest." Uncle Alexander looked very pleased with his world, really.

Ros got up, claiming a kiss from each of them on her cheek, before she went off. She had a lot of thinking to do. Uncle Alexander said something quietly to Mama and Papa. She didn't hear what, then Papa said something back. Just as she put her foot on the stairs, she heard, "As if I would, you'd have my head and you'd be right about it." Then someone closed the library door, and she wasn't going to hear anything more.

CHAPTER 15
JASPER ON DECEMBER 27TH

"Ah, there you are." Master Benton came out of the manor, a leather satchel over his shoulder. Jasper had been waiting on the courtyard bench nearer the stables. "Right on time." That part was pleased. Master Benton was dressed to work, a sensible twill suit, work gloves tucked into one pocket.

It was going to be a busy day. An awful lot of people - all both friends and allies as the Carillons counted it - were going to be out for two pickup bohort matches. There'd be one set for the students, and one set for the adults. Last year's had been amazing to watch, and Jasper expected all the adults had new tricks up their sleeves they were ready to try. Jasper just liked being included, the way they had, automatically and easily, both Jasper and Anna, since Stan hadn't been demobbed quite yet.

Jasper had been glad to help. Anna was off at Stan's cottage for the morning. They'd wanted to catch up a bit more, and well, older siblings got to do that. They'd both be back for the bohort match this afternoon, but it had meant Jasper was the one around to help. Ros and Merry and

Edmund certainly helped with various things on the estate. But Master Benton had specifically asked for Jasper for this yesterday when everyone was exchanging Boxing Day delights. "Good morning, sir."

There was every reason to be polite. From what Jasper had been told - and what he'd picked up the last year, listening to other students - Master Benton's position was a bit unusual. He'd been Lord Carillon's batman during the Great War, then assisted him, then was his valet. When Lord and Lady Carillon married, he became the steward of the estate. That wasn't the usual sort of arc at all, especially since Jasper had begun to realise Master Benton was actually quite adept magically. Even though he'd never gone to any of the Five Schools or, so far as Jasper knew, done a formal apprenticeship in any magical field.

Master Benton paused by the edge of the stable. "Can you get the other end of that, please? It's not as heavy as it looks." There was a tack trunk waiting by the edge of the stable. When Jasper picked up the leather strap on one end, he realised how much lighter it was. The box was a big one. It should be an effort for two men, never mind a man and a still growing boy. Instead, they lifted it easily. Other people would have asked what was in it, but Jasper's parents had trained him well here, not to ask. If it was something he could know, someone would tell him he could ask, or would just tell it.

Master Benton didn't say anything until they'd carried it down the dirt path that ran from the courtyard to the covered arena. Once inside, they set it down in the area that had been set aside for the spectators, marked out with bales of hay draped with ground cloths. Master Benton got it settled where he wanted it with a minimum of fuss before standing back. Jasper took a step back.

"We thought you'd like a chance to see more of what is involved in preparing the space." Master Benton wasn't looking directly at Jasper, he often didn't look at people he was talking at. Mum said that was a way to know he trusted you, that he'd do that.

"We, sir?" Jasper glanced over at that.

Master Benton just smiled. It was a pleased smile, though, and one that was about having just a bit of a secret. "First, let's set everything out. There will be a hamper coming down later with drinks and snacks, such as we can manage. If you'd help me bring that down after luncheon, I'd be obliged. For now, though, we'll want the kit handy. That box on top over there, that's the part that you're not to see the details of."

"One of the goals, then. Or more than one." It was a decent size, maybe a foot wide and a foot deep, and more like eighteen inches high. Jasper waited until Master Benton had put that aside on one of the tables, then helped get out the other supplies. There was a potions case in there. Master Benton added that to the table, opening it and checking the vials and bottles and tins of salve. There were rather a lot there. "That seems very thorough, sir."

Master Benton snorted. "All sorts of things could happen, though we hope the less pleasant ones won't. Best to be prepared, though. These." His fingers brushed along one side, "Are stabilisation potions to hold until a Healer can be summoned. Varying lengths of time and severity. These are for injuries, the kind of thing that can mend with magic without a Healer's touch. These are restoratives, if someone overdoes it. A variety of strengths, we don't want to use something when we don't need it."

Jasper nods. "And those scale in cost and complexity, too." Jasper wasn't taking Alchemy, but he knew that much.

"Exactly so. No point in wasting resources. Here, would you go and take this brush and this jar, and paint a continuous line around the seating enclosure. Top of the bales, on the outer edge."

"Stay inside the bound as I do it, sir?" Jasper took the jar, which felt heavier than it ought to. The brush was substantial, like an artist's brush for filling in larger spaces in a big canvas.

"Exactly so." Master Benton went to move two bales back into place to enclose the entire area. Jasper started there and worked his way around, moving steadily. There was no reason to rush, he'd have been told if there was, which meant steady and thorough was the goal. It meant he had his back to the ring itself for a fair bit. When he came around the back left corner and the front left, he suddenly realised Lord Carillon was standing there. He wasn't doing anything, just waiting, hands clasped behind his back.

Jasper had a task to do, and he kept doing it after one glance at Master Benton. He worked his way around to the front centre again, making sure he'd closed the full area, then he stepped back. "Sir." After a moment, he added politely, "Lord Carillon."

There was something that made him want to go back to a simpler time. His grandparents, his Pride grandparents, would have tugged their forelocks or bobbed a curtsey. Dad talked to Lord Carillon like a person. With respect, of course, Lord Carillon was his boss, had been for decades now. Mum teased Lord Carillon sometimes, but she'd been born into more that sort of family. Not someone with the land magic, of course, but the kind of people who went to parties with them sometimes. Jasper knew how to be polite, and that would have to do.

"Entirely Benton's project at the moment. Good morning, Jasper." Lord Carillon strolled over, closer, but didn't move to come in. Instead, Master Benton did something with his hands, then moved the bales aside once more. Now the bales were joined together, as if they moved on wheels like a luggage cart or wheelbarrow. Tidier than that, actually.

"Well done, Jasper." Master Benton's voice was warm. "Your lordship?"

It wasn't as if Master Benton asked a question beyond the two words, but they seemed to hold a number of specifics somehow. Lord Carillon waved a hand, not quite a salute, and then went off to the doors at the other end of the arena. He went around, apparently checking on something before coming back. "What did you think about the east pole here?"

"How energetic are you intending to be this afternoon, sir?" Master Benton definitely sounded like he was teasing now. "If you were intending illusions, or, mmm, that entanglement charm, we probably want to shore it up."

"Excellent. Jasper, would you be willing to lend a hand?" Lord Carillon asked it so smoothly, Jasper didn't register the question for a moment.

"Me, sir?" He cleared his throat. "If I can help, of course."

"Grand, grand. Would you come here? What we want is for you to stand here, at the point of this triangle, and just let your magic flow out a little. We're going for a carpet over the space, up onto the wall, up to the roof, covering about ten feet here. That's the weak spot." Lord Carillon made an entirely different gesture with his fingers, something precise like a conductor's baton. A line of light rose up from where the side of the arena met the ground, spreading up and down in a line maybe a hand wide. Up where the line met the roof, there was something that got muddy around the edges, unfocused.

"How?" Jasper swallowed hard. "I mean."

Master Benton came over, gesturing to show him where to stand. "Don't force it. For one thing, you want to save your magic for the match as well. But if you can pick up this knack, it's handy for plenty of other things." He considered. "It's like charging a stove, you do that often enough, but there's a lot more space for the magic to flow in. It won't feel like it's filling up. The trick in this case is to stop when you need to."

"It's not something Schola will focus on teaching you, not this kind of application." Lord Carillon was in a somewhat odd mood, maybe. "There you go. Just let it flow and rise. We'll be directing it to fill in the gaps. Think of it a little like water seeping in somewhere, then settling, so everything's in contact."

Jasper did his best. He'd paid attention in class, though a lot of their work was more about theory than this kind of practice. But Professor Fortier had them working on some exercises in physical training this year to feel more of what was going on with them, and with the magic. That helped a bit, actually. Jasper could feel his awareness expanding. It wasn't just about his feet or his shoulders, but how far from the wall he was, that the wall was wood and not stone or brick or something. That the land west of them was a bit quieter than it had been. The bombing range was slowly shutting down.

He just kept breathing steadily, not pushing what was going on, just seeing what it did. He could feel something working around him, using that shaping to do something else. Jasper couldn't follow that at all. He didn't know how to make sense of whatever was going on. Then all of a sudden, it was like the pressure went away, and the water soaked into the ground after a dry spell. A moment later, there was a hand on his shoulder, gentle but strong. "Well done, very well done. Sir?"

Master Benton's voice was even, but Jasper was grateful for the steadying hand when that light came up. Where it had been a thin line, it was now much thicker, more like a century-old tree. Then, after something changed that Jasper couldn't see, all the posts for the arena lit up that same way, evenly. From behind him, Jasper heard Lord Carillon say , "You could do quite a lot of good with that sort of skill. Infrastructure and all. A different kind of land magic, but even more necessary these days."

"Sir?" Jasper didn't even know where to start with questions.

"What his lordship means to say," Master Benton's voice was definitely amused now, "Is that if you'd like some options for learning more about using your magic for this kind of thing, we could arrange for some of that. Finding out if you like it. There are many bridges and walls and houses and cellars that need some help. And will for years to come."

Jasper considered. "What does that mean for, I mean, school? Or, after, I suppose."

"Much the same as you're doing now, for this year and next. If you decide you might want to go that way, there might be some independent study in your fourth and fifth year. We know people who'd help, and so do a number of your professors. You don't need to fuss with that right now. But you have a tremendous strength - like your father. And he and your mother had the sense you wanted to do something useful, but something that was on the land. Not in books." Lord Carillon picked up, smoothly.

Jasper let out a breath, all in a rush. "Yeah." Then he caught himself. "I mean, yes, sir. I'd been trying to figure that out, because the things I like doing don't always fit with how Schola talks about them. Even though that's also, um, interesting."

He heard a snort, and then there was a nudge on his shoulder, encouraging him to turn around. Lord Carillon was outright laughing now. "Oh, that's very politic. You've been listening to Ros, haven't you? Schola has many swots, and swots can do a lot of good in the world. I should know. But it's not the only way to do something. You did well on your tests, you have strong magic. We'll see if we can find you a place that has space for all of that. Not just some of you."

Jasper swallowed hard. "Yes, sir. Your lordship."

"Just so. We'll see about getting you some more training, then. It'd be useful several ways round." Lord Carillon waved a hand. "Anyway. Thanks to your help, Benton and I can now check the warding and protections and finish up. Go have a seat and you can watch. How's that?" Benton cleared his throat once, pointedly, and Lord Carillon waved a hand.

"While we have a moment, Jasper." Master Benton's voice had shifted a little. "How are things going for you at school, then?"

Jasper froze, and he knew they must see it, both of them. And besides, it wasn't like he was going to lie. It was a whole lot easier not to say anything, but maybe Lord Carillon had heard bits from Ros, or even Merry. "My classes are going better this year, so. Pavo's grand, Master Held has me doing a lot more training. I like all of that." He then looked at a point on the ground. "And Ros and Leo and Avigail have been good friends. Peter Wallace too."

"But not everyone." Lord Carillon's voice was clear, that posh accent somehow very precise but not sharp.

"No, sir." Jasper ventured a glance up. "There are bullies. I keep away from them. The teachers are, they've stepped in. But it's always sort of there, a thing to think about."

"And teachers can't be everywhere. That's the thing of it." Lord Carillon brought his hands in front of him. "I'm sorry that's there, lurking at you. May I ask - you don't need to tell me if you'd rather not - what they focus on?"

"Who my parents are, why I'm even there? That I spend all my time with the horses." Jasper shrugged. "Sort of about me and sort of not, all at once? And most of it's just rude, it's not something they ought to get punished for. Professor Hammond took care of things right quick when it was."

"Good man. Isembard and Thesan speak well of him. I'm glad to know that has legs." Lord Carillon considered, looking up into the rafters, visibly thinking. "If there is something we can do to be a help - myself or Benton or Lizzie, or anyone else here - I hope you will let us know. A greeting when we come out to watch the bohort or one of the pavo matches, that sort of thing. Helping you explain things to your professors if you need to." Then he looked over at Master Benton.

"What his lordship means - and says most of, actually - is that you have the estate's support. As is right and proper. You're not like the people who've assumed Schola is their birthright, you're your Dad's son, through and through. Horses included." That part made Jasper smile, even though the rest of him still felt uncertain. "And we're confident you'll find your place. This is a start on it, today, things that can be yours. Not feel like a borrowed coat."

Jasper swallowed hard at that, but he was sure, completely sure, that Master Benton wouldn't fib. And Lord Carillon seemed entirely in earnest, too. "Sir." Then he added, "Ros has had an eye out, too. But she can't be everywhere either."

"I'm glad to hear that. She does hate an injustice. She's asking Lizzie about some things she spotted at the Council Keep over solstice at the moment. Right then. We stand ready to assist, and we hope it's not needed." Then Lord Carillon stopped suddenly, as if someone had just elbowed him, but he'd only been looking at Master Benton. "Let me go check something outside, I'll just be a moment."

That seemed deliberate, all of a sudden, but Jasper certainly wasn't able to argue with it. That wasn't how you did things. Instead, there was quiet while Lord Carillon went out the door. Master Benton cleared his throat. "That was not his most subtle. Her ladyship would tsk."

That Master Benton said so, that made Jasper startle. "Pardon?"

"We haven't exactly asked you what you'd like to do, have we? We are - the estate is, formally and informally - glad to support you. And your brother and your sisters, obviously. But what would you like to be supported in?"

Jasper twitched. "I don't really know. I love the Forest." That was obvious, he assumed. "But Stan's got Dad's old cottage, and Dad's glad to have him in the stables, and I don't know if there's room for me too." He hesitated. "And I love the horses, but I don't know if that's all there is." He gestured at the wood they'd strengthened. "And that kind of magic, I don't know. It's not just for horses."

What he didn't know how to say was that he wanted to

do something that mattered. It was a little about not being old enough to go to the war. That would have been awful, he'd heard enough from Dad and Stan, and what they didn't talk about. But it would have mattered in a particular way. Horses were grand, but they were less and less important in the world.

Master Benton nodded slowly. "It's not. You know there's a good bit you could help with. Bridges, buildings, that sort of thing. We can find out what you'd need for skills for that." He half-smiled. "Possibly more maths, but there are tutors for that."

Jasper did not like the idea of more maths, but he could see it might be relevant. "That's one line of it, sir. But I don't know that that's the right one, either."

"Well, you think about it, this term. Come back in the spring - or write, if you think of something - and we'll see about you spending some time with people over the summer. Different projects and kinds of work. I do know quite a few."

"You know a fair number of everyone in both halves of the Forest, sir," Jasper pointed out. Then he hesitated. "May I ask about something?"

"Of course." Master Benton nodded, as if that were some sort of absolute rule.

"I was thinking, this term, about what other estates were like. How they felt. And I don't even know what I'm asking, but isn't that relevant for some of the magic?"

Master Benton smiled suddenly. "It is. You've been to Veritas. Now, I don't know enough about what you're feeling, that's a longer conversation. But I suspect we could ask Penelope Edgarton to talk it through with you. He'd be best positioned, as on the Council and Heir in his own right. And we might see about arranging visits to a few other estates, as well. Perhaps going along with the horses when there's some reason, and you're home."

Lord Carillon came back at about that point, whistling, but he'd obviously caught the last bit of conversation. "Benton certainly does know a fair number of everyone in the Forest. It's decidedly useful. And we can certainly see about some visits elsewhere. Spring hols, if not before. You also likely want to talk to Gil Oxley, he's dealt with architectural magics on a number of estates, demesne and otherwise." Jasper's face must have shown his surprise, because Lord Carillon grinned. "Oh, he's not that intimidating. He leaves that to Magni. And he likes explaining things from the ground up. Now, Benton, where did you think we should start?"

"North and the doors, sir, working sunwise." Master Benton offered one more smile to Jasper. "Stand where you like, so long as it's behind where we're working. Once his lordship goes off to finish his necessary paperwork, I'll explain what we were doing."

Lord Carillon chuckled again. Jasper bobbed his head. "I'd like that." He immediately trotted over to find a seat in the seating area at the end, and settled in to watch the two of them do a great many things he didn't understand. A lot of them looked very complex indeed, both of them doing different parts of what was needed, with highly coordinated timing. It was like a drill team riding together. Maybe if he understood how it went together, he'd understand the rest of it better.

VESTAL TERM

CHAPTER 16
AVIGAIL ON JANUARY 7TH

Avigail knocked on the door of Professor Morwen's rooms in Salmon House. She could hear the bustle behind her, people still chattering and exclaiming about their holidays. Professor Morwen had a left a note asking her to stop by at ten on Tuesday, when Avigail had a free block.

"Come!" The voice from the sitting room was cheerful, and the door was ajar.

"You wanted to see me, Professor Morwen?" There were several things this could theoretically be about, and Avigail didn't know which of them might have provoked it. Whatever it was, Professor Morwen hadn't written to her parents, they'd have told her.

"Close the door, would you? This won't be long, but I wanted to ask you about something on one of your exams." There weren't any comments about how Avigail wasn't in trouble. On the other hand, Professor Morwen sounded rather a lot like Aunt Mason and Aunt Witt, who didn't give reassurances like that, even when it was true. Or Aunt Doyle, who'd just sit there observing. It made it harder to predict what was coming. Avigail closed the door, hearing the noise outside disappear as soon as the sound charms connected. Then she found a place to sit on the sofa.

It was a sitting room that Avigail found fascinating, honestly. There was Professor Morwen's desk, of course, for routine work. Like all the other professors, she had a proper office elsewhere, up by her classroom. Avigail had wondered if there was a reason for meeting here, or just that Professor Morwen didn't teach classes in the mornings.

The rest of the room was lined in bookshelves, save for the window and a large drafting table. That was currently at an angle, with some sort of diagrams or practical sketches on it. There were bits and bobs of various devices and crafts and objects on the shelves in front of the books, each of them grabbing the eye. It made Avigail wonder suddenly if Professor Morwen were part of Four Metals, it'd be a logical sort of thing with all the different skills Salmon House got into.

This was not the time for getting distracted. Avigail tucked her feet under the sofa and focused on Professor Morwen. "One of my exams." There were two that might be relevant. No, three. Maybe four, but probably not. She'd got good marks on all of them, she knew that already. No use hoping for a clue about which paper without actually asking. "Yes? Which one?"

Professor Morwen snorted. "Two of them, actually. Though it was my class I noticed first." She tilted her head, as if considering something. "You've seen your marks for the term, and your exam. I'm not upset with you. I am, however, wanting to know why you did that."

The exam question had been about identifying items using sympathetic resonances, with items to evaluate in a workroom and then an essay to write up about it. Avigail's actual evaluation had been a page and a half, well-organised, and utterly correct. She was sure of it.

The additional four pages of commentary on the method had perhaps been a tad excessive. Only they weren't. She'd laid out - briefly, but with references she'd read - how the approach would only work with a known pure sample and not in field conditions. Also, how there were several gaps in the provided materials that couldn't rule out common building and clothing materials that were, for example, part of Schola. The sixth page, well, she couldn't help having Aunt Mason's citations in her head now, could she?

After a moment's consideration, Avigail began simply with, "You wanted to know what I knew about that sort of thing. Simply answering the question didn't provide that."

"No, it didn't." Professor Morwen was still keeping her face quite neutral. It was rather impressive, Grandmama would approve. Then there was a hint of a smile. "Do you have a copy of the Mason article? It's not published that I could find."

"I can get one, of course." Avigail caught something. "Didn't you know? She's my Aunt Mason. She started training Papa when he was young, though he apprenticed to someone else, Penelope Lucy Doyle. Also Aunt Doyle." Though once she said it, she wondered if Professor Morwen had already known that, something in her face.

Professor Morwen snorted. "The private habits of the Penelopes are a topic of some fascination, but not one where I know the full extent of their library. Though I have consulted on a few things with Penelope Doyle. It's possible, from the published materials, to see lines of thought developed over the years. But that's not one I knew, in quite that form."

"I'll ask Aunt Mason for a copy. She doesn't share it terribly widely. There are implications for forgery and all that, that's why it was never published. There's one about the general theory of it. I mentioned that one too."

"I did read that, yes. I can see why they might want to keep the specifics private. Please do ask her. I'd be interested in the article if she's willing to share." Professor Morwen considered. "We talked about this when you selected your courses last spring, but you're still interested in keeping your options open to follow your father and your aunts?"

Avigail still wasn't entirely sure what she wanted, but it was a fair question. "I'd like to see. Papa took me out on a few investigations last summer, and we've worked on some projects at home, as we get time." Several of which she was absolutely not going to tell a Professor about. Papa had helped her with an excellent set of charms to help get a better handle on some of how the pretty princesses of her year reacted to things. It wasn't trying to convince them to do anything, it wasn't even giving her more information. It just made it easier to understand some of what she was hearing and feeling and picking up.

Mostly anxiety, in their cases, in a mode that Avigail couldn't make any sense out of. On the other hand, she could at least not do things that made the situation worse. Knowing was a help. She had not done anything less pleasant to them. She sometimes felt she should get a lot more credit for this.

Honestly, she'd been provoked more than sufficiently. There was a list tucked away in her trunk, of all the things she'd discarded. Itching powder, magical dye in the shampoo, a powder that, if sprinkled in their shoes, would give them a feeling like pins and needles. Aunt Charlotte had come up with that one. Only in theory, of course, though they'd worked through what it would take to make it up.

"And you're still thinking about it." That wasn't a question, and that was interesting. Professor Morwen went about conversations differently than Papa did, but not as differently as Avigail had actually expected. She noticed things, and she'd come back to them deliberately later on.

Now, it meant Avigail had to figure out what to say. And that was probably deliberate on Professor Morwen's part, setting it up so Avigail had to say something. Or be rude, and that wasn't really an option. "I am."

"May I ask what you're thinking about, what you're trying to get more information on?" The thing with professors was that they were, on average, perceptive. Certainly Professor Morwen was.

And Avigail hadn't talked this out with Papa yet. She'd been planning to in March, with the equinox hols. Solstice hols were full of social obligations, and Papa had to be right in the middle of it. It wasn't a good time for this kind of conversation. Avigail wanted to start it, but also be able to go away and do other things for a bit, if they needed space. She certainly couldn't explain all of that to a professor.

The thing was, being a Penelope wasn't just a job. It took over people's whole life, even if they went home and did other things. It wasn't just the amount of work - though there was a lot of that, always. Interesting work, but a lot of it. But it was about the way they thought about things. Avigail had seen a bit of that with Papa's last apprentice. She'd seen a lot more of it with Claudio, because she'd been old enough to notice things when Claudio started.

She remembered the first time Papa had him for supper,

nearly three years ago now. Claudio had mostly listened - he'd been really polite and warily quiet. He'd asked a few questions. Papa - and Mama, and Grandmama - had made sure to explain things as they talked. But he had listened like someone who wasn't a Penelope. He was clever. Avigail had figured that out really fast. And he was observant. But it wasn't a Penelope's clever or observant, she didn't know how to explain that to someone who didn't see it for themselves.

What Avigail came up with wasn't remotely all of the truth. But it'd do for the moment. "It's a very important thing to do. And it's been a very dangerous one, and all sorts of new challenges, during the war. I think going into that sort of thing ought to be a very well-considered decision, don't you?" Papa was vastly more likely to be going toward the unstable alchemy lab shaken by bombing, or putting himself between a flood and people who still needed to get out. Or doing some other magical act that no one had asked him to do because no one thought it was really possible. Avigail knew some of the times he'd done that, but not all of them by a long stretch.

Avigail wasn't sure she could do that. And it wasn't something she was willing to do badly. Even without the consideration that doing that sort of thing badly tended to get someone hurt or killed, probably the Penelope. Or worse, someone else. And she'd grown up knowing the Penelopes and a fair number of the sensible sorts out of the Guard as actual people who talked to her and answered her questions and who she liked.

Professor Morwen looked at her for a long moment. "That's an interesting answer." She stood up, going to a table by her desk, and pouring tea - no, tisane, there was the mint - out into a cup. "Mint?"

"Please, professor." It was an easy place to be polite, and it smelled wonderful.

"What feels most important about it to you?" Professor Morwen brought the mugs back, handing one over.

"If you're going to help people, actually help them, not the show of helping them, that's important. And that's a lot of what the Penelopes do. Sometimes it's helping people who are right there. Sometimes it's the Guard, and about finding justice if there can be some." Avigail was certainly never going into the Guard. Not just because Anthony was, and that was too much, but because she knew the things she thought were just weren't always how the law came out. "Sometimes it's figuring out what happened, so people can avoid doing that again, and getting hurt or worse."

Professor Morwen nodded. "There are lots of ways to help people. Not just the usual set. Healing, everyone thinks about that. But there are people who help those who've been injured in other ways. I know someone who does custom wheelchairs, for example. Or a couple of people, actually, now. I've done some consulting about materials, some things work particularly well when you can align sympathetic properties with someone's own magic, or what they're around most."

Avigail tilted her head. "Oh, that's interesting. I read, um, what was it? Richeldis Atherton, about something like that, only that was locking cabinets. Something that moves must have a whole set of other considerations."

Professor Morwen laughed. "Oh, yes. Professor Wain's brother is one of them. You might ask her if he'd come and do a talk on it again. He hasn't since before the war." She then sipped her mug. "Back to your exams. You had a similar - though shorter - response on several of them. We, collectively, are not going to ask you to stop doing that, but we are going to hold you to the standards set for the exam answer. You know perfectly well what those are, so don't be foolish about it. And then, if you have time in the exam, and additional commentary, share it. We'll see what comes of it, in terms of some independent projects in the coming years."

In other words, whatever she said, they'd be shaping something around that. Well, that made some things easier. Other people might just ask. And to be honest, Avigail would ask, too. But seeing what they suggested, that was a lot more fun. Or would be. "Yes, Professor."

"I'm looking forward to seeing what you come up with." Professor Morwen considered. "We're trying to do better with this sort of creativity than when your father and I were students. Your ideas are good, even if old stalwarts would have marked you down - rather a lot - for questioning the status quo. As long as you're making well-considered arguments, not just being difficult for the sake of being difficult, I'm curious what you come up with. Now, let's see. You've read the Atherton. Have you read Lillian Thomas's thing on resonances and the age of materials?"

"No, I don't think so. Unless that's the one that talks about, um, what was it? Victorian furniture."

"That's Clarence Rigby. Though I should grab that, too. Just a minute. Pull up the table there, and I'll have somewhere to stack things." Professor Morwen gestured at the low table near the sofa, and Avigail moved it before sitting down again. Professor Morwen moved around the room, clearly intending to use the rest of the hour to talk about one of her favourite topics. That was just grand.

CHAPTER 17
LEO ON JANUARY 8TH AFTER SUPPER

Wednesday, Leo finished up supper. He'd been making a point of catching up with people, and on Wednesdays, the seating was more relaxed. They didn't need to sit by House. Leo had a theory - he should ask Mum sometime - that it was because they'd all just spent two hours with their housemates, and it was a good time for a change. Of course, some people just continued their conversations from the afternoon, that always happened.

The rest of his hols had been comfortable. He and Dad had spent a bit of time down by the map, going through every spot in Schola. That odd sparkle on the coastline had shown up the first day, but not the second time they'd checked. There had been a couple of times the merfolk were busy round there - Mum had mentioned Jasper seeing them to Dad, and a few times since. But each time Uncle Ibis or Susanna had checked, the merfolk hadn't had anything particular to say about it.

And the second round of checking had highlighted a bit of masonry that had got storm damage and obviously needed tending before it came down and maybe hit someone on the head. Leo had got to help the masons with that, handing things up while they were working and seeing how the repairs were made.

Now, though, it was good to be back in Bear House with people around. They were getting on to some really interesting things in their house magic work, now they were second years and had more basics to work with. A lot of the specific charms and enchantments they were learning were general protection and warding ones. Keeping their things safe, keeping people from peeking in their trunks, that sort of thing.

They had an assignment to take a small wooden chest and charm it over the next fortnight. Then they'd be left out in the House library, and anyone could try to put a stamped token in them. Whoever succeeded, in any box, got a treat. Whoever's box had the fewest items at the end got a bigger one. The tokens couldn't be taken out once they were there, so part of the challenge was working with the enchantments already on the box.

Leo had something of an advantage here, and he'd stopped to ask Professor Hammond about that. It had got a laugh, and Professor Hammond pointing out that it was open to the entire house. Leo knew a fair bit, but there were fifth years who'd been focusing on warding - and on opening them - and who knew things he didn't know yet. It made for an interesting challenge, anyway.

Leo wasn't going to talk to Dad about it - that really was cheating, by Leo's standards. But no one had said he couldn't go look at Dad's personal library. He could do that tomorrow, when he went up for family tea. And probably asking Dad what else he ought to look at was fair. He'd think about that one.

He'd ended up in a knot of students he knew slightly. Most of them were from professional families, the sons and daughters of solicitors and barristers and Ministry staff. Two were the children of people Uncle Golshan and Aunt Dilly bothered on a regular basis, trying to get proper services. It made Leo not sure how to handle things sometimes. But Eloise and Rachel weren't responsible for what their parents did at work. And people who didn't think about whether a wheelchair could get to their supposedly public offices deserved to get called down to somewhere more accessible to do their jobs.

It was possible an awful lot of Uncle Golshan and Uncle Seth and Aunt Dilly's way of looking at the world had sunk in. Leo didn't think that was a problem, but other people apparently did. It meant he'd asked a few questions about their hols, to get the conversation somewhere more comfortable. But he had mostly let them go along and chat without sharing too much himself. He wrapped up supper early, taking his plates to the dish room. As he was cutting back across to the doors, there was a sound behind him. "Fortier! Do you have a min?"

Leo looked over his shoulder, blinking a little. That was Crimson Hettleburgh, taking big strides to catch up with him. Leo nodded and waited a moment. "Yes?"

"Do you mind - um. Somewhere quieter?" Crimson glanced around. The noise from the great hall was rather loud, even with the charms that were used to keep it from spreading all over the room.

Leo considered for a moment. "One of the workrooms? There's probably one free right now." They ducked their way through students milling around. Leo hoped it wouldn't take too long. He wanted to go to the lecture at eight, and it was about a quarter to now. On the other hand, that was just upstairs, and there would probably be plenty of seats. They got lucky. One of the nearer workrooms was open, and Leo gestured for Crimson to go first.

"What's your question?" Leo leaned against the wall. Sitting down seemed like it'd take too long, and if he stood in the middle of the room, it'd be awkward and weirdly formal.

"How are you? How were your hols?" Crimson ran his hand through his hair, pulling it back. "I didn't see much of you. I'd sort of expected to?"

"They were fine. We have a lot of family traditions - some here, some with Mum's family, some with Dad's." Mum and Dad had gone to fewer of the posh parties this year. Leo thought they'd really needed the break, and also things had changed and they no longer had to make quite the same social show now.

So it had been the Council rites on the twenty-second, Mum's family on the twenty-fourth and fifth, Dad's on the twenty-sixth. There'd been bohort at Ytene on the twenty-seventh, and then Mum and Dad had gone out for their anniversary the next night. It left just two parties, one of them for New Year's. That was a reasonable time for a party, honestly, and Leo had enjoyed it. But there were three or so Mum and Dad could have gone to - and Ursula had. And Crimson probably had as well. "Yours?"

"Oh, a lot of coming and going, but so many splendid parties and people to talk to." Crimson nudged the door until it was just ajar. "I'd been trying to catch you, to ask about, um." He let out a breath. "The Council rites and something there."

Leo was beginning to understand why his parents complained that apparently all the Trivium training Schola offered couldn't help people get to the point. "Yes?"

He kept his voice very much in what Mum called polite mode.

"It must be terribly hard to see your sister named as Heir?" From the expression on Crimson's face, right after he said that, it was quite possibly not how he'd meant to say that. But Leo also had no idea how to answer that. That was not what he felt at all, actually, about any of it.

"Pardon?" That seemed a safe enough response, and honestly, Leo didn't know what else might work.

"I mean to say, everyone assumed it'd be you, as your father's Heir. Not any time soon, of course. I'm sure no one wants that." Crimson was stammering a hair now, tangling himself up more and more as he talked.

The reality of it was that no one was sure about Uncle Garin. He seemed more content now - happier wasn't a word that Uncle Garin wore well. He'd been doing lots of alchemical research, some of which was potentially hugely helpful. Not that Leo understood most of it, except that it was about things that would help the land magic restore itself more evenly after bombing damage. Both the physical damage, and he was writing lots of letters to people working on doing it for atomic bomb damage, too, other places. He was working on some things with healing applications, too, from what Ursula had said in passing.

Leo knew Dad hadn't particularly wanted to be Uncle Garin's Heir. They'd talked about that, as a family, plenty of times. Dad would have done his duty, and tended the land, but he hadn't wanted that. Not the way Ros's father or Avigail's father wanted it, and seeing the difference had made things very clear for Leo. Also for Dad, he suspected. There hadn't been anyone else, and now there was. Dad and Mum had checked carefully before talking to Uncle Garin about Ursula.

Oh, he'd been hurt when Uncle Garin had made the decision to name Ursula his Heir apparently overnight last summer. But that was six months ago now, and Ursula had understood the part that actually hurt. The parts that were about things changing faster than Leo could make sense of, having Uncle Garin present it with no warning, those were the tricky parts. Ursula being Heir was great. She wanted it. Leo didn't. And Leo particularly didn't want to be made to.

But all of that was private family business, for the four of them and Uncle Garin and Uncle Alexander. It wasn't for talking about with Crimson, even if Crimson was Heir in his own right. Besides, the Hettleburghs weren't allies of the Fortiers in the formal sense. Their lands didn't border Arundel, there weren't family ties. Or, well, the Great Families being what they were, there were family ties. But it was something like third cousins several times removed. That didn't count. Everyone had that.

Leo considered. "You know that it's something families decide in different ways, yeah?" Granted, a lot of the ways people did were male primogeniture, which frankly seemed a stupid method. They had no idea if the oldest son was going to be any good at it, or want to do it, or wasn't going to get killed doing something else. Uncle Alexander had a particular lecture - well, rant - about the expectations of the land magic, and whether it would do better running down a matrilineal line. But of course, some things were very British, before there was an Albion, so the default was the eldest son.

And honestly, that seemed to work out fine for some people. Edmund Carillon wanted it. And his sisters didn't. Anthony Edgarton wasn't Heir - his grandfather was still quite active. But he seemed fine with it too, from all Leo had heard over the years.

Crimson paused, as if that wasn't the expected answer, either. Leo was doing very badly at giving those today, and that meant he was going to be up thinking about it tonight, and what he ought to have said. And he'd probably end up writing to Uncle Alexander, if he didn't ask Mum and Dad about it at family tea. But if he brought it up at tea, they'd want to do something about it. If he asked Uncle Alexander, he'd get information, but he wouldn't have to do anything if he didn't want to. "Well. Yes." He sounded offended, but what did he have to be offended about?

There was an increasingly awkward silence, then. It stretched on for a minute or two, both of them staring at each other, not knowing what to say. Finally, Leo cleared his throat. "Um. Thanks for checking? But honest, Ursula's much better for it. She wants to do it. I didn't. We talked about it." There, that was a nicely unspecific 'we', seeing as it didn't include who, or when, or how often, or for how long. Uncle Alexander would be proud of him.

Crimson nodded slowly. "Oh." Now he was the one who sounded confused. "What does that mean for you, then?"

They definitely weren't good enough friends for that. What Leo wanted was something Leo was still figuring out, anyway. Leo shrugged a little. "Something else. I've got some ideas. I don't know which way I'll pick yet."

"You sound like Wallace." Crimson grimaced. "He thinks he can pick."

"You could too. You said yes to being Heir. But you could decide what that means for you, how you do it." Leo pushed away from the wall. "There's lots of ways people are Heir. Or Lord. Or Lady." He had no idea what Ursula would be like when the time came. But he was pretty sure it'd be very different than Aunt Livia had been, or Lady Alton, or dozens of other people, including Uncle Garin.

Crimson blinked at him. "That's not how people do things." Then he swallowed. "And I, um. The other thing. Two things."

"Yes?" Leo was now honestly rather baffled.

"First, best of luck in the society invitations. I'm sure you'll be picked, and end up where you ought." Which, coming from Crimson, meant Dius Fidius, and that Crimson was working under a misapprehension again. But Leo wasn't going to correct that here and now. Maybe ever. Besides, he had an easy thing to say.

"I hope you end up the right place for you, Crimson. Honestly." Leo stuck his hands in his pockets. "Anything else?"

This one, Crimson actually looked embarrassed at. "You get on with Jasper Pride, don't you? Despite, um."

"My parents are friends with the Carillons. We've been out there a fair bit, visiting. Jasper's a good sort and a fantastic rider." Leo wondered how actively defensive he ought to be. This was a whole area of protective magics and duelling he and Dad hadn't really got into yet. "Something the matter?"

"Just tell him to watch himself, all right? Phipps and Hector and all." Now, that was curious. That Crimson was actually telling him that. It meant Leo had said something right earlier, but Leo wasn't sure why.

"He knows they're out to get him. Though if you get a chance to talk them out of it as a bad idea, I'd be grateful. So would the professors. I know they hate having to do something about that sort of thing."

"Suppose you would." Crimson ducked his chin. "Don't know if I can, but I suppose we'll see. I just thought someone ought to know. If you want to tell Pride, that's fine."

Seeing as how Leo hadn't promised to keep it private, he certainly was going to. Jasper deserved good information. And he'd tell Ros and Avigail and Peter too, not least because Peter might come in for bullying too. Now he nodded. "Thanks. I will, when we get a chance in private. Right now, I wanted to get up to the lecture. Was that it?"

Crimson opened his mouth, then closed it and nodded. "Yes. Another chat sometime?"

Leo nodded. "Of course." He considered, because there was something he could suggest. "If you want to work together on the Incantation assignment, I was going to be in the library tomorrow after supper." It wasn't one of the more personal assignments, it was mostly research, and Ros and Jasper had picked a different topic. He knew that. Crimson was also interested in the language for incantations. They could look through twice as many books if there were two of them.

"Oh. Thanks." Crimson looked even less certain. "See you then."

Leo managed a smile, though he still felt unsettled under the surface. He went up to the lecture hall without talking to anyone else, lost in his own thoughts.

CHAPTER 18
ROS ON TUESDAY, JANUARY 14TH

"Bonjour, Mademoiselle Carillon. Assieds-toi, s'il te plaît." Professor Knox was settled at the table in his rooms, several books by one elbow, and a larger journal open in front of him.

"Bonjour, Professor Knox." Ros sat, as she'd been asked. She made it through the various routine pleasantries - how are you, isn't the weather being weather today - without thinking about them. This part was easy.

She could in fact do it in her sleep. She'd managed to dream twice in French over hols. French was the most likely of her four languages for that. Mama and Papa both spoke it, as well as Uncle Alexander. They'd had supper entirely in French one of the nights when Merry had been at a friend's. It gave her time to think about what she wanted to say today that wasn't at all about French or learning the language.

She also made it through ten minutes of discussing her week's reading assignment. She'd been asked to read three articles from French newspapers. And then compare and contrast them - in French, of course - to the same topic as covered in either the Trellech Moon or the Times of London. It made for interesting and practical work, since it also counted for Uncle Alexander's assignments.

Ros had started with a number of pieces about the resignation of the United States Secretary of State. She'd talked through both sets with Uncle Alexander and Papa in her journal, but with Professor Knox, she just gave the summary and the comparisons of the French pieces. The other set of articles she'd found had been rather distressing. Those had to do with the fuel crisis, not only in Britain but in Germany and Austria, and places beyond that, too. Some of the articles had focused on the industrial needs, but Ros found the ones about people freezing to death much worse. It seemed particularly awful to come out the other side of the war into that.

They'd ended up in a good five-minute discussion of the differences in energy needs - in the sense of coal and steam - between the non-magical and Albion. The way the papers talked about it made her more and more upset with the injustice of it. That just made her think about other things that were wrong in the world, closer to home. Ros thought she'd been keeping her feelings to herself, but apparently not, because Professor Knox finally stopped and leaned forward, chin in his hands, to just look at her.

There were a number of things Ros could say to that, including in French, but they were all at least a little rude. Even if the French "Quoi?" with the right nasal emphasis was pretty much what she felt. It was an aggravated, angular annoyance. She didn't even know if it was fair to be annoyed at Professor Knox yet. He peered at her again, much more like an Owl than a Fox, then murmured he was going to make some more tea.

It left Ros sitting there, one toe not quite scuffing

against the floor. Again, she wanted to, and she wouldn't. She had manners; she knew how to use them.

When the tea was ready - actual tea this time, which surprised her - Professor Knox sat down again, switching into English. "You are angry at me." It wasn't a question, and why did adults have to be so good at spotting things, anyway? It was utterly unfair. She couldn't argue with him, because she was, even if she hadn't known what to call it right away. And besides, arguing with adults didn't go well, unless they were Uncle Alexander, who liked that sort of thing.

Ros took the cup in her hands, sipping at it, mostly to avoid saying something too fast. When she set the cup down in its saucer, she said, "Why aren't you doing something about them? To help them." That was a sentence utterly lacking in antecedents, and the adults in her life would disapprove, and with good reason. She swallowed hard. "Gloriana Boxer and Alcesta Berring, for two."

"And you and Nancy Trelling and Trueth Nott for the other three?" Professor Knox leaned back now. "What are you willing to tell me about it, then?"

Ros's shoulder twitched. "I'm not in the middle of it." She was just the audience for it, and an unwilling one at that. "Why aren't you doing anything about it?"

Professor Knox considered for a moment, then he spoke clearly and distinctly. "What makes you think I'm not?"

Ros had been about to work up a commentary on things, on how things in her dorm room had been steadily getting worse since they got back. Part of her brain had wanted to make geopolitical commentary about it, but she hadn't quite worked out how. She was trying to be Switzerland, and it mostly wasn't working, and Trueth was about to be annexed like Austria had been, whether or not she liked it. That was about as far as Ros had got with the whole problem.

She didn't know how to answer that question, so she went back to his first one. Telling him the problem was at least a little simpler. "You weren't at the Council rites and the dancing." It wasn't a question. Sometimes professors came - and Professor Knox was more likely to than some of the others. He'd been at the New Year's gala in Trellech, though.

"No, I had a family commitment in France." Professor Knox shrugged slightly. "The first since the war that my Maman's extended family got together. Charming chateau in Anjou, not too badly destroyed by the war, only a modest amount of family sniping. They've never approved of my father, you see." He didn't make that a confidence, more like a piece of information that Ros could have looked up if she wanted, to save time later. Which meant there was probably more there to investigate. She'd have to do that when she got a chance. Ideally before next week. "I've heard about it from several people, but I'm interested in your take."

Ros considered him warily. He'd been absolutely reasonable, all through last year and all through Minerval term, including in her French lessons. He'd given her plenty of interesting reading. He'd answered a number of questions. But she'd been wondering, all along, if there might not be some trade expected in kind. It had the feel of that, like some of the ancient Fatae tales, no chance of something for nothing.

It wasn't the sort of thing she'd been able to talk to Mama and Papa about. Or Edmund and Merry, either. Salmon and Owl went about things differently, inside their heads, that was part of the point of the Houses. And Uncle

Alexander - who might well have understood - had other things to talk about. Much more interesting ones than the scuffles of second year girls.

"You know what it is. There's talk, already - we're only fourteen, all right, Alcesta's fifteen, and Trueth almost is, and so Iseult Crane in Owl." That was getting cluttered. She had to try again. "There's talk about marriages and encouraging certain relationships and not. Some people pay more attention to that than others."

"And right now, it's about having a dance with this boy, and arranging a tea - with others of your age - with this one. Perhaps when the weather turns nicer a ride or a picnic or something. All the customs stretching back before this war and the previous one, and into the Victorian era." Professor Knox laid it out almost lazily, with no heat in the words.

Ros swallowed and nodded, then had a little more of her tea. "No one's actually betrothing us at the age of nine for political reasons. Or six, or infancy, for that matter. But there's a lot of expectations, lurking just offstage."

"Good thing, too. I want all of you under my charge getting a proper education, so you have choices. Though you who are at Schola, you're less of a worry that way. We do get the education into you, even the ones who have a horror of looking clever in class." Professor Knox's eyes twinkled. "So, what happened?"

"I wasn't there when it did? Honestly, there's a whole group - four or five here, a few more who aren't at Schola - who all clump up and giggle. Every so often, one of them will get asked to dance, and then there's more giggling after."

"Your brother, or something like that?" Professor Knox raised an eyebrow.

That had hit it on the head, rather sharply. "Edmund sometimes, yes. And he had to be there."

"As your father's Heir, and that makes him very attractive to the sort of people who want to make what they think is an excellent marriage. And five years is enough older to be very interesting in a, hmm, aspirational sort of way. Especially when the boys your own ages are still gangly and not sure of themselves and, to be entirely fair, often lacking in some key skills. Then there's the practical, lands, estates, homes in several places, no worries about death duties taking out half the income." Professor Knox tilted his head. "And that sort of marriage isn't what he wants."

"No. Sir." Ros tacked it on quickly. "And besides, he's in his first year at Oxford, and an apprenticeship after that. But he was polite, of course. No reason not to be."

"And a great many reasons to be cordial, yes. Your brother has excellent manners. As do you, when you're not annoyed." That last was delivered more lightly, and Ros found herself not quite smiling. "Back to the point of the argument, I am aware that Alcesta and Gloriana are on two sides of a divide and that it is uncomfortable in your dormitory. I am keeping an eye on it. But I am, you have to admit, probably not the right person to talk to them about it. Being unmarried myself, and certainly not a role model when it comes to marriages."

Ros had to admit that was fair. Annoying, but just because Professor Knox was head of House, that didn't mean he was the right person for this conversation. They wouldn't take him seriously enough, for one thing. "They - I don't even know what set them off. Some insult, perceived insult, more like. And it's been awful since we got back. Alcesta and Gloriana won't talk to each other, so Nancy's always having to pass messages to Trueth, and vice versa."

"Not you, then." Professor Knox considered that.

"I made it clear that either of them is welcome to talk to me, but I'm not going to pass messages. They can learn to narrate in the third person if they have something to share." Ros had a line. She was not going to cross it. And honestly, she did have better things to do with her life, like study.

It made Professor Knox laugh. "My. I'm sure they don't know what to do with that. Do keep it up, it's certainly entertaining to me. As I said, I am not the person to interfere, but various teachers are aware. We are consulting regularly about what might lend to a thaw. I would appreciate you letting me know if things seem likely to escalate. Pranks, anything that interferes with studies, that sort of thing. Including your own, of course, being in the midst. Or Nancy or Trueth."

"Like messing with their notes. They're both keeping things in their trunks, and neither of them is good enough to try to break the usual sorts of protections." Ros probably would do better at it, especially if she talked it through with Avigail first. She hadn't actually tried, because if she was wrong and it was obvious, that would be a whole lot of unnecessary fuss.

"Exactly." Professor Knox finished his tea, setting the cup down. "Anything else?" She shook her head. He dropped back into French, just as smoothly as he'd switched to English. Professor Knox began asking her about the ordinary activities of the school, filling in new vocabulary as they went. That was probably Uncle Alexander's request. He was expecting the promised outing with someone who'd want to talk in French soon. Having all the vocabulary she needed would definitely help. In this case, especially the nuances between terms for different kinds of magic and how the French talked about them as compared to other possible translations.

It wasn't at all how she'd expected that conversation to go. But Ros probably should have expected Professor Knox to both be aware of what was going on under his nose and to have some sort of plan about it. Adults were very odd sometimes, but they did sometimes have reasons for what they were doing, or appearing not to do.

It did make Ros think she should sit down with Peter and talk through the dynamics. The boys in his dorm mostly just snubbed him, rather than anything worse. But first, he might as well know what the girls were up to. And second, if they were going to behave like fishwives, Peter might have commentary on how they weren't living up to the skills of the role. That would at least be amusing to both of them to discuss, and he could use some amusement.

CHAPTER 19
JASPER ON JANUARY 15TH

Jasper hung back as Incantation class wrapped up. About half of them were rushing off to go to Ritual class - including his friends. He had no idea what they were doing in class, but Ros and Avigail had both been chattering away about it before Incantation started. Leo had been thoughtful, though he'd made a couple of comments to Peter Wallace about something.

It wasn't any of Jasper's business, though he knew one of them would explain it to him if he asked. Well enough, anyway, to understand why they were excited, even if he didn't follow the rest of it. He wasn't one for fussy, precise ritual workings, he knew that. He did want to understand more of what Lord Carillon and Master Benton had let him watch over hols, but he didn't know how to ask about that. They hadn't needed to tell him that what they'd done was private.

It wasn't wrong, of course. It was just the sort of thing that the estate kept quiet. It just wasn't appropriate to tell those secrets outside certain places in the lands. That was another custom. It was one of the ones that had the weight of law, like the forest rights in the New Forest.

Professor Morwen was tidying up, and she glanced up from where she'd had her papers out on the desk. "Did you have a question, Mister Pride?" She was brisk, but not unfriendly. She'd struck Jasper as being like Island, the current head mare of the Carillon herd, busy with a dozen things that most people wouldn't notice.

"I didn't mean to keep you, Professor." Jasper stood up. "Can I help you clean anything up?"

"Actually, yes, you could save me a trip. Would you be willing to carry these back to my office with me?" She gestured at a stack of books on the corner of the desk while she pulled another together.

"Of course." Jasper went quiet, waiting for her to gather up what she wanted and needed. He followed her down the hallway from the larger classroom space to her office, tucked in with several others on the second floor.

"I've got this block free." Professor Morwen set the books down on top of a long wooden thing. Jasper didn't know the right word for it. It wasn't a bookshelf, it wasn't quite a cabinet. "Thank you, put those there. That's lovely. Do you need to be anywhere? Tea?" She peered into the corner of the shelf. "Well, your choice of mint or red berries, mostly rose hips, I think."

"If you, um." Jasper shifted his weight uneasily. "Why?" That had come out entirely rude, and he coughed. "I mean, have I done something wrong?"

"Oh, no. Let me put your mind at ease. Your work has been quite good in my class." She waited a beat. "Better since winter hols, not that I have a vast sample set to draw on. But it's the time of year when people sometimes put things together differently, and they get better all of a sudden. Like the lot of you suddenly shoot up an inch or two when the adults aren't looking."

Jasper had in fact been trying some of what Master Benton had been talking with him about, figuring out how to use his magic better. Better wasn't quite the right word, it was something about coming to it in the proper time, the pace, figuring out when it needed a walk, a trot, a canter, or a full on charge at a gallop. Today, he hadn't fumbled nearly as much with it, he'd been able to be a bit more restrained.

Now, too, he was thinking about what she'd just said. The way she said it was fond, the way Dad talked about horses. It wasn't scolding and it wasn't blaming. It was just saying how things were, and delighting that they were doing what they ought. Jasper nodded, uncertain. "Mint, please, if it's not a bother."

"Not at all. Nice bit of bracing in the middle of the afternoon. There, pull up whichever chair you like." She had a couple of well-worn ones, nothing at all fancy. It made him think about the professors' offices. He'd seen Professor Wain's a couple of times, but of course, her office was directly off her classroom. Professor Ward's he'd seen a couple of times, that was all books and bits of carved turquoise stone, and also well-worn chairs. Professor Hammond had stacks of file cabinets for sheet music. But he was fairly sure Professor Knox and Professor Leonard had much more posh offices, not that he'd ever seen them.

Professor Morwen's office had plenty of books, of course. Shelves lined both side walls. The desk had books on it, but also a number of small objects, things someone could move around or do something with. Paperweights, certainly, but also a few puzzles, it looked like. Dad knew someone who liked crafting them for keeping his hands busy at the pub. He sat, not quite sure what to say, while she fiddled with the tea, adding a strainer to each cup rather than making a pot, then pouring water into the sturdy mugs.

"Here you go. Give it a minute to steep. Here's something to put the infuser in." She set another mug down in between them, empty. "I'd been hoping for a chance to get a word with you when we didn't have to rush, actually."

"With me?" Jasper had no idea why. She'd said he wasn't in trouble, and he was fairly sure he wasn't. Teachers wanting to talk to him didn't make sense. He was doing all right in both her classes - Incantation and Society and Culture. He had been when he got his marks over the hols, and nothing had changed. He wasn't top of the class, of course, but he didn't expect to be. And he wasn't at the bottom, either. He was about halfway up the ranking, give or take the most recent assignment.

"I knew your mother at school a bit. Not terribly well. We were two years apart. But she had an interest in some of the crafting, even back then, and she'd come to some of the group crafting sessions Salmon House arranges. You know, everyone brings a portable project. We'd do them on Sundays, after the bohort and supper, but before we had to go finish up our prep for the next day."

Jasper blinked a little. "I didn't know that, Professor. She hadn't said. Just encouraged me to do well."

"Oh, no reason you should know. Except that I noticed something then. I know her family didn't much approve of the crafting, not beyond the sort of genteel embroidery of her sort of people. You don't have to answer me, of course. I want to make that clear. But have they been a problem about it with you?"

It was good there was a mug of tea sitting right there, because it gave Jasper something to with his hands. He picked it up, realised it was still too hot to hold comfortably, and put it down again. The thing of it was, things with Mum's family were distant, though she packed them all up and brought them to distant relatives every so often. Everyone on Dad's side had died before Mum and Dad met. But yes, Mum's people had been disapproving.

His family was at Ytene, and Ytene liked crafting, liked people doing things they were good at. Jasper had known that long before Master Benton and Lord Carillon had spelled out that this included Jasper over hols. Then he looked up, trying to figure out what to say that wasn't horribly rude. Finally, he resorted to what Edmund and Ros would do if asked something like this. Merry would ignore it or tear off on a tangent. That wasn't a help. "Why do you ask, Professor?"

He wasn't nearly as good at it as Ros was. Professor Morwen smiled a little. "From what I've seen, you've found some things here you're excellent at. The horses, for example. But you're less sure of yourself in classes. Some of that's understandable. A number of your classmates have benefitted from parents who could prepare them for exactly what would be expected, academically. They've had private tutors and training and tutoring schools."

Jasper nodded, a little uncertainly.

"And you're doing solidly well. Working hard, I gather, from what I've seen and what Professor Wain has mentioned in staff discussions." Professor Morwen hesitated, and Jasper knew he hadn't hidden his surprise at that. "We do talk about students. Deliberately, actually, we set aside meeting time to discuss each class year every term. I find it fascinating, since I don't necessarily teach all of you at some point, like some of our teachers do. I'm not nearly the rider you are, but you must discuss the horses with Master Held. Or your father?"

They did, that was the thing of it. Jasper found it oddly reassuring, to think of it that way. When they talked about horses, it wasn't about judging or blaming; it was about figuring out which way to go with that horse or with their training. A skittish one would be unlikely to settle enough to make a good pavo mount, but might do well as a riding horse or even a carriage horse. "Yes'm." Then he swallowed. "Figuring out what makes sense, there."

"Just so. And when you're riding, you're feeling out the rhythm of it. That day, that moment, that horse, that mood. Am I right?" Now Professor Morwen leaned back a little.

"Yes." Jasper blinked at her. "You're making a point about class?" Of course she'd probably noticed what he'd been trying, he just hadn't expected her to talk to him about it.

She beamed at him. "You are quick. It's a particular sort of cleverness to learn things. Not everyone has it. A lot of people - and a lot of people here - can memorise. It's a lot harder to train the knack for paying attention and responding in the moment. Take the exercise we did second today." It had involved responding to different changes in the incantation they were using, different rhythms and pitches.

"Yes'm?" Jasper considered it. "It took me a while to figure out the differences."

"What did you sort out?" She kept leaning back. She was deliberately using her body language not to rush him. It should probably feel insulting that the same tricks were working on him that he used on horses, but they were also familiar and comforting.

"There's a pace to it, a, pardon. A receptiveness to it.

The first ones we tried, it was stubborn." Jasper didn't know what 'it' went with, exactly. The magic, the incantation, the feeling in the room that was both of those and neither of them, he couldn't tell.

"What did you do? And what would you have done if you were riding?" Now she picked up her mug of tea and took a sip.

"Tried something a little different. The horse can't tell me what's wrong, just that it's not happy somehow." Jasper coughed. "Both."

"The magic has a hard time telling us. There are a lot of ways to do magic. Some things are part of an innate web of relationships and interconnections - that's Materia for you, and a significant portion of Alchemy, if you ask me. Jehan - Professor Knox - would like to argue with me and still hasn't come up with a compelling counterargument. He's only got as far as pointing out that some people do very well with precision of calculations and distillation. I didn't say they didn't." She flipped her hand palm up. "Astronomy is a lot of maps and calculations to begin, but Thesan - Professor Wain - agrees with me that much of the chronological and locational magics are a feeling. There are reasons we teach the Quadrivium still, the interconnections between the four fundamental forms of moving and being in the world."

It was quite a long speech, actually. He'd noticed she mostly preferred shorter back and forths, a conversation, even when she was more or less giving a lecture. After a pause, he ventured. "And I'm better at - or at least maybe better positioned to - work with things that way?"

"Just so. The more you can apply that, the easier you'll find Incantation. Your music classes, of course, but also your Materia. The feel of it is different in the different arts, but more like riding different horses than the difference between two feet, four feet, and a bicycle."

The image made Jasper smile a bit despite himself. She smiled back and went right on. "Now, I'd love to see you put some of that into your next written assignment, the one that's due in a fortnight. If you want some time to go through it, you're welcome to come to my office hours in the classroom, and try things out. Either I'll help you, or one of the older students can give you some feedback. Probably both."

Jasper nodded slowly. "I'll, um." He coughed. "I'll find time." He could tell when something was a good idea. And it would mean he could write home to Mum with something promising. Avigail might work with him on it, too. He was fairly sure she had a knack for working that way, too. Ros wanted to know the underpinnings first, and Leo had his own way of doing things, which worked for Leo but often baffled the rest of them.

And he should ask Peter about it soon - well, maybe Peter and Ros both - because they'd absolutely know which things in the library he ought to be looking at. They always did, though he had no idea how. There wasn't enough time for them to have read everything, not remotely yet.

"Excellent. Do you have time for some free reading?" He nodded cautiously, and she began talking about fiction books, as a way to get a feel for things he hadn't done himself, to hear the song of it. She pulled a couple of copies off her shelves, encouraging him to borrow them and see what he liked. He found himself in the hallway outside her office with three books and a great uncertainty about what had just happened. When he checked the books, they had the Salmon House stamp in them, so she must have brought them up specifically.

He was going to have to read them to figure out why.

CHAPTER 20
AVIGAIL ON JANUARY 21ST

Avigail had been run off her feet all day. Also, she'd been away from her dormitory except for changing her clothes in five minutes between Materia class and her duelling session, and then another quick change between duelling and supper. Then she'd been in the library for a study session until, well, now. She hadn't snuck in the door right before curfew started, but it had been a close thing.

There was a wooden box on the pillow. It was lying perfectly in the centre, heavy enough to indent it a little. She pulled the curtain across her cubicle closed. That was ordinary. Avigail did that when she changed. And she didn't want the rest of her dorm mates to see what she did next. Nor did she want to be distracted by their chatter. The charms helped cut the sound significantly.

First things first. The box was about the size of a deck of cards. It looked like wood, though it could have been charmed or even painted. There were four metals set in the lid, making circular interlocking loops. From the end of the bed, she was fairly sure they were gold, silver, copper, and iron.

How long had the box been there? She thought back, carefully. Avigail was trying to do a lot better at noticing things. It was part of the training she wasn't really talking about with Papa. She'd have to write this up for him, though, except that would mean thinking about the implications. Avigail wasn't ready for that yet.

It hadn't been there when she changed for duelling. She remembered, because she'd leaned across the pillow to grab her notebook, and she'd put her hand right on the pillow. She'd had to smooth it out after, so the house matron wouldn't tsk at her. It hadn't been there when she changed after duelling, either. She'd been very quick. There had been just enough time to grab the day's uniform and change back into it after a quick shower. But again, she'd leaned over to put her notebook back. She knew that because there was the notebook, propped up on the shelf next to her bed.

That meant the box had turned up while Avigail was in the library. That made somewhat more sense, at least. She had a habit of being in the library - or in the evening lecture - on Tuesdays. If they wanted to sneak something in, when she'd have time to deal with it, Tuesdays after supper were an excellent choice.

Avigail was assuming, of course, that whoever it was had been watching her to figure out the best time. That was simultaneously creepy and thorough. Papa would make about six faces over it, probably, but in this case, at least she had an idea why they'd been watching.

She didn't want to open it by herself. It was after curfew now, so she didn't have a lot in the way of choices. She could ask one of the other girls in her dorm to come to the workroom with her, but that would be all sorts of social awkwardness. Avigail was pretty sure Professor Morwen was in her rooms and still working, but that was even more awkward. And besides, the professors knew perfectly well the secret societies flourished at Schola, but there seemed something wrong about bringing it directly to their attention.

After a moment's consideration, she pulled her journal out of her bag and propped it on the end of the bed. She wrote to Ros - who would appreciate the problem, and also not be cranky about Avigail getting this invitation. Whatever Ros wanted, it wasn't the Four Metals. The note was brief, just asking if Ros could meet her before breakfast, somewhere private. She suggested one of the workrooms in the keep that ought to be open at that time of day. They weren't far enough into term for people to be desperately finishing assignments before breakfast. Probably.

That meant figuring out what to do with the box overnight. After some consideration, she rummaged in her dresser, pulling out the smaller box of ritual gear from the side. Mama and Papa had sent her off to school with half a dozen silk handkerchiefs for this sort of thing. It had been something of a surprise to find out not everyone packed like that last year. Avigail found one of the big ones, along with a pair of riding gloves. She carefully wrapped the whole thing up, keeping it facing upright. She tucked it into one of the dresser drawers, taking a deep breath.

Now she had to go off and do all the evening things - brush her teeth, braid her hair, change into a nightgown - all while pretending things were absolutely normal. There was nothing to see here. Fortunately for her, no one asked her any particular questions, and she was back in her own bed within eight minutes. There was a note from Ros, saying of course she'd turn up at seven in the keep. Curling up on her side, she stared off at her dresser in the dark, trying to figure out what she even felt about it.

Fortunately, Ros was waiting the next morning. Avigail didn't have class until nine, but Ros had chores as eight, so they'd need to be prompt. "Hey." Ros raised an eyebrow, but opened the door to the workroom. She waited until Avigail was inside and then closed it behind her. "Can you do the privacy thing? Do you have your book?"

"Is something the matter?" Ros asked it as she was rummaging in her bag for her book. She pulled it open, brushing fingertips against points on the painted image on the page, then tilted her head. "No one nearby." They weren't permitted to bring up certain kinds of wards in the workrooms here, in case something went wrong. Avigail was fairly sure if someone tried, one of the Professors would know, and would also be cranky, especially this early in the morning.

"I came back from the library to find a box. An invitation sort of box. I didn't want to open it last night, on my own." Avigail shrugged a little. "So, you."

"Huh. Which one?" Ros glanced around and grabbed one of the stools in the corner. "Where was it?"

Avigail walked over to the worktable in the centre, pulling the box out of her bag and putting it on the table, using the silk handkerchief to position it. "My pillow. I'm sure it wasn't there when I changed before supper. Ready?"

"I couldn't have restrained myself." It made Avigail snort. For all Avigail herself was endlessly curious, she could be patient about it and do it right. The doing it right part came from Papa - also Mama. But the patient part was definitely all Mama. Where Ros got her impatience from was probably a more interesting question. "Huh. That's beautiful work, isn't it? Not fancy, but well-made. A fair bit of silver and gold, too, that's not a cheap gift."

Avigail considered that. She'd had even more of the training in evaluating portable and wearable wealth than Ros had. It was a custom among Mama's people to wear some of it, as gold chains or jewellery or whatever. The lines of the metals were fairly substantial, up to maybe twice the width of a broad calligraphic pen stroke. It wasn't an exorbitant amount of metal, only it sort of was. Especially given the war and all the metal that had gone to it.

"Let me start there, then." They'd done the basic metal identification charms in Materia class last October, and she'd practised more with Papa over winter hols. She flicked her fingers in the proper patterns four times. Two were pretty much what she expected, but the gold was purer than she'd thought - it might be 24 karat, rather than an alloy. The silver and copper were pretty much what she expected, but there was something odd in the iron.

"The iron's, um. Have a look?" Avigail stepped back to let Ros look.

"Meteorite, maybe? Uncle Alexander has a chunk of one. He was showing it to us. May I?" Ros wriggled her fingers to indicate what she meant, and Avigail nodded. Ros tried the charm herself, then nodded. "It's like that. I hear it as an odd harmonic, an open fourth? I don't know what you get."

Ros would have to work on that one, then, though admittedly random meteors did not appear in her life all that often. So far, anyway. "Do I open it?"

"Any charms you can spot on the rest of it? I don't feel anything." Avigail tried one more time, the charm that sometimes gave a hint of what else was going on. Either there wasn't anything, or she wasn't good enough at the charm yet. It was a tricky one, so that was entirely possible.

"No? I'm, I'm going to open it." She did it with the silk, she wasn't foolish. The lid opened easily. It was well crafted, too. Though honestly, Four Metals was supposed to be crafters of all sorts. If they couldn't make a decent box, something was wrong. And Avigail would be simultaneously more curious about them and less interested in joining, in that case.

Inside the box were four metal coins and a small folded rectangle of thick paper, sealed with a wax seal. The coins had markings on them, detailed ones. She looked up at Ros. "Time for the note?"

"The note. Do you have - no, don't use your penknife. I've got something..." Ros rummaged in her bag and pulled out a bone folder, the kind she used for making little notebooks as a hobby. "There."

Avigail slipped the folder under the wax as a makeshift letter opener. It gave way easily, as if it had been meant to come off in one piece. When she unfolded the paper, the note just said, "Find. Learn. Make." in block letters. It wasn't impossible to match block letters in handwriting. Theoretically. But it involved having samples to work with. She certainly couldn't get samples for every fourth or fifth year in the school, and certainly not in block writing. Part of her brain went whirring off on whether Professor Wain might have them. People used block print for star charts a lot of the time. But that would also mean explaining, and she wasn't going to do that.

"There's a puzzle for you." The bell above them rang for half-seven.

"You need to eat before your chores," Avigail said.

"Thanks for this. I feel better knowing that you were here. And you knowing, too."

"Are you going to figure out what they want?" Ros said. "Here, fold that up, and you can run the box up to your dorm after we eat."

"It's a puzzle. I'm very bad at ignoring puzzles." Avigail frowned. "I don't have to actually, I don't know, turn whatever it is in. Do I?"

Ros snorted. "Being able to and wanting to are two different things. I hope." She shrugged once. "I'll tell you if something unexpected shows up for me."

"Surely something at least a little expected?" If Avigail had got this, Ros was surely an even better candidate for several of them. It also made Avigail wonder who else had a box, or how many they'd given out. Considering the materials, she suspected it wasn't many. Did they expect everyone to make the attempt and succeed, and had only given out that many? She suspected she was not going to get the answer to that question any time soon. Instead, she tucked the note in the box, closing the lid and hooking the little latch before wrapping the silk around the box.

Ros shrugged. "I don't know if I want any of them." Her voice had gone quiet. "Glad someone sees the good in you, though."

Avigail didn't know how to answer that, so she stuck the wrapped box in her bag and held out her hand. "Breakfast?"

"Breakfast." Ros squeezed her hand as she took it. Breakfast was simple. Also probably quite predictable. Right now, Avigail could use a little of that.

CHAPTER 21
LEO ON JANUARY 23RD

L eo was on his way upstairs for family tea when he heard a whole crowd coming down. Ritual class for the 5th years must have run long. Leo was right on time for tea, and usually they were done by then.

Tea on Thursday was one of their absolute habits as a family. Two hours between classes and supper, no matter what else. Mum and Dad had started it when Ursula and Leo were tiny, to make sure they had time together as a household, whatever else happened. Three weeks a month - like this one - it was just them. Just him and Mum and Dad now, though Ursula had come a few times when she could get free. The fourth week, they each got to invite a guest.

Leo was very aware how lucky he was that he got this time with his parents, even during term. He was even more lucky in having parents he wanted to see that often. Near no one else got the chance, except Susanna, now. It meant, however, that he was expected on the fourth floor of the keep in under a minute. He kept going up, keeping to one side. His arms were full of books. He didn't want to stop.

A whole knot of them, boys and girls together, came down, running a little late. They were passing phrases back and forth, not quite duelling with words, but certainly still having a spirited discussion. Leo could follow only fragments of it, and he was concentrating hard when one of the boys bumped into him, and three of his books went tumbling.

"Oh, sorry, I didn't know where I was. Fortier, right?" That was overly casual, it wasn't like they didn't know exactly who he was. Leo just nodded, frozen for a moment with the unexpected jarring of his thoughts. He tried to place the boy's name. Xenophon Anders-Whyte, that was it. One of the girls in the group bent down to gather up a book, handing it back to him once he was standing again. That was, um, right, Antigone Howell. He didn't know either of them very well.

They weren't landed families; they weren't Council families. The next tier down, though entirely respectable and First Families in both cases. He was pretty sure Uncle Garin had commentary about one of the senior Anders-Whytes not being as good an alchemist as he thought he was, but that wasn't actually very useful for distinguishing people. Uncle Garin thought that about most alchemists.

None of them had been rude, and they'd probably not expected anyone on the stairs, not between the third and fourth floors at this time of day. Leo just nodded. "Thanks for helping me pick them up. Have a good night." Then he turned to go back upstairs, hearing their chatter pick up and then recede into the distance.

When he got up to the family rooms, he let out a breath, balancing the stack of books on his hip as he got the door. Before he could actually open it though, Mum was pulling it open. "Afternoon, Leo. Kettle's just about to sing. I've a few apples, but the rest will have to wait for supper."

"Sure, Mum. How was your week?" She ducked into the kitchen before answering, as the kettle sang. Leo set the books down on one of the end tables in the sitting area before blinking at it. He heard Dad coming down the hall. He always knew when it was Dad. Besides, no one else would be up here right now. But what had Leo's attention was an envelope, the corner poking out between two of the books he'd been carrying.

To be precise, two of the books he'd dropped.

"Something wrong, Leo?" Dad came closer, but stopped a few feet behind him.

"Letter, Dad. That wasn't there when I started upstairs." Leo took a breath. It wasn't going to go away, so he might as well deal with it. Leo considered and then sat down. It also wasn't necessary to keep standing, and he felt like he might fall over. Slowly, he moved the books to reveal the letter, which was sealed with an impressively large purple wax seal. He didn't need to look closely to know it had the initials D and F entwined, for Dius Fidius. Not that he'd needed that. The purple gave it away. He was pretty sure Animus Mundi used silver.

Dad made a sound. Leo couldn't have explained what it was better than saying birds had come home to roost. "Letter opener?" Dad's voice was rough, but Leo was pretty sure that wasn't because of anything Leo had done.

It made Leo look up, and Dad looked complicated. Tired, resigned, proud, all sorts of different emotions were right there, though tired seemed to be winning out. "Please. Um. Mum?" He wasn't sure if this was something he could even talk about where she could hear.

"It's all right." Dad turned away, taking a few long steps

over to his desk in the corner and grabbing the letter opener, bringing it back. "Thesan, love, I think we need cider. All of us, do you mind?"

"Water will keep." Mum's voice was clear as anything. "Just a moment." Cider was a particular sort of marker, though mostly he got that - or the mead - for celebrations or rituals.

Leo looked up, and Dad just nodded, so Leo opened the letter, slicing the seal off in one piece. The opener was charmed for that. The seals often had useful magical information, and Dad cared about that. So did Mum, sometimes. Inside was a notecard. The outside was blank, but it was the sort of creamy, thick, visibly expensive paper that seemed out of place given how much paper was still rationed.

Carefully, Leo opened the inside. In formal writing, the sort of copperplate that someone had drilled into them early by a governess or tutor, there was a single sentence. Leo took a breath and then read it aloud. "Do something that demonstrates you should be one of us." Another swallow. "That's all it says. Dad, how do I make sure I don't by accident?" It came out before Leo could get himself under control, and he shivered. He didn't want Dius Fidius, he'd had time to think through that. He knew it wasn't what he wanted to become or do or whatever the right word was.

Dad's hand came down on his shoulder. "Moment, all right? We'll talk about it." The weight was reassuring, and a moment later, there was a bottle of cider in his hand. Then Mum was murmuring there was a square of the precious and hoarded chocolate on the table when he wanted that. Medicinal, as much as the cider was, that was what they kept it for.

Leo managed to nudge the card onto the side table,

curving his hands around the cool glass of the bottle. He took a sip, hearing Mum and Dad talk, the sort of murmur he couldn't make out entirely. When he'd managed a couple of swallows - the cider was delicious and sharp and absolutely the right thing - he set the bottle down to nibble on the chocolate. Mum finished up what she was saying, a little more clearly audible. "Division of labour, love. This one's yours."

Dad didn't grumble. Dad actually was looking at Mum with tremendous fondness, and that was a whole new puzzle. But then he focused on Leo as Mum sat down on the couch next to him. Dad cleared his throat. "How did they do it today?" He held up two fingers. He had something else to explain, then, once Leo gave an answer.

A lot of Dad's training had to do with paying attention, and Leo knew that this was the sort of reason it mattered. "There was a whole knot of fifth years coming down from Ritual, and someone bumped into me. I dropped a couple of books, and two or three people helped me pick them up. It could have been any of them in the group who slipped it in. I didn't see who in specific." Or it wouldn't have been a surprise up here. He added after a moment, "Xenophon Anders-Whyte and Antigone Howell. I didn't see the others clearly." Dad made a small grunt, as if nothing in that surprised him.

"Anders-Whyte came to me last Friday, complaining that you were terribly difficult to get on your own. Apparently, they weren't able to get anything into your House, either. I could have told them that. Bear is always attentive to the protections." Dad wasn't quite meeting Leo's eyes. Mum was just for a moment, but she was half-smiling as if something in this really amused her.

"Oh." Leo swallowed before he had a question. Well, he had a lot of questions, but Dad would probably answer this one. "What did you say?"

"That if they couldn't get the note to you without my help, they really had a lot of work to do on their skills if they want to be responsible for a larger part of the world." Dad shrugged. "And then I gave them extra duelling exercises, and that part might actually have helped a little. They seem to have slipped it to you smoothly enough."

Leo couldn't really argue with that. "But what do I do?" His voice rose and embarrassingly cracked. It hadn't done that for a while.

"For the sake of my sleep, I'd prefer it if you didn't do what your sister did." Dad looked more amused, even while he said it. "She said I could tell you if this came up. I'll let her know it did. Just, um, not a thing to discuss around Uncle Garin."

"As if I would, Dad, honestly." Leo did not need that hornet's nest at all. "What did she do?"

"She got a note. It was on her bed. Of course, there were people in Fox who could. She slept on it, got up the next morning, and came up to get some of the good note cards. Then she sent a terribly polite note back to each and every fifth year in Dius Fidius, formally declining. Sealed with our seal, of course."

Dad's mouth quirked sideways. "We had a delegation up here about an hour later and your Mum had to hide in the bedroom and pretend she wasn't nearby. Ursula got them all right, and I had to make oath I hadn't told her. She'd worked it out entirely on her own, for all it was supposed to be secret. I made it very clear I wasn't getting in the middle of that. And also that she was both one of my students and my daughter, before anyone got any clever ideas about encouraging her to change her mind."

Leo had to laugh at that, a little bark of one. Ursula wasn't a duellist in the salle sense, not like Dad was or Leo wanted to be. But she could absolutely hold her own if she needed to, and she would tear someone to shreds with words and some reinforcing charms if they took liberties. She'd been on her way to that as a second year, even without knowing Dad - and Mum - were right around the corner and handy. "And they left her alone?"

"They did. I had your Uncle Garin complaining at me all that term and through the end of the year when he got a chance. I think it's a fair bit of why he was so fierce about you. But here's the thing, strategically speaking, about that note. They've left things in your hands. If you go along and just do what you were going to do anyway, they might still make you an initiation offer proper. You can turn that down then. But you don't have to make a big fuss and show of it now. It would let them save face. You must be planning something really splendid, all that."

Leo grimaced. That meant it would be looming over him all spring. "Mum?"

"Give me an actual question to work with, please? And have a bit more of your cider, for cushion." Mum paused, and Leo didn't have a question yet, so he waved a hand at her while he had a sip. "I don't know what your sister decided, whether she's a member of any society. Your father doesn't either, she didn't tell us. And you don't need to tell us. Usually, they can invite people without your parents being right here. We know that makes things complicated for you."

Leo took a deep breath. Complicated was a good word. "I don't know what I want, just for myself. And I can't get it all untangled from everything. The family, expectations, all that." He let out a huff. "Uncle Garin, especially."

"You let me handle Uncle Garin." Dad said that firmly, before he glanced at Mum. "Or your mum. She's been doing quite well at it."

"I didn't grow up with him. It helps. He doesn't understand how I was trained. It makes it a lot more work to get to me." Mum was entirely cheerful about that. "And as for the rest of it, if you get more invitations, you can decide what you want to do then. If you don't, that solves most of your problem. We want you to choose for yourself. I promise we'll be happy and proud whatever you pick, so long as you're picking what you want."

Leo nodded slowly. "Are there, I mean. I wasn't trying to impress anyone." Then it came out in a rush. "I want a society who wants me for me, if anyone does. Not the family connections and the traditions. I want something that's solid all the way through, not an outline. And Dad, it's a really nice outline, with curlicues and decorations and rubrication and all? But it's shallow. For me, anyway."

Dad held up his hands. "I'm certainly not going to argue. I've been thinking about what you said over hols." He'd obviously discussed it with Mum later, because she was nodding too. "Go find something that has a proper harmonic resolution. Not the hollow. Right?"

"Right." Leo carefully unpeeled his fingers from the bottle. He'd been holding it tighter and tighter. "So I just go about things, and talk to Ursula, and see what happens."

"Exactly. Which is what you were going to do when you got here, isn't it?" Mum tilted her head.

It was. Even with this massive new thing thrown at him. "How'd your research go yesterday, Mum?" She'd been going to the Astronomy Guild for journals in their library, the ones that were so specialised the Schola library didn't have them. It wasn't a smooth transition, but she just grinned, leaning against Dad's shoulder and picking up talking about it, like there wasn't anything else she'd rather be doing.

Of course, for Mum, that was quite likely true.

CHAPTER 22
ROS ON JANUARY 30TH

Ros felt like she was running late again. It was a figment of her imagination. For one thing, her watch told her she was right on time. For another, she was going to lunch. Being a few minutes late wouldn't be any trouble. She was coming downstairs, from the fourth to the third floor, when she spotted something lying on the landing between them.

It was an envelope, a silver wax seal shimmering in the charmlights of the staircase. Ros raised an eyebrow. "Really?" She asked the empty stairs. She couldn't hear anyone nearby. Then she flipped it over, carefully, with one finger wrapped in a handkerchief. Her parents had drilled proper caution into her. Maybe not quite as much as Avigail's family, but more than enough.

The front of the envelope had her name on it, in elegantly calligraphed black letters. Rosalba Carillon. There was no mistaking that. She considered and then slipped the envelope into her bag. She would open it later, in private, not on a staircase anyone might come up or down. Once she made it down to lunch, she lucked into a chair across from Peter Wallace and worked on figuring out what everyone was talking about.

To her right, it was the coming bohort match between Bear and Seal - likely to be an interesting time. To her left, it was people gossiping about who they knew had invitations, and to which society. Ros heard one of them say, "Well, Fortier, of course," without catching what came before it. It'd be obvious if she asked, so she couldn't, but it meant she missed what Peter said across the table.

"Pardon, sorry, I was thinking." Ros offered it apologetically.

She could tell Peter wasn't entirely buying that as an excuse. Ros was, after all, perfectly capable of doing three other things while she was thinking. Peter saw her do it regularly. Instead, though, he asked a question about the Alchemy practical they had after lunch. Ros did have things to say about that. She'd been reviewing some of her notes from her tutoring over the summer, about the best way to handle a tricky bit of measuring.

As people began to filter out to their one o'clock class, Peter met her at the end of the table. "Something up?"

Ros shrugged. It wasn't forbidden to tell people about invitations, for one thing that was nearly impossible to manage. Sometimes people saw, anyway, or they could certainly guess. She wanted to talk to Avigail about it first, though, and maybe Leo. Leo wasn't taking Alchemy, so it'd have to be after Materia if they had a couple of minutes before he met up with his parents for tea.

"Tonight maybe, all right?" Ros shrugged. "Need to check on something first. And you and Avigail were going to work on that project." They'd got into something from a comment in Ritual class, about different ways of looking at the underlying assumptions in designing a ritual, and

Professor Leonard had given them a new direction to explore. Ros knew herself a more conventional thinker than Avigail, and she was glad Avigail and Peter could do that together. It was also giving Peter more confidence on the magical side.

Peter froze for just a second, as if he expected something worse to come from that. Then he swallowed. "Of course. I didn't mean to push."

Blast, Ros was going to have to fix that now. She smiled back. "I'll come find you later, all right?" He nodded once, and they walked to the Alchemy lab together, picking up Avigail and a couple of others as they went.

Ros did, in fact, get about five minutes with Avigail that afternoon, long enough to mention the invite. But then they'd ended up in a knot of other conversation, with no privacy, and Avigail had wanted to go to the evening's lecture. It was about Sympathetic magic, which Ros wasn't taking. And art, which Ros was interested in, but she'd already had that particular discussion with Mama and Papa with enough detail for the moment. They'd have to find more time that weekend, or something.

All of that meant that Ros knocked on the door to Peter's workroom at around nine, when she'd finished all her own immediate work. He'd got quite good at the soundproofing charms. That meant an ordinary knock wouldn't bother him if he'd set them. Just Professor Knox or one of the prefects, or a specific pattern he'd taught Ros because she wouldn't abuse it. A moment later, the door cracked open.

Ros said, brightly, "Break?" They weren't allowed in each other's workrooms. Leo had explained there was too much chance of people using that for snogging or for things they weren't supposed to be doing beyond snogging. And she certainly didn't want to give anyone the idea she was doing that with anyone, thank you. That would be terribly annoying gossip to manage. Merry had warned her all about it. There was, however, a sofa or two in the corner by the other set of workrooms, and it should be quiet enough. There was also a kettle there. She had her book, she could check if anyone was nearby.

"Sure. Put the kettle on. I'll be a minute or two?" Peter closed the door a tad abruptly, which made her curious. She wasn't offended, though. Instead, Ros went along to start the kettle, set out two mugs, and check if anyone else was around. While the kettle boiled, she settled in one of the corner seats, where she could see anyone coming. She pulled out her book, flicking her fingers to cover the three ravens that would start the charm.

By the time Peter joined her, the kettle was almost ready. She poured and handed over a mug to Peter, then made her own with the strainer tucked inside She set her book where she could see it. Once she sat, he raised an eyebrow.

"I got an invitation today. From Animus Mundi." There wasn't any subtle way of saying it. Ros suddenly realised she hadn't checked with him since that conversation early on, and she had no idea what his thoughts about societies were right now. She'd talked about it with Avigail, quite a few times, and Leo and Jasper some, but thinking back, she wasn't sure Peter had been around for any of those.

Peter leaned forward. "I can see why you didn't want to mention it at lunch. Or supper."

"Have you?" It was rude to ask, that was the thing, but Ros desperately wanted to know now.

Peter shrugged, and for the life of her, Ros wasn't sure how to read that. A year ago, she'd have thought no one had invited him, and now she wasn't entirely sure. "They can take their time, right? And I'm not the sort Dius Fidius wants. And I'm not as good at Ritual as you and Leo are."

"More fools them." Ros tucked her foot under her other knee. "It's got a specific ritual to do, to indicate my interest. And I can't decide what to do about it."

"Is it all right to talk about it?" Peter asked, suddenly. "People don't."

"Some of them are more secret than others? But I asked Edmund over hols, and he said it depends on the society. Talking to friends about it, a lot of people do that. Their allies. But some people don't." Ros felt she'd got herself in a bit of a tangle here. "I know you feel hurt when you get cut out of information."

Peter grimaced. "I don't like it showing. Even with you. Or the others. And I know you all won't hurt me with it, but other people will. Have." His shoulder twitched.

"Have people been bullying you?" Ros could feel herself sounding rather like her mother, actually. It wasn't strident, strident didn't get you the results she wanted. But she felt like she'd got three inches taller, and a great deal more resonance in her chest and voice.

"Not so I'd tell anyone about. Not a lot. As much as they could be." Peter looked away, but at least he kept talking. "It's just talking. I can deal with that. They try to cheat off me, not push me around like they do Jasper."

Ros was quite sure telling him to tell someone wouldn't go over well. And she wouldn't, not unless it looked worse than talking. Not without getting Peter's permission. "And the cheating?"

"Pretty sure the professors noticed. I started out writing a sentence or two that wasn't enough of an answer, then I'd go back and fill it in more later. But now, they word my questions a little differently, so my answer's right and whoever copies me nearby is wrong. A couple of them rearranged seating a few times, too, that helped."

It made Ros snort. "All right. Our professors weren't born yesterday. That's good. And you're sure they're not plotting something else?" It was a delicate balancing act, and she simultaneously was learning things by doing it and not wanting to do it. However, it was exactly the kind of skill that went into diplomatic work, when to say something and when not to, never mind the particulars of what got said. That was a whole different challenge. Finally, she decided on what would do for now. "Tell me if it gets worse, would you promise me that?"

Peter's expression shifted a couple of times, but finally he nodded. "Promise." That meant he'd been a little worried about what might escalate, and that wasn't good at all. "The invitations, I mean. I wondered if it was the sort of thing where someone could do a false one." It made Ros wonder if he'd got one, but was also nervous someone was messing with him. Wanting to draw him out, so he could get hurt. Heart, head, body, any of those would be awful.

"Ah." That was actually a really interesting question, taking it intellectually, so long as it wasn't one's own reputation and well-being on the line. She'd have to pose it to Papa and Uncle Alexander over spring hols. "Most people wouldn't think of that, you know. I can think of reasons why people wouldn't, and there are ways to check, but people do really stupid badly considered things all the time."

Peter waved a hand. "That thing with the exploding confetti that the fourth years put together last week, for a start?" It had stuck to everything, and the dye they'd used for it hadn't set properly. The hallway where they'd set it off had been spattered with dots of impressionistic colour. It had apparently been a fascinating exercise in scrying for students who were studying that, but it had taken hours and several different rapidly adapted solvents to get it off the stonework.

Ros laughed. "Like that." She considered. "So, there are the charms for identification - that the apparent sender and the actual sender are the same. Or the more advanced ones, that can confirm a specific person did."

"But that doesn't work here, because it's someone on behalf of a group, and we don't know who the specific sender is. We haven't learned that set yet. That's fourth year." Peter leaned back, ticking the points off on his fingers.

"How do you know it's fourth year?" Ros was momentarily distracted.

"I asked Professor Morwen about the syllabi for the rest of the class years." Peter smirked slightly. That was good. He was relaxed again if he was like that. "You could too."

"Would you share them with me? No sense in bothering busy professors if we don't need to...." Ros let her voice trail off. She knew more or less what was covered, because Edmund had been pretty informative in what he was doing in class in his notes home to her. An actual syllabus would be much better, though. Also, it would spare her having to dig out the information between the comments on bohort and his friends and the state of the food.

Peter considered. "Sure. If you see if you can get a recommended reading list for the summer out of at least three of our professors. I want to get a head start on it."

That would at least be an interesting discussion, and it would fit right into Ros's language lessons. She could even admit that Peter wanted to get ahead in three of them.

Professor Knox would be amused, Professor Wain would be delighted, and Professor Ward approved of people wanting to learn things for the sake of learning. "Three's a deal."

Peter looked for a moment like he wished he'd asked for more, but then he stuck out his hand to shake on it. He did that automatically, like Ros's family would offer to make oath on it. She shook, then considered the original problem again. "Anyway. I've heard enough gossip about what the invitations ought to look like. Everyone could hear that. It's not actually limiting, but the silver sealing wax is a bit touchy. Animus Mundi isn't entirely secret. They do publish, so I can match it to an existing known seal. But again, anyone could do that."

"None of which proves it's a true one," Peter said.

"I have some checks I can try, but they take a workroom and some time. Saturday, do you want to? We can sign out one in the Keep." Ros wanted to write to Papa and check on a couple of them, but he'd write back promptly in the journal. He'd also know why she was asking, even if she didn't give him details, but she could manage that.

"You've got pavo practice," Peter said. "All morning."

"You like having an uninterrupted morning in the library," Ros pointed out. "I'll sign it out for, um, two? Give me time to change and eat if we run long."

Peter nodded. "You sure it's not a problem for me to be there?"

"I might ask Avigail, too," Ros said, after a moment. "But not a problem."

"Oh, ask Leo and Jasper if you like. Not any of the others. But if you want them there, I mean, I don't get to decide that."

It was one of the things she liked about Peter. Unlike the other boys in their House, he went out of his way to make it clear she should make her own decisions, even if he was at least half doing it because he was self-conscious about family differences. Now she just nodded. "I'll see, all right? And I don't know what they think. I only caught Leo for a moment." She hesitated. "And I don't know if he was hoping for something from Animus Mundi, actually."

Peter wrinkled up his nose. "Oh. Is that going to be awkward?"

"Leo's forthright. With us, anyway. We'll see what he says." Leo was actually quite good at not saying things when he didn't want to, but the things he said tended to be the truth. Ros supposed he'd picked it up from Ursula, talking around the things he wasn't saying. "Right. I should get back to my prep."

"Me too." Peter stood, stretching. "I'll take the mugs downstairs to be washed, though. Done with yours?"

Ros handed it over, dismissing the charm from her book by pressing her fingers to the ravens again. "Thanks. See you tomorrow, if not before?"

"Tomorrow. And thanks for telling me. And showing me the charms." She watched him snag the mugs and head down the spiral staircase that led downstairs, before going back to her own workroom to finish up for the evening. If someone made her take a bet, she'd guess he'd had an invitation, but who from, she had no idea. No matter. He had a right to know if it was legitimate, and besides, it was a rather nifty bit of magical work.

CHAPTER 23
JASPER ON JANUARY 30TH

Jasper made his way along the road to Schola village. It was his usual riding time, before lunch, but the weather was absolutely horrid. He wasn't going to take Dot out in this chilly drizzle, even if she was exceedingly hardy. Schola's weather was usually milder in the winter. He'd been told that over and over again, but he'd only had a winter and a half to judge it for himself, which wasn't nearly long enough to actually have an opinion about this land.

Maybe Professor Wain would know more if she spent time worrying about the orchards and the bees. She certainly paid attention to how often it was cloudy or stormy, that absolutely affected Astronomy six ways round. He could ask her when he got back.

Right now, though, he had a task. Master Held had asked him to run down to one of the village cottages on the road between Schola's keep and the village. Master Isten had hurt his foot, apparently, and needed a hand with a bit of vitality for his stove and such. Jasper would rather be riding, certainly, but the covered arena was in use, so he might as well lend a hand.

His ankles were freezing, though. There was sleet soaking up and down from where his breeches met the ankle boots. And he'd have to tend to the boots themselves sometime tonight. It was no good having the leather dry out. His boots were charmed, but the charms only did so much. Jasper quite liked leather care, honestly, which was good because he did a lot of it. But it was an hour tonight that he'd wanted for his Incantation assignment.

Jasper had been to the village often enough now to know what he was looking for. The road forked, about halfway to the village, and he wanted the cottage just on the left, after the fork. It had a good view of three of the main roads of Schola herself, perched at the crossroads, which was interesting. Most of the cottages on the island either stood quite alone, or they were tucked into the village proper. Through the grey sleet, he could see there were lights on. It was two stories, likely enough two bedrooms upstairs, and a sitting room, kitchen, and bath of some kind downstairs.

Jasper himself wasn't dripping wet. Mum had refitted one of Dad's old oilskin coats as soon as Jasper had grown enough to make it worth the work. It was still a little roomy on him, so he had a bulky jumper under it right now. But it kept out the rain a treat, and a good three-quarters of the cold. He bustled up to the door, and knocked loudly enough to carry over the wind.

"Who is't?" The voice inside sounded a bit more like back home. Not the accent, precisely, the New Forest wasn't Wales. It was something more in the arc of it. People at Schola had the posh accent, the one that sounded educated to anyone in Britain. Jasper more or less did too now, thanks to so much time talking with Ros and Avigail and Leo. He still slipped up on some words, but they at least didn't tease him about it, just made sure he heard how they said it so he could decide what to do.

"Jasper Pride, sir. Master Held sent me to lend a hand."

Jasper waited, and there was a pause. "Ah, come in, then. Come in. Door's open."

The door did open easily under Jasper's hand, everything oiled and moving smoothly despite the cold. The interior of the cottage was on the chilly side, even though there was a fire going in the inglenook fireplace on the wall of the snug. Jasper bobbed his head. "Morning, sir."

"Ah, there now. Hang up your coat, and take off your boots, if you would. No use tracking muck around. I'm proper grateful for you coming out in this. Hooks there." There were several smooth wooden hooks on the wall. Jasper shrugged out of his oilskin and hung it up without spraying water all over the place, then his boots, leaving him in socks. Now he could definitely feel the chill.

"Come in, boy. Your name again? The wind got it, first time." The man in the snug was sitting near the fireplace, lit more by that than the charmlight in the ceiling or the dim light from outside. Jasper could see one of the cupboard beds along the back wall. Mum had told him they were traditional in Wales. Likely where whatever livestock there were had a byre or hutch or whatever out back. He was older, with grizzled hair and a beard, trimmed tidy. The snug didn't have a lot of furniture besides the cupboard bed, the table he sat at, and two chairs.

"Jasper Pride, sir. I help Master Held out in the stables." Jasper folded his hands in front of him, feeling slightly ridiculous now. It was the lack of boots, mostly. It was hard to feel dignified in sock feet. "He said you needed a little vitality. The household things? And that I should see if there's anything else I could do to help."

"Ah, that's kind. Of him, and of you. And you're at the school then. How do you have a few hours to come down here to me? Which of the Houses would you be in? And what part of Albion do you come from?"

It was a lot of questions, all at once. Jasper took a breath. "I'm from the New Forest. Ytene, the Carillon estate, my dad's stable master there. I'm a second year in Horse House, but I spend a lot of time in the stables. And I'm only taking two of the Quadrivium this year - maths and music - so I have a few hours free this morning. Usually, I ride on my own, but I won't take Dot out in this."

"Have your own, then. A mare? Here, if you'd put a titch of vitality into the stove in the kitchen - through there - and fill the pitcher you'll find, we can put a cuppa on. Only have the mint and nettle, I'm afraid, but it's good for what ails you." Then the man nodded. "Oh, and I'm Henry Isten. But I'm thinking Held told you that."

"Yes, Master Isten. Just a moment." Jasper waited to see if there was anything else, then he ducked through down the narrow hall into a tiny kitchen. It was just big enough for a deep slate sink, a stove and oven, and a keep cold box. He fed each a bit of his own magic, feeling it flow out. He'd done that often for Mum in their cottage. Here, it felt almost friendly. Though he definitely wanted a sit down now before trudging back up to the keep, all three had needed quite a bit of help.

He had to lean his hands on the cool slate of the sink for a minute before finding the pitcher and filling it up. He came back, maybe five minutes later, to find that Master Isten hadn't moved other than picking up a book he'd been reading. "Ah, there we are. Pour that into the kettle, hang it over the fire, and we'll have hot water in a bit. Sit, sit."

"Is there anything else you'd like a hand with, sir?" Jasper felt he had to ask. He had been assigned a duty here, and it wasn't properly done yet.

Master Isten looked up, steady. "Sit, please." Jasper sat. Whatever else might come, he knew that sort of look and voice, and he wasn't going to argue with it. Master Isten went on, entirely conversational again. "Tell me about your mare. And your bit of where you come from. You can tell a lot about a man between those two."

There were also topics Jasper felt at ease talking about. Truth was, he tended to go on about both of them. He started with the summary, Dot's virtues of cleverness and steadiness, so long as she got to have her own opinions. How Schola was like and unlike the New Forest took a bit longer, because he was still figuring some of it out. He didn't want to bore Master Isten, who surely had other things he wanted to hear about.

But no, that wasn't it, apparently. Once Jasper had done the summary, Master Isten asked more. It wasn't just about the obvious parts of the Forest, or what Jasper had noticed here so far. He got Jasper talking about watching Dot's birth. He'd been up on foal watch that night with Dad. He hadn't been able to help with all of it, but he'd been able to run and get more help. He'd been rewarded an hour later with the first whuffling exploration of her lips, as soon as she was done getting her first meal from her mum.

They must have talked for half an hour. It was more Jasper than Master Isten, but Master Isten was focused, asking specific questions all through. And the way he talked about the land here, that kept catching Jasper's attention, things Jasper had noticed and a whole lot he hadn't yet. The kettle sang, and Jasper had filled the mugs, without pausing in the conversation. Finally, Master Isten nodded. "You'll do."

"Do, sir?" Jasper wasn't sure what he meant.

"It's the season for invitations, up at Schola. If you're wanting it, we're glad to extend an invitation to the Society of the White Horse. Take your time, give it a think. We're not as fussy and posh as several of them up there. Not so many while you're at school, either, only two right now. And I'm not telling you who. Nor will they, unless you decide to join us."

Jasper really didn't know what to do with that. "How do I decide, please, sir?"

"Go spend some time on the land. When the weather's a tad better. You'll know. If you feel the need to be telling us, you come down here and let me know, before the new moon in May. Or we'll know, likely enough."

That was really no help at all. Jasper was going to have to write to Stan and see what Stan knew. On the other hand, Jasper knew perfectly well when someone wasn't going to give more information. "Sir. Can I see to anything else?"

"If you'd bring down a couple of changes of clean clothes from the bedroom upstairs, on the right. There's a woman from the village, will be by tonight or tomorrow if the storm lets up. And see to the chickens, out the back. Eggs and such. Food's in the bucket by the back door." Jasper nodded and went to check on those without any further conversation. It was a sign of trust, or something of the kind, to be told to do both. The upstairs was the same workmanlike whitewash and well-tended wooden floorboards. Then he got his boots and coat back on. The chickens were huddled together, but otherwise fine. He fed them, made sure they had water, and gathered up six eggs.

Ten minutes later, he was back on the road to the keep, with a slender book tucked in the inside pocket of his coat, against the weather. He had no more information to work with than he'd had before. Maybe Ros or Avigail or Leo could help him figure out what he was supposed to do, or if he wanted to do it in the first place.

CHAPTER 24
AVIGAIL ON FEBRUARY 1ST

"Are you sure it's all right to be up here? And that no one else is?" Avigail glanced around. Pavo practice had only been an hour due to the weather. Leo had suggested they could come talk in the Astronomy classroom, no one would bother them.

Avigail was dubious. On one hand, Leo never said they should be places they shouldn't. He was reliable about that. On the other hand, being in a classroom on a Saturday morning was not the sort of thing that happened without permission. Everything was locked up in cabinets, just the ordinary charts and illustrations that hung on the walls, but that didn't actually help.

Leo glanced up at the set of twelve zodiac constellations mounted along the ceiling on the wall between the astronomy classroom and the stairs. There was a larger panel over the doors, with Polaris and the other constellations near it. Avigail had always found that a little odd. They were sliced up and distant enough that they weren't actually much use as charts to work with. Each of them only had a fraction of the stars, with not much help on how they connected in a sphere. Avigail followed his gaze, but they all looked ordinary, the stars glowing in their proper places.

"Yeah. No one at all." Leo sounded certain.

Avigail caught him looking and raised an eyebrow, hands on her hips. "Explain." Then she swallowed. "How you know that, I mean. Please."

Leo tilted his head, then grinned suddenly. "Promise none of you will tell anyone? I mean, it wouldn't do a lot of harm." The three of them all nodded. Ros hadn't been able to find Peter. He wasn't in his usual spot in the library. And the people Avigail might tell otherwise were here. When Leo had their agreement, he gestured. "Mum charmed the constellations there to glow with who's where. Two for each year, plus two for the staff. It covers everything above the fourth floor. I don't know who's on which constellation. I can just tell when there's no one up here. Even Mum. Besides, it's Saturday. She won't poke her head out of our rooms until lunch."

"Does she show up there, then?" That was an interesting question, magically and symbolically. Avigail gestured at the constellations.

"Mmhmm." Leo considered, and then went to pull a couple of the padded cushions out of the corner, tossing one to each of them, before he said anything. He'd wanted time to think it through. Avigail knew what that pause in him meant. "Mum is Dubhe. Alpha Ursa Majoris." They'd all had enough astronomy - even Jasper, who hadn't taken it as a course - to get that one.

"And your father?" This was Ros, settling herself on the cushion and tucking her feet under.

That made Leo grin suddenly. "Polaris." That was the

alpha star for Ursa Minor. Also, well, the centre of navigation these days.

Avigail tilted her head. "Why that way round? I'd have thought she'd pick Polaris for herself."

"First, Ursa Major is the Wain, and she's always been fond of that as, um, the origin story for Grandad's last name?" Leo said. "And second, I don't know. Parents are full of mysteries. But it makes them both happy. They started doing it before I was born, and I've more sense than to argue. Especially when they've got that kind of head start."

That was absolutely fair. Though it also meant there was a way into the conversation they were all avoiding. Ros, bless her, picked it up. "Well. All right. But we might have some things to argue with. Not with each other, I hope?" Avigail caught Ros's uncertainty there.

Leo folded himself down onto a cushion. "You got an invite from Animus Mundi." That was to Ros, and it wasn't a question at all, so Ros must have told him. "And I got one to Dius Fidius." He nodded at Avigail. "You?"

"Four Metals." He nodded, like he'd guessed.

Jasper cleared his throat. "Society of the White Horse. But it wasn't a note or a card or anything. It was in person, someone in the village." He closed his mouth, then, like he didn't want to say too much.

"Does anyone know about Peter? Or anyone else?" Avigail asked that.

"I've got a guess that he's got an invite, but I don't have a clue who," Ros said. "It'd be nice if other people thought he was worth having round, like we do, but I also worry, I don't know, he'd get hurt, not knowing what to expect."

Jasper coughed. "Peter's sharp about that sort of thing. People try to use him, and he just sort of steps sideways from it. Maybe he'll tell us, sometime, but until he does."

Ros peered at him. "Oh, so you two do talk about other things than your assignments."

It made Jasper smile, just briefly, though Leo thought he still looked unsettled. "Some of us pay attention to body language. I just have a different set of experiences to work with there, when it's just the two of us." Then he considered and added to Ros, "You know Aquila, how she's steady as anything, until she's three feet to the left?"

Ros laughed. "And you can always tell when she's going to, and I can't. All right. Fair." She glanced around, looking at each of them. "So, I guess the first question is how we feel about that. I'll start." She swallowed hard, and Avigail could see how her composure was worn around the edges, fraying a bit, like an ancient tapestry. "I - blast." She looked at Leo, directly. "I'm sort of interested. But I don't want to, if they don't want you. I mean, you're the one who's actually interested in Ritual."

"Why do you think they picked you? I mean, you're doing really well in Ritual. And you're doing lessons with Professor Leonard, and they probably don't know whether that's Ritual or something else," Avigail offered.

"Unless she told them. I mean, we don't know which professors are in what society, or if they are. Let's come back to that. Leo, you next."

Leo shrugged. "I don't want Dius Fidius. Dad's said he's fine if I don't." Leo's mouth cracked into a smile at something, but he didn't share.

"The person who invited me lent me a book. Charmed, so only I can open it, all fancy." Jasper said. "I don't know. There are things I like in there, but it feels high-handed. Like some of it fits me, and some of it doesn't."

"I don't, um. I'm not against the idea of the Four Metals? But I'm not entirely enthused, either." Avigail considered. "But I suppose there's an argument that the societies are a thing we grow into. They're not supposed to fit us perfectly at the start. Like our Houses."

"Lots of different ways we could grow, like Mum says," Leo said, thoughtfully. Usually, he was closed-mouthed about that sort of thing. Then he looked up. "Who else do we know about? Ursula's not in Dius Fidius. She told them no, very firmly, the morning after she got an invite."

It made Ros snort. "Sure they loved that. Did she get trouble for it?" Ros would think about that, the way the ripples played out as they collided with each other and with the unyielding boundaries of the school.

"I think everyone was too afraid of what she'd do next. And Dad was right there, hard to ignore." Leo shrugged. "Mum and Dad don't know if she's in with any of them. So if it was an initiation, it wasn't at night, after curfew." It did put a different twist on what the adults knew, and when, and of course Leo would think about that. Especially with the demonstration of one of the many methods of keeping track of people. Leo added, "It apparently used to be easier, in Uncle Alexander's day or even Dad's. These days, there's a lot more keeping track of everyone, in case we did get a bomb, and Dad hasn't dismantled it. He ignores some of it, sometimes, but that's different."

Avigail tucked that into her head for future analysis. "Tobias Wilton got an invite from the Four Metals. He's thrilled. All his planning paid off." Her shoulder twitched. "I feel sort of guilty about it, actually? Because I didn't try."

"You just went to things they think are interesting, anyway." Ros said, amused. "Well, to be fair, you went to most things."

"Most things are interesting!" Avigail replied. She thought so, anyway, and it meant she was never bored.

Well, almost never. "Do we know about any other Dius Fidius invitations?"

"Crimson Hettleburgh. I'm almost certain," Ros said, promptly. "But not Phipps. Phipps was pouting. Pouting does not suit him. You watch yourself, Leo, if he figures you've been invited and you're not doing anything with it."

"I had it pointed out to me," Leo said, leaning back on one hand and not looking at anyone. "That if I just don't do anything, they can play it like they want it, assume I'm going to do something. Wait, that's a question. My invite said, um." He stopped, then quoted, "Do something that demonstrates you should be one of us."

Avigail snorted. "Mine has a puzzle. I've sorted out most of it. I was going to tackle the rest this afternoon if I got time. Or at least the first part of it. I wouldn't put it past them to have more."

"Mine has a ritual to do. Though I want to confirm it's actually from them, before I do it. It's an odd set-up. And yes, Leo, you can have a look, if you want. Actually, I hope you will? I was also going to see if I could find Peter again, and test it before I open it."

Leo shivered, once. Avigail watched, trying to figure out what to say to that. "What do you think about it, Leo?"

"I think I'm too curious for my own good." Leo bit down on it. "I want to know, and I don't want it, and I don't want someone - a group - who doesn't want me for me. Not who my parents are, or who they think I am. Just me."

Avigail sort of thought that might not be on offer, honestly, but she wasn't going to say so. None of them could be disentangled from who their parents were, even Jasper. Or Peter. Both of them were shaped by it, even if it came out differently than Avigail and Ros and Leo. That made her think. "Really no ideas on Peter, Ros, you talk to him most?"

"No idea at all. I was hoping for a hint this afternoon. You'd be a help there, Leo. But if they didn't take him or Leo, I don't know who else Animus Mundi would have tapped."

Leo shrugged. "I'm curious about your detection charms." That was quiet, a bit muted. "You sure, Ros?"

"Sure I want you there, yeah. So long as you're willing. Do we know about - um. Nine Muses?"

Avigail listed off a couple of names. No one they knew terribly well, but absolutely the likely contenders. "Probably a couple of others, too. I don't know the instrumentalists enough that they'd tell me. Many Are The Waters?"

"No idea," Ros said. "I'd expect someone in Seal, there, honestly."

"Salmon also live in water." Jasper snuck it in surprisingly neatly, and Avigail had to blink at him several times before she grinned.

"Haven't heard anything in my own house, either. And gods know, Merry won't tell me much specific to Seal. She just smiles mysteriously." Ros felt her older sister took that kind of mystery further than she ought. "Society of the White Horse, that's you, Jasper. Anyone else likely?"

"I don't think so? The person who invited me said there weren't many taken in at Schola. Two, and I don't know if that meant, um. Him. Too. Adults. The book says pretty much the same. They're more likely to take people in apprenticeship, a bit older. And nothing says this right out, but more from Snap than Schola."

"Well, I suppose that makes some sense." Ros considered it, then asked, "Dwellers?"

All of them shook their heads after a long, drawn-out

pause. "No idea," Leo said. "Usually, the people they tap are a little, um. Obvious? They're usually not the subtle ones in the class. I don't know, though. And often they've got something to do. Achieve." Leo waved a hand. "More than a ritual in a workroom, I mean."

"It'd fit. So we might discover something later. All right. Ros, you have a ritual to do, and it sounded like you've enough help with that. Leo, you don't want to do anything that could be seen as following that instruction, so helping Ros is fine, it'll be private. Jasper, want to help me rummage in the library this afternoon?" Avigail summed up. "And you just - um. What do you need to do?"

"Decide and tell them by the new moon in May. Or he said they'd figure it out. And isn't that one going to haunt me a bit? It's, um. Seasonal? I like the seasonal. But also a bit spooky in the sense of wondering who's seeing what."

"Makes your ears prick up," Avigail said, sympathetically. "Fair enough. You let us know if we can help with that. And we'll all keep an eye out and share what we discover, right? Promise?" Her voice wavered slightly at the end, because all of a sudden, she wasn't sure. Mama and Papa had both gone through this year on their own, dealing with whatever they'd known, and she didn't have to do that. Probably.

All three of the others nodded, then Leo's chin jerked up. "Mum's on her way up." He immediately broke into asking about something in the Materia assignment. None of them had books or notes out, but by the time they heard steps on the stone, the illusion was good enough to hold. Or at least pass. Sometimes passing was the possible thing.

"Ah, the weather got you? I came up to get my notes. You all should get down for lunch if you want to beat the rush." Professor Wain made her way to her office door.

Avigail noticed the series of passes she made to open the warding, and how at least a third of them were flourishes that didn't do anything. "If you'd tell Helena that I'll be a few, Leo, I'd appreciate it. We're meeting after. She'll wonder where I am."

"Of course, Mum." Leo stood up, and brushed off his trousers, then took the cushions as the others handed them over, to stack them back where they belonged. The four of them went off, talking amiably about things that could be overheard. Then they melted into the stream of students aiming at the great hall and a warm meal on a chilly day.

CHAPTER 25
LEO ON FEBRUARY 22ND

Three weeks later, Leo still didn't have any more answers. None of them did, not about the societies. Avigail had followed the clues from her invitation box. The four coins matched up with four marble busts of admittedly somewhat obscure authors in the library. Those authors each had a book with a note tucked inside with details of something to make. The resulting device hadn't been terribly complicated, according to Avigail. Leo thought her standards were different than most people's, but it had apparently helped to have the Salmon House workrooms on hand. She'd completed the object, but not turned anything in.

Ros's invitation had, indeed, been from Animus Mundi. There was a ritual to do if she was interested - she'd done that one. A note had appeared through the mail three days later, with an additional ritual. That one was both more complex and more binding, in terms of starting her intentions. But it also said she didn't have to make a decision until the new moon in May. Ros, sensibly, was waiting on it.

Peter had been very curious about the charms to make

sure the letter was in fact from Animus Mundi. He and Ros and Leo had talked about it for about an hour, the variations on it. It just drove home that Peter had deep waters to him, he'd gone through the whole conversation not letting either Ros or Leo ask him directly about anything. Leo respected that about Peter, even when it was currently frustrating, but it was frustrating like a Fox controlling the conversation, which Peter was, even if he hadn't noticed that he fit that way yet. He was definitely better at that part than Crimson. At the end, instead, they'd got into a conversation - one that had all three of them laughing - about some of the foibles of the Great Families, stories Peter hadn't ever heard.

Jasper's was easy enough. He had a book. He'd been doing a lot of thinking about it, and even more riding about it, not that the weather was cooperating with that one. He'd also been coming in for more bullying. Some of it was Phipps and Heckle and that lot turning their own frustrations outwards. Some of it was, Leo didn't know how to put this, that Jasper was just a hair more unusual than before.

The thing was, it wasn't about the book or about Society of the White Horse. Or at least Leo didn't think so. He was feeling his way through, thinking more like Mum than Dad here, but it wasn't like he could talk it through with her. Not about societies. He thought it had started over winter hols. Jasper had been paying a lot of attention during the bohort matches, the sort of attention that left a body exhausted but in the best way. And now he was going about what he was doing differently. Connecting things, somehow.

The best way he could put it was that Jasper was like Ursula, when she'd sort of grown into doing what she was going to do, rather than matching the people around her.

Leo could gesture at it in incoherent comments about ritual spaces and the shape of them, and a bit more with musical terms, and none of it went satisfyingly into words. He was trying to pay attention to it more like Mum did than Dad, and that sort of helped, but it didn't actually add up to an explanation.

Whatever it was, Phipps had noticed, and it was like hounds baying after a fox. Even if that was probably the wrong metaphor here. Mostly, Leo wanted Jasper to be happy, whatever that meant, and he didn't have an idea how to help his friend figure that out. Just be there and hopefully keep other people from interfering.

They'd had pavo practice that morning, but in the arena. The weather was still horrid. Snow had fallen and stayed put. The temperatures were frigid, below freezing, and when there wasn't snow, there was either ice or frozen mud. None of that was good for horses, and it wasn't much good for people, either.

At lunch, Leo had let Mum know he was planning to go down to the cave under the keep again. He'd be back by supper, long soak first. She'd nodded, agreeably, before one of the fifth years had a question for her. He absolutely kept the promise he'd made them last year, letting them know when he disappeared downstairs. They'd know where he was, or they'd figure it out, but that didn't mean making them worry was kind. Dad might have lost a few of the lines in his face from all his worries during the War, the last year, but he still had a lot of them.

The soak was reviving, and so was being mostly on his own. There were a couple of girls in the other baths, he thought. He could hear their laughter echo a couple of times. It wasn't Ros and Avigail; they were working on an Alchemy assignment. Jasper was likely still down in the barn, helping out. Peter was almost certainly in the library, but he was working on an extra essay, something Professor Leonard had assigned him. Once he was dry and back in his uniform, he waited until the hallway was clear and ducked down into the storage cupboard, then down the stairs.

Being down here in the winter was perhaps the best. It was warm, the way caves were warm, and cool, the way caves were cool. Not that he had a vast experience of them, just this room and some of the sea caves that opened onto the beaches at the shoreline. And the bank vault caves of the Scali, where Dad's family had banked pretty much since there was a Scali bank in England. But that was a different sort of cave. All the magic felt a little itchy, because of course he was a guest there and on his best behaviour.

When the blue magic came up, Leo settled into his habits. He sat first, just breathing it in. He fancied he could hear the pulse of the school, the places people were happier or quieter. Nothing that was like eavesdropping. He wouldn't want that. Just whether things were tense or more relaxed. Right now, things felt even. They were a month and a half into term, with another three weeks to go. No one was worrying too much yet about exams, and besides, the ones at the end of this term weren't the ones that mattered.

Then, he began to go around, looking at all the lines of the magic flowing and outlining, and more importantly, feeling it. He'd been worried that the ice was going to do things to the walls, especially the exposed part of the curtain walls. Or that someone, with pent up energy, was going to do something that caused a problem. Maybe both. Both was entirely possible.

It wasn't until he got all the way around that he got a sense of something else, though. It wasn't on the map of the school, that was the thing. He could feel something tug at him, off to the north. North and a hair east, possibly. But he didn't know how to pin it down more than that. There was an awful lot of possible north and east, too. First the fields up to the northern orchard, and the couple of cottages up that way. The same sort of place he'd seen that sparkle, what was it, months ago. Armistice Day, that's right, because he remembered coming up and finding that firstie right after.

There wasn't much on that edge of the island. North, there was a stretch of ocean, Cardigan Bay. And then even more north and east was the Council Keep. It probably wasn't that. For one thing, that was a fair distance, and for another, why would that show up here? The only way he could get it to make any sense - that he'd been there enough to get a feel for it - wasn't anything he wanted at all.

In the end, he sat down again to make notes about it. His head was bent over the notebook when he heard steps coming down, then Dad's whistle. "Leo?"

"Here, Dad." He kept the notebook out. "I was going to come find you, but easier to show you."

"Oh?" Dad made his way in, stepping carefully along the paths around the lines of the keep, over to where Leo was. He was moving a bit stiffly. Leo knew the cold was hard on his knee. It wasn't just the usual things about weather and old injuries, though that too. Mum had said two summers ago that it was a bit of lingering curse damage, and it got more riled up in the cold due to some sort of affinity.

Leo shifted over, so there was room to sit on the slate floor. Or something like slate. Anyway, he hadn't actually figured out what stone it was. Dad lowered himself, leaning his back against a wall. "How are things? I didn't get much time on Thursday." He'd had to go fish three people out of the wards, something to do with a society task. Or something people thought was one, which seemed a little more plausible to Leo right now. Leo betted at least a couple of those had been set up, trying to get people in trouble, who hadn't thought to question the legitimacy of the invitation. Anyway, that one had involved gears, springs, an upper window in the sets of rooms above the library and below Aunt Helena's rooms as head of school, and a fair bit of risk.

"I'm fine. Not doing anything eye-catching still, except the pavo's going a bit better. Nims thinks he might put me in the bohort match on the first. It depends how practice goes this week." They could play bohort in the arena if they had to. Though likely enough they'd play outside and the puzzle would be set to make the snow and cold part of the challenge.

Dad grinned. "Oh, then I'll have to cheer for you. We'll see about getting Alexander out for it. Because you've got a sense of the terrain?"

Leo nodded. He was only a second year; Leo didn't expect to play that many bohort matches this year. He wasn't in the starting players for the team, not like Theo Lefton. But he did know the terrain, he did fine in the cold, and Fox was having an off-year. "And Nims thinks I could do a couple of good things. I guess he heard a little about the match over hols from Merry? She was talking me up. And then he asked Theo and Theo said more." That had been a grand day, and he hadn't been playing against Theo. Theo and his sister had been playing with and against the adults, including Dad.

It got a laugh from Dad. "Well, let me know if you both

want to talk through ideas. We can find some time next week. Nims, too, if he'd like. Or the rest of your team."

Leo blinked. "You don't usually, Dad." Dad loved the sport, and whatever else Leo wanted to do with his life, he was clear that the agility needed to be a good player wouldn't hurt. Besides, he loved the challenge of it. But Dad usually stayed absolutely neutral when it came to the school's matches.

"Man can do a thing for his son's House. Besides, I know the Fox team's had extra coaching during hols. This is just evening it up. Even if they aren't making much use of the coaching right now." Dad leaned back a little more thoroughly.

"Someone you played with, then?" Leo could guess at what brought on that sort of mood. Dad had played bohort near enough full-time right after his apprenticeship, before the Great War.

"What gave it away? Maurice Whelk. He's a lousy teacher. Decent player, but he's only good at teaching people who play like him. And that's not this team. Individually, several of them are talented, and some of the reserve more so. But right now? Not all they could be. So." Dad shrugged, spreading his hands.

"So you want to show what being a good teacher can do. And you know all of us pretty well." Everyone on the Bear House team was doing duelling or protective magics in some form, at least anyone who might be playing in the next match. Leo considered. "I'll tell Nims tonight."

"Grand. We'll find a time." Dad paused, then asked, "What did you notice?"

"It's not on the map," Leo said promptly. "And it looks like there isn't anything lasting from Thursday."

"No, we got to them before they tried expansion charms

on ice." Then Dad cleared his throat. "You do know you don't need to," he stopped. "I'm putting this badly. It's your job to be a student right now. Not to feel responsible for this." He gestured at it.

"Did Mum tell you to say that?" Leo watched carefully now, because it was the small things that would give him information.

Dad snorted. "Your Mum said that she couldn't say it, she'd go up in a burst of hypocrisy. I wasn't responsible for much, at your age. Just myself."

"Yourself and all the family expectations and Uncle Garin's disapproval, and I don't know what else," Leo pointed out. "I don't have most of that. Even Uncle Garin, mostly."

"I, look." Dad rubbed his face. "We showed you this because you should get to enjoy it. Being here. But you don't need to feel like you have to fix any of it. That's, I don't know how to put this."

"If it were still the Blitz, I'd be responsible for helping get other people to safer spots. Because that's the decent thing to do. And for making sure all the blackout shades were drawn, and the lanterns shaded properly, and all. I mean, I'm still seeing about chickens and things, when there aren't other people doing it. Bit late to tell me not to be responsible. You'd have to go back to when I was seven."

Dad made a series of faces, and Leo knew he'd won his point when the last one was more or less resignation. "You're doing well in Trivium, I see. The rhetoric is right up there."

"That's talking to Uncle Alexander more regularly. Which is also your doing," Leo pointed out. "Anyway. There's a spot. That way, I don't know how far. Not in the

Keep or the curtain walls. Maybe by the north coast? I can't tell."

Dad closed his eyes, concentrating, and Leo shut up and let him. Neither of them moved or made any noise for quite a long time - Leo counted out at least three minutes with his fingers. Finally, Dad cleared his throat. "I don't know either. I think the coast, but there's no way we're getting down there until we've had a bit of a thaw. The stairs will be all over ice, and cutting around from the east shore's tricky at the best of times with the currents as they are."

"What do you think it is?" Leo asked.

"Well, I'm going to ask Ibis to go chat with the merfolk and see if there's anything that's a problem for them or that they've noticed. Again. Maybe something's shifted since last time. And you know sometimes you have to ask straight out, they won't necessarily mention everything. He can talk to them if we get a day it isn't actually snowing or sleeting." Dad ran his hand through his hair, pulling it back. "It could be something washed up. There are a fair few U-Boats and a few other ships that went down not far from here. I don't think anything further east of us, but there are a couple north, and more west and south. It'll probably keep, in that case."

Leo frowned, but Dad was right on several counts. That the weather was horrid, that this wasn't Leo's to try to solve, and that the merfolk might have more information. None of which Leo could do anything about right now. He'd told Dad. That was what he was supposed to do. He couldn't help that it didn't feel like enough, but he could at least not make things harder. "Let me know if there's anything?"

Dad shifted to pat him on the shoulder. "That I'll do. It's the best way to figure out what you're feeling next time, understand more. Do you want to come upstairs and do a bit of duelling?" It was Dad's preferred solution to an open afternoon.

Leo grinned. "Sure. I was trying to get that shift onto my left foot, still. And it'd be handy for a lot of things." Dad pushed himself upright, and Leo let him have a minute to check on things, before they went upstairs to the salle.

CHAPTER 26
ROS ON FEBRUARY 26TH

Ros pulled back her hands, frowning at the tips of her fingers, which were still sparking with golden bursts of magic. She lifted them slightly, and the other three in the room took a step back. "It's not supposed to do that."

Giselle shook her head. "Well. It's not supposed to do that when you're a second year." She lifted her own fingers, calling up a much more orderly glow from her fingertips. She was a fifth year, though not a prefect. Ros had discovered that Giselle had the sort of innocent face that let her get away with dozens of impish moments, with almost no consequences. It wasn't entirely good for her, and it was a lot better for everyone around her if she had occupation and entertainment to keep her busy. "Most second years can't even manage sparks."

Hermes, one of the fourth year boys, swung his legs. He was perched on the table along the wall in the workroom they were using. "What feels uneven to you, Ros?"

It felt, honestly, like vaulting had, back in the autumn, like she wasn't quite grasping something. The charm was supposed to help trace patterns between people, to make them more visible. Right now, they were running it visible to everyone. Ordinarily they wouldn't do that, they'd use it where only individuals - or maybe their allies - could see the results. It was a way to mark out the next people to talk to at a party, or indicate how to split up the next conversations.

She let out a huff of breath. "I can get it to my fingers, but not from there. And it's all staggering, uneven, that's no good." Mostly, she felt frustrated. "I feel like it's bottled up, somehow, silted?" She'd been talking about silting in rivers with Peter last night, it brought the metaphor to mind.

"There are exercises for that." Giselle considered, peering at Ros's fingers. "Ask Professor Knox, I think. Maybe try running Hamilton's Third a few times, then try it again? Over a couple of days."

Ros had been thinking all along that her parents would find it tremendously handy if they didn't already know something like it. Maybe that was what was catching her up, the idea of knowing things her parents didn't. On the other hand, Uncle Alexander could have passed it along. Or Avigail's grandparents. Teaching the house magics to friends and allies was a thing people could do, even if a fair number of Fox House would look down on it. That was a whole other muddle, and one she felt incredibly unsure how to even bring up with anyone useful. By which, at the moment, she meant Professor Knox, Uncle Alexander, or Avigail's Aunt Charlotte. Instead, she stared at her fingers.

"Give it a rest for a bit. We'll come back to it next week. It's not that you can't do it, it's that something's going odd when you do." Alix patted her on the shoulder. "Try it when there are more people around, too - one of the bohort matches, maybe." Then Alix grinned. "Not Sunday. We don't need the distraction." She was on the team, her first time as a third year, though not starting. Ros was going to have to cheer for Fox, even though she'd really be cheering in her heart for Leo. At least that Leo would make a good show.

Maybe it was her divided loyalties getting in the way. If that was the problem, it was definitely a question for Uncle Alexander. She'd been supposed to get tea with him a fortnight ago, and he'd been stalled by a storm somewhere. Sunday, Leo would want time with him after bohort, both Leo and his dad. Ros could at least sort out scheduling, maybe, for somewhere further down the line.

The other three grabbed their books and wandered off, talking amiably. Ros stayed to tidy up - she was junior. That was her role, among other things. And they were pretty reasonable about it. The study groups shifted around every term, but she liked this one. All three of them listened, and they had good ideas. It didn't solve her problems, but they were decent suggestions.

She was just finishing up sweeping when Professor Knox appeared at the door. "How did it go, then?"

"You left me for last, didn't you?" Ros knew his habits well enough by now. He spent the bulk of the time working with the first years, along with the fifth year prefects or sometimes one of the other professors from Fox House. Professor Fortier, sometimes, or two of the Trivium professors.

Professor Knox spread his hands out. "It's ten to seven, if you want to wash up. Or have questions." He leaned against the door frame. "How did things go?" This time he put the emphasis firmly on 'did' with a smile.

"Everyone else did wonderfully. I got sparks, but they sputter out, and now I'm thinking about whether things are tangled up in a way I can't make sense of." Ros shrugged.

"What sort of tangled?" Professor Knox didn't move. He just stayed there, like he had all the time in the world. He wasn't really blocking the door, but it would be rude if she walked out past him, and she didn't want to be that kind of rude.

"Who else knows this one?" Ros asked finally. "I was wondering if my parents do. If there are lots of people using this charm..." She lifted her fingers, and this time, the glow was steadier, though not actually consistent. "And the rest of us just don't know. Or some people are, and they're the ones who get ahead, and we know why, and they don't."

"Ah." It was a quiet sound, not arguing or dismissing it. "Other Houses have their magics, too. As I'm sure you know, in particular."

"We haven't talked about it much." Ros's shoulder twitched. "I know Bear has a lot of protective magics, making a den. That's what Leo said. The things that make one, control over your space, a place that's restorative, or that you can use as a base for everything else. Salmon has a lot of crafting things - holding something in place, lighting or magnifying it, some of the indexing charms. Owl has those too, but they teach those pretty regularly. Papa taught me some of them last summer, and he said he'll teach me more this coming summer."

"There you are. And what about the others?" Professor Knox twitched his chin. "Horse and Seal and Boar?"

"I don't understand Boar much. Aiming, maybe? I haven't had anyone to talk to about it. Seal, um." Ros knew a lot of their magics had to do with transformation, but she didn't know what scope that had. "Merry and Rowena won't talk much about it." Her sister and Avigail's, both of whom were annoyingly good at keeping secrets, so actually that might be part of Seal.

"Your aunt might, a little. I know she had to leave school, but she would have had some of it. And Richart Hase was a fine teacher. He did very well with Seal House for decades." Professor Knox grinned. "I modelled myself on him a bit. Him and Professor Wain. In how to manage the house, at any rate."

That was a curious thing to say, and she was sure he had a dozen reasons for saying it. Both parts of it. "I don't really understand Horse's magic, either, only I think I like it? I can see the effects of it, more than I can with Bear."

"Talk to me about that, then." Professor Knox considered for a moment, then came into the workroom, nudging the door mostly closed and hopping up on the table himself. He did it just often enough that Ros wasn't surprised by it any longer, but also she was certain it was a deliberate choice. Most things he did were. Probably all of them.

"I keep thinking about it up in Professor Wain's classroom. And her office, even more, the one right off her classroom." Ros had also been in their rooms several times, as Leo's guest for tea, but she certainly wasn't sure how to talk about that. "They feel, um." Ros considered. "The alchemy lab feels very orderly. And it should, obviously, there's a lot that could go wrong if people were too relaxed or careless."

Professor Knox nodded just once, encouraging her to go on.

"But the astronomy spaces, they feel welcoming. Even when it's cold out, up on the top of the keep, it feels like you're just a few minutes from some warm tea or cider or whatever and the way the dark is comfortable, not terrifying."

"And you've seen Professor Wain and Professor Fortier at social events, I know. The sort of social events that are the reason we teach you that charm." He flicked his fingers, calling up the same light. "I use it all the time in house meetings, for the record, with the prefects. Do you think she uses it? Or something else?"

"Or nothing." Ros pointed out that option, stubbornly.

"Or nothing." Professor Knox definitely looked amused now. "Well?"

Ros paused to think through. She'd seen them, after all, at several social events, the public ones, over winter hols. How Professor Wain, in specific, went at things was different than Mama or than Lady Alysoun. She seemed to flow from group to group, having something to say that seemed to make people smile. It was all honest, though; it wasn't hiding things. Cautiously, she said, "People are happy to see her. And she always seems to have something to say to them."

"Ask her about how she prepares sometime. I'm fairly sure she'll tell you. She manages the way she does partly because she's honest. She's not hiding what her interests are. She doesn't bother. It's surprisingly effective in a group of people who see motivations by the dozen hiding under the surface. But she also brings that amiable warmth with her, where she goes. That's a Horse magic. She talks about it as the awareness of the herd, knowing where the risks are, and where your people are." His mouth quirked. "Sometimes I'm counted in the people."

It made Ros snort. "So there are different ways to do the same thing. And a lot of people use them, at least sometimes."

"Exactly. What I want is for you to get good enough that you can choose to use them. I want you to have the tool at your fingertips." He wriggled his this time, without the light. "You were upset, in January, when you thought I wasn't taking action on something. What do you think now?"

It was far too easy to see part of that. "You were using this, the charm. To help sort some of it out."

"Just so. How do you think things are right now?"

Ros shrugged. "Better. I told you that. Gloriana and Alcesta are at least being civil now. How did the charm help?"

"Try it. Figure it out. If you do, I'll give you ten house points." That was a nice chunk, and it'd make the right impression with the older students.

Ros sighed. "I'll think about it." She knew she probably would. For one thing, she was curious now. And for another, she didn't want to be defeated by a charm. It was a bad habit to get into. Maybe she could get someone to help her with it on Saturday or Sunday.

"There you go." They both heard the gong sound, a five minutes warning. "Go find your friends, have a good supper. Come back to it tomorrow."

Ros nodded. There wasn't really anything else to say, and she was, in fact, hungry. Both for supper, and for the conversation about it, if she could get Avigail and Leo and Jasper and maybe Peter together for a few minutes. Also, she really wanted to know how it had gone for Peter, and how he felt about it. He had scruples about different things than Ros did, which was usually interesting and informative, both.

CHAPTER 27
JASPER ON MARCH 6TH

J asper felt there wasn't remotely enough time this week. He was trying to get the last of the set design done tonight, because this weekend was going to be chaos. Avigail had invited the three of them, plus Peter Wallace, out to Veritas for Holi. They had permission to leave Schola after classes on Thursday, stay at Veritas overnight, take part in the festivities the next day, and come back on Saturday.

Jasper found the whole thing a lot, honestly. He'd been to Veritas enough times that it, in itself, wasn't terrifying. He knew how to behave in one of the demesne estates, after all, and the way the Carillons and the Edgartons managed things seemed similar enough. It felt similar enough, anyway, in all the ways Jasper knew how to notice.

But he hadn't been out for Holi since he was about eight. Now there were going to be social expectations. Avigail's father was apparently inviting a lot of people from the Council and elsewhere, which meant all sorts of people who might get offended by who knows what. Even if Jasper knew some of them, that didn't actually help.

But he didn't want to turn it down, either. That would be rude, Avigail had asked him carefully. She'd made it clear he was included, and that mattered, more than Jasper could say. And she'd also said they'd be back in time for pavo, Saturday morning, or at least anyone who got up early enough could be. Jasper was pretty sure the kids would get sent up to bed well before the adults.

Also, he could use a celebration of the spring. February had been almost worse than January, certainly more stormy. Now everything was beginning to thaw, finally, but it all felt sludgy and covered in mud. Probably because a lot of things were, honestly. He wanted something that felt like a cleansing spring rain that let everything start new. Leo and Ros and Avigail all had an assignment for their Ritual class to report about it. Presumably Peter did too.

Right now, though, it meant that Jasper really needed to get this bit of set done. It was the last piece they needed, for the staged readings and recital that would take place Saturday night. If he didn't finish, someone else would have to do the last parts while he went skiving off. Or at least that was what it would look like.

He found the lighter hammer, working on positioning things, humming as he did so. It was one of the songs Dad had taught him. The song was the kind of thing that got sung while working, to help keep a steady rhythm. Or in Dad's case, and often in Jasper's, when wanting to settle a horse. Here and now, he could feel himself settle into the work better, all of it coming together, like it did when he was riding. It wasn't about moving his hand or his elbow or his magic, it was all of it in flow, actually working together and making everything better.

The tune that kept sticking in his head wasn't cheerful, mind. It had come to mind because Jasper had been thinking about Dad, so he'd been singing "William Rufus", which Dad had learned from his dad, back before the Great War. Any song about the death of a king was inclined to be a bit dire, and this was a King that Albion had also cared a fair bit about. He'd got round to the repeated couplet, "When instead of a royal stag that day, the king of England fell..." when he heard a sound behind him. It completely distracted him from the verse with the vulture and the raven, and he stopped abruptly.

"You've a grand voice." Phil Grant had come in. "You're not singing in the performance?"

Jasper shrugged. "I like music. I don't much want to do it up in front of people." Professor Hammond hadn't pressed him, thankfully. For one thing, doing it in front of people made him a target. More of a target. Spots for singers were in shorter supply than people who wanted them. And for another, Jasper had learned most of his singing at gatherings in the Forest. It was a thing to be done with people, communally, to celebrate the good days or that the work got done, or to get through the bad ones. He didn't know how to shape that into something that made sense at Schola, as a soloist.

Grant gestured at the edge of the stage. "Can I come up?"

"You don't have to ask me for permission, yeah?" Jasper waved a hand. "Sure. I'm trying to finish up."

"There's tomorrow, isn't there? No, wait, Professor Hammond said you weren't around tomorrow or Friday. I hope everything's all right at home?" It was an amiable sort of question, but that didn't make it easy to answer.

Jasper could answer with the truth, but it came out curt. "Everything's fine, ta." After a moment, he tagged on, "Thanks for asking." That sounded grudging. He pushed himself upright to at least go do something to keep his hands busy.

Grant didn't move, letting Jasper shift around. He didn't say anything either, just sat there patiently. Jasper knew that sort of pause. He used it often enough in the stables. Grant wasn't staring, though, just - Jasper glanced over his shoulder - looking out into the seats of the audience. Jasper went back to work, letting the sound of the hammer be the only thing he focused on.

When he had to stop - he'd run out of nails right at hand - he straightened up. Grant was still there. Jasper cleared his throat. "Do you sing?" It wasn't what he'd meant to ask, but he hadn't seen Grant perform last time, either.

"Sometimes." Grant shrugged. "My voice was a while changing, not like yours, sounds like. I'm still sorting some of it out. I was a notable boy soprano for a bit. My family almost thought I'd go to one of the choir schools." He shrugged. "We haven't run to strong magic, the last generation or two." Then he cleared his throat. "I'm sorry if I made you uncomfortable. Richelda and I were curious about you."

He had noticed that about Grant, since the last time he'd been a help. Grant and Richelda and a fifth-year boy whose name Jasper hadn't caught spent a lot of time together. They didn't keep people out, there were often a rotating set of others with them, but they were the core of it. There was an ease about how they were together, that was like it sometimes was for Jasper with his friends. But with those three, other people noticed it too, and found it attractive, wanted to be around it. And that wasn't true for Jasper and his friends, not that way.

But the three of them also paid attention to people

around them. None of them were in Horse House, or Jasper would have thought it was the House magics, keeping an eye on the herd. He'd seen them, several times, help sorting out some problem here or there, before it got bigger or worse. The three of them weren't afraid to pull in a prefect or one of the professors, which was actually curious now Jasper thought about it. Most students were.

"You're steady, and that's not always the common sort of thing here." Grant offered it after a moment, as if he needed to add a little explanation to the silence.

It made Jasper snort. It wasn't, no. He'd noticed that. Everyone around him - even in his House, which tended to be a little steadier than some - seemed to get all worked up about all sorts of things. Jasper didn't have time to worry about who was making eyes at someone else, or got a slightly better score on an exam. Not that that made it easier to figure out what to say. After a moment, he offered, "Not really used to talking about myself."

"Also a thing I like about you, actually. The people I went to tutoring school with all blow themselves up bigger." There was something there, a thread that Jasper noticed. Ros was rubbing off on him and Avigail.

He considered, hesitated, and then decided to trust his instinct. "Not people you're close to now?"

Grant laughed. "Goodness, no. I don't have much patience with them. Richelda, Grim, a few others. Figuring out something that's not just show. My parents have expectations, but I'm trying not to worry about that for a bit longer. I figure I've got six months or so. Once I start fifth year, there'll be no help for it. And Richelda and Grim are leaving school, so they can't help me sort through it."

"Grim?" It was an odd name for a person.

"Marco Grimalfi. Everyone calls him Grim, though he's

very cheerful. You may not have noticed him. He's usually off doing something, one of the workrooms. We have to remind him to eat." That'd be the third of them, then.

"That's like Peter." Jasper considered. "And Ros." Both of whom alternated between the library and various work-rooms in patterns they understood and no one else could keep track of. What Jasper knew was which ones to check, like looking for mares out in the Forest. There were tenden-cies that varied week to week, and it was just a process of sorting out which aspects mattered for that mare in that season.

"Carillon?" Grant considered. "Do you know her well, then?"

Answering that would mean talking about his family. Jasper turned to face Grant. "Can I ask why you're asking? Me, Ros, any of it?"

"Mostly just curious. The four of you - five, when Wallace isn't in the library - have some people wondering. Sometimes being nasty, I suppose that's not news."

"Just about me, the nasty?" Jasper tried to ask it casu-ally, but it didn't come out that way. There was an edge to it.

Grant hesitated for just a second. "You and Edgarton come in for a lot of it. And Wallace. No one's sure what to make of her. Carillon terrifies a couple of them. She's sharp. And the people who might make trouble don't know what Professor Fortier would do if someone went for his son."

Jasper grunted. "Good question, isn't it?" He almost lost the sibilant, and finally he swallowed. "My dad's stable master for Ros's father. We grew up playing together, most days, riding when we got older."

"Ah, that explains why you're both so good on a horse." Grant tilted his head. "And Edgarton?"

This was the part Jasper left to Ros. Honestly, who knew what to say to this sort of question? "The families are friends. I don't know all the details? And Leo's been in that mix and his sister." He shrugged. "We picked up Peter first year, more or less. It's not the same for him, not growing up with everyone, but we do our best, you know? And he's a big help to me with my academics." On sudden impulse he added, "I'm glad enough having someone not from their kind of family to talk to."

Grant was leaning back on a hand. "How do they treat you, then?" There was something in the question that made Jasper take notice. It was the way some of the Forest families asked about that kind of thing. How they'd talk about what sort of person Lord Carillon was as Lord. What it was like compared to the old Lord in the southern half of the Forest, before he died. Did they treat you like a person, or like a tool? Most important, did they discard you when you couldn't do the same work or toss you out of a cottage when you got too old to be useful?

"They're my friends." Jasper swallowed hard, because he wanted to say a lot, and it wouldn't come out right. Finally, he looked away, out into the seats. "I trust them. And they're good riders, except for Peter. They treat their horses proper, they treat their friends proper, and I see all that."

There was a short silence, but Jasper couldn't bring himself to look over. Then Grant said, quiet as could be, "I'm glad. A man should have proper friends. I didn't, for a while. No one's sure what to make of Carillon and Edgarton. Titled families, Edgarton's father's on the Council. There are lots of stories about how that goes for people like you and yours, and not good ones."

That was fair. A fair thing to worry about, certainly. And

it wasn't like Jasper could defend it, not without talking about things he knew were private to the estate. He had seen how Lord Carillon was with Dad and with Master Benton, how he treated them like experts who knew their work. How, even more than that, he relied on them to be excellent. He wasn't threatened by it; he wasn't worried about it. He encouraged that. But Jasper also knew Lord Carillon kept a lot of things under his hat, hiding his light under a bushel, as Mum put it.

After a moment, he figured out what to say. "Ytene's grand. They keep a lot of people in work and steady work at that. The land's doing well. Even now we're mending things from the Army bases and all, through the Forest. That matters a lot, to the villagers in the Forest, the families that have been there just as long. Like Dad's."

"You want to do more of that, then? Whatever's after Schola?" Grant made it sound smooth, but Jasper looked up, wondering why he'd asked. There was a lot here that was uncommonly personal, for both of them, which made him want to stamp uncertainly and blow out a breath.

He shrugged. "I like making things better. But I don't want to go into the Ministry, or something. Too formal, too rigid?" He knew Ros was thinking about that, in some form. "And I don't have the skills for what Avigail's thinking about, and Leo's wanting to do more with Ritual. Me? I'm good at horses and sometimes hitting things with a hammer and I don't know what else yet."

"Oh, maybe you'll figure some of that out. There's time yet. I don't know a lot of it either, though I know more about things I absolutely don't want." He shrugged. "Like a lot of what my family would like. You might be luckier there." Then he coughed. "Need a hand with that set again?

I can hold something. I can even lay down paint evenly enough if you tell me what to do."

"That'd be a help." Jasper moved things around. Once that was settled, he said carefully. "I won't be here because Avigail's family invited us out. There's a seasonal celebration for the spring. We could all use a good spring right now, right?"

"Oh, could we! I hope you have a good time, then. You'll be back for the performance?" Grant settled in to brace the frame so Jasper could make fast work of stretching the canvas. It led naturally enough into some conversation about who was performing what, and how prepared they were. Grant was funny about it several times, without being nasty.

Jasper was still trying to figure that out when several others came to do their bits, once the evening lecture let out. By the time Jasper had to head down for curfew, his part was all solidly done. He knew that was in large part thanks to Grant being willing to help and doing a good job with it.

CHAPTER 28
AVIGAIL ON MARCH 7TH

Avigail looked around. As a celebration of spring, this year's Holi was having an uphill battle. It was either snowing or sleeting outside, she couldn't tell from here. They'd all bundled into the duelling salle, with some extra chairs brought down and heating charms laid on. There was quite a crowd, and Papa was bouncing around from group to group, cheerful.

At least last night, they'd managed to keep the bonfire going a good length of time. It had burned down to ashes. Mama had read the tales of demons who had to be chased away, of ogresses. Then she'd told the stories of Krishna's teasing and painting his beloved Radha with colour to match him. Mama and the household had made the proper prayers in the morning. There were fresh offerings and flowers on the shrine. Everyone had spent the morning laying out beautiful bright rangoli on the floor of the salle, in the centre. People were avoiding standing there, still, but that would change.

By all rights, the celebration should have started that morning. But a lot of the people Papa - and Mama - had wanted to invite had other things they had to do with their days. It had meant that Avigail and the others - Ros, Leo, Jasper, Peter, and Ros's older sister Merry - had plenty of time to set everything up. The plates and bowls and bags of all the colours were waiting at the corners of the salle, ready for everyone to enjoy.

Avigail was smug about it, because she'd helped with them. Not just making them for this year, though she'd done that too. But she and Papa had figured out over solstice hols how to mix them out of things that they could get despite the rationing of materia, and that responded to specific cleaning charms. Everyone wore grubbies, of course. But the charms would pull the excess out of the salle and the clothing. It meant people could enjoy the rest of the festival without worrying about smearing the house or the furniture or the books.

Now, they were just waiting for the last of the adults to get here. Mama and Grandmama were doing the final bits of fussing about the food, Avigail suspected. That was also tricky in this time of rationing, so they were going heavily on the rabbits. The estate had been raising them for food for years now, and they did make a lovely stew. Avigail herself made one more circuit of the tables, so she knew where everything was. Satisfied, she came around again to find Leo staring at something.

"What's up?" Avigail sidled over to him and then looked where he was looking.

"That's Uncle Garin. And Ursula, obviously." Leo's jaw had dropped open slightly. "Does he know?"

Avigail reached over and nudged his chin. "He's dressed for it. And Ursula looks really smug. Your parents are coming, right?"

Leo nodded, absently. "Pretty soon. Once Dad was done

with class. They're skipping the staff meeting." Then he looked around, frowning. "There's a lot of people here."

"Papa had ideas. Some of these might be good ones?" It was certainly a fascinating crowd. Avigail glanced around, then reached out to tap Peter on the shoulder. "Peter, want the guide to who's here, by category?"

Peter nodded, also rather wide-eyed. Avigail wasn't sure how overwhelmed he was, Ros knew how to read Peter much better. But it had to be odd, being in a group of so many powerful people, not sure who might be offended by what.

Avigail started ticking them off, including the people Peter had met last night. "Mama, my sister Rowena. That's Grandpapa and Aunt Kate and her husband Uncle Giles and my brother Anthony. They're probably talking Guard things. Um, it's fine to get Uncle Giles with colours. But he won't be able to see anything in here, even people moving, the light's too dim. So be careful of anything that could make him trip or hit his head."

She then glanced around, going clockwise for order. "Those are a dozen of the Penelopes. The three on the left are Aunt Mason, Aunt Witt, and Aunt Doyle. She trained Papa. She's all order and structure except when she isn't. On the other end, that's Isobel who was Papa's last apprentice, and Claudio, who's his current one." They looked like they were plotting something, the sort of thing that would get Papa doused in every shade of colour, probably, if they pulled it off. It'd probably take both of them, though, with some extra help.

"I almost followed that," Peter said, a little weakly. "Your grandmother's been really kind, checking in. And that's your aunt?"

"That's Aunt Charlotte and Uncle Lewis, and two of the

cousins - Theodora's the younger one, and Daphne, you know her." Daphne was in Owl House, prone to living in the library, and Avigail was sure they'd known each other since early in Peter's first year. She'd come out from Schola today, not last night, though. She'd been finishing an essay yesterday. "That's Orion - Lord Sisley - and Hypatia and Cammie and Duncan." Two sets of couples, making their way to apparently plot with Isobel and Claudio from the way Orion immediately leaned in.

"You call them by first names?" Peter frowned. "Wait. How many Council Members are here?"

"Oh, I haven't got to them yet separately." Avigail shrugged. "Names are complicated, but we're at home and it's a festival, and Papa said it's silly for me to call his apprentice something fancy. And they're all friends, so." She then waved a hand. "That's Council Member Landry. Or Leo and Ros's Uncle Alexander, but you've seen him."

"At bohort matches and at supper after." Peter said, a bit more uncertainly. "There are lots of stories about him."

Leo snorted at that. "Not all of them are true. There's Ros's parents, obviously, going over to talk to him. And that's my Uncle Garin - Dad's brother, Lord Fortier - and my sister. Oh, and there's Mum and Dad, they must have just got here." Avigail thought Lord Garin looked rather relieved at that, and Leo's Mum was hugging Ursula and teasing her about something. The Carillons were avoiding that knot of the Fortiers, and that was all about Lord Garin and not about the rest of them. She knew that.

"And the others?" Peter frowned, nodding at the other distinct clump of people.

"Those are all Council Members, sort of clustering." Avigail ticked the names off, but she was fairly sure Peter wouldn't remember them, and they could talk it over later.

"And that's Magister Smythe-Clive and Magistra Teague. They retired last year, but they're still working on projects for the Council."

Avigail checked her watch before tucking it well inside her pocket. "That's Uncle Gil, there, and Uncle Magni checking with Papa. That's probably about the salle magics." Uncle Gil had his back up against one of the walls already. He'd be more cautious in the bustle because of his leg. Grandmama would likely end up next to him, for similar reasons. "And those are Portal Keepers, see Rowena's checking on them. That's Ferdinand, Mama's previous apprentice." Not all of either group, but Papa had been very pleased at the turnout.

Leo leaned over. "Not Silvia Warren, I see." She was famously peeved at Papa, in entirely unsubtle ways. As her son, Claudio was often navigating a very narrow path when she and Papa were in the same place.

"Means Claudio can relax and enjoy himself. Papa said he invited her. Peter, Papa thinks Claudio should figure out what he wants, rather than what he's been told to want." Avigail was pretty sure Papa was winning on that front.

"It makes all the newspaper stories very different, when you see the people right here." Peter offered it just as Papa and Mama walked toward the end of the salle and all the supplies. Everyone fell quiet.

"You all know what we're about today." Papa's voice rang out clear and filled the room. He must be using a charm. "And I'm glad to see you're all dressed for it!" A laugh went up. "As my mother says, we can all use a little more to help the spring along. Just like we can use a little more light in the darkness when Diwali comes around in the winter. Let this open the doorway of spring - the portal of it - and let our fields and forests, waters and air teem and flourish with life and growth. Let our harvest of the coming year fill our cupboards and pantries, overflow so that we can share with many. If our current Schola students would take the trays around…"

Avigail led the other five students - Daphne joined them right away - off to grab the trays and circle around to provide everyone with colour and chaos. It was their job to make sure everyone could grab a bag or three of the colours, and some people had preferences. The trays had a rainbow of them, so it should work out all right.

Mama was grinning next to him, bouncing slightly on her toes. Holi turned her decades younger, reliably, and a match for Papa's energy. She then spoke up, her voice fitting right with Papa's. She didn't speak in public much, and Avigail could see the various Council Members leaning forward and watching her intently.

Mama spoke the Bengali of the prayer, with Papa joining in after a few lines. Avigail translated it along in her head, painting your loved ones with colours, the blessings of joy and plenty, bringing friends closer, and turning enemies into friends. A moment later, Mama spoke it in English. She caught a couple of amused looks at that, but then Papa gave them a nod, and people were reaching for the different bags of colours.

Everyone took whatever came to their hands, and then there was utter chaos. Uncle Giles got Aunt Kate, almost immediately, with bright green cascading down the side of her face. Mama got Papa in brilliant red, and then he was grabbing her and swinging her around. Music picked up, Avigail knew it was a recording, and it didn't matter. The beat of it was contagious, the music she'd learned enough about from Mama's family, when she'd been old enough to remember visiting India, and then from the communities in

London Mama knew. Avigail spun around, handing off the last bags from her tray and ducking to one side long enough to rest it against the wall.

Powder and colour was filling the air, charms making it shimmer and gleam far beyond the materia itself. As Avigail looked, she saw Leo's mum get Lord Garin in the face with bright green. A moment later, Ursula added gleaming purple to the mix, saying something that made him look at her sharply before she laughed. He didn't scare either Ursula or Leo's Mum, Avigail realised, for all everyone else was giving them a wide berth for the moment, even Leo's dad.

Then Avigail was pulled away. Ros had bright pink all over her hands, smearing it down Avigail's cheeks, then grabbing her hands and pulling her into the dancing that was picking up in the centre of the salle. The adults were slower to dance, but then she saw Cammie and Duncan. This wasn't their usual style, but they were bouncing up and down, finding the rhythm of it. Cammie was laughing as she tried to match Rowena's ability to shimmy and make the belled belt around Rowena's hips ring out clean and clear every time she moved.

Papa came into the centre, pulling Mama along with him. He was absolutely caked in colours, every shade of the rainbow, and obviously someone's plot had gone off entirely perfectly. Avigail let her voice trill, just delighting in being able to let loose and not be proper. This was a moment for joy, for chaos, for all the ecstasy she could have with this many people around. It hadn't been like this in years.

Last year, it had just been the immediate family, and the year before that, there had still been the War, and people couldn't gather the same way. Avigail put every ounce of hope she could into the dancing, before pulling more powder out of her pocket, glancing at Ros. Both of them set off to get Leo and Jasper and Peter, who were not covered in nearly enough colours yet.

Later - more than a few minutes, probably less than an hour - everyone had more or less run out of both powder and the ability to keep dancing frenetically. The music wound down, leaving the older adults leaning up against the walls or on wooden chairs, and the younger ones breathing hard. Papa managed to stand. "When we've all caught our breath, we'll do some charms to tidy up a bit, and then we've as much of a feast as we could put together. Rabbit curry, mind the heat, and rabbit stew for anyone who wants something else. Roast veg from our gardens, and the sweet dumplings are traditional and adapted for current times."

There was a lot of laughter, a few calls of cheers, and Papa waving it down with "Toasts come later, toasts come later." He was grinning, ear to ear, and Avigail was going to have absolutely no trouble writing up the analysis of this for ritual class. It hadn't been formal, the way Professor Leonard was teaching them, but that didn't mean it didn't work. More than that, she could see it had, in fact, made people happy. Even Leo's uncle was smiling a little, and so were near all the Council Members. That made it a really good day, honestly. There should be a lot more days like this.

EQUINOX HOLIDAYS

CHAPTER 29
LEO ON MARCH 20TH

L eo looked around the room. The party was tapering
down, with just twenty guests still around. Leo
didn't know nearly enough about this sort of thing,
but he thought it had been a reasonable sort of success.

It was Ursula's first time as hostess at Arundel. The
plans had been for a smaller party by Great Family standards, with about four dozen guests. The Great Hall was
decorated with charmlights and illusion charms and early
flowers. There was a surprising abundance of irises, but
peeking out between the larger and demanding petals, Leo
could see narcissus blooms, snowdrops, columbines, prim-
roses, even a few bleeding hearts. He frowned, considering
the combination.

He didn't think either Ursula or Uncle Garin would care
much about the language of flowers. He was staring up at
it, lost in thought, when Ursula came by and whispered in
his ear. "Uncle Garin likes his garden to be practical. And I
wanted him to feel at home with it."

It was enough of a clue. All of those could be poisonous
or toxic - the thing that had been chasing around inside

Leo's head was the cautions for handling them. But they also all had alchemical uses. Several, in the case of the iris, the snowdrop, and the primrose. They did look well together, purples that went with Fox House and the upholstery in the Great Hall. There were also whites that popped out against the dark wood, a bit of yellow gesturing at the growing strength of the sun.

Right. He could go back to thinking about other things, having solved the puzzle of the flowers. December's solstice had been full of other firsts. Ursula had joined Uncle Garin in the presentations and she'd danced with him when the dancing opened. Mostly, she'd circulated through the gathering afterwards - and the week of parties that followed - talking to dozens of people every evening. She'd also enjoyed it, and Leo was glad someone took after Dad like that.

Leo didn't know how she did it, though. She looked entirely in her element here, making sure everyone felt like they'd had something special from her. It was a bit like Mum when she was teaching, but also entirely different. And it was certainly continents away from what Leo felt he could do. Even allowing for Ursula being nearly five years older, it wasn't enough of an explanation.

He hadn't felt like she was that different before. But now she was. Now she was confident and certain and shining, and it suited her very well. But people were going to expect him to be able to do that now, weren't they? And he didn't have a clue how to. He didn't want to, either. That was the thing. If he'd wanted to, he'd probably be able to figure it out.

Leo was standing there when Dad came up and patted his shoulder. "If you want to go up to our rooms, you can. We'll be a bit yet. Your mum's got her teeth into a conversation." Mum was over chatting with a couple of people. Leo thought they were a set she usually didn't have a chance to talk to. Dad patted him on the shoulder. "If you want company, there's the sitting room. If you're in your room, we won't bother you."

That was fair enough. They were only staying overnight. He hadn't brought a lot with him, but he always had a few books. That part of being part of his family, he entirely understood and was competent with. Leo paused to catch Ursula and let her know he was disappearing upstairs. They both looked at Uncle Garin, who had got pulled into conversation by Mum, and didn't interrupt him.

Five minutes later, Leo had discarded his formal clothing and changed into pyjamas and a dressing gown and slippers. He washed his face and found a book before settling into the sitting room in their family spaces. Someone had got the fire going, and Leo was grateful for that. Schola mostly wasn't chilly. Arundel often was well into May or even June.

He'd only been up there maybe ten minutes when there was a knock on the door. "Mind company?" That was Uncle Alexander, and that was a surprise. When Leo had come up, Uncle Alexander had been in the middle of a knot of people, laughing and chatting. Now he looked a little faded and definitely done for the night. He had a glass in his hand, what looked like brandy.

"Never, when it's yours." It was the truth. Leo would soak up every bit of time with Uncle Alexander he could. He hesitated, but he'd got braver about this sort of thing this year, saying what he saw when he was reasonably sure it was safe enough. "Are you all right? Can I fetch a potion or anything?" Arundel at least had exceptionally well-stocked potions cabinets in about six places.

Uncle Alexander shook his head, looking amused for a moment. "Nothing a potion will help, but thank you for thinking of it. Keep your feet up." He stared off into the fireplace for a long moment. "Your sister looks very much like your mutual grandmother, allowing for entirely different hair colour and about five years." He considered. "Well, and remarkably different fashions."

"Grand-mère Laudine." Because Ursula looked like Grandmum, too, Mum's Mum, but not in any of the ways Uncle Alexander meant. Of course, Leo had only ever seen pictures of Grand-mère Laudine, both photographs and the two formal portraits that hung in the hallways. He hadn't really thought about that for Uncle Alexander. Of course he'd known them, though Leo had to frown, trying to figure out the numbers.

"You're trying to do the maths. I was seven when they got married, Laudine and Dagobert. Nine and a half when Garin was born. A proper adult when your father was. Though I didn't meet him for seven months, I didn't get back to Albion until then."

Leo nodded slowly. "And so it's odd to see Ursula. It was odd for me too. Different reasons, but still odd."

"Do you want to talk about yours?" Of course, Uncle Alexander wouldn't invite talking about his own, but he'd actually nudged the conversational door ajar. Leo would have to be a fool not to take the chance.

"Can I ask about Grand-mère Laudine? And Grand-père Dagobert? Dad doesn't talk much about them." Leo tucked a foot under his other thigh and looked hopeful.

Uncle Alexander let out a sigh. "I suppose it's a night for that. A new generation. May Ursula be far happier here. I think she might actually stand a chance, if she keeps going as she is. There's a different feel to the place." He lifted his glass, making it a proper toast and blessing, before he shrugged. "You know the basics of it."

"You came here with your mother and brother before you were even born. Two months?" Uncle Alexander nodded, and Leo went on. "And you grew up in the gate-house, across the courtyard, and then sometimes in Trellech."

"After my father was killed, Ummi came here. My father's family had connections to the Fortiers, ancestral ones. Vauquelin was a distant cousin. Though he and Papa had got on, from what I was told later. At any rate, they were sufficiently obliged to take us in. As a client family, though that's fallen out of favour since. You understand that, yes?"

"Dad did cover it, yes." It had not been an explanation Dad had been comfortable making, and Leo had consulted the library and then Ursula afterwards to make sure he understood. The whole thing about client families had been all about power, in complex social maths, and only a little about obligations.

"They fed her, housed her - us. They made sure we had a Healer on hand, reasonable comforts. But once she recovered, she was put to work to benefit the extended connections. By the time Garin was born, she'd built up her own consulting work, separate from the family, and we were living in Trellech a fair bit of the time. But we also had the gatehouse, and we were expected back here for the various gatherings and parties and obligations. It made a show, the people who supported the Fortiers in all the ways we did. Phillip was working on his apprenticeship with her, then, too."

Leo nodded slowly. "So you knew Grand-mère and Grand-père when they were young. What were they like?"

"She was a decade younger than he was. It was an arranged match, though they weren't unhappy, I think." Uncle Alexander tapped his fingers together. "He had a mistress, much of their earlier marriage, it was common for the family, but they also enjoyed their time together."

"And?" Leo leaned forward, hopefully.

"Clovis, your great-uncle, he was a more visible personality, shall we say? He and Maylis were a better matched pair in some ways, they fit well politically. But I think Laudine and Dagobert were on average happier, at least after—" Uncle Alexander broke off abruptly. "Different, but more content." He tapped his fingers together. "I've thought, for a while, that Laudine would have intimidated your mother to bits, but if they got past that, they'd have ended up close. Laudine had a sharp sense of humour and an excellent memory. She got along quite well with Ummi, all in all, but at least half of that was that she showed Ummi proper deference. Ummi was a generation older, of course. Between Laudine and your great-grandmother."

Leo had to mentally trace the family trees in his head now. "Great-grandmother Chrodechildis." It was an awfully long name to sort out, though Uncle Alexander's mother was just as bad in an entirely different language.

"I am glad your parents did not continue that naming tradition, honestly. Good, honest, sensible Latin animal names. You've something to live up to, but not Merovingian heroes and queens. And they're quite manageable to spell." Uncle Alexander took a sip of his glass again. "I liked her. Your grandmother. Even after Ummi and Phillip died and I didn't know about a lot of things. I got along with your grandfather, too, but I didn't always like him."

"Uncle Alexander, are you drunk?" It came out before

Leo could think better of it. But none of this was like Uncle Alexander, admitting things like that.

It did make him laugh and set the glass down. "A little unmoored. I suppose that's the thing about coming to the equinox. You pay attention this year, you've started to have enough ritual training to feel it. I feel weightless, like the world could go in any direction all of a sudden. Usually I don't make anyone else deal with that sort of mood. It seems unkind."

Leo considered that. "Is that why the Council rites are at the solstices, when there's a lot more weight on one end? Not the equinoxes?" It was the first thing that popped into his head.

Something in it made Uncle Alexander relax, suddenly. "It's a theory. It is curious, isn't it? And it's not tied to the founding of the Council. Except inasmuch as that was November, originally, and so the next of the four of them would be a solstice, and perhaps that set the pattern. It's an excellent question, though. Cyrus challenged for his seat on the autumn equinox, and I've wondered for decades if that made a difference, somehow. He's always been able to dance away from the weight of things when he's needed to. The magician's illusion."

Leo nodded. It seemed the thing to do, here and now. "You have a reading list?" he asked after a moment.

"Oh, I always have a reading list. And yes, I'll share it and get you started with it." Uncle Alexander waved a hand. "Anyway. This has been an empty house, in a particular way, for a very long time. I worry about whether it will be too much for Ursula, but at the same time, she might be exactly what's needed. Or be able to be, without bending too far from who she properly is." He shrugged. "I'm keeping an eye out to lend a hand. So are your parents, so are other people. Did you think she had her eye on anyone tonight? As a particular friend or anything like that?"

Leo grimaced. "Marrying, you mean? Ugh, I don't want to think about that." Not for him, not for her. Though he knew people gossiped about it. "I'm pretty sure she was working on setting up Olive, and what's his name? The younger of the Bryce brothers."

"Neville. His older brother is Anthony. Huh. That'd be an interesting match, actually, especially if they take to each other. I wonder what made her think of it. I'll have to ask her in the morning. Well spotted." Uncle Alexander now looked pleasantly distracted. That meant the chance to ask more about the Fortier grandparents had almost certainly passed, but that was a bit more than Leo had expected to get.

Before he could think of anything else, there was a noise from the hall, and Mum and Dad were coming in, shrugging off the more formal bits of clothing. Mum dropped a kiss on the top of Leo's head. "I'm going to change, love. Pour me a drink, please? I need to see about getting the charms renewed on these shoes before the next party."

From there, it devolved into agreeable chatter, more about the rest of the spring hols rather than this particular party. Mum and Dad clearly wanted to talk to Ursula a bit more first, before deciding what they felt about it themselves.

CHAPTER 30
ROS ON MARCH 21ST

Ros looked up. She'd settled into the library with a book. Papa, Mama, Uncle Alexander, and Edmund were all still busy with sweeping the house from top to bottom. Ros had started with them at dawn, but she had claimed a bit of sofa around ten in the morning. It didn't need her getting in the way, especially in the box rooms and tighter spaces. Merry had gone off somewhere, probably also with a book. "Aunt Laura. Morning!"

Aunt Laura was not a morning person. She and Mama were very alike in some ways - at least if you looked past the clothing they preferred or chose - but that was a way they were decidedly different. She and Uncle Martin had turned up last night, as they tried to do for the smaller and more private seasonal celebrations. "Morning. Is there coffee?"

"Urn on the table outside." Uncle Alexander half lived on it some days, and several other people in the house liked it. Including, more recently, Edmund. He'd acquired a taste for it the last two years. Ros still felt it was unbearably bitter for her liking. And it wasn't as if she could get either sugar or cream to mute that with the rationing.

Aunt Laura disappeared into the hallway, coming back in a minute or two later with a cup of the stuff and a saucer. She settled on the sofa facing Ros. "It's been a bit. How are you doing, then?" Aunt Laura had been busy over winter hols. Or Uncle Martin had been busy. Ros wasn't entirely sure of the balances there. Uncle Martin worked for the Trellech Moon as one of their senior reporters. And Aunt Laura helped people who'd been seriously ill figure out what made sense for them now. She'd go and stay with them for a few weeks, maybe two months, and sort out what food and clothing and furniture suited.

She knew how to do that because she'd had to do it for herself, not just once, when she'd recovered from tuberculosis when she was younger. But she'd had to figure things out again when she moved in with Uncle Martin. Only it might not have been work that kept them busy, or not the bits that paid them money. That part was, admittedly, a bit abstract to Ros yet.

The other thing that kept Uncle Martin busy was that he was one of the Dwellers at the Forge. As secret societies went, they weren't very. It was rare to go a month without them energetically supporting a strike or leading a protest or loudly explaining what was needed to fix something dire. They were often right about it - Papa and Uncle Alexander both said so. When she'd asked Papa about it a few years ago, he'd rubbed his face, and said there were a lot of ways to change the world. He'd gone on to say that he did some of them, and the Dwellers did things other ways, and the world probably needed both. Though he was also grateful they didn't focus on him too much.

Now - with all the conversations about the secret societies this year - Ros considered the question a bit more. Bringing up Schola with Aunt Laura was something all of them were cautious about. Aunt Laura had been in Seal House, but she'd been ill a lot of her third year - with TB, it turned out - and left school then. It wasn't like she could go back and do it over later. On the other hand, she knew about the Dwellers. And given both Uncle Martin and his best friend, Galen, had been in the Dwellers from the time they were at school, she might know useful things about what they were up to.

That had been bothering Ros a lot, actually. She'd heard rumours about all the other societies, one way or another, and no one knew what the Dwellers were up to. Or, specifically, who they were interested in. Even looking back a year or two hadn't helped a lot, though Avigail had a theory that the war had affected that, like so many other things. And the Dwellers didn't just take people at Schola, and not just when people were school age. They brought in adults. Galen's wife, for one, she was a newspaper journalist, like Uncle Martin.

Aunt Laura snorted agreeably. "You got stuck in your thoughts. I know that expression. Out with it, what are you chewing on so hard?"

"It's about Schola. And the secret societies, mostly." Ros said it cautiously.

Aunt Laura waved a hand. "Go on, ask away, if you've questions." She considered. "None of them invited me when I was a second year. It doesn't sting like it used to. I wasn't ready for it then. And while I like the Dwellers quite well now, I don't want to commit to that, and not be able to follow through on doing my part. I am cheerfully supportive, occasionally bail Martin out when required, and enjoy their parties quite a bit."

Ros contemplated that. "We were curious about, um. How the Dwellers pick? When people are at school." She wriggled her fingers. "I got an invite from Animus Mundi. I'm still not sure about that."

"Huh." Aunt Laura considered, then rummaged in her shoulder bag, pulling out her journal. "Let's see if we can get Martin here. He's far better able to talk about that. What's the concern with Animus Mundi?"

"For one thing, I think they're ignoring Leo, and I don't like that. Or making assumptions about what Leo wants, which is maybe worse. And I don't want to be there without him, if one of us," Ros added quickly. "I mean, not like that, the way a lot of people would think, ugh."

"I promise I will not make any comments about anyone your age pairing up. I know how your parents feel about it, anyway. None of that till you're ready. At which point I consider it my auntly duty to chat and gossip about whatever has now become relevant. Clothes, cosmetics, family intrigues, though honestly, Lizzie's almost always much better informed about those."

Ros gathered her somewhat battered dignity. "If it ever becomes relevant, I promise to let you know." There, that was nicely framed, and all right, it wasn't that she was lousy at Ritual or thought it useless. She just didn't want to do it like that.

Before she had to figure out anything else to say, there was a slight rap on the door, and Uncle Martin's voice. "You called?"

"Come in, love." Uncle Martin did, without a hesitation, settling down on the sofa next to Aunt Laura and sliding his arm around her shoulders. They were a great deal more informal, overall, than Mama and Papa and Uncle Alexander, but that made sense. They spent a lot of time with people who also were. No, that wasn't quite right. They spent a lot of time with people who saw Mama and Papa and Uncle Alexander's formality as something potentially dangerous. That thought was going to keep her busy for a long time tonight. Fortunately, Aunt Laura picked up the explanation. "Ros was curious about the secret societies, and how they choose people when they're at school."

"Without being rude enough to expect things you can't tell me, of course, Uncle Martin." Ros felt it was important to say that. He understood it. He wasn't stupid or careless or any of those things. But saying it meant he knew she understood it too.

Uncle Martin waved a hand, acknowledging it. "Time for that conversation, isn't it?" He grinned. "Your brother and sister asked too, though they haven't told me what they did with it. No reason any of you should."

Ros nodded. That was more or less what she'd expected - and more or less what she knew, too. Leo was fairly sure that Edmund wasn't in Dius Fidius, from what he'd got out of Ursula, but that didn't actually help that much. And she hadn't wanted to ask if he was in Animus Mundi, though that seemed plausible. "We've been talking about it. My friends. Obviously."

"I had no idea what they were thinking when they picked me. I wasn't impressive, not at that age. Scrawny and all elbows and nervous I was going to say the wrong thing to the wrong person and they were going to send me home. And then the Dwellers saw something, and it changed everything for me. Not just Galen, though that's a big part of it. Knowing there was someone with me, alongside me, who cared what happened to me. Like you and your friends, already. You don't need a society for that."

Ros hadn't really thought of it quite like that, not in

those words, but it immediately made her feel better. "So in that case, what I want is for whatever we choose not to get in the way of us being friends. Keeping an eye out."

"Exactly. And the world's different for you. A different war than the one I grew up in." He'd been just too young to fight in the Great War. He'd left school the year after. That was different than Papa or Uncle Alexander, or any of their parents. Even Avigail's Papa, where it was a little more complicated. But he'd served - with distinction, but he didn't talk about it - in this war. "So, my first advice to you is whatever else happens, don't lose that. Friends are too precious. Got it?"

Ros nodded, solemnly. It was good advice, but hearing it said out loud by a grownup gave more weight to what she wanted to do, anyway. "And the rest of it?"

"The thing about being part of the societies is that then you get to look ahead, who to invite in the later years. I'm sure the societies are all different. What I can tell you about the Dwellers is that it's not so much about what you've already done, but what you have the potential to do. And specifically, what being part of the Dwellers might let you do more of." He considered for a moment, one of those rapid-fire calculations she was used to seeing from Papa and Uncle Alexander, not from Aunt Laura or Uncle Martin. "With you and your friends, that might be what the Dwellers could do for you that you couldn't do on your own, nearly as well. Possibly better. I don't know remotely what you all get up to."

He made it come out easily, like a joke, but Ros heard the shift there. She had to smile, though. "Plenty we don't necessarily tell the adults about. Not enough hours in the day, for one thing, to do it and then tell about it." That made him laugh, suddenly. "Not much getting into trouble, though. I mean, there's Leo. He doesn't like to worry his father."

That made Uncle Martin tilt his head. "Oh, I hadn't really thought about that. Huh. Yeah, he'd think about what's dangerous and what's fun differently, wouldn't he? And the rest of you all, because you listen to what you know, together. I'd noticed that much."

Ros had no idea what to say to that, so she didn't say anything. First rule of getting stuck in the deep end of a conversation: stop struggling and float. It worked for swimming; it worked for talking. After a moment, Uncle Martin went on. "The other part of it, of course, is what you could bring to that society. With the Dwellers, it's not that we won't take people with similar interests. Gods know we have enough alchemists with an eye on things that explode to put the lie to that. But we do want some variation in skills and lines of thought. All that."

"Even if you also run to journalists. And so on." Aunt Laura put that in, amused.

"We also serve who report the news accurately and with the emphasis in the necessary places," Uncle Martin said, laughing. "Does that help a bit, Ros? I wouldn't want to be part of a society that only wanted me in a narrow way. And I wouldn't want to be part of one where I couldn't offer them anything worth having. A lot of places can do one, but not the other. And in some cases, it's who you're doing it with that matters."

"You and Uncle Galen." She gave him the courtesy title here, as she often did for adults with that sort of connection.

Uncle Martin grinned, teeth showing. "We make each other much better. And now, Lydia and Laura improve that, improve the range of better we can aspire to. That's the way it ought to work. Narrowing's a fine thing if it's actually refining your skills, making you an expert in something. But it's not much good if it limits what you can do overall."

"But you're not all journalists and alchemists, are you?" Ros had been chewing on that part. "I mean, some of you are more public than others."

"If you're going to effectively change the world, it helps a lot to have people in different places. Not as many in the Guard as might be - it gets a little tricky with the Guard oaths for some to want to balance. And enough of the Guard is not exactly fond of the problems we can create in a good cause." Uncle Martin rubbed his face. "Which they're not entirely wrong about."

"But other parts of the Ministry?" Ros was chewing on that.

"Other parts of the Ministry. And if you're considering diplomacy, well, there's a place where a little understanding of the broader scope can do a lot of good." Uncle Martin shrugged, considering. "Most other parts of the Ministry, though some of them are very private."

Ros was definitely going to think about that one more. "And the schools?"

"And the schools." Uncle Martin grinned, suddenly. "All five of them, so you think about that a little. And of course, a number of crafters and researchers and so on. We're not a huge society. I'm fairly sure Many Are The Waters is actually larger, and Four Metals certainly is. But we get around."

Before Ros could ask anything else, Uncle Alexander's voice cut through from the music room. They must have made it to the ground floor, which meant they'd be in the workrooms and ritual room for a while now. "Depends how we're defining our terms, Martin, doesn't it?" He stuck his head in through the music room door. "Ros, we could use an extra pair of hands from someone nimble enough to get under the tables, if you don't mind?"

Ros immediately bobbed upright. "Thank you, Uncle Martin, Aunt Laura. See you for lunch?"

They laughed and waved her off, and Ros went off to go make herself useful. Edmund could have done it, but first he was a bit high on his dignity still. Second, it probably meant Papa had something to show him about the ritual parts which involved not having his head under a table. Tables were generally lamentably opaque.

CHAPTER 31
JASPER ON MARCH 21ST

"So. What's the problem being, then?"

Jasper started, almost dropping the pot he was buffing by the sink. The pot wouldn't have taken much damage from it, but his toe might have.

He'd been helping Stan since first thing that morning. His older brother had moved into the family cottage last fall. Jasper had spent all last summer working alongside Stan and the crafters Lord Carillon had hired to help. They'd taken down one wall, extending the cottage so there was space for two more bedrooms, plus the loft up above the sitting room, where Dad had slept as a kid. And they'd added a bathing room and proper indoor plumbing for the loo. It had been just about done when Jasper went to school, minus the last of the painting, but that meant this was the first spring Stan was here. And that mattered a lot.

And Jasper had wanted to lend a hand. Dad was busy with the stable yard and would be for a bit yet, though judging by the sun through the window, he could turn up any time. Jasper had come down here. The stable had plenty of people to help. They'd been cleaning and polishing and sweeping out all day, shifting from task to task. Jasper took one more look out the window, but Dad wasn't coming down the path, so Jasper had to come up with some sort of answer.

Jasper took a breath. "What do you think it is?"

His brother snorted. "You're in your second year. You were awful quiet about it over solstice, I have my guesses. Societies and all that."

There was nothing for it but nodding. He didn't want to lie to Stan, even if he could get away with it, which he probably couldn't. To be honest, he felt more than a bit of hero worship for his big brother. Certainly loads of respect. Stan had finished school at Snap, gone off to fight, and come home. Which made them all terribly relieved, Dad most of all.

Dad had lost all three of his brothers to the Great War, and had done his own time in the trenches. Mum had been careful to explain to all of them that Dad wasn't always aware of the places that caught him by surprise. Jasper swallowed. "I got an invite. I don't know what to do about it."

"Did you, now?" Stan's voice went even and agreeable, and Jasper frowned suddenly. Jasper flicked his fingers. "Before you ask, I wasn't invited to the Society of the White Horse. Not then. Might be down the road, who knows? But I hear a whisper here or there, and Dad knows some people who know some things. You know how it is."

"Forest wisdom." Jasper agreed. Dad had the Horseman's Word, which wasn't the same thing as the societies, but wasn't entirely different, either. And if Stan didn't yet, he would soon enough. And Dad had been in and out of a group doing magical work in the New Forest during most of the war. It had been hard to miss when Jasper was living at home. He usually knew when Mum and Dad were about and when they weren't. As he'd got older, roughly how far.

"Eyah." Stan shrugged. "Put the kettle on, would you, if it's cleaned? We could use another cuppa. What about your friends? You needn't tell me their private things. That's not friendly."

Jasper considered, turning to fill the kettle and set it on the hob. "All three of the ones you know have invites. Different societies, you can probably guess a couple of them. I dunno. Ros is sure Peter's got an invitation too but he's right canny about not talking about things he doesn't want a body to know about. Ros and Avigail aren't sure about theirs, Leo really doesn't want his, and I honestly don't know. I'm curious, but curious seems a real bad reason to make that kind of binding oath."

Stan threw his head back and laughed. "There's that, there's that. But you ended up at Schola and not Snap or Alethorpe for a reason, don't you think?"

"Have days where I don't think of much else outside my classes," Jasper said, turning back to face his brother. "That doesn't mean I have any answers."

"Don't have a lot myself. But there's something in you that could do well with Schola. The way they teach. Now, I'll praise Snap up and down, from sunrise to sunset and beyond. You already have the seasons and the rhythms in your blood, at least for here. You're grand with a horse, as good as I am, though you get there a little different. But you've also got more like Dad's range of power, and that's useful, that is, but only if you know what you can do with it and what you can't."

It was something they all knew and never really talked about. Dad had tremendous raw magic at his disposal. When he'd come back after the Great War, it had been barely trained. Lord Carillon had helped him get that training. Dad used it to, well, mend roads and fish ponies and people out of bogs, and shore up riverbanks that were about to collapse. That didn't help Jasper's decisions much. He wanted to be useful, to do things that made the Forest better, but that was a vast sort of question, much bigger than any one person's magic.

Jasper swallowed now. "Do you mind?" It came out before he could think about it, and besides, this was Stan.

"No. Never. For one thing, you're my little brother. Got to keep me on my toes, right? Means I need to know as much as I can about how to use what I have, and how to use it well. And that's settling in. Not that I'd put Plue and Fort out of work." They were Dad's main assistants. They'd been with him since Jasper was a tiny kid. But Dad was training up Stan for eventually, and everyone knew it.

"And the forest rights here." Jasper gestured. The family held all eight rights, not that many did anymore, and Stan could graze livestock, turn his ponies out, harvest yew. All of that.

"I got some good branches for materia work last autumn. And we'll be starting the livestock here this year, just been waiting for the weather to be a little more steady." Stan tilted his head. "You don't have a knack for weather witching, do you? That'd be right handy if you were deft."

"Risky, too." Getting weather witching wrong was a grand way to have a blight or a drought, and the land couldn't take that, not right now. None of it could, between the bombing, the horrific winter that had given way to flooding through the Thames valley and elsewhere, and whatever else might happen. "No one's talked about it much. I could ask in class, though, Professor Morwen's encouraged me to ask her things about Incantation."

"And she treats you right?" There was Stan, all protective brother.

"Not the sort of thing you solve with fighting or shoulders. Or even a friendly darts competition." Stan had an excellent eye for it, which he said was a good way to make friends in pubs as you travelled. "She does. Professor Hammond, too, in Music. Even if he keeps hoping I'll go out for more singing."

"Nothing wrong with a voice," Stan said. "Might be a way to give a bit of a boost, the working songs. You think about that when you think about what you want to do with yourself. What'd it mean if you could share out your magic with a few dozen people working?"

It was a mode Jasper hadn't really thought in, though he'd seen it often enough. There'd be a group getting together to build a new cottage or mend an old one, rethatch a tithe barn, bring in the bounty of the fields in one go. "I'll ask about it. And Schola grows a lot of their own food, these days." He could think about that, they'd be getting ready for planting. Professor Wain must know who to talk to, maybe he could offer to lend a hand, if Professor Hammond or Professor Morwen could help him with what to do.

"There you go." Stan startled for a moment at a shout from outside, then called, loud enough to carry. "Come in, Dad."

Their Dad was a moment or two more, but he pushed open the door without knocking first. "Ah, it looks proper. We're all set up at Ytene. Everything tended. Well, all my bits, I gather Lord Carillon is being his usual exceedingly thorough self about the work, and driving the household staff up a wall. But it's one day a year, we'll all cope." Dad grinned. "Ah, cuppa? And then we can have a go at the thatch."

Jasper took the hint, and went and poured water into the waiting pot. He set it in the centre of the dark wood table to steep, then settled in the chair again. "Stan had an idea about what to try with music. Working songs, giving a boost with vitality. I don't know how to, but I'm sure Professor Hammond won't mind if I ask."

"That's a fine thing." Dad beamed, proud. "Both of you. And it's good to see you here, the both of you." His eyes flicked up to the loft. "Can I ask you to do the climbing today, Jasper? I think you're old enough, and you're probably more nimble than either of us."

"Also," Stan said, amused. "I'm better with a quick catch charm than he is. I use it more."

Dad laughed. "That too. I brought down my Mum's notes, and the runes, and the makings for the charms." He hesitated for a moment. "When I was your age, Stan, I didn't know them. I had her Book, but it was only a sketch of the thing, you've seen that."

Stan focused immediately on what Dad was saying. "And then you learned a bit more?"

"Mmhmm. When his lordship arranged for me to apprentice for the horses, for two winters, doing the training, he found me a couple, the Shipleys. He'd trained up horses for the estate for years. They'd both lived there near all their lives. The East Riding, that was, not too far from the coast and Hornsea. The thatching up there's different from how we do it here. I didn't even know that when I started. Theirs was ridged with turf, though they also used long straw, like we do here. Different design to the spars." Dad waved a hand. "But the missus, she could teach me the runes, what Mum had meant. Not all of them she knew, but she sat with me, night after night, by their fire and helped me work it out. Enough to get it back."

"That's a kindness." Stan spoke very softly. "Did you stay in touch?"

"Letters, aye. And your Mum and I went up to visit them when Anna was just barely toddling. They both passed, a year or so after that, and they were a long way from a portal, so hard to get to. Remind me, tonight, I'll bring out their letters. We have a few other things." Dad shrugged. "Anyway, by then I wasn't living here, and they do need feeding. So last summer, we carved them into the plaster as we built out, and today we'll be, Missus Shipley said it was about breathing life into them. I think you should both get the trick of it quick enough."

Stan reached over to pour the tea into cups. "I've been wanting it all winter. Knowing there was a thing, and it wasn't time yet."

"That's a thing I never had to teach you, either of you. The timing of it. Not rushing beforetime. It's one of the great gifts, understanding that. You can learn plenty of other things, but that one, not so much." Dad shook his head. "Takes a certain skill not to get ahead of where you ought to be, or hang back."

Jasper felt the brush of that, something potent in the saying of it that he didn't understand. He knew himself to be more likely to wait too long rather than rush ahead, and he should probably figure out how to stop doing that so much. Dad must have caught something in his expression. "It's not something you're supposed to have perfect now. But we'll work on it. And today's a good start. There's making the runes, placing them, breathing them alive, and settling them. All the steps. And then we'll see what it's like to have the cottage proper again."

Stan hesitated, but only for a second. "Does you good to see it, Dad? Even with the hard?"

"Does me very good. I didn't know if I ever would. Living at Ytene, it's only a mile and a half or so, but it's a very long mile. Not the same as being here." But of course, he had to be handy for the foaling, and for whatever else came up. And the cottage for the head of the stables was quite a lot bigger and more comfortable, even without the additional space for Mum's looms. Dad reached out to pat Stan's arm. "It's good you're here, and the place is alive." Then he reached for his cup and drank a good third of it, clearly enjoying the silence before they got to work.

CHAPTER 32
AVIGAIL ON MARCH 23RD

Avigail was not enjoying herself. To be fair to her family, no one expected her to. This was a necessary challenge, to be got through as efficiently as possible, for long-term benefits. Once she was through this Sunday afternoon, she'd have nearly an entire week without outside expectations. Of course, a fair bit of that was bribery, so she'd be patient today. No one had bothered to hide it. They'd laid out the choices with a grin.

Papa had promised her the chance to come help investigate something. Aunt Charlotte had invited her for an afternoon in Uncle Lewis's lab. She was old enough now he could start thinking about putting together a perfume that was just for her. Though this would be just the first steps of it, getting to smell all sorts of things and learn more about them. Mama had promised her a trip somewhere interesting by portal, and Mama was picking where, which meant it would be. Not that Papa didn't pick interesting places too, but Mama's were usually interesting for reasons Avigail hadn't thought about yet.

Aunt Doyle had even offered to have Avigail tag along for the day next week, which was a rare treat. Papa was collaborative, perhaps to excess, always wanting to chat while he was doing things, unless it absolutely needed concentration. Aunt Doyle preferred quiet observation, followed by precise action. But she apparently had a bit of a project that could use an extra pair of hands, and she'd asked for Avigail's help especially.

It might just take all that bribery to get through today, though. The Albion Inheritance was one of those society organisations that - like Dius Fidius - talked a great deal about all the good they were doing, and did very little. The fundraising, honestly, was the most useful thing they did.

Ten years ago, Avigail would never have been considered for membership. Grandmama and Aunt Charlotte had gone through the changes in the bylaws with her, because that was actually interesting. It was, as Aunt Charlotte said, an excellent example of a resistant and stodgy organisation being forced to bend to reality. As with so many other things, this problem could be traced back to the Great War. And in particular, to one of those knock-on effects no one ever wanted to talk about, but that mattered a lot.

About twenty years ago, someone in the Albion Inheritance - Aunt Charlotte didn't actually know who - had looked at the birth announcements of the Great Families, and realised they were going to have a problem. Every death in the Great War - and every man who came back, unwilling or unable to marry - mattered a lot to those specific people. But it also mattered to the larger community.

Some people had also fallen in love during the War, with nurses, or other people they met while recovering, but from decidedly un-posh families. They'd tossed aside the expectations about who they'd marry for dozens of reasons. Others just hadn't married, for all sorts of reasons, lots of them rather sad. Even if Avigail didn't want anyone to mention marriage near her for years on a personal level, people ought to get to.

What it meant was that there were a lot fewer children in Albion who descended from the Great Families on both sides. Ros did. Ros's Mama was also a member of the Albion Inheritance, though apparently she'd had a hard time her first few years, because her father's family wasn't nearly so notable. But Avigail wouldn't have qualified a decade ago. Neither would Ursula and Leo. And yet, there was Ursula, across the room, looking immensely grownup. It wasn't just that she'd put her hair up in some fancy way that took at least four hands as well as charms, it was how she was moving.

The newer bylaws made allowances. One parent and two grandparents had to come from the Great Families. Notable contributions by the other parent to the well-being of Albion counted quite a lot. Of course, that was an immensely political argument, the sort Ros could follow and Avigail spent counting knots in the nearest available woodwork to keep from screaming when it came up nearby. Or possibly analysing the places magical disruption might happen and what could be done about it, because Papa had quite an influence on how she got distracted now. At any rate, Leo's Mum and Avigail's Mama counted as notable. No one was actually arguing much about them. Other people's parents didn't.

Ros nudged her lightly with one elbow. "Do you want me to take the tray around to them this time?"

There were certainly a lot of people who had not

adjusted to current standards, despite the Second World War, the Blitz, rationing, and whatever else had come their way. There were three tables, out of perhaps fifteen, who refused to acknowledge Avigail's presence. It made an interesting puzzle, how to do the task she'd been assigned when none of them would cooperate.

Avigail and Ros were, as befitted girls their age, there to fetch and carry for the afternoon. They were being examined closely to see if they suited for future membership. If they did, they'd get an invitation to be a junior member in their fourth or fifth year, maybe the summer after. They'd spend a few years at that, before whatever it was that meant they were full members.

Now, she considered. Ros would deal with those tables handily, of course. Avigail wouldn't lose her temper, she knew better than that. And she knew a couple of people at those tables were the sort that - well, their husbands were in Dius Fidius, and their brothers and their sons. They didn't know what to do with people who wouldn't touch that with a siege weapon.

It was Papa's fault she was thinking about how to break sieges, actually, she'd have to tell him. He and Orion had been tossing around stories a few nights ago, of historical battles and the different ways they might have gone if people had done different things. She considered her options. "Let me see what happens. You come and do the one next to me. You can step in if needed. And then I'll do the other three. They're much nicer."

Ros grimaced, hissing under her breath. "You're not supposed to actually say it like that." Then she straightened up. "Mistress Mortimer, we were just going to take the tea trays around."

"There you go, girls. Do it smartly, of course, and mind

your manners." Mistress Mortimer was one of those families with members on both sides back to the dawn of the Albion Inheritance. Both her mother and grandmother had held key roles on nearly every committee over the years. She wasn't horrible to deal with, just she assumed all the girls serving were at least slightly dim and needed reminding of everything. Avigail didn't need the reminders, her memory wasn't the problem here. Nor were her manners, so long as other people remembered theirs. People so often didn't.

Ros picked up her tray, and Avigail got hers. They were not terribly well balanced, they'd been set out by people who didn't have to carry them, and Avigail noticed that kind of thing. They made their way up the side of the room, and Ros went first to one of her assigned tables. Avigail found a position where she was absolutely in line of the women who were chattering and waited for any sort of opening.

They refused to give her one. She stepped sideways, once, then the other way, then went back to standing still. About the point Ros was coming back, already done with her tables, one of the women looked up, making a show of it. "Oh. You should have said something. We didn't notice you there."

Avigail kept a smile on her face. "I didn't want to interrupt, of course. Tea?"

"Oh, it will be all water, I'm sure. It's so difficult these days, one still can't get tea for love or money." Avigail actually knew some of why. Mama had had a letter from one of her cousins. There was a strike on the docks in Calcutta, and that was slowing everything down. Grandpapa had mentioned there was talk about needing to adjust the ration as a result. Less tea for everyone, then. She held her tongue, refraining from pointing out that she was in sympathy with the striking dockworkers. And she likely would have been even if she didn't know Mama's Papa might have been one of them in a slightly different world.

"I gather Mistress Mortimer went to special lengths for today, ma'am. May I offer you some?" There was a little fuss as she went around the table, offering cups. No cream and sugar. Rationing wouldn't stretch that far, but there were thin wedges of lemon on the tables. Those were a touch easier to justify. Enough people in these circles had orangeries to cover for any black market imports, so long as they weren't ostentatious about the amounts.

It wasn't until she got round to the last of the women that one of them put a hand on her arm. "Whose girl are you, then?"

As if they didn't know. "I'm Avigail Edgarton, Mistress." Avigail said it smoothly, then considered what to say next. She could pull out Papa's name, but that was rather gauche. Aunt Charlotte and Grandmama were across the room. "My grandmother and aunt are here today, there." She nodded slightly. "Lady Edgarton and Mistress Wright." Technically, Aunt Charlotte could use Magistra as an expert in her field, but she didn't.

"And your mother's people, dear?" That was a different woman, one who kept her nails polished and long enough she must have had someone help her put on those silk stockings, speaking of obvious ostentation in several directions.

"My mother is a Portal Keeper. She's still quite busy, all of them are, with tending to the portals so everyone can come and go as we all need to." The smile was becoming a bit gruelling.

"And what House are you in at school? I know your dear

grandmother - we're such good friends, darling Alysoun - so enjoyed her time in Fox." That was an out-and-out lie, because if this had been one of Grandmama's friends, Avigail would have known her. Grandmama didn't entertain in these social circles often, for a number of reasons, but anyone who was actually a friend met the family. Or, more likely, got pulled in by the extended family and circle of friends, like Mama had been.

"Salmon, ma'am, like my father." All right, she couldn't quite resist. "He's rather pleased I'm taking a bit after him. I want to make both my parents proud, of course." There, there was absolutely nothing overtly offensive in that trio of sentences, but half the table pulled back, provoked into an audibly unsettled gasp.

Ros chose that moment to step in. "May I help you with the last tables, Avigail? Oh, good afternoon, Mistress Harris."

"Ah!" The most recent questioner - Avigail was grateful for the name. She could ask Ros for the forename later. "A delight to see you. And you're in Fox House, like your dear father, I know."

Ros bit her lip. Avigail knew she did, because she knew that expression. All Ros said - Ros was better at this than Avigail, by yards - was, "I'll pass along your good wishes, of course. I'm afraid we really must keep going. Dame Whitlaw wants to start the speeches any minute. I do hope you enjoy the rest of the afternoon." Because of course that was wrong too, Ros's father had been in Owl, like Avigail's cousin Daphne. He thought it was funny that people forgot.

Thus freed from the immediate problem, Avigail held the tray while Ros went around and served the other two difficult tables. No one said anything this time. Though that was in large part because anyone with sense could see

Dame Whitlaw fussing with papers at the podium and giving meaningful looks at anyone who might hold up the proceedings.

Once they took the empty trays back, they were permitted to sit in the far corner on uncomfortable chairs and listen. The actual talk was something that didn't interest either of them much - a discourse on half a dozen notable families. As Grandmama had said, it avoided all the scandals, or, for that matter, any sense of the parties discussed having more of a personality than a porcelain doll. Once the presentation got going, Ros shifted her fingers, concentrating hard, and then the sound around them was muffled.

"That's a new one?" Avigail kept her voice quiet. She didn't want to press the limits of the enchantment.

"Ursula helped me, Tuesday. She's a good teacher, turns out. And patient." Ros didn't look at her. They had to keep up the appearance of attention. Fortunately, Grandmama had got a copy of the speech in advance, so they knew what it said and could ask about relevant points if questioned later. "You really did push things. But if anyone asks, I'll repeat just what you said."

Avigail shrugged. "They did ask. And she really was - well. Which Harris is that?"

"Delen, nee Gordon. Her cousin Alcemene has brassier hair, but they look a lot alike otherwise." Ros kept her voice not only quiet but unhurried. That description really wasn't terribly helpful unless she saw them together, but it would do. "Misplaced her husband? I think, ask Mama sometime?" Then Ros let out a breath. "It could have been worse?"

"It could. And it will give Grandmama a laugh, to know she has such dear friends she had no idea about." Avigail held still, rather than shaking her head. "Would your parents let you come over after? You can hear all the debriefing."

"I'd love that." Honestly, Ros would get a lot more out of it than Avigail did, and it was good to share with friends.

FLORALIA TERM

CHAPTER 33
LEO ON APRIL 7TH

L eo slid into his usual chair in his usual seat in the library with only a slight wince. Today's duelling practice had gone hard. Not harder than Leo had expected. He'd guessed correctly that Dad wanted to push them. But he was going to be achy tomorrow, even with liniment and a soak when he could.

It had been an unusually long equinox hols this year, because of where Easter fell. And while a number of people at Schola weren't Christian, and didn't particularly focus on the date, about half of them did. Either they or their families celebrated, or they were in communities that did. Leo had had two solid weeks of doing a lot of reading that wasn't directly for classes. Also, a fair bit of time working through rituals with Uncle Alexander and sometimes with Ros as well, and a lot of time staring out the window at the rain.

Schola had been spared actual flooding, unlike the Thames valley. It helped that everything flowed downhill from the centre spine of the island, as Mum put it, to the cliffs and the ocean below. But they'd had four bits of cliff collapse, and people were still checking to see what was sound. And Dad had been worried enough about Schola herself that they hadn't moved to the Essex house for hols. They'd stayed at Schola other than the two nights at Arundel for the equinox proper and Ursula's party. That bit, Leo didn't mind at all.

It had also just plain been raining, and no one wanted to be out in it if they didn't have to. It was the sort of chilly damp that got under clothes and into one's skin far too quickly. Leo had done as many of the outdoor chores as he could to spare the adults with more aches. But that had meant a lot of chickens and dodging the goats. Now, it was good to settle back into school and a schedule.

Mostly good. He'd had a thing between duelling and supper. He'd been rushing to get into the Great Hall through the side door from Bear. One of the fifth years hadn't quite stopped him. But there'd been a pointed comment about ticking clocks and needing to make a show of things that did his father proud. It had left Leo cranky, all supper, though he'd been eating with his House, and no one had bothered him. Bears did not prod cranky Bears. It was one of the things Leo found particularly comfortable.

Now Leo's head came up when he heard footsteps coming all the way down to their usual spot near the end of the library shelves. There was something a little odd in the rhythm. A moment later Jasper slid into his own chair, not masking the wince he made as he sat. Leo should have considered his words, but he wasn't Ros. Or even Avigail. "You're hurt. Was it Phipps and Heckle and them?" He brought up the charm to muffle sound as he did, automatically.

Jasper flushed, rather dark red, to go with his hair. He

didn't look up, staring at a spot on the table. "Keep your voice down."

"Charmed. You're hurt. Do you need Matron?" There was a list in the back of Leo's head of all the things that could have gone wrong. All the things that people didn't notice fast enough, especially if they didn't know about them.

There was another flinch. "It'll be a thing, if I do."

"It'll be a thing if you don't." Leo swallowed. What he wanted to do - what was sensible to do - was to walk Jasper down there. Now, without any hesitation. And he knew that wasn't right, either. Even if it was sensible. This wasn't something he could ask Mum or Dad about either, not unless Jasper said it was all right, because again, then it would be a thing.

Jasper shrugged. "I'll mend. Had worse falling off a horse."

"You also know all the ways that goes badly. You hit your head?" Jasper shook his head, and that let Leo get enough of a look at his eyes. They were clear enough, and the pupils were the same size. "Kidneys?" Another shake of the head. And honestly, the fact Jasper was moving his head that freely was at least a good sign. "Joints?"

"I'm going to hate having knees tomorrow. Probably for the rest of the week. Good thing we don't have a pavo match Saturday." Jasper sucked in a breath. "If I go to the infirmary, they'll ask questions. Can I wait until tomorrow? If something hurts more, I'll go, promise. I just don't, I can't deal with the fussing tonight."

It would have to do. Leo nodded. "Promise. And come round with me before curfew, I've got a good bruise salve. And a container you can have." He hesitated. "What'd they do?"

"I was late coming in for supper. They got me off to the side, not the offices. And besides, everyone had gone in to eat." Jasper shrugged, then obviously thought better of that movement. That likely meant they'd been aiming for places the bruising wouldn't show.

"So they meant to. Not just taking an opportunity. This the first time they've hurt you that badly?" Leo wanted to make it stop, with a slow fury that he didn't know how to explain. Again, he couldn't talk to Dad. And while he was a lot better than any one of them at duelling or fighting, he probably wasn't better than all of them together, not by himself. If he told Theo Lefton or Avigail, well, they'd help but it'd be obvious. And that got back to not telling Dad. Not that fighting would actually solve anything, that was just a stupid fantasy.

Jasper carefully leaned over and started pulling things out of his bag. Then he stopped, before he silently held out something that definitely did not belong there. That was a fair bit of nice silver, for one thing. It looked like it might have been a spoon once, the sort of metal that got reused as a charm anchor.

Before either of them could say anything, they heard Avigail and Ros coming along, and apparently Peter, Leo heard his voice, quieter. The good part - well, one of many good parts - about playing pavo together is that they all had a certain number of informative one-handed gestures at their disposal. Not quite actual sign language, but enough to convey 'there's a problem'. At the same time, he dropped the muffling charm, because it'd look wrong if people didn't overhear some of the opening.

Ros and Avigail slid into the chairs next to Jasper and Leo, then Peter took the one on the other side of Leo, looking puzzled. Leo held his finger to his mouth, instead just saying. "Hey, we were wondering where you'd got to." No number, no names. Avigail held out her hands for the object. She'd produced a silk handkerchief from nowhere. Jasper handed it over silently, while Ros bantered back and forth with Leo about how he'd bolted his food. Honestly, some people liked avoiding indigestion.

It took Avigail a little, peering at the object, before she took out something from her bag. She dropped the bent bit of silver in a silk pouch, then folded the pouch several times, completely blocking the thing inside from light or presumably sound. Then she glanced at Ros, who pulled out her book and made sure no one could overhear them. Avigail's voice was very even. "They're not doing very well at classes, are they? But that's a nasty little thing. Where'd it come from?"

"Someone slipped it in my bag today. I'm sure it was today, because I had everything cleaned out last night." Jasper hesitated. "Phipps and all. Five of them."

Ros snorted. "Figures." Then she frowned. "That wasn't all they did. Jasper, you promised."

"Let me sleep on it, all right? Who to tell. How." Ros was a force of nature. But Jasper was as stubborn as an ancient oak in a bog. Even Ros couldn't get far with that when he put his mind to it. Then Jasper added. "Don't know what set them off today."

To Leo's surprise, it was Peter who spoke up cautiously. "Daphne - Avigail's cousin, that one - told me that Lowenna Ritt had been at a party with Phipps and Heckle over hols. Not one of the parties Daphne likes, one of the ones they were making nice at for her father's business?"

"Or Aunt Charlotte's plotting." Avigail said, pausing

from her frowning at the spoon to snort. "Both in that case. I think. Though mostly Uncle Lewis, if Daph was there. Ritt hadn't made trouble for you, Jasper?"

"Not since they all got charmed to stay away from me in the autumn," Jasper said. He'd entirely avoided them, which wasn't actually hard. They liked the other end of the library, they were in entirely other houses, and of course they'd not go anywhere near the stables.

Ros reached over to tap his hand. "So she got other people to do her dirty work. Not that she had to talk them into it much, I expect. Idiots. You need to tell someone, Jasper. You know I'll ask tomorrow who you told. And if you want me - or any of us, right?" Everyone nodded. "To come with you, you just have to say who."

Jasper nodded, then gestured at the little pouch. "What's it supposed to do?" Leo was curious about that, too.

Avigail nudged it with a finger covered in silk. "If it worked right, which I'm dubious about, it would let them know where you were. And when you were on your own, or at least if there were other people nearby. Can I write Papa about it, details unspecified? He'll know how to undo it."

Jasper looked resigned. "Sure." Then he let out a breath. "How's everyone else?"

Ros and Avigail were fine. Avigail had come off better in the duelling than Leo had, fairly obviously, though she was visibly distracted by the badly done former spoon, she kept glaring at it. After they fell quiet, Leo said, "Heard someone making pointed comments about making a show of things, make Dad proud. It makes me want to do the other thing."

Ros snorted, then she got the sort of speculative expression that made Leo worry. "Peter, want to help me with something? Leo, can you find an excuse to go off and use your mysterious powers of knowing every secret of the school? Hide somewhere you can overhear, if you like. I want to aim at, mm. Getting some books from up near that knot of fifth years by the Alchemy shelves."

"Tell me what you're going to say first." Leo had an idea for where to go. There was space by the assistant librarian's desk where the sound charms brought everything together. He'd be well out of sight of the Alchemy section.

"Oh, I think some people should have some fundamental truths of the universe pointed out to them. Can I say you spend approximately all your spare time in the Ritual room? Study for half an hour, then find a reason to go be elsewhere, right? You'll hear when I'm done. Meet up and walk back to..."

Leo gave in to the inevitable. Ros had been stalled on one thing tonight. She had got the bit in her teeth about this one. And to be honest, Leo was curious what she had in mind. "Sure. And Bear. I've got some salve for Jasper."

"All sorts of uses." Ros pronounced it like a particular sort of benediction. They got through two thorny bits in their Materia homework together, and Leo was fairly sure that collaborating had been part of the point of the exercise. Then Ros let the privacy charm drop and Leo made a show of packing up his things, saying he needed to go work on an essay. He couldn't do that with them all chattering along. He had to try things out.

Five minutes later, he was tucked out of sight. He'd learned young how the stone and the wood and the charms made it very easy for the librarians to appear omniscient about what was going on around them. A few minutes after that, there were Ros and Peter coming along to look something up - one of the Alchemy books.

"Where did Leo go?" Peter had, perhaps, been

prompted. It came out a hair uncertain, but that could be for plenty of reasons.

"Oh, you know him. Off clearing his head now. Maybe in the Ritual room. It's so funny how some people don't even notice what's right under their noses with how much time he spends up there. He's always on about the differences between the Ritual room's structural underpinnings and the salle's. Over hols, he was reading something about how elevation makes a difference, or directly touching the bedrock. I wasn't actually following all of it."

"You, not following something? Pull the other one, Ros." That sounded a lot more like Peter at his best, teasing back.

She laughed. "Oh, he'd been doing extracurricular reading I haven't done. And we'd been busy all afternoon with other things." Leo wasn't sure how anyone else would take that, which worried him slightly. They'd been doing a ritual with Uncle Alexander, though admittedly one of the foundational Egyptian forms, not something common to Albion. And Ros was ahead of him there, still.

The two of them went off, chatting, gathered up the book they wanted, went back to their table. Leo slipped out by going the long way round the other end of the shelves and out the side door. Twenty minutes later - thankfully, it wasn't currently raining - the other four caught up with him outside of Bear. He was waiting in the little nook where the wall curved around to the tail of the former fourth curtain wall. No one was near them. It was too chilly out for that yet.

"Here. Put some on tonight, first thing in the morning, and lunch, if you haven't been to the Infirmary yet. You can't use it too long on the same spot, the caution's on the label. Does odd things to the skin." Leo held out the salve jar.

Jasper took it, then said, carefully. "Would you come talk to your Dad with me?"

"Always. Eleven? I know you're usually riding, but..." Leo hesitated.

"Probably not tomorrow, yeah. I'll let Master Held know first thing." Jasper hesitated. "What'll happen? Same as before, different?"

"Bit different, I bet, for a couple of reasons. This wasn't them being nasty in the moment, this was them setting it up. That's worse, several ways round. Dad will ask you some questions. And then he'll probably take it to the Headmistress. She can make them tell the truth, if she has to. And then I don't know. Depends how bad they hurt you, and what else they intend to do, probably."

"And, um. Consequences?" Jasper was shifting from foot to foot.

Leo honestly didn't know. Each case like this was different, he knew that. He'd heard Mum and Dad talking through a couple, not in detail, in the past. Were these people who were tangled up in their own stuff, and it was coming out in thorns and fists, but punishing them wouldn't actually help? Or was this something nasty, and punishment might be the only solution? "It could get them sent down for a year or forever. It could get them some sort of punishment. Could mean binding their magic out of class, but that wouldn't help with the physical much. There are compulsion charms that would keep them away from you, but those are a lot trickier when we've got classes together. Classrooms are only so big, right?"

"Oh." Jasper moved for a moment, grimaced as that hurt, then leaned back carefully against the stone of the wall.

Ros cleared her throat. "They had choices. They made

choices. Multiple times. Someone didn't teach them to be decent people yet. Punishing them now might not help that, but it'd keep them from trying it on someone else."

Leo could see that persuade Jasper. After a moment, Jasper just nodded. "Fine." Then he added, almost immediately. "Thanks for letting me decide how. Myself."

"We're your friends." Leo said, as clearly as he could. "We worry, right? But it's no good just telling you what to do. That's rude."

Something in that made Jasper smile, then he moved his shoulder and obviously regretted it, Leo could see the wince. "Yeah. And I just - I can't deal with telling people tonight. Tomorrow." Jasper then shut up, as if he was out of words.

When it was clear no one else was going to continue the previous conversation, Peter cleared his throat. "So why did you do things that way, Ros?"

Ros beamed. "Oh, that's why I asked Leo first. So much easier not to lie. Though if he'd actually gone up, he couldn't have overheard. You heard?" Leo nodded. She went on cheerfully. "At least three of them are in Dius Fidius, I'm almost sure. And I'm pretty sure one of them's in Animus Mundi, so it was a dual goal. Those are the best." Peter gaped slightly, and Ros laughed. "You can also learn how to do this. I'm sure of it. Right now, though, come work through the Alchemy with me for real, would you? And Leo?"

Leo grunted. "I'll walk you back, Jasper. You too, Avigail. No point giving away your skills if you don't actually have to."

As he expected, that was a good argument for Avigail, who hated other people doing for her, but who could see a tactical advantage at a good distance. They took their time about it. By the time he'd walked clockwise around the whole outside of the Keep and back to Bear, Leo was more than ready to buckle down to the rest of his prep.

CHAPTER 34
ROS ON APRIL 20TH AFTER THE BOHORT MATCH

Ros was not pleased with the state of the world on Sunday afternoon. Neither, it seemed, was anyone else. The bohort match had been ridiculously short, only an hour. Ros thought it had been an exceedingly clever match. Seal House had not only been skilled, they'd drawn on their comfort with each other and their individual skills that paid off in half a dozen ways. Ros would be thinking about that, the teamwork of it, for a long time, because that was much more interesting to her than the other details of the match.

Now, however, it was causing a problem for Ros. Most of Fox House was trailing back to their common room to drown their sorrows in something. Some had gone down to Schola village. Ros definitely didn't want to hear at least half the House opine on the unfairness of the match. If they didn't want to get trounced, they could play better. It was entirely logical and also correct. It was just the implementation that was a problem.

Now she was thinking like Avigail, and that was definitely a sign of something. Peter had peeled off to claim his spot in the library as soon as the match was a foregone conclusion. He was working on an essay, and that was no good for working together. Ros was, in fact, done with her prep, because she'd expected the match to be most of the afternoon, followed by celebrations in the evening getting all over everything.

Worse, if she went back to the House, there would be Phipps and Hector and a small Greek chorus of sympathetic girls who thought their ongoing punishments were entirely unreasonable. Ros knew a little of the truth of that, because Professor Fortier had told Jasper. The five who'd been directly involved had their magic bound, outside of the most basic personal charms and specific learning spaces. Perhaps more usefully, they had to stay at least ten feet from Jasper. They'd had to rearrange seating in four of their classes. It would stop when they could sufficiently and honestly explain to the Headmistress what they had done wrong. If they hadn't done it in a fortnight, that would likely take a lot of time.

It was useful to know which handful of first through third year girls Ros didn't need to spend time with, but she was fed up with the whole thing. Why couldn't people just be decent? It certainly made Ros wish Ursula were still around and a prefect. She'd have handled that part of it already. The current fifth years, while quite competent in their own arenas, couldn't bring the history of punishments and restrictions at Schola to bear in the same way.

Now, Ros stayed in her seat on the benches, watching people disperse. Leo was saying something to Susanna, passing on congratulations for Seal's team given the way he was energetically gesturing. Professor Fortier was cleaning up the equipment from the match, but he waved Leo off when Leo went over to see about helping. Avigail and

Jasper were on the far side, but there were more people taking their time going back to the Keep.

Ros shrugged and went over to talk to them. "What do we do with ourselves?" Ros asked. It was more abrupt than she wanted, but it would do.

Jasper groaned. "We could go for a ride, but the fields and half the roads are still too much mud." He was itching to be on horseback, as usual.

"The pubs in the village will be all about the match, let's not. It was great play, but I don't need to hear about it for hours," Avigail chimed in immediately.

Leo joined them part way through Avigail's comment. "What's up?"

"We're trying to decide what to do with ourselves. I'm done with my prep for tomorrow. I definitely don't want to go back to Fox and listen to the moaning. It's still too chilly to sit around outside, though walking would be fine." Ros shrugged. "Do you have any ideas?"

"Actually. Maybe." Leo paused, like he was gathering his thoughts for something complicated. "How do you feel about going down the north stairs and looking at something? Just at the shoreline, probably, but Dad hasn't had a chance. They only finished mending those stairs Thursday." Leo had an odd look on his face, one Ros didn't quite understand. At any other time, she'd have said it was something about ritual work, but that didn't make sense.

"Looking for what?" Avigail asked. "Animal, mineral, vegetable, magical?"

"That's the question. Look, I'll explain if we go, but there's something that might be there. Who knows? Not dangerous in itself, but maybe something that needs someone to come out and look at it. If Dad says we can, we could go at least do the first looking part." Leo was very earnest now.

Ros shrugged, glancing at the others. "Nothing complicated, right? No ropes and climbing harnesses?"

"Put on outdoor gear. I'll make sure we have the right kit. But no, nothing complicated." Leo glanced back over at his father. "Should I go ask?"

Honestly, it sounded a lot more interesting than whatever else they were going to come up with. Avigail grinned. "You know I'm already in. It's a puzzle. I like those. I can probably help. Especially if you tell me more."

Jasper snorted. "You're both very predictable. Sure. I'm in. Ros?"

"Me too. Room for Peter?" Leo nodded. "All right. Go ask. No point in changing if he says no." She waved a hand. Leo grinned and went striding off. Ros watched him for a moment. "He really wants this, whatever it is. Huh."

"Something about Schola itself?" Avigail suggested. "That's the sensible way to bet. How long do you need to change?"

"I'll have to get through the common room crowd, but maybe ten minutes? It won't take me long, I know where my trousers and boots are. I can pack up a few things." All four of them had a proper respect for being out for the day and needing the right things handy. Ros and Jasper were particularly so, given the range and depths and occasional dangers of the New Forest. Avigail wasn't nearly as used to bogs, and Leo barely at all.

It was only a minute or two later that Leo came back, grinning like his face was going to crack open. "We can go. Dad said we can ask the kitchen for a box meal to take with us. Ros, can you do that? They know you, and that you wouldn't lie about it, too. Then I can get the gear. Sunset's at nine, be back by eight, tell him when we get in. Come on, let's go change. We've got hours." Honestly, even without the rest of it, the break in the schedule sounded like a delight.

They split off to their respective Houses to change, planning to meet back by the salle. Avigail offered to go look for Peter, since Ros was getting the food. It took Ros a little longer, both getting through the crowd of cranky people in the common areas, and then to the kitchen. They already had some boxes made up - apparently they'd expected people to want to work through supper - and it was easy enough to get sandwiches and some well-stored apples.

Jasper and Avigail were waiting just inside, and Avigail gestured with her elbow at the storeroom, which had lights on and occasional noises. A couple of minutes later, Leo came out with a couple of well-packed shoulder bags, two larger and two smaller. "Look, so we all know what's there, and in case we need anything else."

Avigail said, "I looked for Peter, but he wasn't in any of the three likely places. Ros?"

"Not in his workroom, either, I did have a look. We can tell him about it later? And he's not so much for the open country, is he?" The four of them all had a lot more experience with it, even if Leo had the most with Schola herself.

Leo snorted at that, and the others all agreed that was true enough. Peter liked a library, he knew where he was in a library, even if his head was in three other places. The four of them, even Leo, enjoyed being outside a lot more.

Avigail took the other larger bag, going through it systematically. They seemed quite complete to Ros. There were a few lengths of rope. Her bag had a portable Healing kit with some potions she hoped never to need. Also it had the more ordinary sort of thing to splint a sprained ankle or put together a makeshift stretcher with some expanding poles. There were four lanterns, candles to go with them if they didn't want to do charmlights. "You sure it's all right to take these?"

"Yeah, I checked. This is the preferred protocol. Two really good Healer kits, the other two are more standard. Plenty of rope and lanterns and light. All of us can do a charmlight, too, I know that. Come on, then." Leo waited until the rest of them were out of the salle and did something with the warding. Ros could tell he did, but not what. He didn't talk again until they were halfway up the north road, toward the orchards and the stairs down. Finally, she asked, "Where are we going, then?"

Leo sucked in a breath. "Without getting into all of it right now, over winter hols last year, Dad showed me something. It sort of helps you figure out what's going on for Schola as a whole. The school, this whole end of the island, not so much the village? Though now I say that, I wonder why. Dad and Mum." He was sounding scattered. "Anyway, there's been an odd spot down on the north shoreline on and off for a bit, and it was back again last I looked, and..."

"And you wonder. And Professor Fortier thinks that's fine?" Ros didn't know why she was checking this, except that it was sensible.

"Mum also thinks it's fine. In general. Though I'm sure Dad let her know about this. And honestly, she's the more cautious one. For lots of reasons." Leo shrugged. "I've got my notebook for them. Ros and Avigail, you have journals. We are being sensible." Then he glanced back at

Jasper. "Mum said you'd asked about it, back in the autumn."

Jasper nodded. "I saw the merfolk out being very active, off the north coast. But I don't know what's ordinary, either?"

"Mum and Dad and Uncle Ibis and Susanna checked, and nothing unusual turned up. But now we can go have a look, so we might as well." Leo seemed very comfortable with the idea.

"I'm still not entirely sure if climbing down a cliff in April is entirely sensible." Ros said.

Avigail elbowed her. "A lot more sensible than in February! Or March. Leo, is that why no one checked?"

"That, and whatever it was that was sort of showing up kept disappearing? Dad thought it might be something washing up and then getting pulled back out depending on the tides. He showed me where there were U-Boats or other wrecks, the ones we know about, anyway. The Great War, too, it could be something that had been on the bottom for ages, and the storms moved it or something." He shrugged. "Anyway. Our task is to go have a look, see if there's anything obvious. Don't poke anything that looks like it might explode in any form. If we see the merfolk, I can talk to them enough to be getting on with. But I'm not that fluent?" Ros suspected this was Leo measuring himself against Professor Ward and Susanna, who were definitely fluent, but she didn't argue.

It didn't take too long for them to get to the top of the stairs on the north cliffs. Ros had only been up to the edge before. She'd always gone down to the sea level by the road that ran east, just north of the Keep. But it wasn't possible to get round to this bit of shoreline from there. There were rocks in the way even when the weather was better.

The staircase turned out to be both fairly solid, and to have some sturdy metal railings bolted into the rock face. "One hand on the rail," Leo said. "But don't rely on it too much? The stairs should be fine, though."

The stairs were in fact solid and even - someone had taken care to avoid spots where someone might slip. There were slight hollows in them, the sort that happened with lots of people going up and down. "How often do these even get used?" Then she hit the stretch that had been patched, and those weren't worn at all, and felt entirely different.

"Not that many people, but I don't know. A couple of dozen trips most years? Maybe twice that?" Leo considered. "That's a great question, actually. I'll ask Mum. She's done more of the research." Then he went quiet, to focus on something. "This is a curve, mind your feet, but it's not iced up."

Finally, they found themselves down at the base of the cliff; the stairs stretching up to the top. They were going to have to climb those again, the hard way, Ros realised. Probably when they were already tired. It wasn't as cold as she'd expected, though, given they were facing north with a lot of open sea on three sides. Ros shifted her weight to something more steady and waited for Leo to figure out what they were doing.

CHAPTER 35
JASPER ON THE SHORELINE

Now that he was down on the shoreline, Jasper wasn't sure about this. It wasn't that they were here, exactly, but that what was under his feet felt foreign in a way he didn't understand. He'd been down to the shoreline a couple of times as part of classes, but all the previous times, they'd had some other goal.

Their natural history class had been looking at plants, and of course being introduced - in general terms - to the merfolk who lived around Schola. They'd come down once as part of their Materia class, as part of identifying different stones. Or in the case of several of their class, not identifying, and thinking sea glass was a crystal of some kind. Professor Ward had been very gentle about the correction. Jasper had thought it was beautiful, though he'd known it had to be glass or something like it.

Now, he felt like he couldn't quite get his balance, and it was nagging at him. The ground under his feet was rough sand, sometimes pebbles, sometimes sand, sometimes larger rocks. Up ahead, it looked like a giant hand had picked up a handful of rocks and boulders and scattered them like seeds. Some were as big as his hands, some as big as his head.

Jasper looked up to find the other three had moved ahead a little, about ten feet. He adjusted the bag on his shoulder. He'd taken Avigail's bigger one when they got to the stairs. Jasper had better shoulders for it. Leo had the other, of course. The girls were every bit as capable, but if they wanted to carry them, they could take a turn later. He'd been glad to bring it down the stairs, where he had a bit more leverage to work with.

Once he caught up, Leo caught his eye. "All right?"

"Yeah, sure." It came out a little more grudging than Jasper really meant to. "Um. Not my native landscape, mostly? I don't know. What's the word?" He was trying to figure out what he'd been learning, and put it into use. It wasn't working here, and he didn't understand why.

"How to weigh the risks," Ros said, promptly, and it wasn't a question at all. "Me too, yeah? Leo, explain the risks, please. Now?"

Leo blinked several times. "You've had the lectures. I know you have. We all did. Last year and again this year."

"Those were more about avoiding swimming - not that we would in April. And probably not in July or August," Ros said. "And not annoying the merfolk."

"Now I think back on it, that was rather unspecific, actually. I mean, I assume one doesn't pitch things into their bit of ocean, which is all the ocean near here," Avigail agreed. "And no, we're not swimming."

"It's actually quite pleasant in the summer! If you're on the west beach, by the cottages. Less of a current there," Leo protested. Then he considered. "We're between high tides - the next one's not until ten tonight. But there can always be a wave that does the unexpected. If you get pulled out to the water, don't fight it, but try to swim back diagonal to the shore when you can. We probably won't see the merfolk here, but let them get on with whatever they're doing, really."

Avigail put her hands on her hips. "Can you talk to them? Properly?" Jasper couldn't quite make sense of why Avigail was pushing at it. There was a slight challenge there, somehow, and Jasper didn't know what.

Leo didn't pay it any bother. "I'm not as fluent as Susanna or Uncle Ibis. But I can get my point across. A fair bit of practical language, finger-spelling to fill in the gaps. It's slower, but it works." Leo considered, then signed three separate things. "This is 'student'. This one's 'help needed'. And this one is 'alert'. That's if there's a U-Boat, I mean, if there was, or there's some other danger they need to know about. But there are agreements about how they handle students. Mostly bring you to a beach where someone can get you, and there's a bell they can ring that will alert people in the Keep."

"There is? I've never heard it? And how was all of that sorted out?" Ros was now visibly distracted by the protocols, which at least reassured Jasper a little. If there had been anything serious to worry about, she'd still be fussing. She repeated the gestures, trying to get the shapes right, and Leo repeated them more slowly so all of them could get it.

"Uncle Ibis has a history. We can ask him when we get back. By which I mean I'll ask him and you can enjoy it." Leo grinned a little lopsidedly. "Avigail, can you do the thing that lets you figure out if there's something strongly magical down here? Oh, and if you've got books with you of any kind, you want to make sure they're well wrapped in oiled canvas and protected. I've got some if you need it."

Leo handed that round to Ros and Avigail, who both had journals, and wrapped one of his own, something smaller. Jasper stared out over the ocean, trying to make sense of it.

Leo was faster about it than the girls, and he came over to stand by Jasper. "Something bothering you?"

"I'm used to forests. I didn't realise how much this would be different, being down here. Or down here like this. I'm fine, just it's queer. Up there has trees, even if it also has meadows and fields and things." Jasper shrugged. He didn't remotely have language for what he was feeling. Maybe he'd figure out more later. "I sort of wish Peter was here. This is open ocean, but there's the thing he showed me about the Thames, last summer, the way the tides go. I don't understand tides properly."

"Let us know if it's a problem, right?" Then Leo turned back, holding his hands out for Avigail, who seemed to have produced a dozen bits and bobs out of various pockets. Jasper was never sure how she managed to have so many things hidden on her person. Now she had a couple of devices, a plumb bob on a chain, a compass of some sort, and half a dozen smooth stones in a wooden case. Leo held them agreeably, until she plucked out an aquamarine, peered at it, and then picked up a stone with a hole in it.

"Hagstone," she said, cheerfully. "Right. What do you know about where this thing might be, Leo?"

That took some back and forth, because apparently it wasn't as simple as knowing the details. But Leo said it could be anywhere along this stretch of beach, it might be underwater, and he didn't know what it was, just that there was something odd.

The next bit was, honestly, the sort of tedious thing that Ros and Leo liked. It had a lot of Ritual bits to it, doing the same thing over and over. Avigail didn't seem to mind. It left Jasper to look out over the ocean. It was different watching the waves from down here instead of up on the cliffs above. Most of them weren't very large, and they broke well out from the bit of beach they were standing on.

After multiple repetitions - one in each of the eight plausible direction points - Avigail pointed further down the beach. "That way. I'll need to try again when we're, let's see. About where those rocks are? Is there a cave or anything down here?"

"We're not supposed to go far into the caves. Ten feet's fine, more than that, Dad said no. We're not kitted out for caves," Leo said. "But that might be enough to get more direction for him."

"Are the caves unsafe, then? Unstable?" Ros asked. They had begun picking their way over the rocky beach. Now and then, one of them slipped slightly on a rock, and another would reach a hand out. Jasper was focusing on being steady. It was like walking on a boggy bit of ground, but of course not a bog proper.

Avigail snorted and answered before Leo could. "First principle of caves. Don't trust them. They're sneaky. We could probably get Papa to do the speech about it sometime over summer hols if we ask right. He's got a good twenty minutes on the treachery of caves, and that's if he's being brief." She ticked off on her fingers. "Getting lost, for one. No idea which way up or down really is, or whether you're going to be able to get back through a narrow bit. Cave ins and collapses and all that. Bad air, and that's a big actual risk. Getting stuck without food or water or people knowing where you are. That one, well, we've got journals, that's a help. Anyone sensible's respectful of caves."

That got the other three off into a discussion about something Leo had read about chthonic beings and offerings before descending into caves. Ros had come across an article about propitiatory something-or-others. Avigail added a bit about the variations in light charms, and why it wasn't possible to do a decent charm to keep good air around someone's head. Jasper let them chatter along.

Then, suddenly, when they were almost at the spur of rocks they were aiming for, Jasper felt something shift. He didn't know why he knew, but he knew it was bad. "Go. Run. Now." He got it out in a burst of air, before he grabbed Ros's arm in one hand and Avigail's in the other. He could feel his magic going out from his feet, keeping him upright and moving forward. He managed a glance at Leo to make sure Leo was keeping up.

They made it to a solid spur of rock, raised up perhaps five feet from the beach around them, and scrambled up on it. Not a second later, a huge wave crashed, soaking where they'd been to some depth. Jasper didn't know how to judge it, but he guessed three feet, maybe more. More than enough to pull them out into the ocean, probably far from shore. As the wave pulled back, the beach looked totally different, too, like something fundamental had changed about it.

All of them were breathing hard, between running and then the shock of it. Leo pulled himself together while Jasper was still gaping. "Well-spotted, Jasper. Everyone all right? No wrenched ankles? Any scrapes?" Everyone shook their heads. Leo looked out, back toward the stairs. "It's not, that's not." Something wasn't adding up for him.

Avigail said, "Oceans, also not trustworthy." She sucked in a breath. "I wish Rowena was here."

Something in that made sense to Leo, but not Ros. Or to Jasper, who swallowed. "Why?"

Avigail peered at him for a moment, then shrugged.

"She's very good with an ocean. That's hers to tell, though. I'm guessing you know, Leo?"

"I know plenty of things," Leo said, distracted. "Um. I'm going to carefully see what the going's like. I don't like the look of what that wave did." There was a bit of fuss, attaching a rope to him, and he left his bag up on the ledge they'd been standing on. Leo climbed down, carefully, but his foot sank into the ground, before he pulled it back.

"Wait a minute." Jasper pulled himself around to dangle his feet over the ledge on that side. "I might be able to help."

Leo twisted. Ros started chuckling. "Like a bog," she said, amiably. To the others, she said, "Jasper's Dad gets called out to help get people out of bogs, I don't know, once a fortnight? He's got really strong magic, and good for that."

"Dad showed me a bit. And your father, Ros. And Master Benton. I don't know if it'll work here?" He offered it hesitantly to Leo, who was the one who seemed to most have anything like a plan.

"Can you try to do a path, maybe four feet across, and steady?" Leo asked. "Here to, I don't know, twenty feet? That rock, maybe."

Jasper curled his fingers around the stone and then tried his best. He could feel the magic flowing through him, like it had at Ytene when he'd practised this, or helped Dad. But where that was effort, but eventually it filled up the space, this felt like it went on forever. It was like he was pouring cups of water out of the ocean into something else, and there was always more.

He fell into it, trying to find a handle that would let him make anything like progress. It was tempting, that's what Dad would say, compelling. Jasper knew it and did it anyway. He didn't know what the options were if they couldn't go back. Then, suddenly, Ros had something sharp, smelling salts, in front of his nose, and he completely lost his grip, coming up spluttering. "What's that for?!"

Ros was sitting next to him. He hadn't even noticed Leo come back onto the ledge. Avigail was on the other side, watching Jasper closely now, like a falcon watched things. Ros cleared her throat. "You got lost in it. That's no good. Leo came back, and we couldn't shake you out of it."

Leo added a beat later. "It helped a bit, but not enough to make it something we could trust all the way back. We'll figure something else out in a minute. Thanks for trying, though. How do you feel? Your magic, you, all of it?"

"Dunno." Jasper felt out of sorts now, grumpy and cranky, like someone had completely upended his sense of self. Leo considered him, then pulled one kit out of his bag. "Drink that. Restorative. Don't argue, just drink."

Leo didn't give commands often, but that one came out like he'd been taking lessons from Ros for the purpose. And Jasper generally did what Ros said. Mostly because what she said was sensible. He drained it in two swallows - the taste was faintly berry - and then suddenly felt a lot better. "Thanks."

"Seemed the thing. You let me know if you feel weird again like that, right?" Leo waited for Jasper's actual agreement, then went on. "We're going to have to figure out our options."

CHAPTER 36
AVIGAIL ON THE BEACH

Avigail let out a huff of breath. "Right. So we need to make some decisions. The first one is about how we decide together." Papa had told her this part. So had Aunt Witt and Aunt Mason and Aunt Doyle, at various points. Often, it didn't matter what system got picked - the Penelopes tossed lots for it, a good half the time, in ways they couldn't manipulate. But they had to pick something.

Ros's chin came up. "Explain?" Ros, of course, was used to someone deciding, usually one of her parents if it wasn't something she could decide herself. Or Master Benton, the same way Avigail would pay attention if Master Frances or Mistress Mirth said to do something. Which was a sensible solution, except that none of those people were here, so they couldn't fall back on tradition and custom.

"If we don't know who's deciding or how we're deciding, we're going to get stuck. That's no good. Jasper was right to get us to run back there." Avigail gestured with her chin at the stretch of beach. "And we're decent at knowing what we know, all of us. But we're not so good with what we don't know."

Ros wrinkled her nose. "Uncle Alexander would dock points for your rhetoric. I think that's circular reasoning?"

"It's a truism. Not entirely useful, but there we are." Avigail glanced at the boys. "Do you have anything to add?"

"I thought I was sensibly staying quiet," Leo said. "You've got a good point. I don't have a good idea how to solve it fairly."

Jasper nodded along with that. "And we've just proved I don't know a beach or a seashore. Not the same as a bog." He rubbed the bridge of his nose, then added. "I'll be fine in a minute. It just feels really odd. Like there's an echo."

Avigail nodded. Not that this moved them closer to decisions, but at least no one was arguing with the idea. "So, how are we deciding things?"

Ros leaned back on one hand, considering. "Leo knows the territory best."

"But I don't know what Avigail knows. About how to find what we're looking for. My thought is to see if we can keep going up the beach. It's tricky, but there's another set of steps - not as nice - round to the northwest point. If we don't want to try for that, we'll have to let Dad know and get someone out with a rowboat or something."

"And you'd rather not bother him? Would he be upset if you didn't?" Avigail knew there were ways in which she was permitted - even encouraged - to explore things. And there was also a long list of things she was not supposed to do on her own. She was fairly sure that 'with my friends' didn't qualify for most of those, not yet. Not until they were all out of school, anyway. Rowena and Anthony got to do a lot more of them now.

Leo grimaced. "Rather not bother him if we can make

our own way home. But I don't want to take risks." He considered. "All right, if I'm the expert on the territory, I say that Avigail does one more look to see if we can track down what we're trying to find. Then we see if we can move to the northwest. If we can't, we write to Dad and get someone to come get us with a boat. And that as we move through different things, the person who's best at that is in charge. So while we're looking for things, it's Avigail. Along the beach, it's me. Like that. If we need some stone steadied, Jasper gets to decide how we go about it. And Ros, you take the lead to help us figure out how to do things if it's not any of those. Fair?"

"Fair." Avigail didn't have to think hard about that. "All right, let me see what direction we're going in. Or if the thing got pulled out to sea again or something." She rummaged for her tools again, setting them up this time on a bit of ledge and running a chain through the hagstone to use it more like a pendulum. The others didn't fuss at her, or make noise, not like some of her housemates did. That was what came from proper magical training from an early age, learning when to shut up.

She was actually rather surprised to feel a stronger tug, something definitive. It was angling in toward the cliff, as if whatever they were aiming for was against the foot of the cliff, or perhaps inside some cave. Avigail looked up. "That way, not terribly far?" she said. "It's a fairly powerful reaction, I think, though I admit, I don't have loads of experience with this?"

"All right," Leo said. "Let's see how the going is this side." He handed the end of the rope to Jasper again, since it was still around his waist. He climbed down carefully, testing one foot, then the other. "Which way, Avigail?"

She pointed, angling it properly, and Leo went that way.

He managed to stay on top of the larger stones without too much trouble. They were mostly flat, and they didn't seem to shift much at all as he put his weight on them. When he was maybe fifteen or twenty feet, he held up a hand. "I can see something here, a bit of wood. I think it's wood? It's buried in the sand."

"Should we come join you?" Avigail asked that, scanning around him. "It looks like you're steady."

"Yeah, sure. Take your time, one person on any given rock. I'll move over a bit, give you more room." A few minutes later, they were all in position in a circle around the thing, and Avigail could see exactly what he meant. There was a bit of wood that looked like it had broken off a crate or something. And it felt odd in her head. Itchy, that was a good word for it. Like it was a little blurry, looking through fog or something.

"Does it make your head feel odd? Scratchy?" She asked the question because hiding what she was feeling would be wrong. Then she squatted down to peer at it more. Leo raised an eyebrow and kneeled. Avigail felt squatting was a lot more sensible, but Mama had brought her up to that, and it was certainly easier on clothes in muddy or sandy ground. Leo's knees were his own lookout.

"Yeah. It does. Like it's hard to look at it? Ros, Jasper?" They both nodded.

Ros considered. "It feels a little like some of the warding Uncle Alexander's shown me? You too, I bet, Leo. But it's not actually warding, is it?"

"Maybe a distraction charm? There's nothing here to notice. Not invisibility, just blending in? But we haven't done those in class yet." Leo glanced at Avigail. "Or duelling. Dad was saving them for next year. The theoretical underpinning's a little knotty, he said."

"Also, I suppose it's the sort of thing you don't want to teach people until you're sure they're going to use it sensibly," Avigail said. She certainly had days she'd like to duck out on being noticed, especially if someone was asking her to do a chore she didn't like. If she actually knew how to, she'd have to spend more time fighting temptation than she really wanted. "Huh. Let me try something."

Papa had taught her a couple of the starting investigation charms, of course. Well, not of course. It's not like it was routine for most second years. But he'd taught her, and it was one of the things where no professor would be surprised at all. She took a breath, working on remembering how it went.

It had an incantation with it, but of course doing it with the incantation was limiting. Sometimes talking was a problem for dealing with situations. Papa could do it silently in about half a second. She had to remember the incantation - it was not very good Latin, actually - and then repeat it, and also hold the proper focus in her mind. For her, it was all about a light glowing, showing things that were hidden.

She also wasn't good enough to hide it from the others. Papa had said sometimes he wanted to show it to people he was working with. And sometimes he wanted not to, if there were people around who might be working against him. It was the sort of thing Papa said very matter-of-factly, even though logically. Though of course, the other reason someone mightn't want it to show was that it would break the Pact because there were non-magical folks around. Sometimes Papa had an admittedly skewed view of who was in the world nearby.

Now, though, it meant she didn't have to try to interpret it by herself. There was a brighter glow around the wood, but then there were little splatters of light leading off toward the edge of the stone. "Is that a cave or something? Could something be inside it?" she asked. "You're seeing that, right?"

"The glow on the wood, then the other spots. I think you're right. Maybe the spots are splinters? They're the right size and shape. Long and needle-like." Ros glanced at the others. "Should one of us look at it? Touch it? Me, I'm volunteering. Avigail and Leo are probably more use fixing things. And Jasper pulling me back if needed."

It was not an entirely sensible suggestion, but the situation didn't entirely permit sense at this point. Sense would have been going back up the stairs early on. And sensible choices didn't get to answers, often enough that Papa would not scold her too much for that. Probably. "Cautiously? One finger, don't grab it or anything."

Ros nodded, and when the other two didn't object, she took several steps to position herself on a rock nearest the wood. Jasper followed her, ready to grab her hand or her belt or whatever. When Ros leaned down to touch it, nothing happened. Maybe ten seconds later, all of them let out an audible sigh of relief. It was enough in unison that it set Avigail and Ros to laughing with the boys a beat later. Then Ros looked over - her angle was different. "I can see more wood in there. Can you make the charm keep going, Avigail?"

"I think so. Let us come join you. Stick right together, don't touch anything until we're all ready. Fair?"

"Fair." Ros said it evenly, with the boys again together a beat behind. They made their way along, following the splintered flashes of light. It was like something out of a prism, twisting in the wind. It had a mobile quality Avigail wanted to stare at for hours. Right at the cliff face, they found a slit in the rock, half-hidden behind another bit of stone, but it opened up almost immediately into something big enough to walk into.

Leo hesitated. "Caves are different. I mean, different rules."

"Should we not?" Avigail wanted to find out what was there. She could feel the pull on her, more strongly now, like something wanted her to find it. "I want to go in there."

Ros twisted around. "What sort of wanting?"

"Dunno." Now Avigail felt stubborn. Unreasonably stubborn, actually, not that it would stop her. Then she sucked in a breath. She had to do this right, she had to do the things that when she told Papa later, he might have improvements or suggestions, but the base was well-done. "I feel like it's pulling."

"Generally, the advice is to go the other way when that happens." Leo said it gently enough, but Avigail felt herself bristling. She made herself take a breath. She couldn't understand why she felt so worked up by this.

Leo might have seen some of the struggle, because he asked, even more cautiously. "Is it going to hurt you if we don't look a little more? More than if we do?"

"Unfair question." She got it out in a huff.

Ros turned fully to face her. "I think it's a very fair one. You're fighting something."

"I want to find whatever it is. It's tugging. I said that. I don't know how to say more than that." Avigail held her hands out, palm up. "I don't know what's going to help, but I don't like feeling like this."

Leo took a breath, as if measuring something. "Ten feet inside? Ros, Jasper, how do you feel about that? Only as far as we can see the light?"

Avigail felt something in that pull let up, hopefully. "Yeah. Like that. That's good."

There was a bit of faffing about with rope and marking in chalk on the side of the cave. Leo insisted on both until Avigail was shifting from foot to foot with impatience. Finally, they could go in, step by step, a rope running between them. Jasper was the last. He was maybe five feet inside, with Avigail able to see something just a little further down, a lump, maybe fifteen or twenty feet further on that was mostly shadow. Then there was a rumbling dangerous noise. Avigail felt like she was moving, then a crash shook the ground and all the light wasn't.

CHAPTER 37
LEO INSIDE THE CAVE

Leo shook his head, trying to clear it, then stopped. Dad had drilled him on what to do in an emergency, and the first thing was not to make it worse. He pushed himself up on one elbow. Leo couldn't tell if the world was spinning, because he couldn't see anything. He could at least tell which way was down - his hand was on cool stone - and therefore which way was up.

"No one move yet. Anyone hurt? Pinned? Say your names, so we know where everyone is." And so they'd know if someone didn't answer, and Leo was trying very hard not to think of that right now.

"Avigail. Ugh. I'm all right, I think. Give me a min." They should all be behind him, to his right. She was closest. That sounded right.

"Ros. Yeah, need a minute." There was the sound of someone moving. "Jasper?"

Further down the tunnel, Jasper's voice came, a bit more uncertain. "Here. Think I'm all right, but a stone hit me."

"All right." Leo knew keeping calm was the thing.

"Light first. Avigail, can you manage a charmlight? Other-wise, candle in the lantern?"

Avigail's voice came out of the dark. "Charmlight or candle. Let me find the lantern." Leo heard her moving, the sound of her bag, and then he set to work opening his up, working by feel to find his own lantern and call a charm-light. It took him three tries, but just about the point Avigail got a candle lit, he got the charmlight to stick for more than a moment. The thing about Avigail was that she had a bunch of the same training about the unexpected.

"Pass yours down to Ros, would you?" Once Avigail had done that, Leo got a better look. They were in a tunnel, comfortably large, further than the lantern cast light. Though of course, these were still set up to cast light on the ground, because of the blackout. He took a breath, cupping his hand, and calling another charmlight into his hand, so they could see more. The roof of the tunnel was a good eight feet. What had come down was near the entrance.

Leo considered. "I'm going to stand up, see about helping Jasper. Avigail, Ros, you stay where you are, so the light's steady and we know where you are. Avigail, how do you feel about the whatever?"

"It's, I can feel something a little further in? I'll stay here, though. It itches, but I can deal with itching." Avigail sounded a little uncertain at the beginning, but she was back to stubborn by the end. That would have to do. Leo pushed himself upright, taking a moment to make sure the world was still where he expected it to be. Then he took a step and another, pausing to hand Avigail the charmlight lantern, keeping the other light with him.

He went back past Ros - sitting cross-legged on the floor - to find Jasper still stretched out. There was a large bit of rock, the size of one of Mum's bigger mixing bowls, off beside his hip. "That's what hit you?"

"Maybe?" Jasper pushed up on his hand. "Let me sit up?"

Leo let him, kneeling down. "Let me see your eyes?" He worked through all the checks he'd learned, from Dad and from other people. "Do you feel like you're hurt?" The thing he was worried about - and he wasn't going to say anything about - was bleeding they couldn't see. He didn't know the charms for that. They were complicated.

"Bit bumped around. Nothing worse than a fall in the arena, even if it's rock? Which, now I say it, is odd. If there's bruise cream or something, I'll take that. Need a minute to get my bearings."

He could hear Ros, behind him, a bit plaintive. "I wish Peter were here, he looked up every possible charm for bruises after, um. Phipps and Heckle and all. I have notes, but I don't remember them enough."

Leo said, as gently as he could. "We'll figure it out." Though he sort of wished Peter were here too. And not just for a charm for bruises. There were a lot of submerged tunnels in London, Peter knew something about those, too.

He turned back to Jasper. "You tell me if anything feels different, even if it seems small, right? Immediately." Then he said. "I think we need to move down the tunnel when Jasper's ready. I don't know how stable this is. And we're not getting out that way. Moment, though, I need to do a charm or two."

First, he got a good look at the rockfall. He couldn't see any light coming through chinks in the rock at all, and that was a bad sign. He heard nothing creaking or moving, but Leo didn't trust it'd stay like that if they tried to move the rocks. Some chunks were huge, too, the size of half Leo's body, and he didn't know enough of the charms to make things lighter like that.

Which meant there was the other question, whether they could keep going the other way. The details for this were actually in the kit he was carrying, but then he realised. "Avigail, your father taught you the charm for checking for good air?"

It took her just a second to catch on. "Oh, cave, right. I can do it this end, you can go further up and do it? Do you still have the rope?"

The rope had held, without even jerking them around too much. Avigail tested the air by the collapse and pronounced it good. That gave Leo a chance to hear the charm, and run through it from the instructions, before trying it himself, which got him a clear green light. "Good here. All right. Jasper, you need a hand?"

"Nah. Just don't go fast yet."

Before Leo could move, Ros said, carefully, "Wait. Did it feel to the rest of you like something pushed us in here? Because I think we ended up further down the tunnel than we should have." She turned, visible in the charmlight, to gesture at the wall of rock behind them. "

"I felt it too." Avigail spoke up, closer to Leo. "Like something shoved me down the path, away from the rock. And Jasper, you got hit, but there's a good five or so feet between where you were and the cave-in. Maybe more."

Leo considered, then shifted to one side of the tunnel, pressing his hand against the stone. "Maybe Schola's helping us. Wouldn't be the first time. Thank you." He murmured one of the things Mum had taught him, an ancient Welsh phrase of appreciation. "We should keep going, though, see if we can get out or to somewhere safer."

They made a slow progression another ten feet or so

before they came across a box. The Box, all in capitals and ornamentation. It had a stencilled marking on it, long since faded by water, and it still looked soaking wet. It was mostly encased in the crate still, but enough had broken off that they could definitely see a box, a different and more elegant shape inside. Avigail was staring at it, hungrily. "It wants someone to do something with it, I think. I think it's the charm on it. Maybe it's supposed to get it safely somewhere?"

There were stories about this, things that would turn up in someone's pocket, getting passed along from person to person until they landed in the necessary place. Sometimes spies had used it, historically, though it was a slow and uncertain method of getting information somewhere. Leo swallowed. "Right. Ros. I think we need to figure out what we do next. Do you have your journal on you? You and Avigail? I've got the book that lets me write Mum and Dad."

"All three of us should write. What are we writing?" Ros's reply was prompt and remarkably even.

"That we were investigating something on the beach, with Dad's knowledge and permission, that there was a wave that made the way back, um, what's the word?" Leo's brain kept getting stuck on odd things.

"Impassable," Ros said. She was rummaging in her bag now. "So we came into the cave. There was a rockfall and we can't go back the way we came. And now here's the thing we'd been looking for, but we don't want to touch it without more instructions. Then can they get in touch with your Dad and Mum, and coordinate and tell us what to do?"

"Yeah." Leo swallowed. "And that we've got good air where we are. And food and water for a day or so, but we can't get out the way we came, and I don't know what's down here. Oh, and I'd rather not stay here. I don't know how much the tide might come in." There wasn't enough light to see if there were water marks, and he had no idea whether the new rockfall was anything like watertight. Probably not.

"Right. Avigail, you got yours? Right. Put the light there. Leo, you write to your parents. Jasper, you have something to drink." Ros was very take charge, and Leo was glad of it. She was being sensible. She wasn't snared by the crate like Avigail was, not that he could tell. Leo settled in to write to Mum and Dad, giving as much detail as he could about where they'd come in. He made a map sketch of where he thought they were and the crate. He was still writing long past when Avigail and Ros finished, finally looking up.

"That was a novel. Lots of details, then?" Ros said.

"I didn't know what Dad might need." Or Mum, honestly, Mum was more likely to look at some of it and have some sort of locational magic plan. He was fairly sure she could actually trace him, magically, without a lot of prep work, and it would take Dad a lot longer. But it wasn't the sort of thing he actually wanted to ask, even if it was Mum, and she would only use it if it really mattered.

CHAPTER 38
ROS, STILL IN THE CAVE

Once Ros tucked her pen back into the loop on her journal, she had to decide what to do next. She'd written to Mama and Papa, knowing both of them would likely notice the notification quickly, and to her sister Merry, too. Ros had also asked Merry to go find Professor Ward and Professor Fortier, and tell them that Leo was writing a note with more details. She'd said they were safe, everything was stable, but they needed help to get out.

Avigail must have written something equivalent, but Leo was taking longer. Of course, he'd know best about what might matter down here. Ros waited until he was done writing, then she cleared her throat. "You don't have a full journal?" It wasn't actually the important thing right now, but she wasn't sure she wanted to ask the important questions, like what they were going to do.

Leo leaned back against the stone wall of the tunnel. "It's one of those tricky political problems. If I have one, and other people in my House and year don't, it looks odd. So instead Mum got a set made up privately, when Ursula started school. That's just Mum and Dad and me and Ursula and Uncle Alexander." Then his mouth quirked up a little. "Also, and this is just for us, promise?"

Ros promised, and she heard Avigail and Jasper echo it, quietly.

"If I don't have a proper journal, Uncle Garin can't write things when he doesn't have any of the context. It makes my life much better, honestly, most of the time. If I make it through this year and he's not awful over the summer about whatever happens with the societies, maybe it'll be easier. But I do not need to wake up with Uncle Garin having been disapproving at length. Especially not with half a dozen quotes in Latin that mean six different things at once. Absolutely not first thing in the morning."

It was, admittedly, not a problem Ros had thoroughly considered from that angle, but she couldn't argue one bit with either the concern or the solution. "And really, the Schola mail runs what, four times a day?"

"Exactly. Any time I want to write to Uncle Seth or Uncle Golshan or Aunt Dilly or anyone else, it will get to them quickly enough." Leo shrugged. "And I don't have to stand out in my House, or worry people are going to try to get into it. This one's blood-locked, the entire set is, and you can't do that with the standard journals."

Oh, that was absolutely fascinating, and sometime Ros was going to have to ask more about that. She opened her mouth to do it, before realising they were getting distracted. "So, what do we do about the cave?"

"That's the question. Jasper, can you get a feel for things? Don't try to move anything, just, um. Is it going to stay a tunnel?" Leo glanced over.

Jasper grimaced. He'd settled with the rest of them, but he was still very quiet, and Ros was a little worried about him. Or rather, more worried about him. It was a growing sort of worry. Jasper shrugged slightly. "I can try. Easier than outside." He put his hands flat on the floor of the cave, one palm on either side of him, took a breath, and then let it out. "Think it's steady, but it might not be if anyone tries to move anything? I mean, without someone who knows how to do that."

"And we don't have people who know about mine collapses right at hand. Not even on the island," Leo said, as if he were running through a list of residents, which he probably was. "All right. We're not going anywhere yet, but I'll lay bets we end up going further down this tunnel."

Ros pursed her lips at that. "Why? What do you know about the tunnels and caves?"

Leo shrugged. "A little. Not a lot. Mum and Dad know more, but they won't talk about it, even with me. A lot of it was not to come down here by myself." He glanced around. "Which, while currently true, is not exactly what they meant. Dad's pretty sure these caves aren't actually particularly dangerous. Mum's tracked it over centuries. They're mostly stable. Which makes me worry about that, why it happened at all." He jerked his shoulder towards the former entrance. "Avigail, what do you know about the thing in the crate? What's left of the crate?"

"My logic says we shouldn't touch it. Certainly not without Papa consulting. The rest of me really wants to, though." Ros realised, suddenly, that Avigail was sitting on her hands. Avigail hunched over a little, her voice the sort of mock-firm that meant she was faking some of it.

"So now we hope no one's gone out away from their journals suddenly, and that they get the message promptly and all that," Ros said. She didn't like having to rely on people outside, not like that. Though it was a thing adults had to do a lot, she'd heard plenty of stories about it, and not just about the war, where it more or less made sense.

No one had anything to say to that, so there was a sort of awkward silence for a minute or two, then Leo started humming one of the songs they'd been learning in Music class as a concentration aid, and all four of them did that for a bit. It had interesting variations in the parts. Leo's voice wasn't quite steady - it cracked twice, and she was sure Leo was blushing a little. Jasper's was more solid, giving them a proper bass line to balance against.

In the middle of that, just when they were getting properly settled into the music, two chimes went off almost simultaneously, and five seconds later, the third. All three sets of adults, then. The singing stopped except for Jasper carrying it through to the end of the repeat, then fading out, while Ros, Avigail, and Leo looked at the messages.

Leo's was again the longest. Or at least Ros thought it was, Leo wasn't as fast a reader as she was, but pretty close. When he looked up, she raised an eyebrow, then asked. "What are we doing?"

"Further into the caves. Mum figured out where we are, and she gave me some directions." Leo looked back down again, considering the instructions. "Dad said your father had some comments, I guess, Avigail?"

Avigail swallowed. Ros could hear it. "He thinks we should bring it with us, but don't touch it directly, so do we have some rope and canvas or something to make a sling? If we can't lift it, that's a different problem. And not yet. He had a couple of things he wanted me to try first. I'll need someone to help, though. Ros? Leo?"

Ros blinked, then looked at Leo. Leo took a moment to answer. "What sort of charm is it? Is it a charm?"

"Charm. Four of them, they'll identify things? It's not

too different from what we were doing in Ritual a couple of weeks ago, or Incantation last term. I can show you." She held out her journal until Leo took it and read it. Twice. Then he handed the journal to Ros at Avigail's nod. Ros read through it, tracing her finger down just above the page. The tone of the whole thing was quite different from Mama's note. Both of them were utterly practical, but Avigail's Papa had written in brief little notes and annotations, most of which Ros could follow, but some she couldn't. The bulk of it, though, she could do.

"Maybe if I help you, and Leo does the warding? Something simple, but enough to avoid what we're doing bouncing out through the tunnels?" Ros suggested after a minute. "I know you can do it, Leo. Avigail told me about the duelling a few weeks ago."

Leo snorted. "No secrets between you two." He wasn't offended.

Ros glanced at Jasper, who just shrugged. "I can keep the rock above us from falling on our heads, I think."

"That seems like as good a plan as we're getting. All right. Let's try that, then, so we can tell Avigail's father what we find out." The charms themselves weren't entirely easy - she had to coordinate with Avigail. It got easier when Leo counted them in.

One charm made the whole thing light up with an eerie blue light, not like anything Ros had seen before. Another made the thing inside the crate sparkle with light, almost like a fireplace, but most of the light was blocked by the remaining bits of the crate. One made a sort of harmony. Ros's job was to hold what she was doing and not change her own pitch. That was a lot easier said than done, because she didn't entirely understand what her part of it was doing. They had to do that one twice to get it to work.

The last one was the easiest, Avigail had kept it for last, because when they were done, she sat down hurriedly. "That was a lot. Food and drink, everyone. Ros, you all right? Leo? Jasper?" The others seemed just as eager for a snack as Ros was. The charms had taken her breath for a moment. Avigail nodded as people got things out of their packs, but she wrote back in her journal first.

It wasn't until they'd eaten and then packed things away that Ros could ask the next thing. "What do we do?"

"Wait for Papa to figure out—" Before she could finish the sentence, her journal chimed again, and she read through it, twice. "Papa says it wants to get somewhere, so as long as we're moving in a - he says 'meaningful' direc-tion - we should be all right. And there's a note from your dad, Leo, saying we should follow the directions you got. We shouldn't touch the box with bare skin, and we should bring a piece of the crate, but not the whole thing."

"I brought the expandable poles and the stretcher set," Leo said. The others all blinked at him. He shrugged. "There are lots of things you might want a long pole for, and they're sturdy! It's not like the canvas takes up a lot of space, and it'd have done for sitting on the beach if we'd wanted to do that."

Ros had to admit there was some logic to it, and besides, it was going to be very handy now. First Leo got out the canvas and the poles - they threaded through loops on the long edges. "Assuming it's not too heavy, we should be all right. Jasper, you up for carrying one end if I take the other?"

Jasper nodded. "Sure."

"We'll trade off, as needed," Ros said firmly. "And we might need you to go up ahead a little."

The crate itself almost came apart when they used one

pole to poke at it carefully. By that point, Avigail had got protective gloves on, the ones that came up to her elbows. They were leather, Ros knew they were silk-lined, and they were made for this exact sort of situation. Well, not this exact one, probably the sea water and the cave weren't that common, especially in combination, but for handling things one didn't want to touch accidentally at all. Maybe she could get a proper explanation of how they were made sometime.

Once they were on, Avigail carefully pulled the wood away, revealing a small box, maybe six inches on a side and three high. There was some other padding in with it, but nothing looked that unusual. The box was metal, but it didn't seem tarnished at all, which was decidedly odd given the salt water. Leo considered the options and then folded the canvas of the stretcher in half.

It rather cleverly made a much smaller square they could use to carry things, with the loops alternating against each other, and giving a double strength to the canvas. Leo and Jasper set the stretcher down, Avigail carefully picked up the box and ceremonially put it on the stretcher, then added two pieces of wood. "That has a marking. And this one shows how it broke, recently. See how that's all new and fresh, not weathered at all?"

There was nothing to do but go onward.

CHAPTER 39
JASPER, DEEPER IN THE CAVES

Jasper felt honestly relatively useless. Leo knew a lot more about the caves - and also about the shore. It was still smarting that Jasper hadn't been able to help more. He hadn't even felt that the entrance of the cave was going to collapse. Ros had a much better sense of how to take charge of things. She didn't fumble it, like Jasper was sure he would. And the others listened to her, too. It wasn't just Jasper, who admittedly had been primed to that from when they were playing together on the nursery floor.

And Avigail was learning all sorts of things Jasper didn't even have names for. That was the difference between her father and Lord Carillon. Penelope Edgarton didn't hide what he knew. Lord Carillon did. And Avigail was learning not to hide it either. Not that she needed to with the three of them, but she didn't in general. That was something Jasper was going to have to think about a lot. Later.

They'd been slowly making their way through a tunnel that got larger as they went. The ceiling was beyond the light, though admittedly, the lanterns they were using had been designed for blackout conditions, and most all the light went to their feet. Whatever they were carrying wasn't terribly heavy. Jasper's hands ached a little from the stretcher's poles, but that was it. Nothing he hadn't felt hauling water or grain for horses. He could do this quite a lot longer.

The tunnel didn't wind back and forth, but it wasn't entirely straight, either. It had a naturalness to it, like the curve of a river or the paths made by ponies in the New Forest. It had a purpose; it had traditions and customs behind it, and it didn't matter that those things weren't made for Jasper. He could follow them.

Which was why it brought Jasper up short when Leo took a handful of steps into some new space and then stopped. As soon as Jasper could look around, he understood why. This wasn't a tunnel, this wasn't anything remotely like a tunnel. There were massive stone pillars, like the tallest trees in the New Forest. The pillars were the great oaks that were centuries old, massive at the base and soaring up to form the ceiling. In each archway, there was some hanging tapestry, and oh, Mum would be fascinated. Mum would want to study them forever.

They glimmered with colour. Those were the old colours, the ones that needed both plants and magic and the secret recipes of the dyers' guild to bring them to living vitality. From where they'd come in, he could see four of them, and there must be three more. Possibly ten more. He didn't know what might be hanging over where they stood. Jasper didn't dare twist round and look.

Ros peered up. "Can we go in?"

Leo nodded once. "Don't, I mean. Just the centre." His voice suddenly had a strain to it, the kind Jasper had learned to hear by spending time in the rehearsal spaces. All the rumble of the lower pitches was blocked up, like silt in a river. Ros frowned at him in the flickering light, but then she stepped out, moving into the centre of the space. Leo didn't move, just said, "Jasper, set it down on three?"

"Three, two, one, yes," Jasper replied. They knew how to count off. That didn't take negotiation. Once the stretcher was laid out on the ground, Jasper stepped over the poles. Avigail patted his arm, and then the three of them went to join Ros in the centre.

There were two rows of banners lining the long sides of the hall or cavern or whatever they were in. There was something up ahead, but it was far away and the light was dim there. Jasper couldn't see any of the details. It was almost like there was a fog that wasn't a fog.

The banners made more sense, at least in some ways. They were massive. Jasper started trying to count up how many hours they'd have taken to weave. That wasn't the earliest maths he'd learned - he'd learned to measure a horse's meal in parts first, that was fractions, more or less. But this had come second, how work translated into fabric, and at what size.

Those looked to be eight yards by five, give or take, maybe closer to four. It was hard to tell. The perspective was tricky, the banners were hung up high. And Jasper couldn't trust his eyes in the flickering of the charmlight. Wait. Not just the light from the lanterns. The cave itself was lit at this end, though he couldn't actually see where or how.

It made Jasper shake his head slightly before he went back to the maths. Done in wool, a single one of those panels would have taken five or six weavers eight months at least. That meant ten would be eighty months. Assuming that nothing went wrong, that the materials were available, that the dyes were, that none of the necessary crafters fell ill or died out of season. Just about seven years, six and two-thirds at best.

He was still stuck on that, the sheer amount of work for something no one saw, no one ever saw. Tapestry was destroyed by being around people - their breath, their touch, their meals. But it was meant to be touched. It was weaving, that was what weaving was for. Jasper couldn't make sense of it. And so he missed the first part of something that mattered more.

Ros had asked Leo something - she was turned toward him, leaning in. And Leo wasn't answering. Leo had, in fact, frozen the way horses did when there was some great threat, and they weren't sure which way to run or kick.

"Ros. Hold." It came out of Jasper louder than he'd meant to, certainly stronger and harder than he'd meant. But Ros had been trained to respond to that from her first steps. Both she and Avigail put their hands up and took a step or two back. Jasper eased around to the other side, letting Leo know he was there by little scuffs of his shoe on the ground. They echoed terrifyingly loud in the cavern. Once he could see Leo's face, he tried to figure out what was going on. He stared, hearing his heart pound in his chest and his ears like Leo's probably was. But Leo didn't move - he was barely blinking.

"Ros, what did you ask?" Jasper kept his voice quiet, and hoped she'd do the same.

"If he knew anything about this. And he started to answer, and." She sucked in a breath, letting it out before words came out in a rush. "I didn't mean to press, Leo."

There was a slight twitch. In a horse it'd have been one ear flicking, checking for danger from all the other directions besides the one he knew about. But Leo didn't move. Jasper considered, then stepped a little closer, holding out his hands, palms up. "Which way do we go, Leo? Can you show us that?"

For a moment, there was no movement. Jasper wasn't actually sure anyone was breathing. Then Leo gave a tiny nod, a jerk of his chin off to the left. "Then we'll go that way. Ros and Avigail, can you take the stretcher?" He kept holding out his hands to Leo, and after a moment, Leo put one hand in Jasper's. Jasper shifted around, so they could walk the same direction. There was a larger opening there, double the size they'd come through. Jasper took one last look over his shoulder, and then led Leo down into the tunnel, calling up a charmlight as he did.

When they were maybe twenty feet along, Leo finally seemed to come back to himself. He hesitated, and Jasper stopped immediately. "Need a drink?"

"I." Leo coughed. There was something complicated and hollow in it. "Sorry, Ros."

"I'm sorry for whatever I did. Which I don't think I can ask about, so I won't." In someone else, Ros's comment would have been light and flippant. This was Lord Carillon's flippancy, the kind that had layers of geological time under it. Master Benton had pointed that out to Jasper years ago, how the surface distracted from what was underneath. "What do we do now?"

"Keep going this way. Can't go the other." Leo's voice had the echo in it still, but then he shook his shoulders out. "Things that are private, okay? Silence-oathed."

Behind them, Avigail's voice said, "I'd more or less figured that out from evidence. You need a drink? Square of chocolate? I have some medicinal."

"Yeah." Leo shook his head. "It's. I hadn't come that close to it before." He said nothing about what fear he'd brushed against. People didn't. Maybe to their husband or wife, if they had both love and trust. Maybe one best friend. Probably not three. If Ros and Avigail knew each other's, it wouldn't surprise Jasper, but he didn't know Ros's. A moment later, Avigail passed forward a square of dark chocolate, then a flask of tea. They were the universal remedies. Once Leo had chewed and swallowed, he looked at Jasper, blinking. "How'd you know what to do?"

Jasper let out a puff of breath. "Horses. Body language isn't so different, yeah?"

It made Leo snort - not unlike a horse - so that was good. "Right." He hesitated. "You all right carrying for a little? I don't think we're very far now, but I'm not sure."

Before any of them could say anything, lights came up - soft charmlights, but still bright compared to the lanterns. Leo peered at it then gestured. "That way, I guess. Follow the light."

"You're sure?" Ros's voice was suddenly uncertain.

"Yeah." Suddenly, Leo was much more confident. "Keep the lantern lit, keep an eye on your feet. And your heads. But I think we're all right. Homeward bound."

It wasn't quick, whatever it was. The tunnels curved around, and at one point, Jasper was almost certain they'd looped under where they'd been a few minutes ago. But the lights kept shining ahead of them, dimming out behind them. The tunnels were big enough to move around in, that wasn't a problem. Finally, they came out in a cavern. There was space at the back, then something along the side that might be a firepit. Jasper barely had time to take in the light coming in that wasn't a charm before there were people in it.

Leo sprang forward, and his father was hugging him, laughing. "Ah, there you are. Everyone all right? We're right out on the shore, near to the east road. Short walk home.

We've Professor Ward here, and - oh, do set that down. A Penelope or two is coming to look at what you've brought back, though your father wasn't able to make it out yet, Avigail. Tomorrow, he thought. We'll make sure it's safe until then."

CHAPTER 40
AVIGAIL ON THE AFTERNOON OF
APRIL 21ST

It wasn't until five in the afternoon the next day that Avigail had a chance to talk to Ros again. And by then, it had already been a tremendously full day. They'd been bustled back to the infirmary to be checked over on Sunday night. Somehow, it was still almost light out when they got back.

Avigail had been honest about the odd effect the thing in the crate had on her. She'd ended up in a bedroom off the infirmary hall by herself until there could be more checks in the morning. Matron had brought her a solid meal, the sort that meant someone had made it specially. Welsh rabbit, with a proper cheese sauce and toast, and how that came out of the rationing, Avigail had no idea. It was comforting in all the ways she hadn't been able to ask for, though.

She'd spent half the night up writing down notes, everything she could remember. It was absolute chaos. The whole thing was half shorthand and half fragments of sentences, but she could sort it out later. Avigail fell asleep eventually. She was tired, even if it was an unfamiliar bed.

She woke up to Papa knocking on the door, and then the bell that meant it was half an hour to breakfast.

Papa had given her a few minutes to get dressed, and then he and Claudio gave her a good check, all the ways Penelopes checked. Matron was right there, of course, though Avigail was fairly sure it was mostly that Matron was very curious about the process. Matron had even asked if Papa - or one of the Penelopes - might come out and give a talk on it to the Healing speciality class before the end of the year.

Eventually, Papa had patted her on the shoulder. "Send along your notes when they're organised. Tonight or tomorrow is fine." Matron brought in breakfast, and again it was filling, though nothing for Papa and Claudio.

"What is it, do you know?" Avigail couldn't help asking, of course.

"We don't know yet, you." Papa considered, then patted her shoulder. "That's why we're here. We think it's something that needed to go by sea, not a portal, so we'll be taking it back by ferry, or something of the kind. Mirth's sorting out the transportation now. I'll tell you more when we know anything, or make sure someone does, but it might be a bit. Very interesting sort of puzzle."

Avigail glanced at Claudio, but he just grinned back, very much like Papa's grin. "Don't try to get it out of me. It's apparently going to be an excellent training exercise." Papa waved a hand and Claudio added, "The opposite end from what I was working on for some of the war. So I suppose that's a fair comeuppance."

"There. And now you ought to get ready to go to class. You're cleared for your schoolwork, but tell me and Matron immediately if you feel anything odd or unusual. Be around other people for the next couple of days, riding and duelling or whatever else you're doing, just in case. Professor Fortier's well aware, obviously. We think that's the most likely place anything unusual would show, but you never know." His mouth quirked up.

"And if it weren't me, it'd just be a fascinating puzzle, but it is me, so you're also a little worried." Avigail considered. "But not too much, or you'd be having me come home or something."

Papa's mouth quirked. "Like that, yes. You're likely to get a package in the next day or so with some amusements, keep an eye out for it. There you go, off to class. I'm hoping we'll be done before lunch or I'd say we'd eat with you."

Avigail knew that meant he'd rearranged the morning's meetings to be here, and the afternoon was less flexible, people who would be offended. Quite possibly Claudio's mother, honestly. At any rate, she'd kissed Papa on the cheek, and gone about her morning, pretending that everything was normal. No one let her get away with that, of course. Before and after every class was full of people asking questions, and lunchtime was even worse. She had to insist on eating before talking, or she'd not have got any food.

Finally, by five, she and Ros were heading out for a quiet ride by themselves. By mutual silent agreement, they headed out toward the north cliff and the stairs. Avigail said, when they were about halfway there. "I don't want to get off or go down or anything. I'm not foolish. But it's in my head, you know?"

"Me too." Ros took a long breath. "How do you feel about it?"

"Queer. Tangled up. Papa checked me out, and Matron, and I'm being sensible and all that. I'll keep track of my dreams. I know all the protocols, at least enough.

It's not like Papa doesn't talk about them." Avigail gestured at the ocean to the north. "It just doesn't feel settled."

"Well, it's not." Ros rode along for a few minutes. "I don't want to join Animus Mundi. I want to do something that matters." It came out in a rush, but the sort of fixed, stubborn rush that was like taking a fence at speed. No backing down once the decision was made. Like Ros had been in the caves, determined to see it through.

"What does that mean to you, then?" Avigail didn't know where to start, except with a question. Fortunately, she was good with questions.

Ros shrugged. "I told you about talking to Aunt Laura and Uncle Martin. What would happen if we sent the Dwellers a letter? Saying that." She then hesitated.

"You said 'we'." Avigail had spotted that immediately.

"Well. I don't want to do it without you. Or without Jasper or Leo, honestly. I don't think we could talk Peter into it. And maybe we've proven we can do something that takes stubbornness and thoughtfulness and bravery and knowledge, all."

Avigail laughed. "Problem-solving. Because we did that. I'm so glad Professor Fortier was right there, when we came out, but we'd made it out ourselves, mostly. Thanks to all of that."

"Rescued ourselves. Not like damsels in distress in some story." Ros considered. "Though I'm pretty sure the boys would take offence to that. And they were amazing."

"Both of them." Avigail agreed. "I don't think Jasper knew he could do that with people? That it'd work. I mean, even though Leo knows him and trusts him. And Leo—" Her mouth closed.

"Leo'll talk about it when he's ready. Or something. I'm

not going to push. And if he tells you things in confidence, duelling, I'd understand. But I'm worried."

"Me too." Avigail let her mare walk on a bit before she said. "So how do we get a message to the Dwellers? And how do we talk to the boys about it? We're going to talk to them about it, right?"

"When we get back for supper, let them know. Find a bit of time in the library. Or the salle, if Leo would rather that. We can work out the wording. But yeah, I - I would do it without them, but I'd rather have them with us. I'll ask Peter, but I think he'll say no." Ros frowned. "There's got to be somewhere they use for communication."

"There's a book about Prometheus I spotted." Avigail half closed her eyes, seeing it in her memory. "It's a bit out of place, I've always thought. It's in with the history, not literature. We can look, see if there's any sign? You'll make the letter sound right?"

"I will." Ros went quiet for a little. There was a lot of quiet in this conversation, and Avigail was good with that. After the noise of the day, it was relaxing. And it was good to have a friend to be quiet with, as well as a friend to talk to. Having both in one person was really wonderful. And rare, Avigail knew that.

When they came to the edge of the cliff, they halted, letting the mares settle. "Papa didn't know what it was. It'll probably take a bit if he didn't write this afternoon." Avigail stared off over the waves. "But I wonder...." She wasn't sure how to go on.

"Yes?"

"I wonder if it saved us. Pulling me in, making me want to go in. Besides Leo thinking it was Schola, which he would. What would have happened if we'd been outside, on the shore, when all that stone came down?"

Ros shivered, hard enough that her mare sidestepped warily. "I don't like that thought."

"Me either. But we were well inside. The tunnel itself held pretty solid. None of us got hurt. Even Jasper only had a bit of a bruise. I can't help thinking that's more than chance."

"Yeah." Ros contemplated it for a bit. "And it's not pulling on you now?"

"I sort of know where it is? Vaguely now, it's a lot further away. A boat back to Cardiff, or on a boat up the Severn to Trellech, I think. Not the ordinary ferry here. But I don't know how much of that was Papa telling me they planned on it."

"Well, you could keep track of if you feel anything odd, even briefly, and I'm sure one of them's keeping a log of what they try, figuring it out. And compare them, independently."

Avigail snorted, amused. "Notebook in my pocket. I mean, better me it happened to than anyone else? I know more about what information matters." She went on, hurriedly, "Not that you don't, too."

"What I know is different, and that's good. If we all knew the same things, it would be very boring," Ros said. "Are you doing more with your Papa this summer, then?"

They hadn't really talked about it, but they didn't need to. "Probably. Claudio's more independent with his apprenticeship now. He'll probably be done within a year or so? I mean, he already knew things when he started. He wasn't fresh out of Schola. And that means Papa would have more time to show me things, so long as I know enough of the safety charms and all that."

"Which is one reason among many that you've got

special duelling practice," Ros said. "Better you than me. And Leo."

"Leo gets a lot more bruises out of it." Avigail was fine with that. Leo was learning different things than she was. Part of the fun of it was seeing how Professor Fortier taught Leo, or taught Theo Lefton, and how he taught her. It wasn't anything about her being a girl - he'd been different with Artemis Lefton last year - but it was about what she needed. What would serve Avigail, almost certainly, was subtlety and being underestimated, right until she did what needed doing. She was learning all the techniques she could that didn't show, not the way it showed in Leo's magic, in who he fundamentally was.

Which reminded her of something. "Leo really cares about this place. And he knows secrets." Saying it out loud made it real for all they'd both been there.

"Don't push at him, all right?" Ros spoke quickly, sounding worried. "When he - that cavern."

"I'm not going to." Avigail did her best to keep any hint of insult out of her voice, because that wasn't really what she meant, anyway. "It mattered to him. It meant something to him. That's what I want to say. And I don't understand how, but there are a lot of things like that. A lot of Papa, for one thing, and a lot of portals for another, and I'm sure there's a lot like that in the Guard, too, or the land magic. Lots of mysteries I don't get the answers to."

Ros snorted. "Just checking. Might take Leo a bit to want to talk about any of it, that's all."

"Are you..." Avigail didn't know how to finish that sentence. But there'd been an odd note in Ros's voice, and she wanted to make sure she understood it.

"Gods, not like that. It's not like it would be with Jasper. That's even worse. But he's our friend, and we make a fantastic team, the four of us. Leo's always in this odd place, standing between worlds. No reason to make it worse. Maybe he'll tell us more sometime." Ros shrugged. "When it's time. He's got a good sense of timing. I mean, it'd be a shock if he didn't, between his mother and Uncle Alexander and all the ritual things."

"Well, that's impossible to argue with." Avigail said. "Did you understand the Ritual assignment, actually, or do we ask Leo to explain it to us tonight?"

"Oh, we ask Leo to explain it. I'm curious about what he says, for one thing. And some of it hinges on some of the history, the sort he explains to Peter best. I'm pretty sure he was doing something similar with Uncle Alexander over hols, too." Then Ros considered. "Come on, let's get a canter in, and then see if Jasper's done. He was helping Master Held with the beginner classes." They turned away, picking up a trot and then a canter.

By the time they reached the stables, the beginner class had finished up. Both Avigail and Ros pitched in to help get all the beginner students and the horses they'd been riding settled. Three sets of hands made light work, so they finished up a good twenty minutes before they needed to go up to wash for supper. Jasper peered at both of them. "You doing all right, Avigail? And um, why were you helping?"

"Can't a woman be helpful?" Avigail grinned at him, which did not exactly reassure him, rather visibly. "The ride was good, but we have something we want to ask you about. Out where it's quiet."

"Give me a min." Jasper wheeled on one foot, going off to talk to Master Held, pause to give his Dorothy a bit of carrot - and then Merla and Capala and Leo's mare Story, too - before he joined them at the door of the barn.

Once they were out on the road, able to see anyone

coming, Avigail found a bit of the stone wall along the edge, and hopped up on it. "Have you made a decision about the Society of the White Horse?"

"That's where you're starting?" Jasper grimaced, but he did sit down rather than backing off. "There's a part of me that wants to say yes. And the rest of me, it's not the right thing. It's, I don't know, this is the wrong way round, but it's riding a fine thoroughbred, all legs and angles, rather than my Dot." Who was decidedly not that. It was indeed an odd metaphor, Avigail agreed, since presumably whatever the White Horse was in that society had a very practical nature, but she got the idea. Jasper added, as if he were still working it out. "I could grow into that sort of person, probably, but I don't know that I want to."

"What do you want, then?" Ros perched on the other side of Jasper.

"Doing things that matter. And things where it's all right to talk about doing them." He swallowed. "That's the new bit I've figured out. Master Benton made a point of talking to me about it, winter hols and over the equinox. Lord Carillon, too. About being able to help with bigger things, like infrastructure. But I want to be able to, I don't know, talk to Stan and Anna about them. Build up connections with people, not have to hide them. There are times privacy and secrecy and all that are good, they're useful? But I don't want to live like that."

"Huh." Ros tilted her head. "Like Mama and Papa do. All sorts of things that some people know, and a lot don't."

Avigail nodded. "That's fair. So, more like the Penelopes. People don't know all of what they do, but they know they do things, and they see enough that there's, I don't know, a shape of it. Even if you don't know all the specifics."

Jasper's head bobbed up and down. "Yeah. I had a couple of questions from people today, about what it was like to find something like that? And I made it clear it was all four of us together, and that was the good part, that we knew how to do different pieces of it. But it also felt sort of good to know people knew I'd done something? Been a part of something."

"Right." Avigail cleared her throat. "Ros and I, we're going to write to the Dwellers and see if they'd be interested in us. You too, yes? I've got that right? And we'll ask Leo, soon as we see him. Peter, too."

"Bet Peter will say no. He asked me some good questions this morning at breakfast, but they were more the sort of thinking questions, not doing? And that's fine. But I think he'd like the less physically adventurous sort of doing things."

That made Ros grin. "There is that. Avigail and I have a bet about whether he'll actually take Protective Magics fourth year, or whether that'll be too much doing and not enough thinking. Right. We'll ask, though." Then she hopped off the wall. "Come on. I want supper, I'm starving."

CHAPTER 41
LEO ON THE MORNING OF APRIL 23RD

By Wednesday morning, Leo desperately needed time away from everyone else. Even Avigail and Ros. He'd split off from them after Maths. It was easy enough, Avigail had Trivium, and Ros was going down to the barn and had to change first. Before she could come out again, Leo was out the entrance of the keep and well away.

The question was where to go. He didn't want to go back to the north point of the island. Leo didn't want to go down to the east road, where it wound down to the shore, where Ros would see him eventually. He certainly didn't want to go down to the village. He could actually have used an hour in the bookshop, talking to Aunt Pross about nothing at all relevant to his immediate life. But the village was out of bounds during the week, except for the fifth years. She'd know something was wrong, she'd tell his parents, and there would be a lot of fuss, even if he didn't actually get in much trouble.

Four directions. That left the west. Leo considered grabbing something more than his cloak and decided against it.

There was far too much chance someone would spot him and want to know where he was going. He was permitted out by the cottages. He knew there were no classes out there this week. Probably not until next week or the one after, depending on the weather. He'd checked the schedule automatically on Monday, like he always did.

The weather wasn't too awful, at least. It wasn't raining; it was warming up a bit. He'd be fine for an hour or two outside. And if he got back late enough to snag a sandwich from the kitchen rather than eat with everyone else, actually, that would be fine. The noise had been getting to him more and more, the bustle of people, and he didn't know how to solve that. Not right now, anyway.

He found a perch on the table, looking out to the west. Dad had said the box likely came from a wreck. He'd been trying not to think of how many there might be down there, in the water between Schola and Ireland. Or north or south, for that matter. They'd heard about some of them, of course. But Leo had learned, maybe far too young, that there were a lot of deaths in any war no one talked about. Or sometimes didn't even know about.

Dad didn't talk about the Great War, not much and not often. Uncle Alexander talked about it even less, proportionately. Uncle Seth and Uncle Golshan would tell stories about their friends, sometimes, or Uncle Golshan would show off card tricks he'd learned in the trenches. But they didn't talk about most of it. Certainly not what it was like to be doing the actual fighting. Dad had told Leo last year to ask Mum about it. Because Dad, after, had been a wreck.

It had taken Leo a good six months to ask. He hadn't until they were out at the Essex house for equinox hols, and Dad and Ursula had gone to Arundel to visit Uncle Garin for a day or two. That had been part of introducing Ursula to the land rites, and Leo had been glad enough to stay put, and just go over for the actual offerings. And a chance for a quiet afternoon and evening with Mum was always good.

There was a thing about Mum. She hadn't known Dad then. Not as more than one of the notable constellations of stars of the Great Families people couldn't help noticing because they were right there, shining in the sky when they looked up. The Fortiers were exactly that sort of prominence. Though these days - he'd listened to Uncle Garin's comments too - rather diminished from former years. But she'd heard some stories before she met Dad properly. And she'd got more out of him, over the years, piece by piece, things he'd never say all at once.

That was what Leo was stuck on. Dad had gone hollow at the centre, trying to fill it up desperately with things that would have destroyed him in a few more years. Mum had said - gently as she could - that Dad had done some horrible things. Things that haunted him, both the doing and the failing to do. Mum had also been clear the things he felt he'd failed at were the ones that tore him up in an endless circle. Uncle Perry's death, in particular, but not just that by a long shot.

Uncle Perry was the uncle he'd never known. He was the one who would have laughed until he couldn't breathe, Dad said, at the idea of Dad settled down, with two kids and a lot of responsibility. And he was the one Uncle Alexander always remembered first at the memorials, any time people shared their dead. Uncle Perry had been Uncle Alexander's heir in all the ways that mattered, everything except actual bloodline.

Leo felt hollow, a bit like that, today. He'd frozen up back in the cave. Leo had been useless until Jasper got him moving. He couldn't have helped anyone, not with anything. There wasn't any way to recover from that or fix it. It wasn't the same. No one had been hurt, but he understood Dad a good bit better now. He sat there, staring out at the water for a bit. Fifteen minutes, maybe twenty, it might have been a half hour. He couldn't hear the bells from here.

He rummaged in the bottom of his cloak pocket, wondering if he had pebbles in there. He didn't, and besides, there was a tiny chance someone was down below, by the shore. Probably not, but. He felt fidgety, and if he'd been able to deal with people, he'd have asked Dad about an extra duelling session. Or something. As it was, he could sit, or he could go climb a tree or something, or he could go back to the keep.

He'd almost decided to go back when he heard the scuff of a sound behind him, the brush of magic he knew. "Mind if I join you?" Dad's voice cut across the space. He was maybe twenty-five feet back, using a charm so his voice carried.

It wasn't like Leo could say no. If Dad had come to find him here, Dad probably had a reason. Even if Leo really didn't want to have any of the conversations he could think of that might happen now. He shrugged. "Sure?" It was grudging. He knew it sounded grudging, but he couldn't get the tone to come out right. Dad came along the far side of the table before settling down on the other end.

"I'm both surprised and not surprised you're not down by the map." Dad wasn't looking at him, which meant Leo didn't have to look back. He could look out at the waves and the bird he could see here or there, circling on the far horizon.

"Did you look there first?" Leo swallowed hard. That had come out badly too. "Sorry. Words aren't great today."

"And I bet everything's too loud and too much and

people keep asking you things. Including me. Your Mumwould have come instead, but she has to teach." Dad's voice was mocking himself, a little, now. "So you get me."

Leo shivered. That was too close to the quick, in so many ways. "Yeah. The everything." He swallowed hard. Now he didn't know how to keep anything steady in his head. "Is something wrong with me? Did I do something wrong? No, that's not right. I know I did something wrong, but I don't know how wrong it was, how big it was, if it's even something anyone can fix." He wanted to go on, but then he ran out of breath all at once.

Dad didn't move, didn't even twitch, from what Leo could see. He didn't say everything was fine, either, and that was good and bad all at once. Instead, he took a breath. That was the breath he took when he was about to say important things, or set up something duelling that was complicated. When Dad had space to take a moment first. "What do you think you did wrong? You told me what happened on Sunday night. It was a very clear report, and it checks out with what Ros and Avigail and Jasper said." Dad was using first names. He was being deliberate about that, making this about Leo as - well, still a student, but everything else too.

"I froze up. When they needed me, and I was the only person who sort of knew where we were going." Leo couldn't even glance over. He had to keep looking ahead, feeling the tension in both his hands now. Fists, they were fists.

"What did it feel like when you did?" Dad's voice was still careful, but Leo could hear that there were other things there, too. Curiosity, mostly .

"The oath. Pressing on me. Only I hadn't made one, not about that. You did. I mean, there are things you and Mum don't talk about, about under the school. I've known that all along. Even before you showed me the map."

"In your heart, deep down, right at the centre, have you made a promise to yourself to keep Schola safe?" Now Dad's voice was a rumble. It was too loud to be a whisper, but Leo felt it, even more than he heard it. He could only nod, once. "And was your fear something like, um." Dad swallowed. "Schola in ruins? Broken, in some way you couldn't name?"

Leo's chin twitched before he could stop himself, his shoulders hunching up at the same time. He got out one word, a grunted "Yeah."

"Me too. Only when I see that, it's knowing people I love are in the ruins, that I can't help them. That I wasn't fast enough or good enough or—" Something in Dad's voice made Leo twist to look at him. Dad went on without too much of a pause. "I can't tell you not to love this island and this school. I love her too. And you've loved her a long time already. I'm fairly sure you couldn't stop without a lot of work, and probably Alexander renaming you thoroughly. Hundreds of choices, to change that."

"I don't want to." Leo's voice sounded thin compared to Dad's. "I don't know what I'd have done if Jasper hadn't. It was..." He hadn't spelled this out before, because other people had been around. "It was the room you talked about, with the banners, the ancient ones. I'm pretty sure Jasper will remember them."

"Jasper would pay attention to wall hangings. I'll have a word with him, though I'm sure he'll keep it quiet." Dad considered. "Did you see the far end?"

"No." Mum and Dad hadn't told him much about that, just that it had given them a view of things they thought they'd never see again. People they'd loved. Leo knew that meant Uncle Perry, and he had a good guess about Mum. "I didn't want the others to know it was there. We couldn't see it. I couldn't tell them not to, because that would have told them it was there. And then I got stuck, and everything was…" His voice cracked, good and proper, and he swallowed hard again, burying his face in his hands.

A moment later, Dad was scooting closer to him. Leo could feel the shift of the wood under him. "May I touch you? Your back?" It was queer for Dad to check, but sometimes he did, other times. Leo managed a nod, and then there was a hand on his back, then another. Steady pressure, enough that Leo could feel how his shoulders moved back and out a little when he breathed. That he wasn't completely floating in space, or collapsed in terror.

He focused on breathing, just on that, for maybe twenty breaths, before he felt a little better. "See. I did things wrong."

"You did many things right. You asked permission, you let us know where you were going. Leo, you and your friends were doing me a favour. Gods, if anything had happened to you." Dad cut that off suddenly, before he went on, his voice funnelled into something more ordinary again. "You thought through problems very well, from everything you've said. All of you, but that means you too."

Dad took a breath, like he was trying to keep control too, but when he went on, his voice was more solid. Leo leaned back a little more against the hands on his back as Dad spoke again. "All four of you listened to each other, though we're going to need to get Jasper a bit more training on some things, obviously. When things went badly wrong, you didn't panic. Your report was quite good, considering it's the first one like that you've done. Everything I needed to know was right there, immediately. You thought to have Ros and Avigail write, too, in case I wasn't available. And as it turns out, it was good to loop Gabe and Claudio in right away. From there, you followed instructions."

"But the cavern." Leo's voice squeaked a little at the end.

"If you had to do it again, what would you do different-ly?" Dad's voice stayed even, but the pressure from his hands got a little more, and after a second Leo leaned back into it, trusting it'd stay there. That he could lean.

"I knew we might come to those caves, I mean, I knew they were there. I could have asked you what to do, if there were places to avoid. I could have gone first and, um. Blind-folded them, maybe? Asked them not to look? Dimmed the light?"

"All of those would have some risks - especially since you were carrying a magical object that shouldn't have been dropped. And that might have been messing with your perceptions, actually, as well as Avigail's. Let me add one more idea, because it happened later. You might have asked the Lady Glaslyn for her help. Not by name, if you didn't want them to hear, but I'm sure she led you out. You came out a different cave than I expected, by a little, for the record. Missed the first two we saw. I didn't even know there was a connection there. Maybe there isn't usually."

"Oh." Leo considered. "But what I did wasn't... wrong?"

"No. A bit clumsy, and the oath, the Silence, was warning you away from going the wrong direction, the only way it could." Dad grunted once. "It's not a subtle tool, it can't be. It's just herding livestock, and sometimes people are an awful lot like goats, and stubborn."

That made Leo smile, then take a deeper breath. "So I'm not in trouble? I didn't do anything wrong?" He needed to hear it again.

Dad twisted around, and now for the first time, he

looked Leo straight on, hand coming up to cup his cheek. "You were everything I could ask for. And I'll tell you so tomorrow, in more detail, when we have tea and your Mum can help. Do you feel a bit better?"

Leo considered. "Enough to go on." Which wasn't what he wished he could say, but he was honest.

"That's a start. And it'll get easier, I promise. I've always found the couple of days after something are worse than the moment. Second-guessing what I should have done, or didn't see in time, or whatever. Do you need a potion against dreams for a night to help? Anything like that?"

Leo shook his head. "That feels like the wrong thing." He let out a breath. "Do you and Mum have anything I can eat upstairs?"

"Oh, I'm sure we can rummage up something. Probably an apple and some toast and maybe an egg or two. Fairly sure we've got some soup tucked away. Spare you lunch with everyone crowding around. And I'll let your Mum know so she comes right down after class."

"Good." The question of how much he wanted to see Mum and be reassured was probably a sign that he wasn't nearly adult yet, and right now Leo didn't care. "That'd be good. Thanks, Dad."

They sat there for another few minutes, comfortably quiet, before Leo gathered his things up, and they walked back to the Keep.

CHAPTER 42
ROS ON MAY 8TH

It was a fortnight later before they got any actual information about what that crate had been. Ros had been increasingly fidgety about it, even though she knew perfectly well that information didn't just show up neatly indexed. Mama and Papa - especially Mama - spent hours making it do that, and lots of other people, as well. And it wasn't as if there weren't plenty of other things to keep them busy.

They were coming up to the last of the pavo matches. Chances were, just Jasper and maybe Ros would get a chance to play at the end of the month, but it did always depend on how things were. Sometimes people decided they really needed the extra time to prep for exams. More rarely there was an injury or an illness or something, not that Ros wished that on anyone, of course.

Now it was Thursday afternoon, and Ros was on her own in the library for a bit yet. Leo was up having tea with his parents, Avigail was doing her chores, Jasper was somewhere, so was Peter. He'd kept slipping off, though he'd reassured Ros that it was for reasons he liked. Short of setting Avigail on following him - which would be rude - Ros had to leave it at that. Ros had settled in at a table. She was working through some of her German homework when there was a cough near her. She looked up. "Crimson. Did you need something?"

"Actually. Can I have a word?" He wasn't quite stammering, but he looked awkward. Of course, he looked awkward a lot at the moment. Ros had decided that everyone at Schola had a few months of being especially spotty, made up of elbows and knees, when they were growing into themselves. Crimson was probably in the middle of his, so he'd come back to school in September taller and having remembered where he'd put his feet. Probably.

"Here? Somewhere else?" Ros considered the options. It was unusual for him to be on his own, actually.

"As well here as anyone else. Anyone nearby?" He shifted from foot to foot.

Ros blinked at him, then checked, silently, before shaking her head. "We've likely got until supper, at this point. Ten minutes."

"Look, can you talk any sense into Leo Fortier? About - um." Crimson sat down with enough of a thump that the librarian looked up, then decided it didn't merit intervention. People did sit down in chairs, even in libraries. Though admittedly, usually more gracefully than that.

Ros cocked her head. "About the societies?" It was an easy guess, given it was May.

"That." Crimson sounded desperately relieved. "Look, it's terribly awkward. Anthony doesn't like being second best, but he got an invitation the other day." That was Anthony Phipps. Crimson was in an awkward place there, sharing a dorm and presumably shortly a society with him. But Ros wanted no part of that apparent friendship.

Ros raised an eyebrow. Of course, Crimson wasn't saying an invitation from who. Of course, Ros could do the simple maths. "Leo turned them down, didn't he? Formally. They'd been pressing him about it. That's not the way to get Leo to do anything."

"But really, it's where he ought to be. Properly. Like he should have been in Fox, certainly." Crimson spread his hands out. He was making things sound terribly reasonable, but they absolutely weren't.

They were sitting in the library. She would lose points metaphorically and quite possibly literally for her House if she lost her temper. Also, her parents and Uncle Alexander would all mock her for loudness in a library shared with other people. She didn't need that. Besides, it would be much more fun to tell the story of how she hadn't burst into guffaws. So long as she could suppress herself.

"Well," Ros said, before she had a moment of brilliance, a way to go forward. "I am glad you came and talked to me, rather than to Leo. You're sure Phipps has an invitation to Dius Fidius then?"

Crimson's mouth opened and closed, as she named the society. Then he glanced around warily, as if expecting the ancient and esteemed senior members to drop out of the rafters. They did not. And, in fact, this corner of the library was almost entirely empty now. In a whisper, he said, "Quite sure. Seen it myself."

Not that she actually trusted Crimson's ability to tell the real thing, but she would have to make do for the moment. "And what did you want me to tell Leo?"

"You must have seen." Crimson coughed. "I mean, people have been a trifle, um. Difficult?"

"To me?" Ros considered that for a moment, then Crimson shook his head, minutely. "Just in private then. I expected that." She sailed on, amiably. "Jasper, of course, everyone knows what happened when they tried that." Then she cocked her head. "Avigail. Peter. Leo?"

"Not to his face yet, but the other three. I thought you should know. Anthony and Malcolm were looking for a chance to make Fortier look bad. The rest of you too, but not perhaps the same way." Malcolm was Malcolm Hector, universally called Heckle among the lot of them, long before he'd made the bullying more obvious.

"More fools them. And you can tell them I said that, if you like. You'd think they'd have learned to keep their hands to themselves. Magical and otherwise." Ros considered. "I think perhaps we'd best not discuss it further until it plays out. Don't you? See you in class tomorrow." At that, she picked up her books and walked out with nothing further. For one thing, she wanted to catch the others as they came into supper. Both as a warning, and because they needed to do some planning.

After supper, Leo led them not to the Astronomy classroom, like Ros had expected, but up to the top of the tower. Ros had never been up there when she wasn't in class before, but Leo knew just where things were. It was perfect, actually. It wasn't remotely near sunset, of course, but the sky was clear. It was warm enough to be comfortable in their jumpers and student robes. "Go on, Ros?" Leo started them off, once they were all sitting comfortably.

Ros laid it out as tidily as she could. Of course, she told them what Crimson had told her - and what he'd gestured at, but not actually said. Leo grunted at the bit about Phipps and Heckle, and Ros wondered if he'd already had trouble. Then she added, "I don't particularly want to make enemies. That's bad strategy. But I also don't need that kind of friend. I've much better ones. I've been ignoring them since what they did to Jasper, of course."

Leo grimaced, then he looked at Avigail. "They given you trouble, Avigail?"

She shrugged. "More the pretty princesses than the boys, but the one might have put the other up to it. The sort of thing I'd care about if I cared about being invited to those sorts of parties, but I don't. I didn't think they'd fuss with you, with your Mum and Dad right there and knowing what's up, but I suppose that's more of a sign they're dense."

It made Leo smile a little, so that was something, though he didn't say anything more.. Ros nodded firmly. "Peter, you?"

"I make sure I'm always with people. Going over to the library or back, or in the House." He hesitated. "And I've got people to talk to, when you all aren't handy. People who aren't like that."

Ros was now absolutely certain Peter had got an invite from one of the societies, she didn't know how she knew, but it was a puzzle piece fitting perfectly into place. Uncle Alexander had told her to trust those flashes of intuition, and she would. Not the Nine Muses, probably not Four Metals, that likely meant Many Are The Waters. Maybe eventually she'd get more out of him. "You're sure?" Ros did want to check.

Peter shrugged. "Bit of a bother, not too much, usually? Besides, they're lazy. I can get up and get a bath or shower in before they're moving."

That was at least wits in action. Ros nodded at him. "And you let me know if you need someone handy, of course." Then she peered at Avigail. "What're you thinking about?" It wasn't, Ros thought, the bullying.

Avigail had been chewing on her lip, considering Leo. "Papa sent me a note today. In the journals, I can't show it to you, trust me?"

They all made the appropriate encouraging noises. No one thought Avigail would lie to them. She might not tell them anything. All of them had their own reasons to keep things secret or private or behind oaths, and that was just getting more so as they got older. But what she said, you could trust.

Now, Avigail took a breath, letting it out. "As far as they can tell, the box and the crate had two things going on magically. One was a fairly thorough invisibility enchantment. It explains why the merfolk didn't find it. It's not so much that it's invisible, exactly, as it makes you forget it's there. Except if it somehow thinks someone can help it get where it's going. Think is the wrong word, of course, but I don't have a better one."

"Huh." Ros considered. "And it kept showing up for Leo and Professor Fortier because maybe they could help? Where was it supposed to be going?"

"They think - this is Mirth, mostly? - that it was one of those things that had to go by sea, that can't go through portals. She found some records about an additional box, in the captain's quarters, on a ship carrying coal from Cornwall to near enough Liverpool in 1917." Avigail looked around. "I didn't think it was that old."

"I'd have thought it was this war, not that one." Leo rubbed his face. "Huh. And they're not going to tell us why."

"I'm not sure anyone's sorted that out yet, actually. Maybe they will, maybe they won't. Anyway. I was wondering if people are being such, such," Avigail grimaced. "I don't have the right words that'd make sense." Which suggested she wanted to break into Yiddish, honestly, what bits Avigail knew of it. "Anyway. If they think there was something special about it that we got to keep, that might explain some of it."

"And jealousy at Leo turning Dius Fidius down. You did actually, didn't you, Leo? Have people given you trouble?"

"I did a lot of talking it through with Ursula in the journals. She said this might happen? To be precise, about three to one that it would, but she didn't think the rest of you would be bothered with it? I'd made a show of doing something unusual. If I didn't decline, there was a decent chance they'd show up and whisk me off, and I don't know if - if anyone could have stopped them. Not without a huge problem. So I sent a note, via the people you'd think, declining." Leo shrugged. "And I can avoid Phipps and Heckle. And any of you can too, if you like. Except, um, Peter, you've got to share a dorm with them, but it'll at least give you warning. I got permission earlier today."

"Permission?" Peter leaned forward a little.

"There are all sorts of warding and identification tools. A lot of them are complicated here, because there's so many people, living in close quarters and so much magic. But there are some that work just off someone's handwriting." Leo spread his hands. "I had to ask for it, but, well, Mum's got everyone's handwriting, going back decades, who's ever taken any of the Quadrivium classes. She made up charms for me. They'll react if they're close. You have to have your hand touching to feel it, but a bracelet or something you can slip into your pocket is fine. You just set them with a slip of paper you tuck in. She gave me beads that will hold the paper."

"And that's allowed?" Avigail was running maths in her head about the various possibilities.

"I mean, they wouldn't allow me - or us - to do things that would let us find them. People can misuse that. But to know if someone's nearby? Not a problem. Our eyes could tell us that if we were looking the right way, or our ears. This is mostly eyes in the back of our head, or a crowd."

Peter considered. "You people who are used to living like that are very odd. You realise, right? But I'm, um. Grateful."

"Me too." Jasper had been quiet, wrapping his arms around one knee and listening, mostly. "I'd rather not be spooked or surprised."

Leo had obviously expected this, because he immediately passed around little knotted bracelets with beads. "Mum said if anyone else, erm, is a concern, talk to her privately, and she'll sort something."

Ros considered what he wasn't saying. "What did Professor Fortier say?"

Leo looked away from them all. "We talked about things down in the caves. And then about this, he said he'd rather not deal with the fuss about me using my skills, but if it came to it, do what needed doing. And I understand that better than I used to. Both when to, and that I'd rather not."

"And you heard nothing from Dius Fidius? Or anyone else?" Ros still felt there was something missing here.

"Nothing. No acknowledgement, other than Phipps getting an invite, which I suppose is answer enough. And you haven't heard anything from your aunt?"

Ros shook her head. "Just that she got the letter." She let out a long sigh. "I don't like not knowing things."

A little to her surprise, it was Peter who spoke up. "Of

course you don't. I don't get why you want that? Too much attention for me." Everyone did laugh at that, both because it was a little funny, and because laughter was the better thing to do with how odd it felt. At least Ros thought so.

Peter went on, when everyone had settled. "I'm glad you told me that you were going to. No reason you had to."

"You're our friend, Peter." Ros said, firmly. "And that's not going to change, is it? Besides, the Dwellers like all sorts of people, that was sort of the point of some of the decision. Not like Crimson thinking some people are more deserving of warnings than others."

Peter winced. "He told you, and not me, yeah. Not that I'd expect him to tell me." Then he shook his head. "Not going to change being friends. Besides, we do pretty well, helping with assignments, right?"

Jasper nodded. "My Latin's much better. And my writing, my last two essays have got actually decent marks, did I tell you?"

Everyone made cheerful noises about that, Jasper had been working so hard for it, it was great it was paying off now. Avigail considered. "And you don't regret turning down the Society of the White Horse, Jasper?"

He shook his head. "I got a nice note back from Master Isten. He understood. And he came down for one of my lessons with Master Held, last week, he was friendly and - it was fine." He let out a breath. "Lord Carillon and Master Benton are sorting out some projects for me to help with over the summer. We'll see how that goes, I guess?"

"I knew Papa would have ideas." Ros said, cheerfully, before leaning over to elbow Peter. "And you?"

Peter waved a hand. "Someone, naming no names, might have sorted out a project for me to work with at the Temple of Healing. Not rivers, but the baths. Nothing formal, nothing, um, directly with patients there, but helping with some of the records and learning how they do things. I don't think I want to be a Healer, but they have a lot of systems for doing things, and I want to learn about that. And being in Trellech a lot, getting a chance to know the city."

Ros said, cheerfully. "See, I told you in September that you'd figure out connections. That was faster than I expected. We can meet up with you, sometime? Show you things? Leo and Jasper, you too." Both she and Avigail knew the city well enough, both their families had townhouses in the magical capital.

There was one of those moments of silence that happened in a group of amiable people. Leo said, after it had dragged on, "We seem to have some plans, right? And we'll keep doing it together, except when we don't."

Someone laughed, and then all of them were laughing, the sort of laughter on the edge of hysteria. But it was theirs, and no one else could hear them, and it would have to do for the moment. Eventually, they'd have to go downstairs and do their prep, and get on with the evening, but maybe not yet.

When they did eventually head downstairs, Ros held back just long enough to get a word with Peter. "You don't have to tell me if you don't want to, but. Many Are the Waters?" She'd been almost certain and then he'd mentioned the Healers and made it not really a guess anymore.

He hesitated, then nodded once. She flung her arms around him, the kind of impulsive emotion that was usually Avigail's. "I'm glad. Really glad." Then she let him go, feeling a little embarrassed, but he didn't seem offended. Instead, they followed their friends downstairs.

CHAPTER 43

"Are you up for it, Jasper? And are they?" Marguerite, the pavo captain, was grimacing. It was one of the key pavo matches for the year. It would decide the cup in the junior league. They were playing against an excellent team made up from guild apprentices. The first half had gone well. They'd started with Marguerite, one of the other fifth years, a third year, and Jasper and Avigail. But the third year's horse had just pulled up lame, and the other fifth year had taken a fall that had snapped his collar bone. It'd be an easy mend, with Matron's touch as a Healer, but it would take a few days to be sound.

Ros and Leo had prepared like the reserves always did. Their mares were tethered to the fence, back from the playing field, with their saddles and bridles ready. Jasper tilted his head. "We've not all been in the same match." He wasn't sure what Marguerite was aiming at.

"No. But I think this puzzle might suit Leo, and he's

good enough on a horse. You all do well together. It would leave me to get on with getting our target." Marguerite was a fearless rider, able to stick to her own bay mare's back like glue. "And if I don't put you in, it's Greg and Amelia, and well." They'd been walking out with each other until last week. While they'd been civil at practice, there was a vast distance between that and trusting the other person as a teammate in a pinch.

Not that Jasper knew about that kind of romantic passion or the breakup. He left that sort of thing for some future year, quite possibly when he was out of school and not in obligatory close contact with whoever it was. Now he coughed. "I'd love the chance. I bet they will too. Ask them. You'll get a fair evaluation."

"That's true enough. Heya, Ros, Leo, to me." Marguerite pitched her voice to carry, and the two of them came trotting over. The field wasn't muddy, at least. It had dried out well, though with a touch of magical help to assist the drainage. She spoke quietly to them, then a minute later, they were off to their mares, checking the saddles and them up swiftly. "Right, Jasper. Strategy."

He and Marguerite worked on how to redistribute things. Someone had to call an object down from a tall pole. It was far enough up that it couldn't be easily identified. Which, of course, limited the sorts of magic they could use on it. That was Marguerite's task. She knew more sorts of magic than they did. The four of them would divide up the other two tasks that would earn them points. There was touching a wand - that was the best name to it - to a series of points. The other was getting a ball through into the other team's goal. "Leo, protecting our goal, yes?" Jasper suggested. "Avigail on the wand, me to see about our goals, and Ros to fill in where she's needed. With

Avigail, probably, blocking people who want to get in the way."

"That's less vaulting for her, unless something gets dropped." Two of the points would involve vaults, maybe three. But Avigail was grand at hanging off a saddle with her hand near the ground in ridiculously impossible poses before she righted herself. And her Capala was tolerant about the whole thing. Within five minutes, Leo and Ros were mounted, doing a bit of warmup away from the others. Within the fifteen minute hold mark, everyone was back and ready to play.

Jasper didn't have a moment to breathe. He'd kept the ball in play - they were using the netted sticks, which meant having a caution about whether they might catch on anything dangerous - but once he got the ball, he could fling it into the other side's goal. Their Defender was solid, with a gelding to match, but not as nimble as Leo was managing. Leo had let one through, but only one, to Jasper's five points so far. Every time he glanced around, he got a better sense of the entire field, the way all the pieces fit. It was magic coming together, this was a thing he could be really good at, if he could do it beyond pavo.

Avigail was riding like a centaur, one minute hanging off the saddle with her fingers knotted in Capala's mane, the next vaulting off to touch a point. She'd flung herself in the saddle. As he got a look at her, she bounced up to stand in her stirrups, then balance on her knees. That got her a touch on a point hanging in midair before the other team could collect it. She'd whooped with sheer joy as she landed in the saddle again and urged Capala faster, claiming point after point.

Ros had settled into keeping pace with her, a block between Avigail and the opposing team who might want to get in the way. It wasn't flashy play, but it was the sort of thing that required far more competence than a lot of the flash - and Avigail's complete trust. A couple of times, Ros had positioned her Merla barrel to barrel with Capala. She deftly kept both mares cantering while Avigail did what she needed, circling them back so Avigail could vault on. It needed exquisite timing if Ros didn't want to get kicked in the face. It made Jasper think for a second like the sun and moon as twins. Ros was all golden and pale, and Avigail all darker and shadows, and they were an absolute match for each other.

The first time he'd got a look at Marguerite, she'd been standing in her stirrups, trying charm after charm to get the flag down. The second time, he'd almost startled enough to confuse his Dot, because Marguerite had been shimmying up the pole, and she'd only had a couple of feet to go. Her gelding's feet were planted, even though one of the other team was trying to lure him away.

Then he managed another shot at the goal, though this one bounced off the frame. When he looked back, Marguerite was shimmying back down, quick as can be. Avigail whistled, the bird call that brought his head up instantly, and she was galloping at him, to hand off the wand. He knew what that meant. Get the last points, as many as he could, before Marguerite got the flag that had been on the pole back to their own goal.

He didn't need to urge Dot on. She'd always had a fine sense of when something mattered and it was time to do her best. She surged forward, all the power in her hindquarters launching her into the world like an unyielding boulder. Jasper squeezed with his knees and calves, showing what they needed to do, a serpentine pattern that cut across the field to line up the maximum number of points. She curled around one, like she was more snake than horse, and he vaulted off as she slowed, hitting the marker dead on with the wand. Dot was already picking up speed when he vaulted back on, then they did that twice more. He could hear Avigail and Ros behind him, making it hard for anyone to stop him and Dot, clearing the way.

Finally, there was the last marker. As soon as he was in the saddle again, Dot was flying, like one of the great mediaeval battle mounts, until they were just ahead of Marguerite and her gelding. He touched their net an instant before Dot pulled up to a stop just in time to avoid the ring's fence. He could feel how they'd won, even before Marguerite ended the match by touching the ball to the top arch of the goal, right in the centre.

"Hold!" The call went up loudly, and all of them pulled up. The horses were breathing hard, the riders perhaps even more so. Despite the spring weather, it was warm enough all of them were dripping with sweat, and all of them were grinning fit to burst. Master Held and the other referee announced the match. Those last few points had counted more than Jasper had realised. It meant they'd have an excellent chance as a team going into the final rounds of competition at the Midsummer Faire. They'd be able to watch the qualifying matches and save their mounts.

Now, he couldn't stop grinning. He managed it long enough to congratulate his team, then to make the proper sportsmanlike compliments to the other team. They'd played well, very well. It had been a proper challenge. But Jasper and the Schola team had played better, and everyone knew it. Everyone knew that the second half had been splendid, well-played on every level. When Jasper looked around, Leo's parents were there, handing him a flask of water before they left him alone. Jasper wished Dad could have seen it, and Lord and Lady Carillon too. But now they'd be playing at Midsummer, and they'd have first dibs on the play, because of this, as the team that had finished this match.

Now it was time to walk the horses out, gently, praising them every bit of the way. All of them were talking to their mares, not to each other. They were giving the little scratches that each preferred, a little treat from a pocket and the promise of more to come. Once they got back to the stables, a good half-hour later, to be sure, there was plenty to do. They worked through currying and brushing, checking their feet, making sure they had food and water and a bit of restorative warm mash. Master Held came round to check on them, pleased as anything, but he waved off a discussion of it for the next week. "Time for that then."

It wasn't until they took the tack back to the tack room that any of them noticed anything odd. Sitting on each of their saddle holders was an envelope of plain parchment. Marguerite had just beaten them in and she waved a hand. "Didn't just catch my eye, then? Well done, you lot. We'll be planning for Midsummer. I'll find a time we can talk past matches and how to approach that one." She was gone before any of them figured out what to say.

Ros swallowed. "Shall we?" She balanced her saddle on her hip, reaching with her fingers to see if the envelope moved. It came off easily in her hands. Then she slipped the saddle onto its rack, opening the letter with another touch and a murmured charm. She didn't quite whoop - they were inside, and some of the horses were more nervous sorts. But she did wave it. "Read yours!"

Jasper got his saddle on the rack, then opened his own. Red seal, an anvil. He held his breath. Inside was an invitation - not to prove themselves to the Dwellers. Instead, they just had to confirm their willingness by presenting themselves at a particular time on the road by the stables. Just stand there, let themselves be seen, and go away again.

"Huh." Leo looked up over his. "That's an interesting location. We're doing it, though, right?"

Avigail snorted. "We asked them to ask us. It'd be rude to not turn up. And they did the thing properly. I wonder how they made the letters stick? It's tricky, unless they have a hair or a link somehow. And I can think of lots of ways they could get something from one of us, but all of us?" She waved a hand. "Tack now, tack later? We're going to have to clean it sometime."

Ros said. "I should say now. But I'm starving. And grotty. Bath, lunch, then come back down here and deal with the tack when it's settled?"

Jasper nodded. "That's fair. And we can check on the horses, too, make sure there's nothing we missed."

"Also a good idea," Ros agreed. "What did your parents say, Leo?"

"Mum said it was absolutely worth getting up for." Leo was laughing. "And I know she had a late night last night, actually. Later than usual. And Midsummer Faire! We'll get to play. Uncle Garin will fume, that's great."

"I do not understand you and your uncle," Avigail said, slightly primly. "Uncle Lewis isn't anything like that, and he's also an alchemist."

"There are quite a few things different between them," Leo said. "Anyway, then your parents can see you play, and that'll be great. And we'll get another chance together."

"Fairly sure if we have another good match, we'll all make the team next year, too. And Marguerite's leaving school. Papa will be delighted. Four of the horses in the match out of his stables." Ros was thinking through the dynamics. "Who do you think for Captain?"

"Lunch, first. Bath, lunch, then politics." Avigail and Leo each took one of Ros's elbows, nudging her along and back out the barn to the road back to the keep. Jasper trailed along, grinning as broadly as he could. The rest of this year was going to be fabulous, and so was next year.

CHAPTER 44

AVIGAIL ON SATURDAY, JUNE 6TH

Avigail's fingers kept twitching. It had seemed like one thing when she and Ros had sent the letter off. And, like as not, there would have been tedious parts for whatever Four Metals did for their initiations. She'd not only paid attention in Ritual class, but she'd grown up hearing Papa talk about things. And the more so when he'd gone through several magical shifts in his life in a single year, as an adult, seven years ago. Once stuck in the midst, the only thing to do was keep going forward with as much grace and care as possible.

And she was definitely in the midst. Each of them had got a note a week ago, so they could prepare themselves. They had the morning for their usual amusements - pavo practice, of course, in all of their cases. Then they'd been told which of the bathing rooms were reserved for them. They'd been told to come out to the cottages on the west coast of the island when they were ready. There'd also been a list of what they could bring and what they shouldn't. Yes, to any personal ritual items they wanted with them, a book or personal notebook, but not to bring their journals or any other item that might communicate with others. And they should bring anything they might want overnight. All they'd been told was that someone would come and collect them sometime after eight that night.

When they got there, they found one cottage comfortably arranged for an evening, though not overnight. None of the beds were made up, nor was a fire going in the fireplace. And of course, it would be light out until half-ten that evening, this close to summer solstice and with double summer time still in play. There was a hamper of food, all the things the kitchens could manage under rationing, but more individual than the student meals tended towards.

Ros had brought her book of magic and her sketchbook. She'd spent the afternoon into the evening making sketches for some new piece of magical art. Nothing terribly refined. She was - from what Avigail could tell - playing with the design of it. Jasper had his penknife and some wood he was whittling. Leo had gone to sit on the table in front of the cottages for a long while, staring off at the waves.

Avigail had joined him silently for a bit, before she'd wandered around the cottages, considering the materia that grew around them, as well as the nature of the local stone. She'd had the lectures on both, of course, but it was something to do, and she spotted three plants that hadn't been on the class lists, though she'd have to check if she'd identified one of them properly.

A bit after nine, two people came to the door of the hut. With Leo in front of them, they must have collected him from the table. "Good evening." Avigail didn't know either of them by sight, which was true of many people, but also interesting. They were perhaps in their forties now. "Do you come to dwell at the forge, knowing all we may ask of you? Please, each of you give your answer in turn." There was an element of trust here. Any of the usual sort of signals didn't make sense when it was strangers, and the four of them hadn't been brought into the society yet. Leo cleared his throat.

"Pardon, please, how may we know it is you we are supposed to come with?"

The woman laughed. "You've won me a bet." She had dark hair piled on top of her head. Then she leaned over and pulled something out of her pocket. The letters they'd written, signed by all of them.

Leo considered once, and then nodded. "Mistress." He made his formal request smoothly enough, and the rest of them followed.

Something in that made the woman in charge laugh, rather a lot, but then everyone was picking up their satchels and walking. They'd been told to wear comfortable clothing, shoes they could walk in, and Avigail understood why. They went past the turnoff to the keep, though it was silhouetted against the sky behind it, and they kept going down toward the eastern shore.

Once they were down on the beach itself, the woman turned to them. "We must blindfold you for the next few minutes. You will hear what is going on. When you can see again, you may wish to make some gesture of acknowledgement. But there are no formal words other than the oath. You may speak freely from your heart. We ask again, do you come to dwell at the forge, knowing all we may ask of you?"

Again, all four of them agreed, though Ros reached for Avigail's hand and squeezed it once before dropping it. A minute later they were blindfolded, then there were the sounds of more people on the gravel of the beach. Avigail's arm was taken firmly, guiding her along across the beach, onto stone. She heard the hammering first, a hammer on metal, then she felt the heat of the fire.

Whoever was guiding her kept her well away from whatever caused that heat, bringing her into a cooler chamber. She could hear the hammer and anvil still, steady rhythm that let her sink into it, before there was a tiny pause. When it picked up again, it was as if someone new had taken over. That happened six times, all told. None of the four of them spoke. Avigail wasn't sure she moved other than breathing. There was something gripping about the sound, about knowing they were in the cool dark of a cave. Besides, she had no idea what was around them.

Then, before she knew it, Ros had disappeared from beside her, then she thought Jasper, then Avigail herself. Perhaps in order of age, then, Leo's birthday wasn't until later in June. She had no time to think more about it, because she was led to a point, asked one more time, "Do you come to dwell at the forge?" This time, there were more questions about whether she had come freely, if anyone had pressured or threatened her to join - though she could hear the laughter barely repressed there. And then, she was asked to share her understanding of the expectations.

"The fire of inspiration, the tools shaped by the forge, and the community of brothers and sisters who do this work in the world." Avigail knew the proper response, they'd shared that up front, in the invitation. She added, after a moment, "People who understand the need to do something more." That got a murmur. No single voice she could pick out, but she suddenly realised there were a lot of people there. More than she'd expected.

She was guided off to one side, and then she heard Leo

asked the same questions. He answered clearly enough, then he was moved away. There was a moment where there was more movement, before she heard a voice say, "Sponsor, lead this one toward the flame." Twice, it wasn't her - but she heard Ros's little gasp, and a murmur of Ros's voice, too soft to understand, then Jasper's.

Next it was Avigail's turn, and the blindfold was removed. She stood in front of a massive fire pit with an anvil and forging tools right next to it. She understood, immediately, what they'd meant about making some gesture, and so she did what she'd learned from Mama, the instinctive reaction to the fire and the gifts it brought, one of the prayers to Agni as she bowed. One of the briefer ones, because she remembered where she was.

Then Leo was brought forward, and his face lit up at it. Not at the fire, exactly, she didn't think. But something about the place or what the fire felt like, or that this was a ritual that he was enjoying immersing himself in. Possibly all of those. Probably.

"It is our tradition that we welcome you, now that the darkness is gone, banished by the fire, with a cup of welcome, and an introduction. Each of you has someone who has offered to sponsor you, who will speak for you when that time comes, and then speak for the next sponsor." Avigail was increasingly sure she didn't know the man, but that implied that some of the people here knew her. On the other hand, it would be rude to crane her neck. And besides, the light of the fire - and the heat of it - made looking behind where the four of them were standing tricky.

They began at the left of the man leading the rite. As Avigail got a better look at him, he seemed to be perhaps in his fifties or sixties. Older than Mama and Papa, but not quite into Grandmama and Grandpapa's generation. Each person gave some bit of descriptive praise, and a good two-thirds of them made it clear there was some story behind that which might be shared later. Several times, people laughed loudly and freely, though no one quite called out teasing comments.

She had a suspicion, by the time it came round to Ros, but then the man next to her was saying, "My year brother Martin is a great man for a bit of detail. Here, he's been glad to vouch for the truth, not the show of it, and we should all be glad for his gifts with that."

Someone called out across the circle. "And we are."

That was Ros's Uncle Martin, married to her Aunt Laura. He stepped forward, so Avigail could see his face, grinning. "I'm delighted to welcome Ros here to our circle. I've had the pleasure of watching her grow up when I visited, and how she's always treated everyone fairly. Even the posh ones." It made Ros's nose wrinkle, but then she was smiling, and her uncle was clapping her on the shoulder before he went on. "Phil here asked if he could stand up for Jasper, and I'm proud to know that our younger generations are as clear-sighted as we want them to be."

Jasper did crane around to look beside him, and someone - a fifth year, probably - stepped forward. "Jasper caught my notice because he insisted on doing the right thing, even when it brought him some trouble. More to the point, he did the right thing sensibly. He didn't make it worse, except for being a tad too stoic. Jasper, I'm right glad to have you here. We can use your construction skills, along with everything else. Everyone knows I'm no good with a hammer."

It got another laugh, and then Phil went on. Phil Grant,

that was the name, fourth year. "He told me, at one point, that his friends treated him proper, much like they treated their horses, and I think that's a grand way to put it. I look forward to a year with all of you here, next year, what we can do. But it was also good to hear from someone who'd known Avigail her whole life."

Avigail didn't crane round, but only because there was someone right next to her and she knew who it was as she stepped forward. She blinked, her jaw dropped. "Aunt Doyle?" She could hear the squeak, then the hand on her shoulder.

"I've had the pleasure of knowing Avigail since before she had a name, properly. Having had the training of her father, I'm quite clear what sort of things she might get into. Might as well have a bit of that on our side, don't you think?" Aunt Doyle had been Papa's apprentice mistress. She was one of the pinnacles of order and structure. If she was a Dweller - obviously she was - Avigail had a lot of rearranging of her assumptions to be doing. Aunt Doyle leaned in and whispered, "I know you have questions. We'll have a chance later."

It would have to do. Besides, Aunt Doyle went on to say, "And there's someone who claimed the right to speak for Leo, also with a different angle than might be. Tabitha?"

Professor Morwen stepped forward, grinning. "Now, I've not had the pleasure of knowing Leo here since he was tiny - just from when he was five or so. But I know how deeply he cares for this place, how far it runs in his bones, and how much that can matter when times get hard. I hope very much tonight brings all the blessings for the years to come that it can." Leo ducked his chin, and didn't say anything. A moment later, Professor Morwen - did they just use first names, even with whole proper grownup adults who were also teachers - was going on. She introduced the man who'd been leading the ritual, mentioning he was a Healer who focused on long-term magical damage.

From there, it was a round of the sort of ritual bits she'd expected. They were each presented with copper tokens and three iron items. Avigail wanted to examine hers properly in better light and with her tools. The three were a scribing tool, a twisted circle - Aunt Doyle pulled hers out from under her shirt, showing it could be worn - and a length with a spiral. Then the whole thing devolved into plenty of beer and cider and a bit of mead. Professor Morwen had brought some, with a "One of the Wain traditions, mead for special occasions." Avigail thought that almost fractured Leo into pieces.

Everyone took turns telling stories. There was less dancing than Holi, and far less coloured paint, but the rest of it felt like that. It was a community, together, of all sorts of ages and skills and interests, and yet here they all were, and it was so excellent. Avigail laughed until her sides ached more than once.

When it got quieter, people peeled away, until there were only a dozen left. "You're welcome to sleep out here, all four of you, if you like. People do, we've set it up with the necessary things." That was Professor Morwen - Tabitha, apparently, in these settings and only these. Of course, she'd be responsible for something like that. "Take a few. Think about what you want. You needn't be back in school until luncheon. And yes, Leo, your parents know not to worry. There's three other initiations tonight, mind, so it's not terribly specific information."

Leo looked deeply amused at something, but he nodded. Avigail knew they'd stay. She only had to look at the other three for that. Aunt Doyle gathered up her things, glancing at Avigail. "Walk me out?"

"Of course." They paused out on the beach. It was still twilight - it'd technically be twilight all night, but the sky was clear. Finally, it burst out of her. "Does Papa know?"

"About me? No. Or at least I've never told him. Witt and Mason know, but it hasn't come up directly with your father. If you want to tell him about you, that's your choice. But there's a reason I'm almost always the one seeing to Dweller cases that just need checking. And never the ones that might turn into something legal. We'll go through those agreements this summer, so you know what to expect, the judicial magics and all that. But it's not a problem. Does everyone some good to have a Penelope or two at the forge."

"Huh." Avigail let out a long breath. "I didn't expect most of that. And it was so much better than I'd guessed."

Aunt Doyle laughed, amused. "Oh, there's a lot more of that coming. Good night, Avigail. See you when you're home from school. We'll make sure we get some time to talk."

"Good night, Aunt Doyle." Avigail waited until the people who weren't staying disappeared up the beach and onto the road. Phil Grant was staying, and Richelda and Grim, the fifth years of the Dwellers, and a third year who Avigail didn't know well at all. Someone had laid out plush sleeping mats and plenty of pillows, and the fire was burning down. They could talk and laugh and dream all night, and that was also excellent. Together.

CHAPTER 45

LEO ON JUNE 13TH

By the end of the term - just a week later - Leo still felt more than a bit overwhelmed. Far too many things had been crammed into seven days, between reviewing their exams, lists of reading to do over the summer, and everyone bubbling over with their plans. And of course, there was quite a lot of gossip about who'd ended up in which societies, though Leo was fairly sure at least half of that was dead wrong.

The four of them had been told to take the summer to think about how public they wanted to be. Of course, they could tell their families if they wanted, the whole thing was up to them. Professor Morwen had been cheerful about pointing out that she was more effective if most people didn't know, and once it was out there, you couldn't take the knowledge back. Leo hadn't told his parents yet, but he was pretty sure he was going to. It was just a question of whether he told Ursula first, and he wasn't seeing her until tomorrow.

He'd got through the end of term comfortably enough. Phipps and Heckle had tried something, more than once. The first time, they'd made the mistake of trying when Avigail and Leo were working on their own, sitting in a different spot in the library than their usual because the other three were working on something else. Heckle had made an attempt to grab Avigail's braid and yank it - not even anything competent. At the last moment, she'd twitched it away, and Heckle had overbalanced, going down in a heap. Leo had grabbed his forearm, pulling against gravity. "Might want to keep your hands to yourself, so you don't fall over your own feet." It had been a nice bit of defensive work from Avigail, and Leo had told Dad and Mum about it privately. Both because Avigail should get the praise from handling it right, and so Mum knew the charms were useful.

The second time, Phipps had tried to spill all Leo's books while they were coming out of lunch. Phil and Richelda and Grim had been right behind them, with a few of their friends among the older students, and they'd immediately gone off on a full-scale teasing. It hadn't hurt that Leo had been carrying his extra reading for Dad and Uncle Alexander, so the titles were all far more advanced than the usual second year run. They'd drawn in a good dozen fourth and fifth years until there was a net of people laughing and making it impossible for nastiness to take any root.

Ros had managed to talk to Crimson about it, and Crimson said he'd made it clear he wasn't going to have any part in that kind of stupidity. He'd also stepped in once or twice, in their dorm, Peter said, when things got messy. Next year, they'd have their own rooms, and Leo had already promised to make sure Peter knew all the best warding for things that he could learn. Dad had offered to help with that over the summer, for all five of them.

And on the academic side, Leo's marks ranged from solidly good to excellent. Highest in his year in Ritual, with Ros right behind him, and he'd done better in Materia than he'd been afraid of. Highest in Astronomy, too, but it wasn't like it was hard this year. They were still in things he'd grown up with.

Fourth year would actually be more of a challenge, but he had a year yet. He'd talked to his professors about what to study this summer as preparation for doing the exams for Oxford and Oxford's Academy. And Ros's father apparently had a tutor to recommend, the same one who'd worked with Ros's brother Edmund.

And they all had good plans for the summer. Penelope Doyle had some projects for Avigail, when she wasn't tagging along with her father and Uncle Claudio. Peter was going to be busy in Trellech, but they had plans to show him more of the city, and maybe do another visit to London or two. Ros was doing a lot of language study, and she was probably going to join Leo in prepping for university, at least so she had the option. And Jasper was spending about half his time with horses, and half his time learning about buildings and bridges and things.

All in all, it was a good end to the year and a promising summer to come. Leo had therefore gone down to the village to spend his Saturday seeing people off. He'd amiably wished his housemates well. He'd also said goodbye to Ros and Jasper, then to Avigail, as they went through the portals. Not that he wouldn't see them all next week. They'd left the horses here at Schola until it was time to take them to the Midsummer Faire, and they had training practices four days out of five.

It wasn't until the last of his year went through the portal that Leo found himself standing alone. The ferry had already gone, so that horde of students wasn't there. It just left the teachers, the others waiting for the portal and a few from the village who'd been tending to various pieces of the great migration. It was an event, beginning and end of term.

The island felt different. As usual, Leo didn't have words for it. He stared off at the portal before turning around. Mum was standing there - Dad was talking to two other teachers. "Walk back with me, Leo?"

"Of course, Mum."

It wasn't until they were well out of the village that Leo said, "I can help with the chickens tonight." Someone had to. He was here, and all the teaching staff still had all sorts of things to wrap up from the year. They had reports to write and requests to make for next year's books and materia and all that. Aunt Helena - it was no longer term time, so he could think of her that way again - had to put in all the orders in good time. Rationing wasn't just about food.

Mum stopped on the road. "I know you want to help, Leo. And you're a grand help, and yes, we do need someone to collect eggs. But we've barely had time to talk since last week." Leo went still, and she turned to face him. "We're very proud of you. And we'll tell you so, properly, later. I think I understand why you've been worried about it, but I'm not sure, and I don't want to assume."

"That's the thing, Mum. You don't assume. It's what I find easy." Leo turned back to take a step or two up the path, and Mum joined in. "Why aren't you upset? Or why isn't Dad upset? Like Uncle Garin is upset. Not that he's done it directly at me. Yet." Leo could feel his shoulders hunch up.

"Is there something you think we ought to be upset about? Your Dad will handle Garin. Well, and your sister, she seems to be doing remarkably well with that, honestly."

Something struck Leo. "Uncle Alexander said, back in March, that party, that Ursula reminded him a lot of Grand-mère Laudine at that age. Maybe she reminds Uncle Garin of his mother?"

Now Mum stopped dead, and then she started laughing. "You know, I wouldn't be surprised. Care to make a bet about whether your sister's figured that out? You can ask her tomorrow."

"Dad's the one you make bets with, Mum. I won't take that, anyway. Chances are excellent she has by now, even if she hadn't then." It helped Leo feel rather better about the whole thing, even though Ursula was entirely distinct from the rest of it. They went further along, past the split in the road, before Mum spoke again.

"We meant what we said, both of us - and your Uncle Alexander. We want you to be your own person. Dius Fidius wouldn't be that for you. And your Uncle Orion might have helped a bit with that argument, actually. He's one who got forced into ways of doing things that never quite suited, and we helped, but..." Her voice trailed off.

"You helped a lot. I mean, I've seen what Uncle Orion's been like. What he's like when he gets here, and what he's like when he goes." Leo imitated it, once all stiff, shoulders up by his ears, and then more relaxed, easy with it. "Not so much difference now, but a couple of years ago? And before the war?"

Mum snorted. "He's doing a lot better, yes. And we

want you to have that kind of good. Ideally without fifteen years of not so good and a year or two of truly awful first."

"Dad had some awful bits." Leo was trying it out now, saying it out loud. "What if the hard parts are what make the good parts matter?"

They'd stopped long enough that Dad in fact caught up to them. Leo didn't notice him until Dad was right there. That suggested Dad had been using a charm to duck out of half a dozen gossipy conversations he didn't have the patience for. Usually Dad - and Ursula - were the charming social ones of the family, but Dad definitely had his limits for that. "That's a question for your Uncle Alexander. He can meet us at Arundel for the afternoon tomorrow and supper, so you know. Make up your lists." He added to Mum, "We owe Jehan for dealing with Phipps and Hector and all that. And he says he's some thoughts, depending on the summer."

Dad was letting him hear that deliberately, Leo knew that. But it wasn't as if he could say anything. Instead, Leo waited for Mum to nod, then he cleared his throat. "And what do you think, Dad? About the hard bits?" Leo swallowed hard, but it was a good question. He knew it was, and it was also an important one.

"I don't think you need the hard parts to have the good ones. Or to appreciate them. The good parts are something that's part luck and partly our choices, and how we go about those choices. Even when things are hard or dark. But I appreciate the good more now, because of the hard. I never want to go back to that, and I hope I won't ever. What brought that on?"

"I said I hoped Leo would have the good bits without what Orion's had," Mum said, promptly. She didn't mention the part about Ursula and Grand-mère Laudine.

Which probably meant she'd let Leo do it when he chose. Or Ursula. Mum was like that.

"That's true. Anything else?" Dad slipped his arm around Mum's waist and nudged her forward. "If we stand on the road, someone will come talk to us."

"Isn't that usually my line?" Mum started walking, Leo picked up on the other side of her.

It wasn't until they were back through the keep, upstairs, in the family rooms that he cleared his throat. He trusted the warding and the privacy here, absolutely. "Mum, Dad?"

Dad had been teasing Mum about something, then shooing her to sit down so they could split a bottle of cider. He looked up. "Yes?" It was instant, immediate, as if he knew it was something serious.

"You meant it, about whatever I chose?" Leo knew asking was going to give it away. But he also knew Dad knew - and presumably now Mum - that he'd not become part of Dius Fidius.

"Yes." Dad's response was nearly as instant. "You don't have to tell us anything, you know. Ursula hasn't."

"If I'm informative and she isn't, doesn't that average out? Basic maths."

Mum laughed at that, then waved Leo at a seat. "Sit. Or loom, whichever you like. I swear you've gained another inch in the past fortnight. Remind me to put looking at your uniforms for what needs letting out or charming in mid-August, so we don't have to do it twice."

Dad pulled a notebook out of his pocket and wrote it down. Leo cleared his throat. "Dwellers at the Forge. Last Saturday, I mean, you probably knew that part."

Mum blinked at him. He'd actually startled her some-how, and then Dad was grinning. "Oh. My." Then, right on the heels, he said, "That's what you chose, then. Or they choose you?"'

"Both." Leo had talked this through with his friends. "Um. In confidence? Even from other parents?" Mum and Dad looked at each other, and Leo added, "Usual bounds." Which meant that it wasn't anything dangerous to any of the students, what adults needed to do something about. Secret societies sort of lived in a liminal boundary space with those rules, but Leo was fairly sure no one was going to let any of the students do anything too dangerous until they left school.

Mum nodded. "Usual bounds." Dad echoed it a beat later.

"All four of us. Not Peter, he's doing something else, and we're all good with that." He let out a huff of breath. "We asked. We'd had different invites - all four of us, different societies. Not going to tell you where. Don't guess where I can hear?" He'd give it away, if he did, at least to his parents.

"I promise we will leave our guessing for our own excellently warded bedroom when you are somewhere else entirely," Mum said cheerfully. "Oh, I like that. And that means Tabitha's keeping an eye on you, at least enough. I wondered, but it's not always clear if there's just a teacher who's the contact point, or actually in the society."

Dad snorted. "And we do know about her. But that's because the warding on the cave needs a little attention from time to time. Your Mum has been helping with the locational magic parts even longer than I've been here."

"And you - um. What do you think?" Leo didn't even know how to ask that question.

"I think I'm glad that you're in with your friends," Mum said promptly. "I only had one good friend, most of my time at school, and a lot of people to talk astronomy with, who turned into better friends later. But I wanted that for you. People who like you and want you and help you out, and where you get to do the same with them."

"You had sisters." Dad picked up cheerfully. "And Seth and Golshan. Different. But yes. I - things with Perry were some of my best memories. But we were young scandals, on and off. I think, on the whole, I'm pleased that whatever you end up busy with, it's trying to do things better. You planning on telling anyone else?"

"Ursula." Of course Ursula. "They told us to take the summer before telling too many people. And I don't know if Ros and Avigail and Jasper are going to tell their families or not. Or when or how. They were still thinking about that. And Jasper's parents will worry." There were ways in which Jasper was taking the most risk. Ros had been talking that week about the differences between her Uncle Martin and his friend Galen. Specifically, how Galen was the one who bailed Martin out a lot, because being posh and in Fox House gave all sorts of protections.

"You tell us when that changes, then, if that's something you want to share," Mum said. "And until then, we'll see about things. Passing on gossip that might be handy for one, though I tell Tabitha a fair bit of it."

Dad was looking Leo up and down. "I'm thinking we could get you a proper cloak, fully enchanted. And some more gear for your regular bag. A cloak, it won't matter too much if you get another inch or two of height, compared to a jacket." Leo had two or three to match Dad, so that was still entirely possible. He glanced at Mum, who nodded. "And if your friends all want the same, especially Jasper, I think we could see our way to making that happen."

"Bet Avigail's parents and Jasper's Mum might have

some ideas. I'll talk to them about it when we're done with pavo this week and ask?" It might be a good incentive for telling various parents. "Why now?"

"Because I suspect you're going to get into a few more things, being helpful, and I'd rather have you prepared and well-supplied. Changing the world isn't exactly safe. A lot of people don't like that sort of thing. They can get over themselves. But in the meantime, a bit more protection won't hurt."

"And Uncle Garin?" This was one of Leo's ongoing concerns, after all.

"Leave him to me. Or your sister." It was so like what Mum had said earlier that Leo started laughing until his sides ached, and then he had to try to explain. That got him into the comment about Grand-mère Laudine, which made Dad look really thoughtful. After that, well, Leo didn't want to go anywhere, and Dad got encouraged to tell a few more stories from the family, the kinder ones.

Next year was going to be splendid. Tomorrow was, and next week, and the Midsummer Faire might be a triumph. But it wasn't just one good day on the horizon. It looked like there might be too many to count, like Mum's stars.

THANK you so much for joining me (and Leo, Ros, Avigail, and Jasper) for this adventure. If you enjoyed *The Magic of Four* and would like to read more of this series, please sign up for my mailing list to get all the latest news and fun extras.

Your reviews (on whatever review site you use) are much appreciated, too! Read on for more about these four, Schola, and their parents as well as a few historical notes.

AUTHOR NOTES

Thank you so much for joining me for *The Magic of Four*, the last book in the Land Mysteries series. I hope you've enjoyed a bit of Schola and the lives of these four.

As always, thanks to my friend and editor, Kiya Nicoll. And to my early readers, who among other things also made sure my (very responsible) teenagers still acted like teenagers.

Of course, all four sets of parents here have their own romances. Jasper's parents met and fell in love in *Outcrossing*. Lizzie and Geoffrey Carillon fall in love in *Goblin Fruit* (and Alexander Landry becomes part of their family thanks to the events of *Best Foot Forward*). And Avigail's parents met in *The Fossil Door*, with *Old As The Hills* and *Upon A Summer's Day* picking up with the family in 1940.

Finally, when it comes to Schola, Leo's parents fell in love during *Eclipse*, and have adventures in the caves below Schola during *Chasing Legends* (found in the *Winter's Charms* collection).

You can also find extras for many of these folks via my website (celialake.com).

If you'd like more of these four and their families, I do have some future plans. I do not intend to write past 1950 for a variety of reasons (which means I have no plans to write any of these four and their romances). But I do have a few books in the writing stack that will definitely include them.

I have plans for Ursula Fortier's romance (Leo's older sister) in 1947, coming out in May 1925. Edmund Carillon's romance (Ros's older brother) will be out that November, set around 1948 while he's at Oxford. Claudio Warren's romance will take place in 1950, and will almost certainly involve a bit of Avigail and her family. That'll be out in May of 2026.

Before I get into a few author notes for this book, I wanted a moment for school stories. I grew up reading Enid Blyton and the Chalet School at a time when they were nearly impossible to get in the United States. My father would often go to London once a year in December (he was a theatre professor, so this was partly to see productions in the West End). I'd send him with lists of which specific books I wanted. During the two trips we made as a family when I was little, we also picked up a number of titles.

One of the things I've given a lot of thought to was how a magical school should actually work, as well as how it worked in the British schooling systems of the period. On the practical level, besides going to (American) boarding school myself, I also worked in an independent day school for a decade.

Schola presents the challenge of being a magical school with a priority for magical education, but also having some students who will integrate with non-magical society. Thinking through how that works took a lot of time.

One thing that was true in the period was that people specialised very early. (My parents were educated in the 40s and early 50s. They took basically no maths or science after the age of about 13, because they both went into history and languages.) I wanted a system that would be flexible enough for overlapping magical needs, but that would also keep that specialisation.

A number of drafts of class schedules later, I had a system that worked. Those rare students (like Avigail and Peter) who would like to take all the classes ever can do so. Those who want to specialise more (like Jasper) take fewer. Others are somewhere in the middle, or supplementing structured classes with additional tutoring (as both Leo and Ros do). Schola - with 350 students - is small enough to allow flexibility a lot of the time.

Then we come to the magical aspects, like the house magics and the secret societies. A book allows only so much space, alas, so while we get glimpses of several of the house magics, it's by no means a complete picture. The societies, though, were a delight to dive into. I have books to come that will spend more time with the Four Metals and the Society of the White Horse, and ideas beyond that for the others. (If you want more of the Dwellers, *In The Cards* and *Point By Point* both focus on them, including more of Martin and Galen and Ros's Aunt Laura.)

On to a few specific historical notes

The aftermath of the Second World War is threaded through all of this book. I do have a series of prequel extras

411

(currently available through my Patreon for patrons, I'll be releasing the whole set as an extra in due course). Those posts cover the first year of our characters here, the 1945-1946 school year. It includes their sorting into houses, settling in, and a few other key events around the end of the Second World War.

The various points around **rationing** are historical. It's sometimes a shock to realise that some of the most restrictive rationing actually happens in 1945 and 1946 (flooding in 1946 and 1947 did serious damage to grain crops in the British Isles). While Schola is mostly spared the worst of that, and they have a lot of resources to support their own food, it's a constant balancing act. Rationing didn't end until 1954 in the United Kingdom.

It's worth mentioning here that rationing was managed differently for schools than for individual households, and that places with resources to supply some or most of their own needs also had greater options. Schola - and estates with a home farm, such as Ros and Avigail's families - could supplement rationed food from their own gardens and livestock within reason. (In all three cases, they're sending surplus to the Temple of Healing in Trellech and other institutional uses within Albion.)

Similarly, magic does draw on the body's natural vitality. I've fiated that rationing for people actively engaging in war work (or education) that draws strongly on their magic have additional rations, similar to some other professions during the war. That covers basically anyone at Schola proper. But we're talking more like 4 or 8 ounces of cheese a week (instead of the usual ration of 2) than "all the cheese you like".

On to the specific notes!

Chapter 6: Pavo as a game is based on some of the

mediaeval training exercises used by mounted knights. As noted, it has a played-on-foot equivalent in bohort. Both involve doing specific tasks using a combination of skills (including magic) to win points.

Dot, Jasper's mare, is an authorial insertion of my pony Dorothy, who was the joy of my teenage years. She's as described in the text, both in terms of her appearance and her brains.

Chapter 10: I love a bit of grammar. Here, Ros is getting deep into a bit of nuance. Latin - like other declined languages - has different cases for nouns that indicate different things. You commonly use the ablative for concepts like from, with, by, or in and at. The ablative of attendant circumstances can be thought of as being about the surrounding situation, the way something happens. Why this one and not one of the many other cases? I love the name.

Chapter 25 : The **weather** in the spring of 1947 was truly awful. The year began with a lot more snow and ice than usual for the British Isles. It was the coldest February since 1895. In the spring that turned into severe flooding in many locations, and substantial damage to crops and fields. The floods were in many places the most severe that had been recorded, including flooding of the Thames that rivalled the earlier 1927 flood.

Chapter 33: The **tea strike** is entirely historical. It did mean the reduction in tea rations for the UK in the following months. Avigail's sympathies are naturally with her mother's extended family.

Chapter 39: The **tapestry** maths are drawn from calculations from the Metropolitan Museum of Art. How long tapestries take to create varies quite a bit based both on the design and structure and what period of time we're talking about. However, Jasper is very aware of what time is involved, thanks to his mother.

Chapter 44: Regular readers will know I am continuously baffled by historical time zones. That's for good reason. During the Second World War, the UK had gone on what is known as "British **Double Summer Time**" in order to make use of the later light for factories. (This put clocks two hours ahead of GMT for the summer, and one hour ahead in the winter). They went back to GMT at the end of the summer in 1945 with the end of the war. However, the fuel shortages from the harsh winter of 1946-7 meant the country went on Double Summer Time again during the summer of 1947.

Thank you again for joining me for The Magic of Four and the lives of these students. Please sign up for my mailing list (or follow me in other spaces) to hear about new books as they come out. And as always, you can find more info about my books, characters, and plans at my website, celialake.com. Happy reading, wherever it takes you!

ALSO BY CELIA LAKE

The Mysterious Charm Series

Outcrossing

Goblin Fruit

Magician's Hoard

Wards of the Roses

In The Cards

On The Bias

Seven Sisters

The Mysterious Powers Series

Carry On

The Fossil Door

Eclipse

Fool's Gold

The Hare and the Oak

Point By Point

Mistress of Birds

The Mysterious Arts Series

Bound for Perdition

Shoemaker's Wife

Perfect Accord

Charms of Albion

Pastiche

Sailor's Jewel

Four Walls and a Heart

Land Mysteries

Best Foot Forward

Nocturnal Quarry

Old As The Hills

Upon A Summer's Day

Illusion of a Boar

Three Graces

The Magic of Four

Other stories

Complementary

Winter's Charms

Forged in Combat

Learn more about the world of Albion and future books at my website, celialake.com. Additional information linking characters, places, and timelines is available at my authorial wiki at bit.ly/celia-lake-wiki (or get there from my website under the menu that says "more information").

Sign up for my newsletter to be the first to hear about future books and learn about fascinating bits of research. Happy reading!